GW00645298

THE LAST STARS IN
THE SKY

KATE HEWITT

Storm

ONE

"It's the next left."

My voice comes out a bit too sharp, and I see Daniel's mouth purse as he flicks on his turn signal—unnecessary because we haven't seen another car in over thirty miles, but city habits die hard, I suppose. In the backseat eleven-year-old Ruby, having been asleep for the last hour, shifts and then sighs before curling up again, like a snail. Fourteen-year-old Mattie, sitting next to her, holds her phone up, squinting at its bright oblong screen in the darkness, as if it contains all the answers of the universe, which to her, of course, it does. Or at least it could, if only it still worked.

"There's no *signal.*"

There hasn't been a signal since just after we crossed the border two hours ago, so this complaint is not new. At least without a signal she can't complain about the social media apps I deleted from her phone, resolutely, ruthlessly, because at some points as a parent you have to wake up, like a slap to your face,

1

finally face your own inertia and *do* something, even if it makes things worse. Especially if it does.

Now I remain silent as Daniel slows down and then turns the car into the dirt-and-gravel road leading right down into the woods, a dense, impenetrable thicket of evergreen on either side of the track. The tires crunch on the gravel, loud in the sudden, hushed silence of the car. I let out the breath I hadn't realized I was holding.

Welcome home.

Or not.

We drive in an increasingly taut and expectant silence down the road, the trees on either side of the narrow dirt track looming above, dark and menacing, or maybe that's just me, reading into a difficult situation. After all, none of us really want to be here.

Thanksgiving is in just over a week, and we're meant to be having turkey, watching football, relaxing—*reveling*—in our comfortable home back in Westport, Connecticut, in front of the big-screen TV, the turkey in the oven, spinach dip and pita chips on the coffee table, a bottle of red breathing on the sideboard. Except that home isn't ours anymore and we had nowhere else to go but here—my parents' ramshackle cabin in rural Ontario, Canada that hasn't had a single visitor in seven years.

This is a chance to reset, I remind myself. Reboot. Refresh. Re-something. Take deep breaths and mindfully remember what is good about life, what we're grateful for... or so all the glossy magazines and curated Instagram feeds tell me. All I need is a matcha iced tea and the space to recalibrate. Throw in a yoga mat and it's all good.

I close my eyes against the dark, winding road. It didn't take much to make me cynical, and yet I still want to believe in it all. I want to believe that six weeks away from reality is really what we need to restart our lives, get them back, better than ever.

What actually happens between Thanksgiving and Christmas, anyway, besides holiday parties and Christmas concerts, a never-ending merry-go-round of pointless social events to the frantic soundtrack of 'Carol of the Bells' and endless trays of luridly frosted Christmas cookies? We'll leave it all behind—school, the social stuff, the news, the worry—and we'll come back stronger than ever. We *will*.

Daniel will get a new job, Mattie will straighten out, Ruby will rebalance. All at Lost Lake, in the isolated backwoods of Ontario, Canada.

I realize, belatedly, that I have not included myself in that equation, mainly because I don't yet know how I fit into it. In any case, I have my doubts as to whether any of that will happen. The truth is, we really had nowhere else to go.

"Shouldn't we be there by now?" Daniel's voice sounds loud and a tiny bit strident in the quiet confines of the car, and it makes me jump a little.

"It's two miles from the start of the road to the cottage," I tell him. Remind him, because he's driven it plenty of times, as I have, although not since the kids were small. Sam, my oldest, now at Clarkson College in upstate New York, was only eleven when we last came here for a vacation, the summer before my dad died. I picture Sam hanging between the two front seats, poking his head toward the dashboard, as eager as a puppy. That was a sort of golden age of the cottage—young-enough kids who didn't mind the isolation, as long as they could swim and canoe and fish. Epic games of Monopoly, toasting marshmallows on the fire, sitting with my head on Daniel's shoulder after the kids had gone to bed, watching the fire die to embers and feeling that bone-deep sense of peace only this place could bring.

Seven years later, I am trusting in that promise.

I've wondered, in a distant sort of way, why we never went again, after my dad's funeral that next winter. We always meant to but, every time we were poised to make actual plans, we never did. Memories made it too hard. Teenagers resisted the remoteness. And five hundred miles, a lot of it on back roads, made it easy, or at least easier, to keep putting it off.

Until now.

"I don't really remember the cottage," Mattie says, like a confession, her voice hushed. She's forgotten about the lack of phone signal, for the moment at least. "Besides from photos, I mean."

"It might not look like the photos, not anymore," I warn. I'm bracing myself for a falling-down wreck; Darlene, a kindly local woman my mother hired years ago as an ad hoc caretaker, has been coming by every so often to make sure the place isn't *actually* falling down, but seven years of emptiness take its toll on a house, especially here, with the harsh winters, the endless snow, the mice.

"We should be there soon, surely…" Daniel half mutters as the car grinds into a lower gear. "I remember this hill."

"It's another half-mile." I know every inch of this road, *still*. I spent every summer of my childhood up here, bare feet in the dirt, legs crisscrossed with bramble scratches, mouth stained with raspberry juice, face freckled from the sun. The last seven years suddenly stretch behind me like a vast and empty tundra of time, when I made myself stop thinking about the cottage. About what it meant to me, what it could have meant to my kids.

Another turn, and we'll come to Lost Lake, glinting silver under the moonlight. I find I'm holding my breath, leaning forward—and yes, there it is. A darkly opaque oval, fringed by dense evergreens; it is no more than a swathe of blackness now, a stretch of emptiness. The moon, however, is hidden beyond a bank of clouds, so there is no silvery reflection, but I know the lake is there, simply by the space. The darkness.

"Are we there yet?" Mattie asks, her voice caught between

impatience and anxiety. She has even less of an idea than me of what to expect.

"Almost..." Daniel mutters, although I can tell from the way he is squinting ahead at the road that he doesn't realize how close we are. He doesn't know every turn and bump the way I do. This place is part of me in a way I can't explain, not to my husband. Not even to myself.

"Remember the rock," I say quickly, just as the bottom of the car scrapes hard against the granite boulder in the middle of the road, gray flecked with pink, opposite the old barn. Daniel curses under his breath.

"Dad." Mattie sounds both impressed and scandalized by his unexpectedly fluent swearing.

"Sorry." Daniel passes a hand over his face. "Long day."

Long year, I think, but don't say. I'm not about to bring that all up now, right when we are about to embark on our supposed second chance.

Because the cottage has now come into view, a dark hulk against a darker sky, its pine boards interspersed with once white, now graying pitch, looking smaller than I remembered, and definitely more dilapidated. A gutter is hanging askew, and moss has spread across the boards, over the windows, turning the wood fuzzy, the glass greenish. The place looks completely forgotten, and it is—or at least it was.

Daniel brakes, bringing the car to a stop in front of the back door, which basically operates as the front, since the front of the house has a deck that faces the lake.

"This is it?" Mattie demands. She sounds horrified, and I'm not surprised. Compared to the sprawling, modern McMansions back in Connecticut that she's familiar with, this place is an unappealing rural ghetto. And yet already, improbably, my heart is lurching, warming. This is, in essence, my home, even if I pretended for seven years that it wasn't.

5

Next to Mattie, Ruby stirs and stretches, blinking sleep out of her eyes, looking around. "Are we here?"

Daniel slides me a look that's hard to interpret in the darkness of the car, but I think it's something like *Satisfied?* It was my idea to come here after we'd lost our house. I knew I'd rather be at my family's cottage than in some depressingly affordable two-bedroom apartment in Bridgeport or Stamford, eking out an existence with Daniel as a delivery guy for Amazon, Ruby and Mattie in the mediocre public schools. At least the air is fresh here. We might remember how to breathe. How to be. Or at least I will. Maybe.

Not that I've ever said that aloud. If I did, I think Daniel would laugh at me for thinking such things were possible, the cottage as some sort of magical cure-all, a Hallmark movie come to life, with all the accompanying sugar.

"Come on, let's go." Resolutely I reach for the door handle. "Darlene said she left it open for us."

I step outside of the car and take a deep breath; the air is definitely fresh, pure, and sharp with cold. Already my lungs hurt and the inside of my nose tickles, and it's only November. What will it be like in December? January? Will we still be here then?

"Come on," I call to the girls, and I walk toward the front door. It's unlocked, just as Darlene promised, and as I step inside, the familiar smell of the cottage—pine, woodsmoke, a hint of leather, and dust—hits me, and a thousand memories rush through my mind like a flock of sparrows, wings beating, bodies rushing by. I'm six again, happily huddled by the fire; I'm eleven, reading *Archie* comics in the loft, dust motes dancing in the air; I'm fourteen and bored out of my mind. I'm twenty-five, bringing Sam here for the first time, dipping our toes in the crystalline water of the lake as he laughs, and then I do too, reveling in this simple pleasure. I'm thirty-nine, aching with grief as I gaze at my father's empty chair, the silence reverberating all around me.

I blink, and the memories fade away, replaced by this new reality. Nobody is here. Nobody is waiting to welcome us. I step into the laundry room, which serves as an inelegant foyer to the rest of the cottage—the washing machine and dryer on one side, and a clutter of old boots and coats on the other. My gaze skims over the narrow wooden shelf my dad built decades ago that still holds a jumble of keys, old receipts, some bug repellent, probably ten years out of date. A lump rises in my throat, surprising me. My dad died seven years ago, and yet for a second, it almost feels like he's here, like he'll walk around the corner, arms outstretched, smile wide.

Alex!

"Mom, are you going to let us in?" Mattie huffs from behind me, and I step into the kitchen to give the rest of my family room to enter.

"Sorry."

"This isn't so bad," Daniel remarks in surprise because the cottage is not nearly as derelict inside as we might have feared. Darlene has left a few lights on, and everything is clean and tidy, if well-worn. It feels like entering a time capsule; nothing has changed, and yet everything has.

I was last here for my father's funeral, three days after Christmas, a world of ice and snow and frozen grief. My mother was in a daze; my older brother mostly silent, my younger sister having flown in just for forty-eight hours from some far-flung place where she'd been working as a freelance photographer, eager to get away again as soon as she could. With three small children in tow—Ruby had been little more than a toddler—I somehow managed to feed everyone, find funeral clothes, get us to the church, *exist*. I can barely remember any of it now. I don't really want to.

"Shall I build a fire?" There is an enthusiasm in my

husband's voice that hasn't been there in a long while—months, at least. Being laid off and losing our house, our whole way of life, both humbled and embittered him—or maybe it just embittered me. We haven't talked about it enough for me to know, and I don't know which of us is more reluctant to have that conversation, painful and necessary as it surely will be. Maybe we can have it here, or at least *want* to have it? That, I suppose, would be a start.

I take a deep breath, inhaling those familiar, cottagey smells. I walk into the living room, the heart of the house, with its massive stone fireplace, wooden beams, faded sofas and the loft area above where my brother used to sleep. My sister Jenna and I shared a little bedroom off the living room; it's filled with boxes now, or at least it was, the last time I came here. I haven't looked inside yet. My parents had a bedroom on the other side, with windows facing the deck and the lake, and the bedroom opposite theirs was for guests—a motley crew of cousins and friends who were gamely willing to make this journey to the outer boondocks of Ontario. Add a kitchen, small bathroom, cellar, and a porch, and that's the cottage in total. Sprawling in its own way, yet essentially small.

How many summers did I spend here, watching the fireflies blink and weave outside my window, listening to the melancholy late-night call of the whippoorwill or the persistent whine of mosquitoes, the desperate *rat-a-tat-tat* of moths hurling their tiny bodies against the screen window? How many winter evenings, huddled under a heap of blankets, the comforting crackle of the fire the only sound in the still, icy night, making me feel safe and warm, loved and protected? How many card games around the table on the porch, how many sun-drenched mornings pouring homemade maple syrup over my pancakes, how many gray, wet afternoons, the lake obscured with mist, the rain dripping from the eaves, feeling relentlessly bored?

Yet it was all so long ago, it feels like it happened to a different person. A different me.

"Alex?" Daniel prompts.

"Sure," I say after a second; it takes a moment for the memories to recede and my brain to kick in gear. "A fire is a great idea. I think there should be some firewood stacked on the porch."

Daniel goes off like the proverbial hunter, while I walk slowly around the living room, running my hand over the fireplace mantle, the back of a chair, reacquainting myself with this place. Mattie and Ruby follow me like a pair of lost puppies.

"Where are we supposed to sleep?" Mattie asks, looking around, her lip curling a little. It is basic, for sure. Rustic is the kinder term, I suppose, but I doubt my daughter feels like using that now. Compared to our five-bedroom house with its finished basement, bonus room, and three-car garage that we left back in Connecticut, it's going to seem *rustic*, indeed.

And that is without telling her that the pipes are probably frozen, the water turned off for the winter; there will be no hot baths or showers, no washing dishes or even flushing the toilet for the entire time we are here, at least not without drawing water from the lake.

I realize I'm not entirely opposed. My kids' lives have been soft, at least until Daniel lost his job and pretty much all our money, and then lied about it, to boot. Not that I'm blaming him. Not exactly.

"There's plenty of firewood on the porch," Daniel announces as he comes back into the living room, his arms stacked with logs. "So, that's good."

Yes, it is, because we'll certainly need it. The fireplace is the cottage's only source of heating, besides a few ancient electric heaters buried away somewhere whose wires have probably been chewed through by mice. I shiver because even though Darlene texted to say she put a fire on earlier to warm the place up—its woodsmoke scent is still lingering in the air—it's died out now and the place is freezing.

"I'll get us warmed up in no time," Daniel says, and I wonder if I've spoken aloud.

Mattie is still looking around in something close to distaste. "So, where am I supposed to sleep?" she asks again plaintively.

"You can sleep in the loft, for now, with Ruby," I tell her. Some long-ago instinct makes me save the guest room for, well, guests. Sam can use it when he comes in a week; after that, we can move Mattie and Ruby around as they like. "Tomorrow we'll clear out the little bedroom," I continue, "and you can have that, if you'd rather, although I think the loft might be warmer. Heat rises, you know." I try to smile, but my lips feel funny. I can't escape the feeling that I'm stuck in a time warp. Everywhere I turn, I expect to see someone else—my father, who's dead; my mother, who has been in a nursing home for five years, clinging to the last fragments of her memory; or my old self, who is long gone.

"Why don't you help me get the groceries from the car?" I suggest. I turn to Ruby, who has been wandering around silently, her thumb in her mouth even though she's eleven years old. "Rubes?"

"What?" She glances at me, blinking slowly, lost in her own world as she so often is; at least it seems like a peaceful place.

"Can you help with the groceries?"

Another blink, and then she silently follows me out to the car, along with a harrumphing Mattie. As we step outside, I breathe in the freezing air, and tilt my head to the sky, which is scattered with a million stars. There are so many that they blur together, a jumbled canvas of connect-the-dots.

"Look," I say to Mattie, nodding upward, but if I'm hoping for an isn't-nature-great moment of bonding, it falls spectacularly flat. She gives me a typical teenaged glare and stomps over to the trunk of the car, hauling out one of the cardboard boxes of groceries we bought in Kingston, a city by the border and the last major outpost before we headed deep into the woods. Mattie takes the box and stomps back into the house.

"See the stars, Ruby?" I try again, and my younger daughter simply smiles at me. *Sam might appreciate them*, I think with a sigh as I reach for another box of groceries. He's only been gone for three months, enjoying freshman life at college, but I miss him, more than I expected to. After three or so years of being mostly monosyllabic, communicating by grunts, he turned pleasant and chatty right before he left. He texts me more now than he spoke to me a year ago, which feels like a bittersweet victory, and yet one I'm grateful for. He's planning to come for Thanksgiving; he's meant to fly to Ottawa the Tuesday before, in just one week. I know he'll love it here, the way he used to, with an enthusiasm that isn't marred by teenaged angst or anxiety. I can't wait to share it with him again.

Mattie and Ruby and I finish bringing the groceries inside; I bought a ton because the nearest supermarket is forty minutes away and I wasn't sure when we'd next be able to get there. Besides, there is something about being so far out in the sticks that makes you want to bring in the supplies, hunker down.

"Is there Wi-Fi?" Mattie demands, as I start stacking cans in the pantry; Darlene swept it all out, emptied out what had been there the last time I came—the ancient bags of sugar and flour, the dented cans of fruit and vegetables. They must have been quietly moldering for all the years someone was supposed to come up but never did. First me, with my vague promises, then my sister, floating the idea of working remotely from here for a few months. My brother, too, talking of turning the place into some sort of business, a vacation destination for the tourist looking for the seriously remote. None of it came to anything, which was completely unsurprising.

"There's no Wi-Fi," I tell Mattie. "At least not like there is—was—at home, but there is a satellite that connects to the TV, and you usually can get some internet access through that." Not much, though; emails and single pages are pretty much all its speed offers; TikTok scrolling or YouTube streaming will definitely not happen. "It hasn't been turned on yet, though," I tell her, keeping my voice matter-of-fact but also enthusiastic, "but maybe we can make it work."

Mattie gives me a disparaging look. "So, what's the point of having it if it's not turned on?"

"I thought we could take a break from all that, for a little while," I say as lightly as I can because it's still a difficult topic for Mattie, not to mention a painful one for me. Two weeks ago, she was suspended from school for having marijuana in her locker, which prompted me, among other things, to take a look at her phone—and discover a world I would have much rather had not existed at all, and definitely not in relation to my daughter.

Now she lets out a growl of frustration and hurls that phone onto the sofa, the ultimate act of teenaged melodrama. It's usually attached to her hand.

"What are we *doing* here?" she cries wildly, and I glance at Daniel, who is crouched in front of the fireplace, propping kindling into a pyramid like a proper Boy Scout. He's too busy with his fire-building skills to notice Mattie's outburst.

What we're doing here, I think, *is getting away from everything that was bad back at home.* The social media. The toxic friends. The older, drug-dealing boyfriend. The lies. The shame. So maybe it is a good thing we're in the middle of the woods, away from all the influences that were derailing Mattie's life at an alarming speed, faster than I could even keep up with.

"Look!" Ruby exclaims, and points to the fire that Daniel has started, a few small flames tentatively licking at the kindling. He grins and straightens, and something in me aches at the look of pride on his face. That's something I haven't seen in a long time. And yes, it's only a fire, and a small one at that, but right now I want to hold on to what is good; I want to nurture it. I smile at him.

"That looks great."

Mattie lets out another groan and reaches for her phone again. I go back to the kitchen and resume unpacking, finding a surprising little lift from stacking cans in the pantry, hauling sacks of flour and sugar, packets of pasta and rice. The twenty-first-century version of homesteading, I suppose, including plenty of stuff for the freezer.

After a few moments, Ruby comes in and starts poking around, while I wonder if I should make hot chocolate, turn this evening into something celebratory.

"Look." Ruby tugs at my sleeve and then shows me a photo she's taken from the front of the fridge—faded and old, its corners curled up. It's of my father and me; I must be about ten. We've been fishing in the lake, and we're holding on to our rods like walking staffs. He's smiling down at me, a look of laughing tenderness on his face, and I'm grinning straight at the camera, my gaze blazing with fierce pride and joy, my finger hooked through the mouth of a rainbow trout. I don't actually remember the moment, but I remember the photo. My dad reminisced many times about how proud I was, how I'd reeled that trout in like a pro. "It was your Walter," he said fondly, naming the fish from the old movie *On Golden Pond*, one of our favorites, about cottage life.

I wonder if the lake still holds any trout, if my daughters will want to fish, never mind actually touch those slimy scales.

I smile at Ruby. "That was me and Grandpa, way back when."

She nods, smiling back, and puts the photo back on the fridge.

I take a deep breath, will the memories back, and keep unpacking.

TWO

I wake up when the sky is still dark, just starting to lighten at its edges, because I'm so cold. The fire must have gone out in the night, and I can see my breath, a frosty puff in the air, as I huddle under the heavy comforter, Daniel snoring gently next to me. It felt strange to sleep in my parents' bed, like I was stealing something, or maybe pretending. Daniel snuggled right down, though; we lay close to each other—closer than in our king-sized bed back home—but not quite touching, which felt apt.

This morning, there is frost etching the inside of the windowpanes in delicate patterns of wintry lace, and when my feet touch the icy wooden floor, even in thick, woolen socks, I suppress a gasp. Next to me Daniel stirs and then burrows deeper under the covers. I reach for a few more layers—fleece, scarf, slippers—and then head to the living room to build up the fire.

Last night we were too tired to dig out the electric heaters from the little box room, but we should today, definitely, and see if they still work. I tried to make a jolly game of it all, going to sleep in the freezing cold—heaping blankets on beds and finding the hot-water bottles under the sink, along with quite a few mouse droppings.

I tried, but I don't think it worked. Everything felt too strange, too hard, and when I looked outside it was so *dark*, relentlessly so, my eyes straining to see something, anything, under the pale light of a sliver of a moon. I used to find the quiet and dark peaceful, at least I think I did, but now it unnerves me. Mattie stood next to me in her shortie pajamas, shivering theatrically, while I told her to put on some extra layers.

"I know you have them, and it's cold here, Matts, really cold." I tried for an encouraging smile, although I suspected she was being difficult on purpose because she was angry. What fourteen-year-old kid wants to upend her life to spend six weeks in rural Canada? Not this one, at any rate.

I build up the fire and then put the coffee on, having first to fill the coffeemaker with water Daniel got last night from the lake. Just as there was throughout the winters of my childhood, there is now a big barrel in the corner of the kitchen, our fresh water for the day. He thought it was all something of a lark, strapping on the head torch he brought from home and picking his way down the stone steps to the black expanse of the lake, which hasn't frozen yet, although chunks of ice bob in its freezing waters. He filled two buckets, and, huffing and puffing, brought them back up, time and time again.

"This will get me into shape," he exclaimed, and I was glad that he was willing to enter into the spirit of the thing, although I wondered if he still would a couple of days from now. Well, it was only for six weeks. We could all manage that.

All in all, I'm amazed that most things in the cottage still actually *work*, when everything is seven years old at the very minimum, but they do. The coffee machine sputters and hums to life, and soon the comforting smell of fresh coffee fills the kitchen. I take a mug and, wrapping my hands around it for the much-needed warmth, I head to the living room.

The fire is a cheerful, welcoming blaze and I curl up on the sofa. Outside, it is still dark, but I make out the shape of Lost Lake as dawn creeps along the horizon—the dock jutting out, the leafless trees on the shoreline, its surface in the early dawn light still dark and opaque. I realize I'm eager to go out and explore, to reacquaint myself with the haunts of my childhood. Reacquaint myself, even, with the girl I used to be.

Spending my summers here—and all my school vacations up until about age sixteen, when I finally put my foot down, and found a summer job waitressing at a Sizzler back home in New Jersey—shaped me, more, perhaps, than anything else in my life has. It amazes me, now that I'm back, that I managed to avoid truly thinking about the cottage for seven whole years. I managed to forget what it was to me, who *I* was when I was here, and live my Westport life—running a home, a family, and a book club—without much more than a flicker of sentimental regret for all those summers and holidays, weeks, months and even years—in this place, my home.

A sigh escapes me, and I take a sip of my coffee. For twenty years, I reflect, I've managed to fill up my life with what now seems like the paltry and the insipid. At first, it was all well-intentioned, valuable even; after an unexpected pregnancy—Sam—right after Daniel and I got married, I became a stay-at-home mom, thinking it would only be for a few years that somehow slid into a decade without me even realizing.

Having had to give up my entry-level position in publishing, I made being a mother my career—organic everything, all the baby and toddler classes, perennial parent volunteer, dedicated class mom, on and on, ad nauseam, until I started to annoy myself with my own earnestness. And then, as some kind of self-protective measure, I started to make fun of it all, in a self-deprecating sort of way. When your kids are teenagers, you don't want to *still* be the mom who brings in the pumpkin-deco-rated cupcakes for Halloween.

At that point, I toyed with the idea of restarting my career, but after a decade and a half out of the workforce, and only a couple of years' early experience in it, it felt impossible. Who, really, wants to hire a 42-year-old as an entry-level editorial assistant? And as Daniel was making good money—*was* being the operative word—I had no desire to hire myself out as a lunch lady or retail assistant just for the fun of it. But that didn't leave me with very much—the aforementioned book club, tennis twice a week, and making sure every year of our lives was documented in curated photo collages going up the stairs was never meant to be my life's ambition. But what is?

I think of the girl I was in this place, the girl who strode through the raspberry patches, mindless of the scratches, who plucked a leech from her leg with scornful fingers, who barked at a bear to make it run away.

I was that girl, and yet I can't quite believe it. I'm not sure if I can remember how to be her again, or even if I know how to try. I look at her and I see a ghostly Laura Ingalls, a TV-toned fantasy; and yet once she was real. Wasn't she?

As I watch the sun coming over the tops of the evergreens, I wonder if that's part of the reason I wanted to come back here—to find myself in this place again, before it—and that version of me—is lost forever.

In the weeks before we lost the house and life as we knew it blew up, I began to dream of the cottage—or, really, have nightmares. In my dreams, the place was always falling apart in a dystopian, mystical sort of way; the lake had turned into a treacherous swamp, filled with writhing snakes; or, in one vivid dream, huge slug-like creatures that surfaced from the dark depths like malformed walruses and then sank again, bubbling back into the dark water.

The house fared no better; in one dream it was on fire; in another a great big pit had opened up in the living room while I backed away in terror, clutching Ruby to me. In yet another dream, lava flowed down the hill outside, a great, molten river rushing toward us as we huddled in terror, right here by the fireplace. I always woke up from these dreams first gasping from fear, only to have it replaced by relief that it wasn't real, and then an ache of realization that in some ways it sort of was.

You didn't have to be Freud to know why I was having the nightmares. My mother's nursing care was expensive; a few months earlier my brother, as executor of her estate with power of attorney, had emailed my sister and me about the necessity of selling this place. Not that it would sell for very much—fifty acres in the back of beyond, even with its own small lake, wouldn't fetch more than a couple hundred grand Canadian, if that, but my brother wanted to be rid of it, had for years, which was understandable considering none of us came here anymore. I was the one who held on, arguing it was for my mother's sake, but really it was for mine.

And now I'm here, having this last gasp of cottage life, while framing it as a necessary reset for my family. We'll have to sell it in the spring, I know; my mother needs the money for her care, and Daniel and I obviously can't afford it now. The prospect still hurts me, though. Even if I've been avoiding it for most of the last decade, this place still claims a part of my soul.

I finish my coffee, add a log to the fire, and then head to the kitchen to make a start on breakfast. I want to banish the melancholy thoughts of what once was and do my best to live in this moment, simple as it is. This is why we came here, I remind myself. Not because we didn't have any choice, but because this was the best one. And bacon frying is the best smell to wake up to, especially with a lake now shimmering under wintry sunlight, the fog hovering over the water beginning to melt away in ghostly shreds.

Nobody wakes up until the bacon and scrambled eggs are warming in the oven, and I'm on my second coffee, standing by the window as the last of the mist rolls across the lake, like fragments of a dream. The water is a deep greenish-black and as smooth as glass, the sky above the color of pewter, with pale patches of fragile blue breaking through, like hope itself.

The trees that densely fringe the lake are either leafless and skeletal-looking, all barren branches and claw-like twigs, or thickly, densely evergreen, utterly impenetrable, a forbidding wall of nature stretching toward the sky. The dock, I can now see in the morning light, has rotted; half of it completely gone, the other half fallen into the lake, now no more than a tumble of mossy planks. After seven years, I shouldn't be surprised at the extent of the decay, and yet so much here is still the same. The old canoe, made of red tin, is still hoisted up on the beach, from when my dad last pulled it up there, after he'd taken Sam fishing.

I remember that morning perfectly—the sun shining high above, the sky so blue it almost hurt to look at it. The whole day hurt, in its purity and beauty, because I knew that it was almost certainly the last time my dad would take my son fishing; he had terminal cancer, and his prognosis was in months, not years. He died just four months later.

Even now I can picture him and Sam heading down to the dock, my dad with his rod and tacklebox, Sam trotting next to him, alert, excited, jumping up and down a little. I see my dad steadying Sam with his hand on his shoulder as he clambered into the boat, making it rock to and fro. The eagerness on Sam's face, to finally be out on the lake with his beloved grandpa; I think even he, at that age, sensed the solemnity of the moment, and yet also felt its joy.

"Do I smell bacon?"

I turn, managing a smile as Daniel comes out of the bedroom, dressed as I am, in fleece, sweatpants, thick socks. His hair is sticking up in several directions, and he has a day's growth of silvery beard. He looks like a mountain man in the making, and I can tell he's pleased by this version of himself.

"I don't think I've slept so well in years," he exclaims, as he heads into the kitchen. "It's so quiet here."

"The girls must have too," I reply, "because they're still asleep." Although, glancing at the clock above the mantle—something else that's still working, after Daniel wound it last night—I realize it's only just after seven o'clock. Still early.

Daniel comes back into the living room, holding a mug of coffee. "I forgot how beautiful this place is," he says, his gaze on the lake. The mist has now cleared, the sky already lightening to blue from the gray, like color bleeding through cloth. The lake shimmers beneath the watery sunlight. "Why didn't we come up here more?" he muses.

"I don't know," I reply, although I sort of do. Because a cabin in the woods with teenagers isn't much fun. Because a water park or Disney World always seemed like an easier, if more expensive, alternative. Because five hundred miles always felt too far, and I was afraid to so much as brush up against the memories I knew would still be here, ready to crash over me the moment I opened the door.

Daniel gives me a direct look. "So, what should we do today?" he asks, and I'm not sure if it's a challenge—a not-so-subtle *why are we here again?*—or that he needs a project. For months, we've been like this, a continual parry and thrust of barbed questions, meaningful sighs, deliberate silences. Neither of us can quite keep from showing, in myriad, minuscule ways, how injured we feel, each one of us the wronged party, and yet I know, I *know*, we both are. We both contributed to this mess in our own ways, even if I can't let go of my anger. In truth, I haven't tried all that hard.

"That's up for discussion," I say in as upbeat a tone as I can. "Make this place more habitable for the next six weeks, I guess? Mattie wants to move into the small room, so we'll have to shift some boxes. We should check on the firewood in the cellar too—we'll probably need more. And a good vacuuming. Darlene has done a great job, but there are still a lot of mouse droppings everywhere."

"That's life in the woods for you," Daniel remarks sagely, and I smile and nod. He loved it here, back when the kids were little; a week or two every year when he could pretend to be a mountain man, get out the chainsaw, drive the truck. He was good at it all, too, I remember; far handier than I was with a power tool, taking the vagaries of cottage life—mice, mosquitoes, damp—in his easy stride.

"And we'll need more water," I add, because already I know that will be a constant refrain—up and down the steps to the lake several times a day. "Maybe that can be Mattie's job. It might be good for the girls to have chores here. Feel part of things."

Daniel doesn't reply, but I feel his wince even if I don't see it because despite what I just said, my reaction is the same. We both back away from the thought of asking Mattie to do anything she doesn't want to right now because getting her to comply with even the most basic requirements of family life brings both resistance and drama.

"And we could explore a little," I add, not wanting the day to be nothing but a to-do list, cottage style. "The old four-wheeler is in the barn, and the truck too, I think. I doubt they work now, but we could see. Maybe you could fire them up." A few years ago, Darlene would drive both once in a while to keep them going, but when it became ever clearer that none of us were coming back anytime soon, I think she probably stopped.

"Sure," Daniel says expansively.

"Great," I say, and I nod toward the kitchen. "There are eggs and bacon in the oven."

He nods, and for a second, we just stand there—Daniel by the fireplace, with his back to the fire, me in the middle of the room, as if I don't know where to go. Then he puts his mug down on the mantle and comes over and slips his arms around my waist. It's both deliberate and awkward; we've moved around each other these last months, making sure not to touch. I didn't actually realize how much until this moment.

After a second or two, which feels like too long, I clumsily put my arms around him. There's a familiarity to it, but without the ease, which makes it feel even more strange. We stand there for a moment, arms around each other yet somehow it feels as if we are not quite touching.

"This could be good," Daniel says quietly, which is what I've been telling him all along, but he makes it sound as if it is a new sentiment. "For us."

That is new, and it gives me a jolt—of hope, at the possibility of it, but also alarm because even though neither of us has said so, *us* is a concept we need to address. "Yes," I say at last. I'm under no illusions that it is anything more than a brief detour, a step out of time, although one that I hope will bring us closer in the long term. In six weeks, we'll be back in Connecticut, or wherever Daniel finds a job, trying to carve a new life out for ourselves, falling into patterns, making new ruts. It's what I crave and dread at the same time, and living in that paradox is exhausting. I close my eyes as the morning sun sends its bright, healing rays across the pine boards of the floor.

"Yes," I echo, with more conviction. "For us."

THREE

"What, am I supposed to be impressed?"

Mattie tucks her chin toward her chest as she scuffs one sneaker along the dirt road. It has not been an easy day for her—or for me. There have been, I've come to realize, too many unwanted surprises here, too many strange and unexpected things for my suburban daughter. Last night, in the blur of getting to bed, Mattie didn't fully appreciate the complete rusticity of our situation. Now she's starting to—although *appreciate* may be the wrong word. Actually, I know it is.

I suppress a sigh as I scan the barren landscape—leafless trees, frozen ground, everything muted and brown and utterly, eerily still in the dead zone of late autumn, early winter. No snow, no vivid autumn hues, just the *lack*, like color has been leached from every living thing. Even though the woods are still, I feel as if I'm being watched.

I know there's nothing out there right now except for maybe a hungry squirrel, a hibernating bear. I'm not being watched by anyone at all, and maybe that's what's unnerving. The utter and absolute remoteness of this place, where you could scream as loud as you wanted, and nobody would hear.

If a tree fell in the woods, would it make a sound?

The answer, here, seems obvious.

Mattie certainly hasn't been bowled over by the wilderness. She's eyed everything askance on our little nature walk, just the two of us, as Ruby opted to stay back in the cottage with Daniel. Our chance to explore our surroundings, have a little mother–daughter bonding time, although precious little bonding has happened so far.

We've ventured out to peer into the pump house, now a shadowy, cobwebby clutter of old and probably broken tools, and then the root cellar, the door too swollen from rain and age to open, its latch rusted. Just as well, perhaps, as I have no idea how much stuff is moldering in there.

We walked down the dirt road to the old garden, turned into a tundra of thorny, barren raspberry bushes and frozen, stony ground, and now we are up at Maple Manor, the whimsically named shack where, for a decade or so, my parents made maple syrup.

It was a shabby-looking place in its heyday, and it is more than half falling down now. Mattie nudges a pile of rusted tin pails heaped outside the walls with her sneaker. "This place is, like, *so* decrepit."

I let out a huff of laughter because of course it's true. "But you used to love Granny and Grandpa's syrup," I remind her, although maybe she doesn't remember. It's been years since we've had any.

Mattie scowls and digs her hands deeper into the pockets of her coat. The wind coming off the lake is cold and cutting, and it makes my eyes water and my cheeks sting. Dead leaves swirl and eddy about our feet and the wind soughs through the bare branches above us before it dies down again, leaving that almost unnatural stillness—the silence of the woods stretching all around us, unsettling in its totality. Our nearest neighbor is, I believe, more than five miles away, down a rough dirt track. The nearest gas station is ten miles, and the nearest town over twenty.

I have an urge to shout or to clap my hands over my ears, I'm not sure which. Something, to break the silence, or maybe just to get a reaction from my daughter.

"How long are we staying here for?" she asks on a martyred sigh, even though I'm pretty sure she knows the answer.

"Through Christmas, probably, and then we'll have to see." Hopefully, then Daniel will have a plan. We all will.

Mattie shakes her head, in a weary sort of disbelief, which I suppose is better than her ranting at me yet again. This morning we cleared the little room of its boxes, to be a bedroom for her; Ruby was happy to stay in the loft. I had visions of making it cozy, piling up the pillows and duvet, but a mouse had made a nest in the mattress, and Mattie squealed in horror at the sight of the mess spilling out onto the floor—crumbs and corn kernels, mouse droppings and mattress stuffing.

"We'll bring a mattress down from the loft," I told her quickly, placatingly, but she backed away, hands held up as if in self-defense, declaring she'd never sleep in a room where a mouse had been making its home.

"Then you won't be sleeping anywhere in the cottage," Daniel informed her cheerfully, which did not improve the situation.

"Sam will be here soon," I remind her now. "That will be fun, won't it?"

She shrugs, and I try not to sigh. They'd only just started to get along before he left; Mattie was finally old enough for Sam to take seriously, and I'm hoping that when we're all together, it will feel... right, I suppose, in a way it hasn't in a long time.

I'm also trying to think of a way to make this whole proposition more appealing—in all my memories of happy times at the cottage, it was never mid-November, the whole world frozen, everything the muted brown of dead things, and so *quiet*. We should have come here in March, when the sap is running, or, better yet, in summer, when the lake is sparkling and blue and *warm*, and the woods open up with birdsong and berries. Unfortunately, that wasn't when our lives fell apart.

"Is Dad going to get a new job?" Mattie asks unexpectedly, and I hear a note of vulnerability in her voice that makes me both tense and ache.

"Yes," I reply carefully. "That's the idea."

"How can he even find one, if we're stuck up here?"

"His resumé is with a head-hunter, and once we get the internet going, he'll able to make some enquiries." We'd already discussed the logistics of it—making sure the phone and internet work, a short flight from Ottawa to New York if need be, for interviews. If he gets to that stage.

"Why are you so mad at him?" Mattie asks, and I stiffen in surprise.

"I'm not mad at him," I tell her after a moment, which isn't exactly true, and, from the look she gives me, Mattie clearly knows it. But why is this about me being mad at him, rather than how Daniel let me—us—down? Not, of course, that I want to frame it that way to Mattie, or even to myself, but still. *I'm not the bad guy here*, I think, and then quickly remind myself that no one is.

"It's not his fault he lost his job," she states, her tone turning truculent, and I draw a deep breath, inhaling cold, fresh air and woodsmoke, letting it both steady and buoy me.

"I know that, Mattie," I say as gently as I can.

"So?" Another challenge, this one a sneer.

"I told you, I'm not mad at Dad." At least, I'm trying not to be. It's the lying that's been the hardest to take, but some part of me knows I've punished him long enough for it. I continue, my tone turning a little repressive, "It's been a difficult, complicated situation, and we're working through that. Together."

She lets out a snort of disbelief and then starts walking away from me in a way that feels deliberately dismissive. I let her go, clenching and unclenching my hands to keep my fingers warm, and to give myself a chance to regain my calm. It's typical that Mattie wants to blame me, rather than Daniel. She's always been a bit of a daddy's girl, and I'm the one who insisted we come up here, away from everything she knew. The fact that she's been suspended from school is probably my fault, too, in the warped world of her teenaged mind. I should have done my best to bail her out, the way so many parents at her private school do, rather than let her face the school's wrath for breaking their rules.

A sigh escapes me, long, low, and defeated, and slowly I follow Mattie back to the cottage.

Inside it is warm at least, and there is the disconcertingly loud sound of the TV filling the space, making me want to clap my hands over my ears. It feels so incongruous, so *wrong*, compared to the peaceful quiet of the morning, the needed still-ness, when I allowed myself to begin to hope.

"I got the TV working," Daniel says jubilantly. "And the Wi-Fi too. I called the satellite company—they just had to flip a switch."

"So I see." Mattie has already snatched her phone, swiping at it frantically, looking for the Wi-Fi signal, longing to be plugged in and connected to *something*. I look around for Ruby because I know that she doesn't like having the news on. So much of it is so grim.

"She's up in the loft, reading," Daniel says quietly, and he mutes the TV. I go into the kitchen to see what we can have for dinner. "We need to stay in touch with the world at least a little bit," Daniel says, as he follows me into the kitchen.

"I know." I take out a box of macaroni and a hunk of cheese.

"It was just a little strange, hearing it blare out like that. I'm sure we'll be glad for it in the long run. One day in and Mattie is already getting bored, I think."

Daniel rocks back on his heels. "I'll take a look at the four-wheeler and the truck, see if I can get them started. I'm sure she'd like blasting around on the four-wheeler."

"Yes, great." I rest my hands flat on the counter and give him a smile, conscious of Mattie's accusations, the uncomfortable kernel of truth burrowed inside them that I know I have to dig out and examine. "Thank you, for everything you're doing. I... I know this hasn't been easy."

Daniel nods gruffly, his hands shoved into the pockets of his battered cords. "Well, it hasn't been easy for you either."

"No, but..." I take a breath, trying to choose my words with the utmost care, each one both precious and dangerous, because, amazingly, this is the most we've talked about this whole situation in months, since the first time Daniel came into the kitchen, hanging his head like a naughty child, scuffing his shoes on the floor. *I have to tell you something*, he'd said, and I'd stared at him in complete bemusement because I was certain he would never have an affair, so it couldn't be that, and yet his tone suggested something secret and shameful.

"I haven't really tried to make it much easier," I say now, a concession—or a confession? Both, perhaps, and both are needed.

Daniel is silent for a long moment. I go to the pantry for an onion and then start chopping it while he simply stands in the doorway of the kitchen, staring at the floor. From the living room I hear the crackle of the fire, Mattie's squeal of success as she finally gets her precious Wi-Fi.

"Well..." he says at last, which isn't much of a response, and yet it tells me a lot. It tells me he agrees with me but is reluctant to say so, and it makes me wonder if I'm not the only one who is still angry.

"Maybe tomorrow we can go into Corville," he suggests after a moment, and it feels like a kind of truce. "See the sights."

"The sights of Corville?" I let out a little laugh. "They are few, but sure." At twenty miles away, with a population of thirteen hundred, it is the nearest town, its main attractions a fair-sized grocery store and a hardware and a feed store and not much else.

"The girls might enjoy it, though."

"Yes, they might." And after just one day, they need a break from the boredom?

"Do you remember," Daniel says quietly, "when we brought the kids here when they were little? It always took a few days to relax into cottage life, you know, the slow pace of it. We'd be edgy and restless for about half our vacation—"

"And then by the time we left, we wanted to stay another week at least," I finish with a small smile. "Yes, I remember."

Daniel smiles back at me, and for a second, we simply stand there, letting the cottage work its time-worn magic. It seeps into our bones, settles our souls. We just need to be patient and let it. Not resist its soft, sweet tug, its quiet promise that here and only here can you set your world to rights.

From the living room Mattie lets out a howl of frustration. "This Wi-Fi is *so* slow!"

After dinner, we manage to recapture a little bit of that magic. Mattie and Ruby clear the table while I wash dishes in the sink, and Daniel dries. Then we build up the fire, and I get out the marshmallows; we toast them over the dancing flames as night draws in, an unending blackness outside, unrelieved by the moon, hidden behind by a bank of clouds.

"It's so *quiet*," Ruby says, as she snuggles into me, her mouth rimmed with stickiness, her body warm and solid curled into mine.

"Yes." We have all said that so many times already, in varying tones—wonder, disbelief, trepidation, peace. I squeeze her shoulders, and she leans her head against me.

Mattie is curled up in the old wicker chair opposite, where my mother used to always sit. I can picture her there, with a cup of coffee in hand, or maybe some knitting. She was a diligent, determined knitter—all my kids have baby cardigans and booties she knit, in various, elaborate styles, with crocheted lace, colorful patterns of dolls or sheep. I didn't appreciate it all nearly as much as I should have, accepting the blankets and booties almost as a matter of course, putting them away in drawers with barely more than a murmured thanks.

It wasn't until my mother stopped, about six years ago, after trying to knit some mittens for Ruby and being unable to follow the pattern, frustrated by her inability, and maybe a little scared by it, too, that I started to realize the level of concentration and effort they took, not to mention the sheer amount of time. None of which, I realized, I possessed in the slightest. I'd never even knit a scarf.

"This is nice, isn't it?" Daniel says, and I blink the apparition away, the memory lingering in my mind like remnants of mist, the whispers of ghosts. Mattie is in the chair, not my mother.

"Yes, it is." I smile at Mattie, who has thawed slightly since having connected to the outside world via her phone. Although we deleted all her social media, we still allow her to text her best friend Lily, who is a genuinely nice girl and was not part of the problem that engulfed my daughter's life in the shape of a seventeen-year-old boy named Drew and his gang of no-good friends. He, thankfully, is out of her life, hopefully forever.

And it *is* nice here now, I think, with the fire crackling, the cottage finally warm, or at least warm*ish*, the night outside so dark and making us feel even cozier. Is there any sound more comforting than that of a crackling wood fire, the shower of sparks, the settling into the grate? Daniel and I share a smile that feels both conciliatory and complicit, a bridge being built, a joke being shared. Mattie licks the marshmallow off her fingers and Ruby burrows more deeply into me, elbow digging into my side, but I don't mind. I want to live in this moment; I want to quietly glory in it, spin it out.

Then the contented quiet is split by an unearthly sound from outside—a long, lonely howl that echoes through the still night, on and on, before finally fading away into silence.

Ruby jerks up straight, her eyes wide. "What was *that*?"

"A wolf," I reply after a moment, reluctantly, because I fear the girls are going to freak out; and the truth is the back of my neck is starting to prickle. The sound is unlike anything you'd hear in the Connecticut suburbs, ghostly and eerie and alarmingly close.

"A *wolf*?" Mattie stares at me in incredulity. "Are you serious? There are *wolves* here?"

"Mattie..." I stare at her helplessly. Does she not realize we're in the Canadian wilderness? There are wolves, and bobcats, and bears, not to mention all the other fauna—squirrels, chipmunks, foxes, deer, and, yes, snakes, although harmless ones. I think. Has she never seen a wildlife documentary on PBS? Maybe she hasn't.

"Of course, there are wolves here," Daniel says, the voice of calm and reason. "We're in the woods, Mattie. But that wolf sounded far away—its howl was echoing over the lake. I think it's probably on the other side."

Ruby shivers and then burrows even deeper into me. I put my arm around her again and we all sit in silence, waiting, I realize, to hear the howl again.

"The wolves won't hurt you," I tell Ruby, but I realize I don't sound convinced because I'm remembering the moment of sheer terror when I once came face to face with a wolf on the dirt road. I was about eight or so, walking as quietly as I could, so as, ironically, not to attract the attention of wolves. It came out right in front of me, stared at me for an endless moment while I stood there, trembling; its eyes were a vivid and surprising ice blue. Then it trotted silently down the road, *toward* me, for a heart-stopping second, before, indifferent to my presence, it loped off into the woods. "They really won't," I say, more firmly this time, and Mattie just shakes her head and reaches for her phone, as if the internet will somehow ward off the dangers of the wild.

"Do you know where your dad kept his guns?" Daniel asks quietly, a while later when the girls are getting ready for bed. "He had a .303 rifle, didn't he? And a .22."

"Yes..." I don't want to think about guns. My dad had them only as a precaution, mostly.

"We should find them, make sure they still work," Daniel says. "Just in case."

As if to punctuate his statement, the wolf howls again, and I wonder if it sounds closer. "I think he kept them in the bedroom closet," I tell Daniel. "They really should be in a gun safe, but..." That wasn't so much of a thing, back in the day.

Daniel nods, mountain man in action. "I'll take a look."

The wolf is still howling intermittently, its long, lonely sound making me tense every time, as I put Ruby to bed up in the loft, arming her with plenty of blankets and a hot-water bottle. Her eyes are wide, the blankets drawn right up to the tip of her nose.

"Why do wolves howl?" she asks, and I pause, trying to think, but then I realize I don't know.

"I think," I say slowly, "they're just saying hello to their wolf friends."

Ruby gives me a look of blatant skepticism, but then she snuggles under the covers, and I know the answer has satisfied her enough to go to sleep. And it's mostly true, isn't it? It's about marking territory or something like that, I think, but again I realize I don't know.

There's so much I don't know, I acknowledge as I climb the ladder back down to the living room. Daniel is in the bedroom, the guns in their cases laid out on the bed. I look away. I'm not that courageous wild woods girl of my childhood, I realize with a lurch. Maybe I never really was.

FOUR

Corville is exactly as I remembered it, everything unapologetically unchanged, from the hardware on the corner to the bridge over the Bonnechere River, to the Country Depot feed store and supermarket on the outskirts of the town, on the road out to the larger town of Pembroke, another thirty miles away. The only difference in the whole town is a tiny, hipster-ish coffee shop by the bridge, advertising lattes and free Wi-Fi, and I notice as we drive past, completely empty.

There really isn't much to see in Corville, but Daniel had a look at the truck and four-wheeler this morning, and he wants to get some spare parts from the hardware, and I'd like to stock up on a few more groceries. Even though I bought plenty in Kingston, there are a couple of gaps, and who knows when we'll be back here again? I somehow doubt that Ruby and Mattie will want to experience the delights of Corville for a second time.

"People actually *live* here," Mattie remarks in a wondering tone as we park in town; the parking lot is mostly empty, and half the stores are still shuttered. While Daniel goes to the hardware, Mattie, Ruby, and I will stroll around.

"Don't be a snob, Matts," I say cheerfully enough. "It's a

perfectly nice place." Although I fear any town without a Star-bucks or an Abercrombie will seem deficient to my daughter. "Let's walk down by the river," I suggest.

I can't remember the last time I've been down here, under the bridge, where the water rushes by in white, frothing rivulets, diverting around several, large flat rocks that stretch far out into the water.

The girls wander alongside the river, glancing at the rocks, perfect for stepping out onto, but neither of them does, and why would they?

That isn't the kind of life we've lived—which has been sani-tized, suburban, and safe. Even "risky play" at school is super-vised, a series of balance beams and knotted ropes where kids can play only with careful instruction and teachers present.

"Let's go out on the rocks," I suggest, and Mattie looks at me in her typical teenaged disbelief, scathingly eloquent in her silence. It's like a superpower, the way teenagers can give such excoriating looks of sneering disdain. Do they practice in the mirror, or is it a skill they obtain at a certain age, like getting your Hogwarts letter, aged eleven? *Here is how you sneer...* "Come on," I say, my tone somewhere between cajoling and insistent. "It'll be fun."

"The water's very cold," Ruby says in a small voice. She has always been very cautious, to the point of timidity.

"It's *freezing*," Mattie corrects, folding her arms. "No way."

Their intransigence saddens rather than irritates me. They're *children*. Where is their sense of fun, of adventure and play? "I'll go first," I say, and I eye the first rock. As I size it up, I realize it is a little farther away than I thought. It's a matter not simply of stepping from shore to stone but of having to make an honest-to-goodness flying leap. I am, for a millisecond at least, going to be entirely airborne.

"Well, Mom?" Mattie says, and there is a laughing chal-lenge in her voice that makes me brave. I jump.

I hear Ruby's quick intake of breath as I land on the rock, stumble slightly, and right myself. My heart is pounding. I turn to my daughters, arms spread out, smile in place. "See?"

Mattie shakes her head. "Why do you want us to do this so much?"

Because I want to them to have fun? Because I need to prove something to them—or to myself? I don't exactly know, but for some reason it feels important, this little leap into the river, far more, I know, than it actually is.

"The view out here is amazing," I reply, as if that's an answer. Mattie huffs. Ruby hunches her shoulders and looks down at the water rushing by fast, foaming white. I stare out at the river, tumbling over rocks, rushing forward, and wait for one of them to act.

Then Mattie lets out a long-suffering sigh that makes me smile. "All right, *fine*," she says, and, crouching a little, she leaps onto the rock with me, as nimble as a ballet dancer, legs outstretched, hair flying, except like me she stumbles as she lands, and we end up clutching each other for a few taut seconds as we stagger around. I realize I can't remember the last time we've touched each other. Hugged, or even given a pat on the arm.

Mattie releases me quickly, dropping her arms and stepping away. I pretend it's no big deal as I turn to Ruby. "Rubes?"

"I don't know..." She nibbles her lip, eyeing us on the rock as if we're all the way across the Grand Canyon. For her, maybe we are.

Ruby has had low-level anxiety about a lot of things, ever since she was little. Not enough for a diagnosis, and I know because I've taken her to several specialists over the years, to try to figure out why she has her quirks—a hatred of seams, a fear of loud noises, periods of selective mutism. Acronyms have been bandied about—OCD, GAD, PDD. None of them have stuck, and in the end, the doctors decided Ruby was just Ruby, quirks included. And right now, she looks like she doesn't want to jump.

"Come on, Ruby," Mattie says, surprising me. "It's not too bad, and it *is* pretty cool out here."

My heart surges with love and pride and gratitude. Mattie's encouraging remark is something so small, and yet it's progress. "Only if you want to, Rubes," I tell my youngest daughter. "But Mattie's right. It is pretty cool out here."

And then, without warning, my daughter jumps. She flies through the air, her expression one of total terror, her strawberry-blond hair flying out from underneath her bobble hat, before she lands practically on top of me. I grab her, and so does Mattie, and for a few precious seconds we're all in a strange, desperate hug, and it feels like the best thing that's happened to me in a long time.

Then we separate, and, after a few seconds of wandering about what is essentially a very small space, Mattie lets out a bored sigh, and Ruby asks if we can go back now. But it still happened, I tell myself. No one can take that away from me.

We make the jump a second time with a bit more confidence and then we head back up to meet Daniel in front of the hardware, before going to the supermarket to stock up on a few more staples. I buy five more five-pound sacks of flour, another two dozen eggs, along with an entire cartful of other stuff. Daniel shakes his head wryly even as he pulls out his credit card, happy enough to go along, despite the cost.

"What is it about the cottage," he asks in a musing sort of way as we box up the groceries, "that makes you want to start homesteading or something? Buy a cow and a plow and, I don't know, a barrel of salt?" He smiles good-naturedly, and I smile back, enjoying the feeling of complicity.

"My mother and I used to pretend we were pioneers," I tell the girls as we push the cart toward the parking lot. I have a sudden, piercing memory of picking wild strawberries with her in a meadow halfway around the lake. Kneeling in the sun-touched grass, prizing the tiny strawberries from the fragile plants like red pearls from an earthy shell, filling up a drinking glass of green plastic, and presenting it to her like a treasure. I had slipped a few into my mouth as I picked, my lips and chin stained scarlet with juice.

"Pioneers," Ruby says, her eyes alight with interest. "How?"

"We were picking strawberries," I explain, "wild ones that are really, really tiny. I was getting impatient and so she said we should pretend we were pioneers, and that we needed the strawberries to survive."

"Strawberries to survive," Mattie repeats a bit scornfully, but then she remembers that this is her grandmother, whom she loves, and she adds in a grudging sort of apology, "That sounds like Granny."

"It was." It was *exactly* like my mother, who loved the cottage and all it stood for, who would have been a real-life pioneer if she could, with her knitting, her maple syrup making, the strawberries and raspberries and apples she picked and made into jam and sauce and pies. "We only picked the strawberries that one year," I finish, on a small, apologetic sort of sigh. "After that the pine trees grew up over the meadow and so the strawberries didn't grow there anymore, without the sunlight. We never found them anywhere else."

And for a second, I'm hit by a sudden wave of grief, so intense and overwhelming that it feels like slamming into a wall. It leaves me breathless and reeling, so I'm simply standing there in the parking lot, the cold wind blowing over me, as Daniel and the girls keep walking to the car.

"Alex?" Daniel asks, frowning a little, as he sees that I've stopped walking.

"Yeah... sorry." I smile at Mattie, and I ruffle Ruby's hair. I tell them we can get poutine—chips with gravy, a Canadian specialty—if the chip wagon by the gas station is still open in

November. I slide into the passenger seat and stare out the window, and I remind myself that my mother is alive, even if in moments like this I feel as if I've already lost her. I used to visit her at least once a week, back in Connecticut; her nursing home is half an hour from our old house. Before we left, I explained to her that we'd be away for a little while, but I'm not sure she understood. Even though she's always glad to see me when I visit, time doesn't seem to have any real meaning to her anymore.

Back at the cottage, we all help to unload the groceries; there's now so much that I have to stack some things on the floor. Already I'm thinking about Thanksgiving, the pies I'll make, the turkey in the freezer that will need to defrost for three days, at least. Maybe Mattie and Ruby will want to help me; I can teach them to make pastry, my mother's recipe, with vinegar and an egg, a tablespoon of brown sugar to sweeten the crust.

"We're certainly well stocked," Daniel says, and I nod, feeling satisfied, almost happy at the sight of all those sacks and cans.

"We should call Sam tonight," I say. "Tell him to make sure to pack some warm clothes."

"I'm sure he will, upstate New York has got to be as cold as here, or almost," Daniel points out. "But yes, let's call him."

That night, with the fire blazing merrily, the curtains drawn against the icy night and, thankfully, no wolves howling, we call Sam on the old-fashioned wall phone, the kind with a rotary dial and a curly cord. My parents never upgraded this, along with so many other things here.

"Hey, are you up there already?" he asks, sounding so cheerful it heartens me, makes things feel easy. "How is it?"

"Good. Rustic."

"Rustic, huh? Is that codeword for, I don't know, a wreck?"

He laughs; everything is fun to him, as well as simple. I'm envious as well as proud.

"No, not exactly," I answer on a laugh, and Mattie grabs the phone and says into it, "Basically, yes."

I hear Sam chuckle, and I find I'm smiling. I miss Sam so much, and the thought of seeing him again fills me with joy. Ruby takes a turn on the phone, standing on her tiptoes to speak into it. "We're pretending to be pioneers."

"Pioneers," Sam repeats, sounding impressed. "Cool, Rubes." I take the receiver back to hear him ask, "So, are you really going to stick it out until Christmas?"

"I think so." We haven't told Sam the specifics of what happened—the loss of Daniel's job, as well as the house, Mattie's suspension from school. It felt like too much to burden him with just as he was starting his first semester away from home, and also I felt too humiliated. I'd failed on so many fronts. So had Daniel.

Instead, we constructed some rambling story about needing to take some time out, Daniel deciding to do something else, the girls needing a break from school. We didn't mention the house at all. Daniel wanted to tell him the truth, which was a bit rich, considering he didn't tell me the truth for nearly six months, but I was adamant. We'd tell Sam what had really happened when we were face to face, when we could explain, reassure, promise. It wasn't the kind of conversation you could have over the phone.

"Well, it's all pretty wild," Sam says, sounding so cheerful that I wonder if he's simply not letting himself think about it. After all, it's pretty strange to have your entire family decide to up sticks and move to rural Canada for six weeks. He must suspect something, but he sounds untroubled, taking it in his stride. He's got his own life to live now, after all, with all the pleasures and pursuits college has to offer, a subsuming universe that's a world away from high school, family, the life he lived only a few months ago. And thankfully it's not at risk, since he's got a scholarship and some financial aid. The knowledge of his life apart from us makes me happy for him, as well as sad for myself. This is how it's meant to happen, the natural order of things, and yet as a parent it can still feel wrong, or at least hard.

"We'll see you on Tuesday," I tell him. "Just four days! Your flight gets in in the morning, right, to Ottawa?"

"Yeah, eleven or so. I'll email you the info. Can't wait." He pauses. "It'll be weird to be up there, without Grandpa or Granny."

"I know." My voice is soft. "But it's good too. Better than I expected, in a lot of ways."

"Good. I'll have to get the fishing rods out. The lake hasn't frozen over yet, has it?"

"No, not yet."

"Cool."

We share a few more pleasantries and then we say goodbye, and I feel that little rush of sadness, like an emptiness blowing through me, as Sam ends the call. Like my mother, but in an entirely different way, it feels as if I've lost him too.

Daniel must sense something of this because he puts his arm around me, and we go back to the living room, where the girls are curled up in chairs by the fire, Ruby reading, Mattie on her phone.

"How's the Wi-Fi working out?" I ask her, and she rolls her eyes.

"It's atrocious," she says, but she doesn't sound nearly as scathing as she once might have, and I wonder if the detox process is already happening. Away from the bad influences of social media, Drew, the in-girls she was so desperately trying to be friends with, the *drugs*, my daughter can finally start to thrive. The cottage can work its age-old magic. I'll take that vision of the Hallmark movie now, all the sweet, sappy senti-mentality. Bring it on. Let it bring us together, healing and helping us to grow. Cue the movie montage, the swelling music right now.

I'm smiling at the thought as Daniel and I sit on the sofa, his arm still around me. I let my head rest against his shoulder and close my eyes, enjoying the novelty of us being together like this, another new beginning, just like he said. I believe him now; at least I am starting to.

I listen to the comforting sounds of the fire—the crackle and hiss of the logs, enjoying the way the flames cast dancing shadows across my eyelids. Maybe I'm being too hopeful, but tonight I'm happy. I'm at peace.

Later, I will recall that feeling, examine it like an artifact, try to remember how that sense of contentedness felt, stealing through my bones, turning them soft. Making me hope. It will be a long, long time before I ever feel that again. In fact, it will be never, at least not in the way I did then, with such a blessed ignorance of all that was to come.

I thought I'd already suffered then, I'd *done* my time, what with Daniel losing his job, Mattie being suspended, as if these laughable trivialities somehow *counted* for something. The truth was I had absolutely no idea. No idea at all.

I'd hold on to the memory of that night for a few seconds at most, trying to imbue myself with its peace and power, before it evaporated like the mist on the lake, ghostly shreds of another time, another life, when everything was so very, very simple.

Because just eight hours after I sat there on the sofa, feeling so happy, so hopeful, the world as I knew it, as *anyone* knew it, had ended.

FIVE

I wake to the sound of the generator crankily kick-starting to life. After a three-day power outage fifteen or so years ago, my parents invested in a large propane generator that squats outside the kitchen window, to use if any such outages happened again. None did, but the generator was a reassurance to them, a way to feel at least a little self-sufficient, the way they wanted to back in the seventies, when it seemed like everyone was looking to own a couple of chickens, call themselves a commune.

As I blink sleep out of my eyes, I wonder why it's starting up now. I'm amazed it can still run after ten years; hazily I recall that Darlene might have tested it every so often.

I blink some more and then sit up. Outside the window the lake is like glass, as smooth as a mirror, reflecting the trees on its shoreline perfectly, the dense evergreen as well as the bare branches of the maples and birches. The sky is the hazy blue of morning; by breakfast it will have hardened to a deep, penetrating blue, a cold, sunny day. The weather matches my mood —bright, determined. I clamber out of bed.

I dress quickly, my breath creating frosty puffs in the air. There is frost on the inside of the windowpanes again, and the railings of the deck are dusted with snow. I imagine Ruby's delight; when we first told her we were coming up here, she asked if she could bring a sled. By Christmas we could very well likely have several feet of snow. The thought makes me smile.

As I come into the living room, I feel a flicker of exasperation that Daniel is already up but has let the fire die down. The room is cold, and he is crouched in front of the TV, his fingers pressed to his lips. The screen is full of fire, some explosion somewhere, no doubt. I don't want to know about it.

"It's freezing in here," I say, making sure to keep my voice mild. Daniel doesn't respond. I press my lips together and go to poke at the ashes before throwing another log on the stirred-up embers. He still hasn't spoken as I go into the kitchen and discover he hasn't made coffee either. The generator is still whirring away outside, and I return to the living room; Daniel has not moved an inch. A flicker of unease ripples through me.

"Daniel?" I ask. "Did the power go out?"

He gives a little shake of his head, almost like a twitch, and reluctantly I move my gaze to the TV screen. I thought it was the news, but it looks like a home movie of some kind, the camera swinging all over the place, from a distance. The sight is of fire, an awful, indistinguishable blaze filling up the whole screen.

"Good Lord," I say. I can't make out any buildings or people, just fire and smoke. "Where *is* that?"

Daniel doesn't reply for a second, his gaze glued to the screen. Then, in little more than a whisper: "New York."

For a second, I can't speak. I can't think. That surreal, burning landscape of destruction? *New York?* "What?" My voice is thin. "Where in New York? Why aren't they showing anything else, some commentary or something?" I want him to explain it to me, give me an answer that's neat and tidy, but already I'm sensing, on a deeply visceral level, that it's not going to happen.

Slowly Daniel turns to face me. He reminds me, weirdly, of an old man. Something about his eyes, his mouth... he *has* changed. Aged, even though he looks the same. "It's New York," he states in a low voice, the words coming hesitantly, as if he has to find them, then lay them down. "And Washington DC. And Chicago. And Los Angeles. And Houston. And... Miami, I think. Phoenix..."

I take a step toward him, then freeze. For a second, I'm caught in a maelstrom of emotions; I feel suddenly, incredibly furious, as if there is something to blame him for, and I'm also terrified, frozen in indecision, because I don't want to ask him any more questions, yet of course I have to know. "What," I ask in an oddly cold voice, "are you talking about?"

"Alex..." He pauses, takes a breath, then starts again. "There have been nuclear strikes, Alex. Several. Many, even. Overnight."

He stares at me, his expression stricken and grim, and I stare back, refusing to let the words compute. *Nuclear strikes?* I have a sudden urge to laugh wildly. *Are you serious, Daniel? What do you think this is, some stupid action movie about a tornado or an asteroid where we all have to escape the destruction?* The world as we know it ends? Cue the action scene, the car chase, the explosions when I decide to take a bathroom break because I can't even tell what's happening?

I close my mouth, which has dropped open, and turn back to the TV. I'm searching for something recognizable in the blazing, flattened landscape that looks like something from Mars, a lunar landscape of nothingness but fire.

"How did they film that?" I ask almost belligerently. It is an absurd question, but I'm searching for loopholes. My mind is already racing, considering hoaxes, cyber hacking, conspiracy theories, someone has taken over a TV station...

I need this not to be true.

"I think it must be a drone or something. I don't know." He shakes his head slowly. "All of Manhattan has been... has been destroyed." He speaks almost wonderingly, if he can't believe what he is saying. "There was a newsperson earlier before it cut off. The whole metro area—" He stops, and realization slams into me. The metro area... Westport, where we used to live. Where all our friends are. Our lives are, or at least were...

My gaze swings back to the TV, but it's just the same aerial shot, a canvas of orange and red, impossible to make out anything but fire. Is it running on a loop? Is it even real? There's no other footage, no voiceover, nothing.

"You said Washington," I say slowly. "And Chicago. LA..."

"I think so. That's what they said before it cut off. The whole infrastructure of the country must have been completely damaged, even destroyed..." He trails off, his gaze drawn inexorably to the screen, also looking for answers that are not there. *Nothing* is there.

I think of the generator, waking me up this morning. The annoyance I felt a few moments ago, at the fire going out, the lack of fresh coffee. I'm edging closer to an abyss, but I don't want to look down. I can't. I won't.

I blink slowly, trying to frame this in a way that makes sense, that is possible. I want to say *okay, so what we'll do is...* but I can't get there. It's an impossible, fathomless leap.

And then it hits me, and I gasp if I've been punched, winded, reeling. "*Sam...*"

"He's upstate," Daniel says quickly, automatically, as if I don't know this. As if it makes a difference. Does it? "I think it's far enough away from, you know, the radioactive cloud..."

Radioactive cloud? I have another urge, utterly inappropriate, to laugh. We can't possibly, seriously be talking about radioactive clouds. This is some awful *would you rather* scenario, the kind that Sam likes to suggest over dinner. *Would you rather be in the epicenter of a nuclear strike, or one hundred miles away?* Cue the debate about radioactive clouds and nuclear fallout. Mattie wants to be incinerated in the blast; Ruby would prefer to live underground for five years until it's safe to come out.

No. *No.* This can't actually be happening. The TV screen suddenly goes black, and it feels as if we have been plunged into silence even though there had been no sound.

A panic is creeping over me like a mist, blurring the edges of my mind. My heart is thundering; I'm hyperventilating. I take a few, deliberate, even breaths. *Think, Alex.* My gaze moves to the window; outside the sky is blue, the lake is gleaming in the morning light.

Without even knowing why, I run to the door, wrench it open, and then stumble outside, the cold air hitting me hard in the face. There is a loon on the lake, swimming placidly, cutting a smooth ripple through the water. The world is still.

I glance at the horizon, half expecting it to be a livid red, a mushroom cloud billowing up, but it's as calm and blue as the rest of the sky. I stand there, shivering, clenching and unclenching my fists, my mind a frightened blank. I'm trying to think, but I physically can't. Everything is buzzing static, getting louder and louder until I have the urge to press my hands to my ears, block it all out, but I can't because it's inside me.

Behind me Daniel steps outside, closing the door carefully behind him. We stand there in the freezing cold, my back to him, the lake, shimmering and beautiful in the dawn, before us. Neither of us speak.

Finally, I ask in a wooden voice, "What do we do?"

Daniel doesn't answer for a moment. "We need to find out

more," he says at last. He sounds calm, but also resigned. Unshakeable, even in this, and it occurs to me how I've counted on that about him, for so long. No matter how I veer or vacillate, he remains steadily the same. It is why, I know, I took his lying so hard; it was so completely out of character for him. But that hardly matters now.

"See if the US has retaliated," he continues, "or if there have been more strikes. How... damaged everything is, I guess. I have no idea what the—the consequences of this are. Will be. I don't even know who sent the missiles, what happened to cause..." He trails off, sounding dazed. "No one could have seen this coming."

"How do we find out those things?" I ask in that same wooden voice. I feel as if I have no idea how to do anything anymore; as if I need operating instructions for absolutely everything, even breathing.

"I'm not sure." He sounds more certain now. We are both trying to be practical because that feels stronger. "The TV isn't working, besides what you saw. But the internet still might, since it's connected to satellite, and not a router."

I whirl around to face him. "We need to call Sam."

I haven't bothered much with my cell phone since we arrived at the cottage, since there is no signal here, but now I race to our bedroom, practically pushing past Daniel to get inside, and then fumble among the detritus on the bedside table —my watch, a glass of water, a tube of hand cream. When I press the button on my phone, I see that the battery is dead, and I let out an anguished cry.

"Mine works," Daniel states quietly, from behind me. He thumbs a few buttons while we both wait, breath held. He can't make a call without a signal, but he tries to load a web browser. Already painfully slow at the best of times here, the Wi-Fi, such as it is, cannot load a single page. That's not unusual, up here, but it still frightens me.

48

"The landline," I practically gasp.

But when we race to it, in the kitchen, like two children on a treasure hunt following the clues, the line is dead. "I think," Daniel says hesitantly, placing it slowly back into the receiver, "the electromagnetic pulse from the strikes would have taken out the phone lines, along with the electrical grid. Everything's connected between southern Canada and the US."

I have a feeling he's garnered that kind of information from the many sci-fi movies he's watched, but right now it's all we have.

I shake my head slowly, my mind still racing yet unable to keep hold of a single thought. "We have to go and get Sam," I say, because that's all I can think about. I can't bear to think about all the others yet—my brother, my sister, my mother, my friends. Mattie's friends. The girls' teachers. Daniel's old work colleagues, university friends, aunts, uncles, cousins... Everyone, absolutely everyone, we ever knew—*what's happened to them?* Are they dead? Injured? Stumbling around in some apocalyptic universe I can't even envision? "*Daniel.*"

"Alex..." He looks at me helplessly. "I agree with you, of course I do, but how? He's about three hundred miles away."

"Still." A plan is forming—unthinkable, maybe impossible, but still. "We'll drive," I say. "We'll drive to him. You said upstate New York will be safe from the—the nuclear fallout, right?" It still feels ridiculous to say it, to *mean* it. "We have to get him back up here." Because the cottage, I realize suddenly, might actually be the best place we could be right now. It's the one place we know of where we might be safe. Although *will* we be safe? Or will some nuclear ash cloud drift its way up here?

Is this the kind of scenario where we all think we're fine, laughing in relief, and then in a couple of days our hair will start to fall out, our skin will turn black and begin to bubble? A horrible mash-up of movie snippets and scenes from books is running through my mind—a documentary on Chernobyl crossed with some action movie with Tom Cruise, with Nevil Shute's grim tome *On the Beach* thrown in for good measure. A montage of Armageddon moments drifts through my mind, untethered yet presenting itself as anchored in fact.

"Alex," Daniel says, and I realize I'm hyperventilating, gasping for air. "*Alex.*" He puts his arms around me, and I press my face into his chest, hard enough to hurt, because I need some kind of escape from this, some kind of distraction, if just for a few seconds. I crave comfort, even though the empirical part of my brain knows there isn't any.

Daniel doesn't murmur that it's going to be okay, or that we'll figure this out, because of course those sentiments are absurdly, offensively paltry. He just holds me, and for a few seconds, I let that be enough.

Eventually, I ease back, take a deep breath. My eyes are dry, my breathing even. "We need to get Sam," I state again, a fact, one I refuse to argue or debate.

Daniel nods. "We don't have enough gas," he says slowly, thinking through it. "To get all the way there and back."

It hits me again, how much has happened. How much has changed. Will there not be gas stations along the way, will there not be *gas*? Will it be anarchy from here to his college, a fiery world of violence and chaos, death and destruction? *We're only one generation from extinction*, I think, and then wonder who said it. Some president, maybe, during the Cold War. It seemed alarmist, an exaggeration, even then, but right now, amazingly, it feels true. It might even be understatement because maybe everything has already ended, I realize numbly. Life as we know it. Society, structure, culture, government, laws... it might all be gone, and I have no idea whether we'll ever get it back.

"Can we listen to the radio?" I ask suddenly. "There might be someone transmitting somewhere, right? Someone who can

give us more information about what has happened out there."
Again I'm thinking of various vague sci-fi scenarios, the lone
pilgrim in an apocalyptic world, fixing up their ham radio,
trying to find another person out in the wilderness. *Can you
hear me? Can you hear me? Come in...*

Daniel nods, his forehead furrowed. "Maybe," he says. "It's
worth a try."

The only radio is the one in the car. We sit huddled in the
front seats, our breath coming out in frosty puffs, as Daniel
twiddles the dial.

"I think we'll have better luck with AM," he says, but there
is only static on every station. Thoughts are flashing through my
mind like streaks of lightning—Westport is sixty miles from
New York. Would it have been destroyed in the blast? No,
surely it's too far. But what about the fallout, the radiation dust,
all that stuff from the sci-fi movies that I don't really know
anything about? I have no idea at all about the answers, how
much danger everyone is in. My brother, my sister, my mother.
She's maybe eighty miles from the city, in her locked memory
care unit... my mind races.

Have the carers left? What about all the hospitals that no
longer have electricity? What about the people on life support
or in desperate need of dialysis, breathing therapy, defibrilla-
tors... what about the *babies*? Preemies in NICUs, toddlers in
pediatric wards... or even all the children at home, including my
own, whose future has been wiped away in an instant.

I can't let myself think about all the repercussions, not until
I know more. I strain to hear something amid the radio's static,
but there is nothing. I shiver as I hunch my shoulders and fold
my arms, trying to keep warm; I should have put my coat on.

"From the news report I heard before it shut off," Daniel
says quietly as he continues to twiddle the dial, "it seemed the
strikes were only on cities."

"*Only?*"

"I mean," he explains with a preternatural sort of calm, his face set and grim, "that they didn't target our own nuclear warheads or oil refineries, or anything like that, which apparently would have made everything much, much worse in terms of radiation and fallout, ongoing pollution, that kind of thing." He glances at me. "That's the world annihilation scenario. This isn't."

I suppose I should take some small semblance of hope from that, and yet I can't.

We don't even know who's responsible for the strikes. Has anywhere else been hit—South America, Europe, Asia, Africa? Or is it just the big bad US that's been, yes, *annihilated*? I remind myself that I don't actually know anything, that all I've seen is a TV screen of smoke and fire, that this could, *maybe*, be one giant hoax. Outside, the sunlight shimmers on the lake.

Then the static on the radio breaks, and a voice comes on, scratchy, tense, cutting out every few seconds. We both hold our breath, strain to listen to the faint, tinny sound. It takes me a second to realize it's the president of the United States speaking.

"The most important thing is for everybody to stay calm," he says, and a laugh escapes me, torn from my body, high and wild. Seriously? "If you are outside," he continues, "please find the nearest shelter. Anyone within ten miles of any of the strike zones should stay inside, with the windows closed at all times. If you have a basement, shelter in it. Do not leave your residence. I repeat, do *not* leave your residence. Water and food will be distributed to those in need as soon as possible. We are working hard to restore our infrastructure, and hope to have electricity working again, along with running water, in the affected areas, within the next few days. Please be patient and do *not* panic. This is a devastating moment for our great country," he concludes, his voice choking briefly, "but we will, with time and effort and, most of all, unity, rise above it. God bless you all."

I let out a shuddering breath as the radio briefly goes to static again, before another voice comes on, this one a woman's; she sounds shaken but firm. "That was the president of the United States, speaking from an undisclosed location. I'm Shelley Stevens broadcasting from KYZ Watertown. To summarize what we know so far, early this morning, nine nuclear missiles have hit major metropolitan centers in the United States—New York, Washington DC, Miami, Chicago, Houston, Phoenix, Los Angeles, San Francisco, and Boston."

"Boston." The word comes out of me in a something between a shriek and a groan; Sam's college is close to the border with Massachusetts. I turn to Daniel. "How far is that from Sam?"

His expression is shuttered, his gaze focused on the radio. "About a hundred and fifty miles. I think."

I gulp back the scream inside me, the shrill insistence that we go get him *right now.* I know we need more information, we need a plan, even if I can't imagine what that might be. This isn't a hoax, and the numb terror inside me feels too big to absorb, to allow.

"It appears that there is a power outage over most of the country right now," the broadcaster continues, "as well as severe disruption to water and gas supplies. Telephone and internet services are also currently not working across, it is believed, most of North America. As you heard, the president is advising people to stay in their homes and wait for assistance, and to that end martial law is in full effect across the entire country until further notice. There is no word from government sources about whether retaliatory strikes have been either considered or planned, or if further strikes are expected."

I press my fist to my mouth, bite my knuckles. Hard. The broadcaster continues, her voice wavering a little, "Until we know more, we advise, as the president of the United States has instructed, for everyone to stay in their homes and wait for assistance. This is Shelley Stevens, broadcasting from Watertown."

When the radio goes to static again, I slump back against the seat. My heart is racing, but I feel, quite suddenly, completely exhausted, as if getting through the next few minutes is as inconceivable as getting through the next few years.

"I think I should go into Flintville," Daniel says, naming the tiny town ten miles away from here, in the opposite direction to Corville; it's nothing more than a gas station that offers a few groceries, a couple of houses, and a church.

I turn to him. Every thought is coming so slowly it's as if I'm half-asleep, fighting my way out of a stupor. "Flintville? Why?"

"We might be able to find out a little more about what's going on. Some people might have a better satellite service there, better reception. And I might be able to get some gas."

"Okay." I nod slowly, my mind seeming so sluggish that every thought is hard to hold on to. The frantic energy that was racing through me has vanished; I feel as if I'm moving through molasses, mind and body. "Should I come with you?"

Daniel shakes his head. "No, I think you should stay here with Mattie and Ruby. I... I don't think we should leave the cottage empty."

"Empty?"

"I don't know." He rubs a hand over his face. "People can panic in situations like this—"

"Situations like this?" I let out a hollow, hopeless laugh. "When have we ever been in a situation like this?"

"You know what I mean. There's a power outage for a couple of hours and people start looting, smashing windows. Times that by a factor of, I don't know, a thousand. A million." He blows out a breath. "We don't know how quickly services will be restored anywhere. Or if there will be further strikes. If the US retaliates—"

"Stop." I hold up a hand. "I can't think about that." I can't think about any of it. "Go to Flintville," I tell him evenly. "Get some gas." Daniel nods, and I keep his gaze as I finish, "And then we'll get Sam."

SIX

After Daniel leaves for Flintville, the cottage feels strangely empty. Mattie and Ruby are still asleep, and I'm afraid to turn the TV on, so I end up simply prowling around, rubbing my hands together, trying both to think and not think at the same. After a few useless minutes, the steady rumble of the generator suddenly jolts through me. *What if we can't get any more propane?*

I run outside and fumble to switch it off, and the world is plunged into a sudden, absolute silence. I didn't realize just how loud the thing was until I turned it off, and I wonder how much propane we've wasted, running the lights, the heaters, the damned TV. The trivialities of life, now, when we have to start thinking differently. I'm not sure I even know how or where to begin.

Back in the cottage, I start putting away the dishes from last night's dinner. Part of me wants to hurl each plate to the floor, watch them shatter. I want something to *break*, but I keep myself from such a pointless exercise of frightened futility. Besides, I think with a sort of macabre humor, who knows when we'll be able to buy a new set?

I focus on the minutiae of the mundane—pick up each plate, open the cupboard, stack it inside. Take the next one, stack it on top. The clatter is somehow comforting, and yet it takes effort to do this simple chore. I have to concentrate.

As I work, my thoughts leapfrog from one impossible idea to the next. If Daniel can get gas in Flintville, he can drive to Sam's college. Find Sam, come back here, and we'll all hunker down together until the world rights itself again, within the same six weeks we'd been planning. I want it to be that simple, but already I know it can't be—even though I have no idea what it *will* be. Will Daniel even be allowed to drive on the roads, if martial law is in place? Is it in place in Canada, if there were no nuclear strikes here? What is happening in the rest of the world?

As for the route from here to Sam's college... will there be places to stay, people to help, or will the world have descended into instant anarchy like Daniel seemed to think might happen, maybe already has?

And even if he manages to get all the way there, get Sam, get back... what then? I think of what the president said, about restoring services. He made it sound as if it could be a couple of weeks, maybe months at the worst—patch a few wires, flip a few switches, and then life could get back to normal, or almost... a new normal, perhaps, but something still resembling what we knew and took for granted before.

But then I recall that footage on the TV, the nine cities that are now nothing but radiation and rubble, and my stomach cramps because there is no normal now, new or otherwise. How many people whom I know have died, including my own family?

I leave the dishes and go to the living room, slumping onto the sofa as I drop my aching head into my hands. I breathe in and out as I feel panic creeping over me like a cold mist, obscuring all thought, making my heart race and my palms dampen and my mind blank again, that awful snow-screen of static buzzing in my brain. *Think, Alex. Think.* But what is there even to think? Do I want to think about my sister, who lives in Russian Hill, in San Francisco, and is, if this news is to be believed—and I still can't quite make myself believe it, not in totality—almost certainly dead, her body, her apartment, her whole building caught up in the blast, vaporized in an instant or maybe just burning in endless fire? Do I want to think about my brother, in eastern Ohio, who—again, if I can truly believe what has happened, if I can *accept* it—is, at best, hiding in his home with his wife and two children, with no electricity or water? His youngest son has diabetes. How will they manage his condition in this chaotic world? What if they run out of insulin? What if he has a hypo-glycemic attack? Will hospitals be working there? Ambulances, doctors?

Or do I want to think about my mother, in her nursing home, half an hour from where we used to live, outside Worcester, Massachusetts? Worcester is only about fifty miles from Boston. Is she already dead? If my mother *isn't* dead, is she waiting for the radiation cloud to fall on her, having no real possibility of understanding what has happened, what is coming? She's with it, mostly, my mom, in terms of recognizing people, *getting* stuff, but she's in a wheelchair, suffers from confusion and anxiety, and has significant memory loss.

Will the care assistants stay in the home to give her and the other residents their medication, their food, as well as the reassurance they will most certainly need? Or will they panic and run for their own homes, their own families, and leave the elderly residents behind, confused and helpless and alone, locked in their memory care unit with no one at all to help them or even tell them what's going on?

A shudder escapes me, a sound close to a sob. I can't think about any of that. I *can't.* I have to focus on the here and now.

Take care of Mattie and Ruby. Get to Sam, somehow, *somehow*...

"Mom?" Mattie has emerged from her bedroom, wearing a fleece and sweatpants, her hair in a dark tangle around her face. There is a soft sleepiness to her expression that reminds me of when she was a little girl, a snuggly armful, smelling of sunshine.

She blinks slowly at me, and I wonder how I look—like I'm in a silent scream of horror and despair? That's how I feel. There is something raw and wild inside of me, and I can't let it out in front of my daughter. I don't even want to let it out in front of *myself*.

Mattie looks around slowly, as if she already senses something is wrong; without the generator running, and no background electrical hum of anything at all, the cottage feels quieter than ever, a penetrating stillness as if the whole world has stopped, and in a way it *has*... but Mattie doesn't know that. And, I realize dully, I have to be the one to tell her.

"Has something happened?" she asks uncertainly, and I press my lips together to choke back the howl rising in me, forcing its way out. If I give in to it, I don't trust myself to keep from breaking down completely, and that's something my daughter can't see. I take a gulping sort of breath, swallowing it all down. "Mom?" she presses, and now there is an edge to her voice, a wobble.

I gaze at my daughter, only fourteen years old, a child who likes to pretend she's jaded and street-smart, twisting a strand of her hair around one finger, her head tilted to one side, her eyes narrowed as she waits for me to respond—already I can see her uncertainty is morphing into annoyance, just as mine did with Daniel earlier, because God knows irritation is far easier an emotion to handle. I ache for my daughter in this moment, her very last one of ignorance, of innocence. The sweetness of not knowing, and yet already it's there in her face, the hint of suspicion, the creeping of fear, although she can't possibly imagine what I'm about to tell her. "*Mom.*"

"Mattie..." How can I tell her? The words feel too big for my mouth. "Something has happened," I state, striving to keep my voice even, although already it is wavering, breaking. I draw another breath while my daughter stares at me in growing alarm, her body tense and practically twanging, her eyes wide and dark, her finger now still, the strand of hair wrapped darkly around it. "There have been... there have been..." It's as if the words physically won't pass my lips.

"*Mom.*" This comes out in a yelp, a squeak of fear. "What's happened? Is it Granny? Sam?"

It's everyone. "Mattie, there have been nuclear strikes across the US," I tell her, and as incredulous as it seems, as completely and absurdly unbelievable, I no longer have the urge to laugh whatsoever. I feel leaden inside, both heavy and empty with the impossible weight of this knowledge, even as I resist it, still. *It can't be true. It can't be...* "It happened last night. Nine US cities were... were hit."

"*What?*" She stares at me, looking both disbelieving and stricken, and then she reaches for her phone and starts swiping frantically. "Nothing's loading!" she tells me shrilly, an accusation, and I realize that this, of all things, is the sign to her that something is wrong with the world.

"Mattie," I say, as gently as I can, "the internet has been taken out all over. The power is out over most of North America. Nothing is working right now."

She looks up from her phone, her eyes wide and terrified, her jaw working, yet no words come out. "What..." she finally gasps out. "What... no..."

"I'm so sorry."

"We need to go back to Westport!" This in a shriek, a demand.

I shake my head, striving to keep my voice even, my manner calm even though my hands are clenched into fists, my nails digging deep into my palms. I'm afraid I don't have the emotional strength to handle Mattie's disbelief, the wildness of her anger and pain, and yet I have to. I'm a mother; this is my job. My duty. And, I know, this brief moment of panic is only the very beginning. "Mattie," I say, still striving to keep my voice gentle, "we can't."

Her eyes widen further, her face taut with fear, her hand clenching her phone, pressing it against her breastbone as if to anchor herself. "What about Sam?"

"We'll get Sam," I promise steadily. It's a sacred vow—to her, to myself, to all of us. "We *will* get Sam."

"If we can get Sam, then we can go back home," Mattie retorts, and for a second, I can only stare. Then I remind myself that she's fourteen. She's thinking about her friends, her old life, as if she can somehow gather its shattered fragments and glue them back together again, if she can just go home. If she can just get there.

"Well, yes, theoretically, I suppose, *maybe*," I finally answer reluctantly, "but Mattie, we're safer here, farther away from the blasts, the radiation, all of it."

"The *radiation*," she practically screeches. "Is everyone dead? Back home? Is everyone *dead*?"

"No," I say quickly, too quickly. "I mean... I don't know. I don't think so. Not in Westport." I rake my hands through my hair, pulling it back from my head, hard enough to hurt. The pain anchors me in this moment in a way that's necessary. "I don't know what's going on," I tell her, an admission. "How badly things... places... have been affected. I don't think the blast would have killed people in Westport outright..." *But the radiation might?* I can't make myself finish that sentence, but I don't need to because Mattie is smart, and her eyes narrow in appalled understanding.

"If we can get Sam," she says, her tone turning cold, "we can get Drew."

Drew? I drop my hands from my hair as I stare at her in disbelief. Drew, her punk, drug-dealing waste-of-space boyfriend who gave her weed to keep in her locker at school for him? Who took her to parties with all his druggie friends? Who got her suspended and very nearly expelled? The boyfriend who was waiting in his car outside our house while she blithely told me she was going for a walk—and I believed her? Trusted her, in too many things? More fool me, but I can't *believe* she's even thinking about him now; I thought we'd banished him, along with her social media apps—but then I realize I shouldn't actually be surprised, that nothing's that easy, and affections don't disappear just because you delete an app... or because as a mother you are desperate for them to.

She's fourteen years old; she had her heart broken, much to my own grief and sorrow. "Mattie," I state levelly, "we are not getting Drew."

"Why not?" she screeches at me, working herself up into a fury, fists clenched, looking ready to fly at me, tooth and nail. "You're willing to get Sam, but not Drew? That's not *fair!*"

I make a choking sound; I'm not sure if I'm swallowing back a laugh or a sob. That's not *fair*, to choose my son over her horrendous boyfriend? Nuclear war or not, there is no way in hell I'm expending a single iota of energy, emotional or physical, in bringing Drew here, or anywhere. "We're not getting Drew," I tell her again, flatly this time. There has been a *nuclear war* and yet we are still arguing about her boyfriend. There's something absurd about it, and even funny, I'm almost tempted to laugh, hysterically perhaps, but Mattie has now worked herself up into a rage.

"You never liked him—"

"Drew has a family, Mattie," I interject, "to take care of him." Not that I have any idea what they're like, nor do I want to know. "He's not—he's not our responsibility." For some reason it sounds callous, when I say it out loud, but it's true. It's absolutely true.

"You don't even care if he *dies*," she flings at me, and, as much as I'm trying to hold on to my temper, I can't. Not about stupid *Drew*, when there is so, so much else at stake.

"Mattie, about thirty million people have died," I snap. "So excuse me if I'm not shedding tears over the boyfriend who almost got you expelled from school."

Not the most measured response, I can admit that. My daughter lets out a cry like a wounded animal, and turns and darts back into her room, slamming the door behind her so it rattles on its hinges. Teenaged tantrum, Armageddon-style.

A groan escapes me, and I start to sink back on the sofa, only to still at a small, hurt sound coming from the other side of the room. I turn and see Ruby standing by the ladder to the loft, her face pale and stricken, utterly silent.

Daniel returns two endless hours later. The girls and I have hardly spoken to each other in all that time; I tried to explain to Ruby what had happened, in stilted, fragmented sentences, but she turned away from me without a word, and I decided to let it go.

There would be time enough to let the reality of our situation sink into us, ripple out endlessly. Even now, realizations come to me like aftershocks of an earthquake: Ella, my best friend from college, works as a consultant for Deloitte in Manhattan. I texted her right before we came up here, to tell her we were going. I hadn't been very good about keeping in touch since Daniel had lost his job, embarrassed by the whole situation. Is she dead now? Almost certainly, I think, with a shudder of incredulous horror; she lived in midtown.

And what about Daniel's sister? She lives—*lived*—just

outside LA, with her husband Matt and their little bichon frise, Zuzu. For some reason my mind snags on the dog, a furry white puffball with a pink bow in her hair and a yappy bark. My sister-in-law Jennifer absolutely doted on her. All of them surely dead, or at best shut up in their house to protect themselves from the radiation, with no electricity, no water, no *hope*.

How many others who I know, or knew, liked or loved or even just had a passing acquaintance with? Friends from high school, from college, distant cousins, friends of my parents... so many in danger. So many dead.

When I hear the crunch of tires on the driveway, I'm relieved to escape my own harrowing thoughts. I need to focus on the practical, the future. *Sam.* I race to the back door as Daniel climbs slowly out of the truck, looking both haggard and resolute.

"I got some gas," he says, and a small, trembling sound of relief escapes me.

"They were still pumping at the station?" This prospect sweeps over me in a warm wave of reassurance, that things are still going on as normal somewhere. *Here.* Gas is being pumped, money is being exchanged, life goes on, in Canada, at least. It's a different country, after all. It can't be as bad as we'd feared.

Daniel shakes his head. "No, the tanks were empty, and the store was completely cleared out," he says in a low voice. "I don't know if it was looted or what, but every last thing was gone. Shelves totally bare. Nobody was even there, the door had just been left open. It was like..." He pauses, a long, low breath escaping him as he runs his hand through his hair. "I don't know what it was like."

A shudder runs through me, and I force myself to shrug it away. I need to stay practical. "How did you get the gas?"

"Darlene saw me driving back here and gave it to me."

"Darlene..." Even though she's been coming in to take care of the cottage all this time, I haven't seen or even spoken to her in years. Probably not since my father's funeral, and even then, only briefly, because I was exhausted, overwhelmed, in shock. She hugged me, I remember, pressed her powdered cheek to mine, told me how much she'd loved my dad, how kind he'd been. I returned the hug on autopilot, my gaze fixed on a display on the other side of the church hall, photos of the Sunday School's nativity play. Even now I can envision the slightly blurry picture of a child in a donkey costume that I stared at while Darlene told me how sorry she was.

"She wanted to help us," Daniel says. "And she remembered Sam, you know, from when he was little. Said it was for him, as well as for... for your dad. You know how he looked after her, since she was on her own."

I nod because I remember, many times, my dad stopping by Darlene's to give her a hand stacking her wood or to fix something in her house; he even left her a couple of grand in his will. My throat tightens resolutely, and I swallow to ease it. "And she had gas?"

"Yeah, in her shed, gallons of it. You know how people are up here. They've been waiting for Armageddon for the last twenty years."

He smiles without humor, and I try to smile back, but my lips tremble and I feel my expression collapse on itself. "I told the girls," I tell him on something close to a gasp. "They..." I can't finish that sentence. I don't even know how to; I don't know how they are. Ruby is curled up on her bed, reading her book like her life depends on it, and maybe it does. Mattie has been sitting by the fire, staring into space. When I tried to talk to her, she just shook her head.

Daniel nods slowly. "It's hard to take in." He takes a step closer to me, dropping his voice to little more than a whisper, which frightens me. "Listen," he says, "I think it's worse than we thought." We're huddled in the laundry room, the door still open to the outside, cold air rushing in. I take a step toward him, bend my head to listen. "I got some more radio reception in Flintville," he continues in a whisper, "and Darlene saw some stuff on TV that we didn't get."

My stomach swoops, cramps. "And?" I force out quietly, even though I have the urge to clap my hands over my ears, sing *la la la* until Daniel stops speaking, until *everything* stops. I don't want to listen; I can't bear to know.

"No one can say for sure," he explains slowly, "because no one really knows. But there have been reports of the sky going dark over the whole east coast... from the chemicals released, you know, from the ensuing fires as well as the initial nuclear blasts. Chemical plants, oil refineries that were near the blast centers... it all went up along the whole eastern seaboard. The air pollution will be as bad as, if not worse than, the radiation, all along there, and it will travel with the wind."

"To here?" My voice is barely a whisper; I struggle to form the words.

"I don't know. The wind's blowing from the west, at the moment."

Is that a good thing? I can't imagine any of it, but I absorb what he has told me and swallow hard. "Okay."

"It looks like millions have already died, but even more will die in the coming weeks," Daniel continues. He is staring fixedly ahead, not looking at me. "From the fallout, the fires, but also other things. Nothing is working—no water, no electricity, no public services, just about anywhere. Canada is affected too, they're connected in a lot of ways to the US. Apparently, the countries have one of the most integrated power grids in the world, so nothing's working, at least near the border, and, as you know your dad liked to point out, ninety percent of Canadians live within a hundred miles of the United States border." He rubs his hand over his face as I nod; I can practically hear my dad say it, in his now-this-is-really-interesting voice.

"In the States," Daniel continues, "they can't even get close enough to put the fires out in any of the cities. And then there's all the people in hospitals, people who need to go to hospitals, the emergency services are a mess, and first responders want to stay at home, where it's safe, especially because of the radiation..."

I swallow again; my throat feels dry, my lips numb. "You learned this all on the radio?"

"And from Darlene, what she saw on TV early this morning. But... there's no easy fix to any of this, Alex. There's no fix at all."

I nod mechanically. I'm thinking of my mother in her nursing home, so helpless, so alone. Does she understand? Is she scared? "But the president said things would be up and running in a few days." I offer this as if it is evidence, paltry as I know it is.

Daniel shakes his head, resolute, utterly certain. "I don't think so."

We are both silent, staring ahead, simply breathing, and all of it feels hard enough. It takes effort to keep going, as if I have to tell myself to breathe, force my heart to beat, my body to work, second by agonizing second.

"Will you be able to get Sam?" I finally ask, and while I mean to sound practical, like there is a reasoned discussion to be had, a note of challenge hardens my voice, a tone of judgment that I know Daniel hears. I didn't mean it like that; at least I didn't want to. But I know it's there just as he does, and I know all that one note represents, all it accuses. *You failed us once, as a family. You lost us our house, our happiness, our whole lives. Don't do it again.* I stare at him, half in apology, half in defiance.

Daniel's lips tighten as he stares at me bleakly, understanding everything, I think, that's just gone through my head as if I had said it out loud. I practically did.

"I'll try," he says.

SEVEN

"Breathe out, close your left eye, line up the sights, squeeze the trigger. Keep the gun tight against your shoulder, otherwise it might hit you in the face and that would sting a bit."

Daniel's voice is steady yet holding a wry note of humor I recognize, and am amazed he can hold onto considering our situation. I don't have the strength to reply in kind; I simply nod, his instructions running through my mind in a loop as I try to do what he says. My squinted gaze is focused on the tin can perched on a log fifty feet away. I breathe out, let the air slowly trickle from me, even as my heart pounds. *Focus, Alex. You can do this.* I squeeze the trigger.

The gun kicks hard against my shoulder and the bullet goes wide. My breath comes out in a rush, and I lower the rifle.

"Damn."

"It's okay," Daniel replies as calm as ever. "Try again."

"I don't want to waste the bullets."

"We have a few to spare. Your dad kept quite a bit of ammunition around." He smiles, but I can't smile back. It's been twenty-four hours since I woke up to the sound of the generator, the world changed, and every single second counts. There is absolutely nothing to smile about.

Daniel was adamant that we make some kind of plan before he left to find Sam. "I'm not rushing off half-cocked, Alex," he told me sternly, his expression so obdurate that I realized he would not be moved on this point. "Too much is at stake. I need to make sure I'm prepared, and I need to make sure *you're* prepared."

Hence the shooting lessons. We've been out here for almost an hour in the freezing cold, deep in the woods, the sky a hard, bright blue, the trees bare all around us, a silent army of stark, skeletal sentinels. My fingers are numb even in gloves, and I can't feel the tip of my nose. I have yet to so much as nick the tin can.

"Why would I need to shoot a gun, anyway?" I ask Daniel, trying not to sound petulant, but we've been at this for a while and I want to move forward, I want to do something that *counts*. It's a futile desire, I know, but I feel it all the same.

"Because I want you to be able to defend yourself," he replies in the kind of patient voice he uses with the children. "And the girls."

"Against what?" Now I sound belligerent. "A wolf?"

"No," Daniel replies, his voice still steady. "People."

I forget the rifle and its barrel swings down toward the ground as I stare at him. "*People?* You think someone like Darlene is going to—what, *attack* us here?"

"No, not Darlene," he replies. Now he sounds as if his patience is being tried. I'm being difficult, maybe even on purpose, because I don't want this to be the reality. I keep pushing up against it, kicking at it pointlessly, the way Mattie did against us taking her phone away, insisting we were unreasonable, that life didn't work this way. Except now it does.

"But someone we don't know," Daniel continues, "who doesn't know us? Who stumbles upon this cottage, this lake, the barn and the garden and everything else, and thinks they might like some of it? Yes." His eyes are hard, his mouth a grim line as he nods toward the rifle. "Try again."

And so I do, as grimly purposeful as he is, because even if he's just trying to scare me, it's working. I don't want to be attacked, but if I am, I'm damned well going to be able to defend myself. Or at least try, I amend, as I miss again.

There hasn't been any news in the last twenty-four hours; the TV was nothing but static when we turned on the generator for a few precious seconds, and the internet is still out. Daniel and I have gone out periodically to the car to try to listen to the radio, but we haven't been able to hear any broadcasts, just static nothingness, like the whole world is on the fritz.

It's eerie as well as terrifying, being so out of touch. Normally, I've appreciated how isolated it is here; I've effused to both family and friends how it's the kind of place where you can *really get away from it all*. And while that's certainly a good thing considering the current situation, it's also incredibly disconcerting. I want to know what's going on in the world even as I dread to hear—if the US has retaliated, if there have been more strikes, if the world really is on fire the way it was reported to be.

Because besides the lack of electricity, nothing here has actually changed all that much. The sky is still blue, the lake placid; yesterday evening it snowed, an inch or two dusting the ground like icing sugar; it had melted by the afternoon. The fire, if we keep it built up all day, heats the cottage adequately enough. Yesterday afternoon, Daniel found an old wood stove in the basement that my parents had once used for finishing off the maple syrup. He brought it into the kitchen, cleared a place for it by the electric stove, now rendered useless.

"Just like *Little House on the Prairie*," he remarked, and I didn't know whether to laugh or to cry at the thought. I did neither; I simply stared at him, resolutely dry-eyed.

The stove came up to my thigh; it reminded me of the Holly Hobby play oven I had as a kid, and what a fire trap *that* was, smelling of burning plastic no matter what you baked in it. This, at least, worked fairly well, once I'd been able to get the fire stoked up hot enough; I was able to make a beef stew on it that took hours, and a lot of wood, to cook, but still. It worked. We ate dinner.

"We'll need to keep an eye on supplies," Daniel told me in a low voice after we'd eaten, when the girls were tucked up in bed. It was dark save for the light from the fire, casting flickering shadows across the wood floor. Peaceful, save for the sense of numbness that surrounded me like a shroud. With nothing else to do, the girls had gone to bed at eight. They'd been so unsettlingly quiet since I'd told them about the strikes, not even asking any questions, barely saying a word, their eyes dark and wide and a little vacant as they wandered around the cottage like they were lost.

I knew they were processing and grieving; they were exhausted, emotionally and physically, just as I was. I also knew I should talk to them about it, but I didn't know how, or whether I had the strength. What comfort could I possibly offer them right now? What possible reassurance? And so I let us all be quiet, at least for now. There would surely be time to talk later, to figure things out. Too much time, maybe—or not enough.

"Supplies," I repeated neutrally to Daniel. "You mean food?" We'd already put all the refrigerated and frozen stuff in the shed outside, in sealed crates, to stay cold, but how long would it last? My beloved turkey, the centerpiece of our glorious Thanksgiving dinner, would now have to be rationed carefully, precious sustenance that it was. And after that? I'd bought a lot of food, but enough to see us through however long it took for some kind of normal life to be restored? How long would that even *be*?

"Yes, food," Daniel answered, "but also firewood, matches,

batteries, everything. Your parents were great about keeping everything here well stocked, but some of it is really old, and in any case, it's not going to last forever."

I stared out at the endlessly dark night, thoughts forming slowly, painfully, coalescing in a way I resisted, with every atom of my being. *Forever.* "Do you think conserving will be enough?" I asked after a moment, even though I knew Daniel couldn't really answer that question. I was acting as if his predilection for bingeing on *Star Trek* spin-offs gave him some sort of expert knowledge, but it was surely more than mine.

"I don't know." Daniel was silent too, and both of us stared out at the darkness while the fire crackled and settled in the grate. A few days ago, this moment would have felt like the height of peaceful contentedness; now it was its frightening nadir. "The good thing," he continued slowly, "is we are actually living in a place where it *is* possible to survive, if we need to. We can shoot game, we can grow food, we have a supply of fresh water that, as far as I know, can't be contaminated." The lake is fed by deep underground springs, something I never before thought to be thankful for, or think about at all. "We can survive," Daniel stated with matter-of-fact certainty, "if we need to."

If this speech was meant to rally me, it didn't. At least, not much. *Shoot game?* Was he actually serious? As for a garden... "But it's November," I pointed out, and Daniel gave me his old, wry smile.

"Yes, I know."

I rested my head against his shoulder and closed my eyes. I wished I had his calm, quiet optimism, but I didn't. It was late November; we couldn't plant a garden till May, and then the vegetables would have to grow. That was six months or more to survive before we could think about homesteading properly, if that was even going to be a thing. Considering my track record with our houseplants, I wasn't sure it could be.

We keep at my shooting lesson until, after another hour and far too many bullets, I manage to nick the tin can. The ding of the bullet hitting metal is a sweet, sweet sound, and I lower the rifle, my shoulders aching from both the tension and the effort.

"I did it."

"Yes, you did."

Daniel smiles at me, and I try to smile back, but the bleakness I see in his eyes, despite his cheerful tone, tears at me. I'm the one making him get Sam, and neither of us have any idea of how dangerous a journey it might be. I feel like I'm sending him into battle without so much as a pocketknife, and yet I'm still doing it. And I'm not going to change my mind. I don't even feel guilty, and perversely it's the lack of that emotion that gives me a sense of guilt.

This is my *husband*. We've been married for over twenty years. He held my hand through every labor; he stayed up all night with Sam when he had croup, singing lullabies as he ran the shower to ease our son's tiny chest. He makes the best blueberry pancakes; he knows what makes me laugh even before I do. He'd die for me, I know he would, and the terrible thing is, I'm afraid I'm asking him to.

"We could all go together," I blurt, and of course he knows immediately what I'm talking about.

"No." His voice is firm, unwavering. "That would be more dangerous, especially for the girls, and we can't leave the cottage unoccupied."

I know he's right, but I still resist, although whether I really do mean it or I'm just virtue signaling—to my own *husband*— I'm not sure. "Maybe it would be better, for us to all be together," I say, my voice starting to wobble. "No matter what happens."

"The cottage is actually the best place for us to be in this situation, Alex," Daniel replies gently. "You know that. Think of Ruby and Mattie. We can't put them in danger." He rests his hands on my shoulders, his fingers curling around to my shoulder blades, anchoring me in place. "We really can survive here, if we try," he tells me. "I want you to try."

I give my head a little shake, still resisting the notion. I might have, briefly and whimsically, thought about being the wild woods girl of my youth, raspberry-stained and briar-scratched, but not like this. Never like this. "We can't play pioneers," I protest, my voice wobbling all the more now. "I mean, we *could*, but we wouldn't survive." The idea is laughable. "Have you ever skinned a deer?" I try for one of Daniel's wry laughs, but it comes out uneven, like a discordant note. "Or made soap? Or, I don't even know what, ground *wheat*?" I let out another laugh, the sound sharp this time. "We can't do this, Daniel. I can't. Not..." *Without you.* I don't say it because I don't have it in me to make him feel guilty, not when I'm the one making him go. I close my eyes against the hot press of tears. I don't want to cry. "I'm sorry," I whisper, and Daniel gently draws me to him.

We haven't hugged much in the last six months, and the hug we had just a few days ago felt awkward and forced, but this doesn't. I wrap my arms around him tightly as I burrow my head into his shoulder, as if I'm trying to fuse my body to his. He hugs me just as tightly and, for a few precious seconds, the whole world and all its terrors falls away, and there is just us, together.

Then Daniel steps away, putting his hands back on my shoulders, gazing at me with a steadiness that makes me want to cry all the more.

His voice is as steady as his gaze. "You can if you have to, Alex. I know you can. At least, you can try." He pauses, his voice thickening enough that I have to wipe my eyes. "I need you to try."

"And what if someone gets sick?" My voice splinters as I wipe my eyes again, trying to step back from the verge of emotional overload. I'm so close to losing all the tightly held parts of myself, and I can't, especially not if Daniel is going to leave. "Or injured? What if Ruby breaks a leg, or Mattie needs antibiotics?" My voice rises, no longer wobbling. I sound angry when what I really am is afraid. Daniel doesn't have the answers to my questions.

He gives a little shrug, managing a small smile. "What did they do back then?"

"What, like a hundred years ago?" I raise my eyebrows, wiping my eyes one last time. "They *died*. From practically a paper cut." My voice is shaking now, the fear audible. "Daniel, I can't do this."

"What's the alternative, Alex?" His voice turns gentle again, and I cover my face. "We can't go back home. It would be worse, much worse, anywhere else in the entire country. More danger from radiation, from pollution, from other people—"

"Canada wasn't hit, though, was it? We could try to get to a city. Ottawa, or Toronto—"

"When all the power is knocked out across all of North America? When there's no water, no plumbing, no medical services, and the only food people have is what is in their fridges?" He shakes his head. "We'd be competing for resources with thousands, millions, and we don't even know if Canadian cities have been affected. A radioactive cloud could be heading toward Toronto right now."

"It could be heading here," I point out, and Daniel concedes the point with a nod.

"Even so, you're better off here." He pauses. "But after I leave, I think you should try to camouflage this place a bit. I know the neighbors like Darlene know it's here, but other people won't. If you cut down a few trees and lay them across the road..." He frowns. "I can help with that before I go. We can't give any reason for people to wander up here and take a look."

"I don't want you to go." The words come out of me quickly, a whimper of protest, as if I'm a child. It's foolish for me to say, to feel, because we both know I'm the one making him go. Would Daniel try to get Sam if I hadn't insisted? I hope so, for our son's sake, but I'm not sure—and I'm scared. I don't want to be alone with the girls, fending off wolves or wild woodsmen or whatever else might be lurking out there. And what if I'm sending my husband to his death? *Or consigning my son to his?*

"I know," Daniel says quietly, and a sob escapes me, an unruly sound and one I've managed to keep myself from since all of this happened. Daniel takes me in his arms again, and I bury my head in his chest, breathe in deep as I try to still the sobs. I don't want to cry because there is too much to cry about, but I can't keep from shuddering as I hold back the tears.

He doesn't speak because there is nothing to say, no promises to make, no assurances to give. Just as he did when this first happened, he simply holds me, and once again I have to let it be enough. Even if it isn't.

It still has to be.

Daniel leaves the next morning, forty-eight hours after it all started—or ended, really. He has stocked our SUV with forty gallons of water, plenty of food, most of it dried, a sleeping bag, matches, a flashlight, gas. He is dressed in several layers, his coat on the seat next to him along with hat, gloves, scarf. His face grimly set.

Mattie, Ruby, and I stand on the front stoop of the cottage to see him off, and it feels like an absurd tableau: *the womenfolk bid the gunslinger farewell.* I'm half expecting Clint Eastwood to come down the road on an Appaloosa, the director to call cut, everybody to sag and smile. But, no. This is our reality, and yet everything in me continues to resist it.

"You'll take the 401?" I ask, even though we went over his

itinerary last night, pored over the ancient map we've found in a drawer, considering the different roads he could take to the border. We wondered whether the border crossing would be manned; if he would be allowed to cross at the Thousand Islands Bridge where we crossed into Canada, marveling at all the tiny islands dotted in the river below, some barely bigger than the cottages perched on them.

"I don't know if I'll be able to cross there," Daniel said, his finger following the line of the St Lawrence River, which forms a natural border between most of Ontario and New York. "If I can't, I'd have to drive all the way to Hamilton or Cornwall. That's over two hundred miles. I won't have that much gas."

Neither of us had admitted the glaringly obvious fact that he did not have enough gas to get to Clarkson, halfway between Utica and Syracuse, and back, anyway. We were both, for some not-articulated reason, participating in the fiction that he was going to be able to drive all the way to Clarkson, New York, without impediment, pick Sam up, and come home again, as easy as that.

"Well, I'll figure it out," Daniel had said, folding up the map, as if it was a matter of simply picking another route, being slightly inconvenienced. Reprogram Google Maps, find another way, preferably with a Starbucks, but if not, go without the caffeine. I remained silent because I did not know what to say.

I still don't know what to say as he hugs us each in turn, with a solemnity that I resist because it feels far too final. The girls are pale-faced, silent, clinging to him, but then letting him go. Daniel turns to me.

"Keep the gun close," he says, and I nod. "Don't run the generator unless you have to."

"I know."

He nods, smiling a little, and somehow, in the midst of everything, this heartens me. He believes in me, even if I don't.

"I know you do," he says. "You'll be fine. This place is a part of you, after all."

A choking sound escapes me, and I suck it back in, for the sake of the girls. I want to tell him I love him; I want to hold him and imbue him with the love I know I've felt for him all along but have withheld these last few months because I was so angry.

Last night, in bed, Daniel took me in his arms, like a question. We hadn't made love in months; we'd basically been acting like strangers, but last night we fumbled and clung to each other, and while it wasn't passionate or frenzied or desperate, it held its own unbearable poignancy, hands sliding over familiar flesh—how absolutely I *knew* this man—lips brushing in the dark. I didn't let myself consider that it might be the last time.

He hugs the girls one more time each, and smiles at me, his eyes crinkling at the corners, and there is that wryness again—like he knows what I'm thinking before I do, like he accepts it and understands. I try to smile, but my lips tremble.

In the frozen, still silence of a November morning, the ground dusted with snow like a scattering of breadcrumbs, he climbs in the car and drives away while the three of us silently stare, watching the car bump down the drive and around the corner. Even after it has disappeared, we stay there out in the cold, listening to the sound of the motor fade into the distance. It is a comforting sound, the soundtrack of modern life, a false reassurance that things are normal.

"When will he come back?" This is from Ruby, who has said maybe six words since I told her about the nuclear strikes two days ago. Selective mutism has been her default in times of stress, and the doctors and therapists we've consulted over the years have told us to let her be, and so I do. It's easier, anyway, especially now.

"I don't know," I tell them both. "A few days, maybe?" It is only a six-hour drive to Clarkson from here; in theory, in normal times, *before*, Daniel would be back tomorrow. But we all know he won't be, and he probably won't be back in a few days either. The fear none of us is willing to voice is that he won't be back at all.

When the sound of the car's motor finally dies away, we all troop silently into the house. For the last forty-eight hours, we have been focused on getting ready for Daniel to go, but now that he's gone, I don't know what to do. The thought of tidying up or making breakfast feels ludicrous, almost offensive, as if I'm pathetically clinging to some sort of normality when the whole world has been upended, destroyed.

And then it comes to me—my shoulders straighten, my spine stiffens, and I feel a sudden surge of resolve, like a much-needed shot of adrenalin in the arm, waking me up, giving me strength. *This place is a part of you.*

"We need to take stock," I announce.

Mattie looks at me warily. She has been almost as silent as Ruby, drifting around the cottage or spending hours curled up on the sofa, simply staring into space. When she realized she might not be able to charge her phone again, she turned it off; it felt like a funeral. "Take stock?" she repeats. "What do you mean?"

"Of our supplies. Food, first aid stuff, batteries, blankets, firewood, everything. We need to know how much we have. Make a list of it all. An inventory, so we can make a plan, a... rationing rota." Saying it out loud bolsters me. Daniel was right; my parents kept things here pretty well stocked. And while everything is at least seven years old, that doesn't mean it's useless. At least, I hope it doesn't. Besides, the three of us need a project. A reason, or at least a distraction from all the emptiness around us.

"We'll make a list," I say again, in the manner of someone talking about Christmas presents. "We'll write everything down. Ruby, you can do the writing. Mattie, you'll help me with the inventory."

For an awful second, I think they're not going to comply. Mattie is going to flounce off, Ruby drift away. I don't have it in me to jolly them along, I know that already. But to my relief, they don't resist. Quite the opposite, in fact, which fills me with relief and a strange, sudden sort of joy. *We can do this*, I think, *together*. Just like Daniel said. The trouble is, I'm not sure what *this* encompasses.

And so I'm glad when Ruby scurries off to get a pen and paper, and Mattie cocks her head thoughtfully.

"Where should we start?" she asks, and I could hug her just for asking.

"We'll go room by room," I decide. "Who knows what we'll find? You know how Granny and Grandpa kept just about everything." And who knows what might come in useful—a spool of thread, an old pair of glasses, a loose screw. I might have to turn into a female MacGyver, which is laughable considering the extent of my DIY knowledge, especially without any access to Google or YouTube, but I'm going to try.

We start in my parents' bedroom because it seems like the easiest to manage. The dressers are still full of my parents' clothes; I'd planned to bundle them up for charity, so Daniel and I could place ours in the drawers, but I hadn't gotten that far. We've been living out of suitcases, but now I realize I'm grateful that I wasn't so industrious straight off the bat. My father has three heavy, cable-knit sweaters bought from a mail order catalogue, still in their plastic wrap. They're warmer than anything I own, and they'll come in handy, as will the hiking boots in the closet—ten years old, but never worn.

We list all the clothes and shoes and boots in the bedroom's dressers, as well as three blankets folded on a shelf in the closet above my mother's hanging clothes—which comprise a bunch of evening gowns she wore on a cruise about twenty years ago and never touched again. Not so useful, but who knows. Maybe we'll find some surprising use for sequins, and at least the blankets have, miraculously, not been attacked by moths or mice.

We find other things, too, things that are poignant without being useful. In the small top drawer of my father's dresser, we discover a collection of homemade cards and letters my children, and my brother's children, wrote to him over the years—complete with clumsy writing in thick marker, dried glue, a few shiny grains of glitter. Mattie reads one she wrote when she was about eight and sniffs audibly. I put my arm around her, and she lets me, and then we move on.

The linen closet is no more than a little cupboard set in the wall between my parents' bedroom and the guest bedroom we'd meant for Sam; Darlene has left everything pristinely folded, scented dryer sheets between every neat layer to keep the mice away. Ruby carefully writes down everything we have—a dozen each of fitted and flat sheets, twenty-two faded pillowcases, five more blankets.

We move onto the guest room, which, like the little room was, is now filled with boxes from when my parents sold their house in New Jersey. There are boxes of old photos, of Christmas decorations, of my mother's knitting, balls of yarn and several sweaters half-made, missing a sleeve, still on their needles, along with dozens of dog-eared knitting patterns. We make a record of it all.

The closet is filled with more clothes—my father's tuxedo, more of my mother's fancy dresses, and, in a jumbled heap at the bottom, a box of ice skates from my childhood. I have a memory of skating across the lake one winter when I was about eight. There had been no snow, and the lake had been like a sheet of glass, an enormous, private rink for my personal enjoyment. The sense of freedom as I'd skated all the way across, arms outstretched, the cold wind rushing past me, had been exhilarating.

"Three pairs of ice skates," I tell Ruby. "Sizes four, seven, and nine." I put them back in the box and then slowly, painstakingly, with an intent focus that serves as the best sort of distraction, we continue to move through the whole house. The bathroom has three drawers full of old medicine—some of it prescription, for my mother's thyroid and my dad's blood pressure, as well as a host of crumpled packets, half-full bottles, semi-squeezed tubes, all of it at least five years out of date, a lot of it much more. Once I would have swept it all away, straight into the trash, but now I don't know what we might need one day. We keep it all, document every last pill.

In the kitchen, we take stock of the food. There is an entire cupboard full of stuff my mother canned at least seven years ago —apple sauce, tomato relish, pickles, spaghetti sauce. Mattie opens her mouth as if to protest the very notion that we might want to eat this stuff one day, but then she closes it again. Ruby writes it all down.

We go through all the groceries I bought, writing everything down. Five dozen eggs. Ten kilograms of flour. Eight cans of diced tomatoes. Three cans of puréed pumpkin, for the pies I now know I will not make. Seven packets of pasta. Four of rice. Two liters of sunflower oil, one of olive oil. On and on it goes, and, while it seemed like a lot when I was boxing it all up in Kingston, it certainly doesn't now.

The stuff from the fridge and freezer is outside, and we inventory that too—milk, butter, juice, bacon, sausages, a turkey I'll have to cook in the wood stove because I'm not going to waste twenty pounds of good meat, and as it has already started to thaw, I'd better do it soon. Chicken breasts, green beans, broccoli, Caesar salad kits.

"We have a lot of food," Ruby says, sounding almost cheerful, and I manage a smile. Already I know it won't be enough to make it all the way to summer, even if we ration it as carefully as we can.

As we work, my stomach tightens and I struggle to keep my

tone cheerfully practical, as if this is a helpful exercise and not the detailing of our eventual demise.

But maybe Daniel is being an unnecessary doomsayer, and things really will be restored in a few weeks. Restored enough, anyway. Won't the army get involved? The government will come up with a plan. I resolve to check the TV once a day for news, just in case. This might only be weeks, months, maybe, at the worst, and we could have enough food for that, if we ration very carefully.

The trouble is, I realize as Ruby writes down in her careful handwriting *1 turkey*, I'm not sure I really believe that, even though I desperately want to. It won't just be months... and we won't have enough.

We finish the kitchen and pantry, and move on to 'Grandpa's room', as my kids used to call it, back when he was alive—a walk-in cupboard between the kitchen and porch where my dad kept all his bits and bobs—nails, screws, wood glue, and, yes, lots of batteries. Except when I tip them into my hand to count them, most of them are corroded with age, flaking off in my palm. Mattie sucks in a breath and Ruby looks at me questioningly, pencil poised.

"A dozen AA batteries," I say as cheerfully as I can. I throw the rest in the trash and then dust my hands off before gazing around the little room, its jumble of junk I don't have the energy to sift through right now. My dad used to know where everything was, could locate a certain kind of nail in seconds, but I certainly can't. We've been going at this for two hours, and we still have the box room, the loft, the living room, as well as everything outside—pump house, barn, and root cellar, if I can figure a way to open its damned door.

"Let's take a break," I say, and silently Ruby puts down her paper and pen and then she and Mattie both, as if by unspoken mutual agreement, drift away. I stand there, staring at that room of who knows, maybe one day life-saving junk, and feel a wave of emotion crash over me—a mix of terror and grief, too great for me to withstand.

Abruptly, I whirl away from the room and dig in one of the kitchen drawers for a crumpled pack of cigarettes I saw earlier, back from when my parents used to smoke. Health scares finally made them quit in their seventies, but it was still the cause of my father's death.

I take it and an old lighter, grab my coat, and head outside. The sky has turned a flat, whitish gray, and the air is breathtakingly cold. I perch on a pile of damp logs behind the pump house and light up. I've never been one for cigarettes except for a bit of social smoking at parties in college, which was more about waving them around importantly than actually inhaling, but now I suck the smoke into my lungs without missing a beat, as if I've always known exactly what to do.

My head swims and my chest expands, and then tightens, and I close my eyes, amazed at how, for just a few seconds, I feel something almost like relief flooding through me. I bow my head, and instantly it crashes over me again—the fear, the grief, the *regret*. How could I have let Daniel go without telling him how much I loved him, how sorry I was? Instead, I hugged him as if he was going to work, waved him off with a firm smile. *Bye bye now. Have a nice day.*

I allowed things to matter that simply *don't* anymore, holding on to old hurts instead of letting this tragedy, this complete and total *catastrophe*, put them into perspective. I'm as bad as Mattie in that regard—and then I think no, I'm worse. I'm an adult, and I should know better. I should know a lot better. I should have been completely honest with Daniel, instead of holding some part of myself apart because I was simply too scared to admit what this meant. I should have told him everything—how sorry I was, how much I loved him. I tell myself he knew, anyway, but it's no comfort. I should still have said it. I should have been a strong and good enough person to say it.

The cigarette has burned down nearly to the filter, and I take another drag, but this time it just feels like tar entering my lungs, sticky and black. There is no light-headed buzz to bring me relief. I throw it onto the damp leaves and grind the butt with the heel of my boot as I stare into the stark and leafless trees, everything barren and brown, a forest now devoid of beauty, a palette of nothing—nothing but potential danger.

I think of the wolves howling the other night, the bears that I know freely roam this area, and probably more confidently and aggressively now, because no one has been around for years, and they might not have started to hibernate just yet. I think of the iron hardness of the earth, the bleakness of winter coming; soon it will snow, *really* snow, several feet deep, and the temperature will plummet to well below zero on a regular basis. We might freeze before we starve, I think bleakly, and that's only if no one stumbles upon this place like Daniel seems to think they will. Yesterday, he cut down some trees that he instructed me to lay across the road at various points, to discourage potential explorers. Will it be enough to keep people away? I have no idea.

I take a deep breath, and then another, trying to summon the strength to get up, to keep going, for my children's sake if not my own. This is day one of how many? When will Daniel be back? When will this *end*?

From the cottage I hear Mattie's voice, sounding small and uncertain. "Mom?"

Still, I can't move. My limbs feel leaden, my head heavy. *Get up, Alex. Get up and be strong, for your girls.*

"Mom," she calls again, more stridently this time, yet with a tremor of fear in her voice.

Slowly, I heave myself up from the woodpile and walk around the pump house toward the cottage. Mattie is on the driveway, her hands lost in the sleeves of her sweatshirt, looking around apprehensively. When she sees me, she breaks into something close to a run.

My heart stills, suspended in my chest. *What now?*

"Mom," she says breathlessly as she reaches me, "there's someone coming down the road."

EIGHT

DANIEL

He does not let himself look back as he drives down the road, the car bumping gently over the rocks and ruts, away from his family. His hands clench on the steering wheel, and he forces himself to focus on the road ahead, its twists and curves. At the barn he remembers the big rock and steers to the right, going over it gently, a soft bump and then a thud. He drives onward, down the quarter-mile of private driveway to the dirt road, then two miles to the main road as Alex reminded him only four days but what feels like a lifetime ago, an epoch, when they were arriving and all he had to worry about was his wife's accusing silences, something he'd become used to over the last five months but that still wounded... or, really, annoyed him. You can only be hurt by something for so long, Daniel has come to realize. Even his own grief gets tiresome, a thought that is comforting, considering the circumstances.

He doesn't know what will happen when he gets to the main road, and he hasn't let himself think about it too much. When he drove the ten miles to Flintville two days ago, he didn't see a single car. He doesn't know if martial law is in force in Canada, although of course it is in the United States; he is not so naive as to think he'll be able to cross the border even close to the normal way, no matter what he and Alex discussed, in their determined naivete, their stubborn optimism. Hand over his passport while they check his license plate and then wave him across, *welcome to the US*. No, that's not going to happen now.

How he will get across, he's unsure. The St Lawrence River cuts across from here to Hamilton, two hundred miles away at least with every bridge—and there are only a few—a border point. He needs a plan, but the only one he could think of was to *go*, and so he did.

He comes out to the main road, utterly empty and silent under the bright blue sky. For a moment, he simply breathes, enjoying the beauty of the day, the simplicity of the moment, when he can, for no more than a second or two, pretend he's just heading to Flintville for gas, that back at the cottage the girls are playing a board game, Alex is baking cookies. Such simple things, and yet so infinitely precious, so utterly out of reach.

He banishes the image and then he turns left, toward Flintville and the hundred and fifty miles to the border. He has a full tank of gas and enough to fill it at least once more. How far will that take him? Six hundred miles? It's around two hundred and eighty miles to Clarkson, and then, of course, back again. He could manage it, maybe, if he doesn't have to detour. If he can even get across the border.

He drives on.

He doesn't see a single car in the ten miles to Flintville; when he gets there—a right turn at the shuttered chip wagon, then past the gas station—it feels, quite literally, like a ghost town. Curtains are drawn across every window, and he doesn't see so much as a shadow move. The town, he knows, has never been a bustling hive of activity, but there's an eerie stillness about it now, a wariness, like a held breath, and his heart beats hard as he drives through, to the open road beyond.

There are about a dozen towns between here and the highway, none of them anything more than a gas station and a couple of houses and stores on a single street. As Daniel drives through each one, they are all the same: still, silent, empty, and yet he feels watched—a prickling on the back of his neck, his hands slick on the steering wheel. He's waiting to be stopped by the police, hijacked by renegades, *something*, but nothing happens, and he feels, *almost*, a little ridiculous for thinking in such a melodramatic way. Despite what they saw on the news, heard on the radio, nothing feels as if it has really changed, and yet he knows it has. He remembers the looted store in Flintville; there hadn't been so much as a box of matches left. People are scared and desperate, or perhaps just anticipating feeling desperate soon.

As he drives on, he wonders if, forty-eight hours after the strikes, people are still in shock; maybe he can get to Clarkson and back before the world erupts or implodes, if it ever does. Maybe, he thinks, people will be docile and compliant, meekly obeying the law until order can be restored, the army mobilizes, the power grid is fixed, refugee centers are formed... his mind is a mash-up of disaster movies but, despite the certainty he showed to Alex, he doesn't know if any of it actually applies.

He drives twenty empty miles with nothing but skeletal trees on either side of the road, semi-submerged in swampy, half-frozen lakes, the sun glinting off their dark surfaces, turning the desolate landscape briefly beautiful.

Once, twenty miles from where Route 41 meets the highway, a truck passes him on the other side of the road, careening wildly. He catches a glimpse of the driver, another man next to him in the cab—both wearing baseball caps, grimy brims pulled low down over their faces; he sees the flash of their plaid shirts, their wild eyes. They disappear down the road with a screech of tires.

He drives on.

After two and a half hours of driving, he gets to the intersection with the highway and hesitates; the large rest stop for truck drivers on the side of the road where they stopped for coffee four days ago, with a gas station, diner, and gift shop selling dreamcatchers and fishing tackle, is completely deserted. One of the gift shop's windows is broken, as if someone took a baseball bat to it, shards of shattered glass still in the window, gaping like broken teeth. The inside, he sees as he squints, has been looted, racks turned over, the shelves that hold the useful stuff—engine oil, lighter fluid—emptied. A cheap-looking teddy bear lies trampled on the ground, one black, plastic eye staring forward unblinkingly, unnerving Daniel more than it should.

He is reluctant to turn onto the highway, where he feels he'll be more conspicuous, and perhaps more likely to be stopped by the police, but if he doesn't take the highway, he knows, he'll use a lot more gas, on the twisting back roads that meander toward the border.

Yet he can't bear to be stopped before he gets to the States, at the very least; if he's turned back here, a mere hundred and fifty miles from the cottage, when he's encountered nothing but empty road, he'll feel like a failure, and that's almost as unacceptable to him as returning without Sam. He has felt like a failure far too many times over the last year—and yes, he knows it was his fault, completely his fault, but that doesn't ease the burden or make him feel any better.

He felt like a failure when he was laid off from his job after only a month at his new company; starting afresh meant he didn't get any severance pay. He felt like a failure when he pretended to go to work for six months rather than admit to his wife he was out of a job. He felt it when he took out a second mortgage on their home without telling Alex, even though it had meant forging her signature; he felt it when the bank coolly foreclosed on their home three months later. He felt it when he saw the indifferent pity in the eyes of the guy at the storage facility who told him his credit card was declined and he realized he didn't have enough money even to store their possessions—Ruby's teddy bears, Mattie's bedroom furniture that she'd picked out for her thirteenth birthday, their wedding china, everything. Their whole life packed in boxes, and he had nowhere to put it.

He'd had to call a friend from his old workplace and basically beg to store it all in his barn, out in Old Greenwich; Alex still doesn't know about that. She'd already been giving him the icy silent treatment for months by then; they'd been staying in a suite at the Hampton Inn, and they couldn't really afford even that. He hadn't been willing to make it any worse. Of course, those boxes mean nothing now, just more collateral damage, a paltry sum in light of absolutely everything else that's been lost.

Still, Daniel resolves, he is not going to feel like a failure in this. He will succeed, no matter what it costs him, even if it kills him. Maybe that will be enough penance for his wife, for himself. Maybe. And maybe he will even be able to get Sam— for a second, he pictures his son as he last saw him, standing in the middle of his freshman dorm room, hands on hips, looking around in quiet pride, but with a hint of childish apprehension in his eyes. When Daniel had hugged him goodbye, Sam had held on for a second longer than he normally would have, then laughed and stepped back, clapping him on the back, a boy turning into a man in front of his very eyes.

Resolutely, he turns away from the highway and follows narrow, country roads toward the border, Route 5 to Route 6 to Route 19, twisting through cornfields, the occasional farmhouse barely visible in the distance. He stays as close as he can to the highway, which is no more than a winding flash of grey in the distance, the occasional road sign or rest stop visible between the bare trees, all of it utterly empty. He heads southeast, cutting through now barren farm fields, devoid of all life; he doesn't see a single car or person. He feels as if he is completely alone in the world, an alien in a lunar landscape, shipwrecked, stranded, and yet moving forward.

Hours crawl past; he left the cottage five hours ago, but already it feels like an age, an eon. He hasn't stopped once, even though he is hungry; his shoulders are cramped, the back of his neck throbbing, along with his fingers clenched on the wheel. He won't stop, he decides, until he is safely across the border.

Of course, crossing the border will be a big problem. He knows that, and he has yet to think of a solution. He packed food, gas, even a gun, but he has not prepared for this inevitable eventuality. He does have two thousand US dollars secreted in various pockets and pouches on his person, all in twenties; three hundred of it he took out at an ATM in Watertown, before this all began, simply as a sensible precaution. The rest he found in his father-in-law's top drawer, along with some old birthday cards from his grandchildren.

Daniel is hoping a bribe at the border might work, although he suspects it won't. He knows he should have come up with a better plan, just as he should have before, when he was out of a job and running out of money and still telling no one, but the difference now, he thinks, is that there *is* no plan, for anyone. At least none that he can think of, except to drive on, down this unknown and uncertain road.

A few miles from the border crossing, he turns onto the Thousand Islands Parkway, amazed at how quiet and empty it continues to be. It's eight miles to the Thousand Islands Bridge across the river, and then the border itself—barricades, immigration officers, questions, being turned back or arrested unless he can think of another way. His hands grip the steering wheel tightly. His mind remains blank.

A mile passes, and then another, shuttered summer cottages glimpsed between the trees, the occasional glint of sunlight on the St Lawrence River. He is so close now, so very close, and still nothing. No one.

Then, just after he rounds a curve, he sees a police car pull out from a hidden road, lights flashing blue but no siren. His stomach drops and then clenches, and he feels sweat bead coldly on his forehead. He pulls over, gravel crunching beneath the tires, the exhalation of exhaust the sound of defeat.

The police officer is fiftyish, graying, with a paunch and a grim expression. His hand rests on his holster as Daniel rolls down the window.

"You know it's illegal to be traveling right now?" the policeman asks, not aggressively.

Daniel takes a deep breath. "My son is at college in New York state," he says. "I have to go get him."

"The border is closed." The policeman's voice is, surprisingly, gentle, even regretful. "No one is able to cross. No one. You need to go home."

Daniel turns to squint up at him; the glare of the sun is creating a halo around the officer's head, making it hard to gauge his expression. "Please," he says, because he has no other words.

The policeman hesitates. He glances up ahead at the road, as if looking for something, then back to Daniel. "Look," he says, leaning in and lowering his voice, although there is no one, no one at all, who might hear. "There's a guy in Rockport who is taking people over on his boat. It's by the boat works, on Front Street." He steps away from the car. "You heard what I said about going home." Then he walks back to his car while Daniel lets out a shaky, shuddering breath, lowering his head and closing his eyes for a brief moment, in something almost like prayer.

When he checks the map, he sees that Rockport is just a couple more miles down the parkway. The policeman has driven on, and the road is empty again. Slowly, Daniel pulls out on and keeps driving.

He finds the boat works in Rockport, a touristy town right on the river that, like everything else, is silent and empty, everything shuttered. He drives on, realizing he will need to hide his car somewhere. All the stuff he brought—the food, the water, the gas—he will have to leave, and he doesn't want it to be stolen. God willing, with the help of a miracle or maybe several, he will return to use it—with Sam.

A mile or two on the other side of the town, he finds an old, abandoned barn, weathered sides mostly intact but with its roof falling in; there are dozens like it up and down this part of Ontario, forgotten farms, abandoned generations ago thanks to the stony ground. Now the ground is frozen, and the car makes no tracks as he drives right into the barn. He has to get out and shift some fallen planks and logs, sweating with effort in the freezing cold, before he can park the car fully inside. There is no way to disguise it, so he will have to hope for the best, that no one will venture into this ruin.

He takes out a rucksack, packs it with as much water and food as he can reasonably carry, a flashlight, a pocketknife, a first aid kit. He straps a sleeping bag onto the bottom, and puts on his coat, hat, scarf, gloves. He slings the rifle over his shoulder. He feels weirdly ridiculous, yet also grimly intent.

As he clicks his key fob to lock the car, the electric beep and flash of lights seems already a relic of a bygone age. He steps outside, glancing around, but there is no one in sight—not a human, not a house, not a car, just fields, sky, and road. It is three o'clock in the afternoon and dusk is drawing in, the color being leached from the sky, and there is a deeper chill to the already icy air. He starts walking down the road, the crunch of his boots on the gravel sounding unnaturally loud in the stillness.

Half an hour later, he comes to the boat works, with its deep-water marina; there is a ferry boat, red and white, with *Rockport River Cruises* painted on the side, but no other boats at the dock this time of year. He walks past the main building to a house around back that's as shuttered as everything else. He wishes the policeman had given him a bit more detail, but he has to go with what he has. He knocks on the door. There is, unsurprisingly, no answer.

Daniel waits because, just as with every other aspect of this surreal journey, there doesn't seem to be another option. It is coming onto dusk properly now; the river is already lost in shadow. He shivers in the cold, even though sweat is prickling between his shoulder blades, trickling down his back. Five minutes pass, each one endless. He knocks again.

"Please," he says, raising his voice a little. "I'm here to ask for help, to cross."

The minutes tick by. It is now almost four o'clock, and almost dark. His feet are numb, his face too. Should he give up? Go back to the car? If he returns to the cottage now, after less than a day, Alex will never forgive him. He will never forgive himself.

He knocks again.

The door opens.

Daniel instinctively takes a step back as he glimpses the man standing behind the screen door, his expression, behind a bushy, graying beard, inscrutable. He wears a grimy baseball cap pulled down low over his forehead, and his face is seamed with wrinkles. He smells of smoke and oil, like a chainsaw. His mouth, beneath the beard, is a hard, uncompromising line. He is, Daniel thinks, almost a parody of a redneck woodsman, like a northern version of *Duck Dynasty*, but then Daniel realizes he must look like a parody too; he is, after all, wearing a fleece vest and a button-down shirt underneath his coat, his old Rolex strapped to one wrist.

"I need to cross the river," he says. The man has not yet spoken. "Someone told me you take people across."

The man scratches his cheek, almost absently. He seems relaxed, and yet Daniel is under no illusions. He might be the one with a rifle slung over his shoulder, but he suspects this man could gut him like a fish before he managed so much as to put his finger on the trigger.

"What have you got?" the man asks. His voice is a rubbly sort of smoker's voice, with an Ontario twang.

"I have some money."

"How much?"

Daniel hesitates, knowing he will have to negotiate, and that he is decidedly at a disadvantage. "Three hundred dollars," he says at last. One hundred seemed paltry, but in any case, the man remains unimpressed.

"What else?"

"You mean besides money?"

The man nods.

Daniel thinks. He has only packed essentials, nothing he is willing to give up. He doesn't want to give away the location of the car, or the other supplies he has. "What do you want?" he finally asks, and he hears the wavery edge of desperation in his voice.

The man sighs, as if Daniel is being tedious, and then he shrugs his assent. "I'll take the money. We can't leave until dark. You can wait in the boathouse. I'll get you when I'm ready." And then he closes the door with a firm click, and Daniel is alone again.

He walks over to the boathouse; the door on the side is unlocked, and he steps inside. A wooden boat, looking very old, is up on trestles, and takes up almost the entire space. Daniel slides to the ground on the other side, his back against the wall, his elbows resting on his knees. He takes out his cell phone, but there is, of course, no signal, and he turns it off quickly, not wanting to waste the battery.

When he gets to the other side of the river, he will be in upstate New York, but still over one hundred miles from his son. He will have to walk or beg rides the whole way, but right now, for the first time, it actually feels as if it could be possible. Crossing the border, he tells himself, will be the hardest part, even though he can't possibly know that for sure. But simply walking somewhere, even in winter, feels doable. If he walks four miles an hour, ten hours a day, he can be in Clarkson in three days. He has enough food for that long, if he's careful. Of course, this doesn't account for detours, for dangers, fatigue, illness, or any number of problems he could encounter. But he holds on to it all the same—three days. He will see Sam in three days.

For a few moments, he lets himself think about Sam. Not as he is now—trapped at college, away from his family—but as he was as a little boy. He remembers when Sam was about eight years old and had an obsession with Chinese checkers, would play a dozen games, winning almost all of them, constructing elaborate jumping routes for his marbles and shouting in glee when he completed a particularly intricate jump.

The memory of his son's triumphant shout has Daniel laughing aloud, the sound bursting from him, surprising himself, before he slumps against the wall and closes his eyes. *Sam.*

His mind skates toward Mattie and Ruby, Alex. He wonders what they're doing now. Making dinner? Building up the fire? Huddling together on the sofa? He trusts Alex will be okay; she'll protect their girls. Maybe, he reflects with a faint smile, this will be the making of her. The making of *them*, as a family, except he isn't even there.

By six o'clock the sun has completely set, the river lost in darkness, and the inside of the boathouse is absolutely frigid. Daniel has gotten up to walk around and restore feeling and warmth to his limbs; he aches with exhaustion, yet he feels almost unbearably alert, every nerve twanging with awareness. He hears the squeak and bang of the screen door, the crunch of boots on gravel. The man appears at the door of the boathouse; in the dusky light Daniel can't make out his face.

"I have the money," he says. He's taken out the three hundred dollars and put it in the pocket of his coat, and his numb fingers are now clenched around it.

The man holds out his hand. Daniel gives him the folded bills and he pockets them with something like a sigh. "Don't know how useful money will be," he says, "but at least it's something."

"Thank you," Daniel says, heartfelt, and the man just shrugs, without looking him in the eye. For the first time, Daniel realizes that he is with someone who might have information, more than he has. "It's so quiet everywhere," he says. "All the way here—one hundred and fifty miles—I didn't see anyone around at all."

The man shrugs. "The government told us to stay inside, so everyone's staying inside."

"I expected it to be different."

He raises shaggy eyebrows. "Do you remember the pandemic?"

Daniel considers, realizes he has a point. For better or worse, people have become compliant. Scared. "Do you know what it's like?" he asks. "In the States?"

"No. I take people across, that's it." He folds his arms across his chest. "I don't want to know." Daniel nods, chastened. "I'll take you to Iroquois Point," the man tells him. "We'll have to go without a motor because the Border Force has been patrolling the river. Don't speak, don't make a sound, and whatever I tell you to do, do it." His voice is low, almost menacing, and Daniel does not want to think what might happen if he disobeys. What this man might be capable of. "Got it?" he asks, and Daniel nods again, quickly, because it sounds like a threat.

Twenty minutes later, they are on the water, in a rowboat only a little bigger than the one he used to take Sam fishing in, back at Lost Lake; he remembers how proud Sam was of catching three little bass. Now the only sound is the creak of the oars, the gentle splash as they hit the water, the boat gliding smoothly along the bank of the river, through the darkness. The air is icy.

This part of the St Lawrence River is dotted with islands, some like postage stamps, some a bit more substantial. Daniel remembers Alex once telling him that for an island to be counted as part of the Thousand Islands archipelago, it must be at least one foot square above water all year round and support a living tree. He sees several such islands that barely meet that requirement as they glide past them, shrouded in darkness, through the water.

The man keeps to the banks of each tiny island, crossing open water only when he must, the wind cutting and frigid when he does, making Daniel's eyes water and his cheeks sting. He remembers some of the islands' names from the map he and Alex looked at—Baby Tar, Little Grenadier, Cleopatra, Fancy Rock, Ball, Huguenot, Steamboat, Maple, Manhattan. They slide past each one in the dark, the night completely still. When the moon emerges from behind a bank of clouds, the water glints silver. He can see the opposite shore now, a long, low smudge in the darkness. He can't believe it has been this easy.

Creak. Glide. Creak. He is holding his breath, straining, half of him wanting to leap out of the boat, wade through the water to shore, now only about twenty feet away. The water is utterly freezing; there are chunks of ice bobbing in it already. They are so close.

Then, in an instant, everything changes. Bright lights suddenly flood the river, making them both stiffen and squint, and a voice sounds on a megaphone.

"Stop where you are. This is the Canada Border Patrol. Stop immediately where you are, or we will shoot. I repeat, we *will* shoot."

The man immediately stills the oars. Daniel glances back at him, sees the resignation in his face, and realizes that, right when he is about to make it across, he is going to be thwarted. He will be arrested, shot, or sent back. Which would be worse? He glances down at the water; there is still twenty or so feet or more to shore, and it is swirling with ice. He won't make it.

Then he feels a hand hard on the center of his back, pushing him over. He starts to lose his balance, and he realizes the man is pushing him into the river. Is it an act of mercy, he wonders as he feels himself fall, or ruthlessness?

He falls as if in slow motion, and then, for a second, the icy water closes over his head, and his mind goes blank, his body into shock as the freezing water penetrates his clothes, his very bones. Then he finds his feet—it's shallow enough to stand, a little over chest deep—and he starts wading through the water. It is like walking through treacle, through tar, thick and impassable, and his body, strangely, feels as if it is burning.

"Stop where you are. *Stop where you are!*"

He keeps putting one foot in front of another, even though now the water feels like wet cement, turning everything heavy. Even only a few feet from the shore, it is almost impossible to move. His limbs are slow and clumsy; his brain is a swirl of fog. Everything is numb, his clothes sodden and already starting to freeze on his body. He can hear the steady chug of the border patrol's motorboat, its lights sweeping the water in frightening arcs. He keeps moving—one foot, another. *I can do this*, he thinks. *I* must *do this*.

A gunshot cracks through the freezing air just as Daniel throws himself onto the bank. The patrol boat is coming closer, the chug of its motor reminding him of the savage pant of a wild animal. With what feels like the last of his strength, he clambers up onto the bank and then, stumbling at first, he starts running into the darkness.

NINE

I don't recognize the woman walking down the road. She's thirtyish, with a lean and wiry figure, wearing a puffy coat and leggings, cheap hiking boots. Her hair is dip-dyed hot pink and pulled back into a ponytail. Her expression is resolute.

"Do you not remember me?" she asks, a very slight sneer to the words, and I still, my mind racing. *Remember her?* I don't remember anyone from up here.

"Sorry," I reply, my voice guarded.

"I'm Kerry. Darlene's daughter. You used to babysit me when I was a kid."

I did? A vague memory of watching a little kid with armbands splash in the lake, while I sat on the dock and felt bored, drifts through my mind, but I could be making it up. The woman in front of me is entirely unfamiliar, and her expression, while not hostile, is certainly not friendly. I stare at her blankly for a second, and her lip curls, just a little, but I still see it. *Stupid rich American*, she's probably thinking, and I don't entirely blame her.

"Sorry," I say again, and I wait, at the top of the road, until

102

she stops, about ten feet away from me. An impasse, a face-off. Mattie is behind me, huddled and shivering in the cold.

"I need help," Kerry says without preamble. "I think my mom has had a heart attack."

"Darlene?" I say—stupidly, it's true—and her lip curls again as she nods. "I'm sorry," I tell her—a third apology, but this time it also serves as a no. How could I possibly help? "Have you gone to the hospital?" Another stupid remark.

"Do you think the hospitals are working?" she asks in an are-you-actually-dumb tone. "There's no electricity or anything anywhere, and no one is supposed to be out on the roads, anyway. Besides, my mom's car is broken down, and I'm out of gas."

I don't know what to say to any of this, so I remain silent.

"Your dad had a heart attack once," Kerry tells me, as if I don't know. That was eight years ago, a year before he died of a related cancer. "My mom thinks she saw some nitroglycerin in your parents' medicine cabinet."

Once again, I don't reply; I already know there is nitroglycerin in the medicine cabinet because we inventoried it just a few hours ago. I held the little brown bottle in my hand as memories of my father's heart attack—the call that came early one morning—filtered through me, the sudden clutch of terror I'd felt at this first brush with mortality and suffering, the sudden, terribly certain knowledge that life *does* end.

Now I realize I'm not sure that I want to confirm to this woman, this stranger, about the nitroglycerin. I'm not sure I want to give it to Darlene.

Then, it hits me in a rush; Darlene gave Daniel gas, gas her own daughter could clearly have used, to get her to the hospital, or at least somewhere safe. *For Sam*, she'd said. And here I am, reluctant to give her some potentially life-saving nitroglycerin that we don't even need? I'm ashamed of myself, and yet the urge to protect my family, to circle the wagons and preserve our supplies, is still strong.

"There might be some," I allow, my tone guarded. "Did you walk all the way here?" She nods. I think it's about four miles to Darlene's little house, on the way to Flintville. "I'll look," I tell her, and then add, as a somewhat reluctant afterthought, "Why don't you come inside?"

Kerry follows me into the cottage while Mattie trails behind, and no one says a word. As we come inside, Ruby appears from the loft, her hair in a tangle about her face, her eyes wide, her hands lost in the sleeves of her sweatshirt. She doesn't speak either.

"Nice place you've got here," Kerry says, as she looks around the kitchen, and I wonder if I'm imagining the edge to her voice. I think of what Daniel said, about people looking at the cottage and lake and wanting what we have. I walk quickly to the bathroom.

I find the little brown vial of nitroglycerin easily enough and slip it into my pocket. As I straighten, I catch sight of my reflection in the mirror—my face is pale, my dark hair pulled back too tightly, the lines around my eyes and between my nose and mouth look deeper than they were just a few days ago. I look strained, anxious, *angry*... and older than my forty-six years. I take a deep breath, let it out, and then turn to go back to the kitchen.

Mattie, Ruby, and Kerry are all standing in the same places, silent and waiting. I take the vial out of my pocket. "I have it here," I say, and Kerry holds her hand out. The peremptoriness of the gesture annoys me, and so I keep hold of it, my fingers closing around it. Her mouth tightens, her eyes flicking to my hand and then back to my face.

"Are you going to walk back?" I ask after a second when no one speaks, and she just shrugs. "I'll drive you." I'm not sure why I'm offering, only that I am. Maybe I'm trying to make up for the way I've held on to the vial, or maybe I want to see more of the world.

"Dad has the car—" Mattie protests, and Ruby interjects softly, "There's the truck."

My dad's truck, an ancient beast of a machine, twenty years old, hard-used and careworn. Daniel tinkered it with yesterday, to make sure it worked while he was gone, the engine sputtering to life after he'd stepped hard on the gas. For some reason this, at the most inopportune of moments, makes my eyes sting as I remember his thoughtfulness. As he opened the hood of the truck, I had stood there restless, anxious, even annoyed. Why?

Kerry shrugs her assent. "All right," she says, and then, as an afterthought, "Thanks."

It takes me a second, but I realize her prickliness and her reluctance—they remind me of me.

"We should all go," I say, because I don't want to leave Mattie and Ruby alone; but then I remember what Daniel said, about not leaving the cottage unoccupied. But it's only four miles, I reason, and we won't be gone that long, maybe half an hour at most. I'll lock all the doors; it will have to be enough.

The girls pull on coats and boots, and we walk down to the barn, where the truck is kept. It's already starting to get dusky, the light fading, shadows gathering along the road, on the far side of the lake. The air is colder, with a hint of icy dampness that promises freezing rain rather than snow. Daniel has been gone for—what? Six hours? Where is he? Has he crossed the border? Is he safe?

For a second, I falter in my determined stride, and I have an urge to drop to my knees, to wrap my arms around myself and *howl*. Mattie gives me a sharp glance, as if she senses my impulse, and I give her what I hope is a reassuring smile and keep walking.

· · ·

It's been years since I've driven the truck, probably decades. I learned to drive on it, bumping over back roads while my dad sprawled back in the passenger seat, the epitome of relaxed, except for his hand clutching the door handle.

Now, having slid open the door with a loud, protesting creak, I stand in the entrance of the barn, its shadowy, cobwebby interior hiding all sorts of useful things—a snow-blower, a lawnmower, a log splitter; all, I realize, running on gas. There are coils of rope and some ancient folding deckchairs, a couple of vintage-looking toboggans and a pair of cross-country skis I think I used when I was a teenager. I see about two dozen pails, used for maple syrup making, and a couple of ladders, along with the metal chute my parents used to load the firewood into the cottage's cellar. There are some extra planks of the kind used for the cottage's siding, and half a dozen spare windows too, propped against a wall. All of it, I think now, could have some purpose, some benefit... or not. Would I even know what to do with some extra planks, a spare window? I don't think I would.

In the middle of all the junk is the truck, dented and battered, with the four-wheeler next to it. I have the keys in my hand.

"Mattie, Rubes, you guys can get in back," I tell them; the truck has a double cab and can fit six people in a pinch, along with the open bed behind. The girls rather gingerly climb in, and Kerry swings up into the passenger seat next to me as if she's ridden there a thousand times. I glance at her, taking in her set expression, her pink-tipped ponytail swaying as she moves. There is something hard and unfamiliar about her; instinctively, I don't trust her. I have no memory of her beyond the hazy one I'm not sure is real. Is she even Darlene's daughter? No, I'm being stupidly suspicious. I take a deep breath and start the truck.

No one speaks as I back slowly out of the barn; I'm concentrating on not hitting anything. Then we are on the driveway, heading toward the open road, the first time either I or the girls have left the cottage since everything happened, bumping slowly over the rutted track.

As I turn onto the main road, it feels like nothing has changed. We see no other cars, but that's not that unusual, and as I drive along, I can almost believe I'm just heading into Flintville for some gas, maybe some milk. I can even almost imagine that my dad is next to me, telling me to go easy on the brake or carefully around a curve, laughing a little as he grips the door handle.

"It's here on the left," Kerry says, the first time anyone has spoken since we got in the truck, and with a jolt I realize I've been so lost in my memories that I almost passed Darlene's house.

Not that I'd even recognize it, at least not for certain. I can't remember the last time I've been there—when I was a kid or a teenager, at least. It's like a lot of other houses in this part of Ontario—small, weathered, built of clapboard, with a steep tin roof that allows the snow to slide right off. There is a small, fenced-in vegetable garden, bare now it's winter but still looking neatly tended, and a henhouse surrounded by chicken wire, a front porch stacked with wood.

We get out of the truck.

Kerry goes in first and we follow, to a small sitting room with a large TV, a wood stove, and a single sofa. Darlene is stretched out on the sofa, her head back on the armrest, her face grayish. Her eyes flutter open as we come inside.

"Kerry...?"

"Mom, I got the nitroglycerin." Kerry glances back at me, a bit accusingly, and I realize I never gave it to her. Wordlessly I hand it over, and Kerry administers it to Darlene, telling her to put it under her tongue.

Behind me, Ruby and Mattie fidget and shift; everything

about this is strange to them, I know. It is strange to me, as well, and as I look around, I wonder how Darlene and her daughter are going to wait out Armageddon. There's no generator here, and the little wood stove can only heat the house so much. There's no water supply, either, although maybe there's a stream or lake in the woods nearby. How much food do they have? And what if Darlene needs more care?

I glance back at her; I'm not even sure I would have recognized her after all these years, although I doubt she's changed that much. I'm the one who has changed, who has let myself forget so much. Darlene is a petite, sturdy-set woman with curly gray hair surrounding her kindly face like a halo. She smiles at me when she catches my eye; I struggle not to look away.

Kerry slowly straightens. "Thank you," she says, and it sounds like a rather curt dismissal, which should be a relief, because I want to go, but for some reason I don't move.

I owe Darlene, I'm realizing, quite a lot, and I've never even bothered to say thank you—for keeping the cottage clean, for making our beds, making sure everything *works*. "Are you going to stay with her?" I ask Kerry, and she jerks her head in a nod, looking scornful; of course she's going to stay with her mother. Besides, where else is there to go? I don't know where Kerry lives, what her life is like. Does she live locally? She looks to be mid-thirties; what kind of job is there out here for someone like her? Does she have a husband, kids? Somehow, I doubt it. She looks like a loner; she acts like one too.

"Will you guys be okay here?" I ask, and Kerry juts her chin out, just a little.

"We'll be fine."

The little house feels cold; the fire in the wood stove has gone out. How much wood do they have on the porch? Enough for a normal winter, yes, certainly, but for *this*?

"If you need anything else..." I say slowly, "will you let me know? I want to help."

Surprise flashes across Kerry's face, but then she nods. "Yeah. Sure."

Still, I don't move. I'm remembering, quite suddenly and vividly, how it was Darlene who showed my parents how to make maple syrup. It was Darlene who helped them with the garden, who taught them that a plastic cup of beer planted in the soil will keep slugs away from your tomato and zucchini plants, the kind of tip I could have googled, once, but not anymore. Darlene is the one who gave them a haunch of venison for the freezer from a deer that she'd shot herself; who said that scented dryer sheets placed between towels and blankets will keep the mice from nesting in them.

Darlene, I'm realizing, is a fount of backwoods wisdom that I have no other way to access now. I need her much, much more than she needs me, even if neither she nor Kerry realize that yet.

"Look," I say, my voice a little too loud, and I feel everyone stiffen. "Maybe you both should come back and stay with us."

Kerry simply stares at me, clearly completely nonplussed by this suggestion. Darlene's eyes have drifted shut and her breathing is unsteady.

"I don't like the thought of you guys here alone," I continue, pretending, even to myself, that I'm not being mostly mercenary. "Especially without a car." Still Kerry says nothing. "And, honestly, we could use some help." For a second, her lips twist in contempt and I wonder if she thinks I mean with housecleaning or something absurd like that. "What I mean is," I continue hurriedly, "we're not hardy pioneers the way my parents liked to pretend to be, you know? We don't really know how to survive out here, and the reality is, we need to learn. Fast. And maybe if we pool our resources, our knowledge, and our stuff, well... maybe it could benefit all of us."

No one says anything for what feels like a long, taut moment. I can't tell anything from Kerry's expression, and Darlene looks as if she's almost unconscious.

"So, what are you saying?" Kerry finally asks. "We come live with you like, for good?"

I can't tell from her tone what she thinks of that idea. I'm not sure what *I* think of that idea. I don't know this woman at all. "Well..." I reply after a second's pause. "Yes."

Another silence. I glance at the girls, who are standing by the door, looking as if they're longing to leave.

"I don't know how long things are going to be like this," I tell Kerry, and she makes a scoffing sound I can't interpret. "Maybe things will be up and running in a couple of weeks—"

"Yeah right," she cuts across me, and I nod in reluctant acknowledgment.

"However long it is, surely we'll be better off together?" I let the question hang there for a moment, unanswered, before I continue, "We can load anything you want into the truck, take it with us now." I've already clocked the chickens, the stacked wood. Who knows what else they have that could be useful? Like Daniel said, people up here have been readying for Armageddon for the last twenty years.

Daniel.

I can't think about him now; I can't let myself. I focus on Kerry. "What do you say?" I ask her, half wondering if I'm making a mistake, already knowing I can't afford not to take this risk. "Do we band together?" I smile, like we're about to embark on an adventure: *jolly high-jinks together, let's go!*

Slowly, after what feels like an age, and still looking suspicious, Kerry nods. "Okay, fine."

From the sofa, Darlene's eyes flutter open, and she smiles at me.

"You are your father's daughter," she says, "looking out for everyone just like he did."

I look away from her without replying because right now, as I eye up the wood and wonder what's in it for me, I don't feel like my father's daughter at all.

TEN

We load everything up as twilight falls, the darkness dropping like a curtain as the air sharpens with cold. Mattie and I heft boxes and suitcases into the bed of the truck; now that Kerry has agreed to come with us, it seems she wants to take everything. She's packed all of Darlene's clothes, her toiletries and trinkets, her cookbooks and dishes that we definitely don't need. I've got my eye on the firewood and the chickens, but Kerry seems more concerned that we bring her mother's decorative plate from the Queen's Silver Jubilee in 1977.

She flutters around Darlene while we heft and hoist; neither Mattie nor Ruby have said a single word and I'm starting to worry. I should have talked to them about all this first, I realize. More importantly, I need to listen. But the parenting books that tell you, so pompously and portentously, how you need to set boundaries and give consequences and listen without judgment, blah, blah, *blah*, are not really relevant when it comes to end-of-the-world scenarios.

In any case, I know I need to have a conversation with each of them. I need to offer reassurance, even if I don't know what that could possibly be.

It is completely dark by the time we finish, and the truck is completely full. As I look around the emptied house, I feel a pang of both sympathy and solidarity for Darlene; how would I feel, if I had to walk away from the cottage and all it represents? Of course, I did that already back in Connecticut, but still, I don't think it felt like this. Darlene, Kerry told me, was born in this house and has lived here ever since. It belonged to her parents, who passed it down to her. And now she might be walking away from it forever.

I wonder when I will get used to all the endings we now encounter. I wonder if I should.

As we prepare to leave, Kerry helps Darlene up from the sofa. It seems the nitroglycerin has helped because, with her daughter's assistance, Darlene is able to walk to the truck, and then clamber, slowly and painfully, into the front seat of the cab.

"Aren't you going to lock it?" I ask Kerry when she walks away from the front door after merely shutting it. She gives me a look I'm starting to recognize, as well as dislike—scorn mixed with weariness, like she simply does not have the energy to explain everything to me.

"What's the point?" she tells me with a shrug, and she gets in the truck.

Mattie and Ruby have already climbed into the backseat of the truck's cab, and I can't see their expressions in the darkness. Already I'm starting to regret inviting Kerry and Darlene to live with us. It's not exactly an invitation I can rescind, and there can't really be any *hint, hint, nudge, nudge, it's time for you to leave* scenario. I'm becoming more aware by the second that I don't actually know these people. Why did I invite them to move in with us basically forever?

Oh, right. Because I had no choice. No matter what optimism Daniel was clinging to, I know I can't go into survivalist mode without a little help. Hopefully, Darlene and Kerry really can help us.

I start the truck, and it coughs and gasps into life. We drive back to the dirt road without seeing a single person or car.

Later, after Darlene and Kerry have gone to bed and the cottage is quiet, I sit curled up on the sofa by the fire and gaze unseeingly into the glowing embers. The last few hours were a hassle of unloading and unpacking, helping Darlene into the cottage, wondering what on earth I was doing. Trying not to think about Daniel, where he might be, what might have happened to him, while actually thinking about him all the time, the background noise to everything.

Now Kerry and Darlene are both asleep, Darlene in the guest room and Kerry in the box room. Mattie moved up to the loft without a word of protest, which alarmed me. It's not natural, the way the girls are silently drifting through their days, like ghosts. But then nothing about life right now is natural.

I lean my head back against the sofa and close my eyes, knowing I should go to bed yet unable to summon the energy to move. I miss Daniel with an intensity that feels like a physical pain, a gnawing of my insides, hollowing me out. *How* could I have sent him out there, with no way to be in contact, no possibility of understanding what dangers he might face? And yet what choice did I have?

"Mom?"

I open my eyes and see Mattie in her pajamas, standing by the ladder to the loft. "Sweetheart, it's late." It must be nearing midnight.

"I couldn't sleep." She walks toward me slowly, hesitantly, until she's standing by the fire, gazing down at the glowing embers just as I was. "Where do you think Dad is?" she asks softly.

"I don't know." I pat the sofa next to me and, to my relief and gratitude, she comes, snuggling in the way Ruby does and resting her head against my shoulder. I can't remember the last time we've sat like this; it's surely been years. "I hope he's crossed the border," I tell her quietly. "That was going to be the tricky part, I think." Although God knows, it's probably all going to be a lot more than *tricky*; it might be impossible.

"But if he hasn't?"

"I don't know, Matts. I—I suppose it's a good thing he hasn't been sent home yet." But has he been arrested? Attacked? I'm not going to stoke those fears in my daughter. I don't want to stoke them in myself. Daniel is sensible, smart, cautious. All good things in a situation like this.

"What do you think it's like out there?" she asks. "I keep trying to imagine it, and I just can't."

"No, I can't either." Which is something of a mercy.

"Sometimes..." Mattie ventures, "I wonder if this is all a big hoax. I mean, besides the electricity being out, nothing's really changed, right?"

"Not for us," I agree slowly. *A hoax.* I'm thinking of the picture of fire and devastation on the TV screen, the president's voice on the radio. *If only.* "I know what you mean, though," I tell my daughter. "It feels so unreal. I almost want to drive to Corville or somewhere, see what it's really like. How everyone is affected."

I don't actually mean it, but Mattie lifts her head from my shoulder to look at me seriously. "Could we?" she asks. "Could we drive somewhere and see?"

I hesitate because I really didn't mean it—although, I realize with a jolt, I sort of did. I long for some connection to the outside world, a way to gauge what's really going on. "I don't know," I say slowly. "It could be dangerous, Mattie."

"Corville, dangerous?" Her tone is not quite brave enough to be scoffing.

"And we need to conserve gas. Who knows when we'll need it?"

"Where else is there to go?" Now she really does sound scoffing. "I mean, by the time there's somewhere to go, the gas stations will be open again, right?"

I don't reply because I have no idea. Everything, absolutely everything, is unknown, and my ignorance is exhausting. "Mattie," I finally ask, "what would we even do in Corville?"

"We'd just *see*. And, I don't know, maybe buy some groceries."

I shake my head because if the world really is in Armageddon territory, we're not going to be buying any groceries.

"I just want to see," she insists. "Because what if this is all, like, fake?"

I think of the footage on TV, the radio broadcast, the president's voice sounding so tinny and yet so real. The empty gas station in Flintville, the generator kicking on with its gusty rumble. "It's not fake, Mattie."

"Wasn't there some time in history, when people believed some radio broadcast that was just a science-fiction story, and then they like, killed themselves?"

"*War of the Worlds*," I confirm, "but I think the mass hysteria is mostly an urban legend."

"Well, still."

Still what?

I'm trying to think of a practical reason to go to Corville, to justify using the gas and leaving the cottage unattended, that isn't just about *going to see*. Because the truth is, like Mattie, I *do* want to see. I want to know, to be sure; I want to get a sense of how bad things really are. But it feels extravagant as well as foolhardy, to go on some jaunt right about now, simply for curiosity's sake.

"I'll think about it," I tell Mattie, and she sighs, a sound of relenting, before leaning her head against my shoulder once more. I put my arm around her, and she snuggles in a little more, and for a second, I'm almost able to feel happy. Not actually happy, of course, but an approximation of it, a fleeting sense of gratitude, as wispy as the fog that melts away from the lake as the sun rises.

"Do you think things will ever go back to normal?" she asks after a moment.

I consider the question seriously. "Not the normal that we once knew," I say finally. "But a new normal, yes. I hope so, in time."

Mattie gives a snort of disgust, which makes me smile. "What does that even mean?"

"I have no idea."

She laughs then, softly, and I laugh too, a huff of sound. When we've both subsided, Mattie says quietly, "What I mean is, will we ever go back to Connecticut?"

I'm silent as a montage of memories from Connecticut rolls through my mind—the five of us snuggled in the family room, watching movies; Mattie practicing piano in the living room, the sound drifting to the kitchen as I made dinner. Birthdays, Christmases, Thanksgiving dinners... and all the normal, nothing sort of days that I now treasure, because mundanity has become precious. "I hope so," I say at last.

"*You* hope so?" she retorts with some of her usual sass, her lips pursed. "I'm *fourteen*. Do I really want to live the rest of my life out here, like Laura Ingalls on—on Mars, or something? I mean, if we have to stay out here, who am I supposed to marry?"

This makes me laugh properly, from my belly, in a way I haven't in a long, long time.

"I'm serious, Mom," Mattie says, but she's smiling.

"Do you miss Drew?" I ask. The question surprises us both. I didn't realize I was going to ask it. I'm not even sure I want to know the answer.

Mattie glances away from me. "Yeah," she says, her tone turning both guarded and thoughtful. "But I know you thought he was kind of a jerk."

He was a complete and utter ass, I think, but thankfully don't say. Still, Mattie's too smart not to notice; she turns back to me, her lips quirking, eyes glinting. "What, you're not going to agree?"

"I know," I say carefully, "that he was important to you."

She lets out a hoot of laughter. "Great, Mom. That's straight out of one of your parenting books, isn't it? The *How to Talk to Teenagers* one or that one about kids and power struggles."

I let out a little laugh of acknowledgment. "I'm not sure which one, actually, but definitely from one of them."

She snuggles back into me, and it makes my heart sing— such an unexpected joy in a time like this, and one I both savor and marvel at. Neither of us speak, but the silence feels comfortable, contented even, if only for a little while. I can live in this moment, or almost, and not think about Daniel. Sam. My brother and sister, my *mother*. The whole world...

So maybe I can't live in this moment, after all. My mind is racing again, down blind alleys, coming up against dead ends, making my heart pound and my eyes sting. There are no answers.

Mattie wriggles away from me again. "So, can we go to Corville?" she asks.

"Maybe," I say, but I'm pretty sure I mean yes, and judging by her small, catlike smile, Mattie knows it, as well.

The next morning, I wake up early, mainly because I'm cold. Without Daniel's solid warmth in bed next to me, the freezing air penetrates; I had stretched out a leg and encountered an empty expanse of icy sheet that woke me up, even though it was just a little past dawn, feeling lonelier than ever.

Even though it's barely light out, I can already tell it's going to be a beautiful day. There is a clarity to the air that promises dazzling sunlight and deep blue skies. Already the lake is glinting like a mirror as the mist clears away; there is a thick dusting of snow on the ground, maybe an inch. Gazing out at all that beauty, I'm reminded of when I first brought Daniel here, back when we were around twenty. We met in college, became friends in our freshman year, then began dating as sophomores. He came that spring break with a few of my other friends, ostensibly to help my parents make maple syrup, but really all we did was sit around and play cards, take a few walks.

The cottage was in prime, wintry beauty, everything softened by snow; it lay heaped on the boughs of evergreens like mounded icing, the lake a stretch of snow-covered smoothness, the sky the same deep, piercing blue it is today. Daniel shook hands with my mother and father and then turned to the picture window, his mouth dropping open, his eyes creasing in delight as he took in the view.

"Isn't it *beautiful*," he exclaimed, so sincerely that for some reason we all laughed, Daniel last of all, a little abashed.

Twenty-three years later, I can't believe he's gone. That I don't know when I'll see him again, if ever. That I'm the one who made him go.

I pull on some extra layers and head out to the living room to do the usual morning chores, already becoming normal, routine—build up the fire, start the stove, boil water for coffee. The coffee machine doesn't work, of course, and so I've been making it in a pot on the stove and then pouring it through a fine-mesh sieve. It seems to do the trick. I'm conscious that coffee is a precious commodity; we have the five two-pound bags I bought last week, and an unopened five-pound vat of Folger's that expired five years ago. After that, no more morning coffee, I guess.

I haven't really thought about what will happen when the

food runs out; I'm still clinging to the hope—the belief—that some kind of normal life will be restored before that occurs, especially now we've added Darlene and Kerry's small stash of food to ours. *As long as we're careful,* I think, but I'm not even sure what careful looks like, especially since I have no idea how long we have to be careful for.

"That smells good."

I turn to see Kerry coming into the kitchen, her hair in a bedhead mess about her face, her arms wrapped around her wiry body. She looks a little more approachable than she did yesterday, and yet I'm still, I realize, a little intimidated by her. There is something tough about her—the pink-tipped hair, the ropey muscles of her arms, a tattoo on one wrist of a bird in flight. The way her expression always settles into something between a challenge and a sneer. Is it a form of self-defense, or is it just the way she is? Will I come to know her well enough to find out?

I deferred to her all yesterday evening, relying on her exper-tise about everything—at least the expertise I assumed she had. I asked her where the chickens should go, whether, without a chicken coop, they needed to be inside—she looked at me like I was an idiot, and I probably was.

"Just put them somewhere sheltered," she said, as if it were obvious, but I didn't know what that actually meant. Inside? Outside? Under trees? I ended up locking them in the pump house; we'll have to build some kind of coop at some point, I guess.

"Do you want some coffee?" I ask now, and she nods. I fetch two cups. "How's your mom?"

Kerry shrugs. "She seems okay. She's sleeping."

"Do you think she had a heart attack?" I ask. "I mean, actually?"

Another shrug. I hand her a cup of coffee, and she wraps her hands around it. "I don't know. She had something. Her heart's been bad for a while." A pause. "Thank you for the nitroglycerin."

"Oh. Well." I'm embarrassed because we both know I was reluctant to give it to her. "We don't even need it, so..."

"You might one day."

I try to smile. "I hope not."

We both subside into silence, sipping our coffee as the sun rises and the first streaks of light filter through the kitchen window. "I recognize," I say after a moment, awkwardly, "that I'm a real newbie here. I feel like I grew up at the cottage in a lot of ways, but I didn't, not really." Kerry looks at me over the rim of her coffee mug, saying nothing. "I could use some advice," I continue, the words heartfelt yet sounding stilted. "About, you know, surviving. How to, um, live off the land. Hunt. Grow things. And stuff like that." I sound ridiculous. I feel ridiculous. I basically have no idea what I'm talking about.

"Advice on how to survive?" She sounds amused, and now I feel both embarrassed and a little angry. She's certainly not making this any easier for me. Surely, she understands what I'm talking about. "Like what, exactly?" she asks.

"I don't know..." I keep an edge from my voice, but only just. "What do you think we need to do to prepare for winter here?"

This question, at least, is taken seriously. She cocks her head, her gaze sweeping through the room as if assessing its possibilities. "You'll need more firewood, for a start." She nods to the porch. "Is that all you have?"

"And what you brought." She purses her lips, and I know what she's thinking. *So that's why you asked us to stay.* "There's also some in the basement," I recall. I haven't actually been down there to take a look, never mind make an inventory of what else can be found. "But probably not that much."

"Well, you need more," Kerry states matter-of-factly, "a *lot* more, especially if it's for all your cooking and heating. You should get it in soon because it will need to dry out before it's used." She raises her eyebrows. "You know most people have their winter wood in by August, right?"

I recall my parents buying a couple of cords of wood from our neighbors, the Kaminskis who live a few miles away, at the end of every summer. "Yeah," I say. "I know."

Okay, so we need to go out and cut some firewood. *I can do that*, I think. That is, at least, in the realm of possibility. "What else do we need to do?" I ask.

Kerry shrugs, the gesture dismissive. "Get some more food, I guess."

Wow, what a font of homesteading wisdom. I'm not sure what I was expecting—for Kerry to dash outside, pick a few plants and whip up a stew? Bag a rabbit and cook it for dinner, show me how to trap, how to shoot, how to distill dandelions for some kind of medicinal elixir? Did I think she was some kind of wise medicine woman, simply because she lives in the backwoods of Ontario? I feel like an idiot, and I know it's because she's making me feel like one. Is it on purpose? Maybe. Probably.

"And where," I ask her, "would you suggest we go to get more food?"

Her eyebrows arch again, her lips curving. "Corville?"

Seriously? "You think I can just walk into Foodland and pick up some groceries?" The edge is definitely audible in my voice now.

"Probably not, but there are other places to get food," she replies with certainty, and my interest sharpens because she sounds like she knows something, something I don't.

"Where?"

Kerry shrugs, a small smile playing about her mouth. I think she likes keeping me guessing. "Places..." she says again, and I wonder what she means. I wonder if I even want to know.

"All right," I tell her. "Let's go to Corville then." I say it evenly, like a challenge, and her smile widens. Mattie will be pleased, at least.

"Okay." She nods, pushing off from the wall she's been leaning against. "My mom will have to stay here. She's not up for the trip."

"Okay, if you think she'll be all right."

"And," Kerry finishes, "we'll need to bring some bolt cutters."

ELEVEN

I found the bolt cutters in my dad's little tool cupboard, next to a bunch of mousetraps. They're in the back of the truck, along with a couple of cardboard boxes from the barn that Kerry thought we should take, for the food presumably, although where we're going to get it, I still don't know. Somehow, I doubt the supermarket in Corville is operating as usual, but who knows? I'm caught between fear and a hope that feels delusional but remains persistent. *Maybe, just maybe...*

The girls are in the back of the cab, anxious but excited, almost as if this is a normal outing, a day trip to the supermarket and the chip wagon and the river, just as it was before. Even in the midst of Armageddon, it seems, a teenager can get bored.

I am not excited. Dread swirls in my stomach like acid, making it cramp. My hands clench the steering wheel, white-knuckled and aching, as we drive the twenty miles to Corville in virtual silence, having had to move the logs that camouflage the driveway; Kerry heaved one end while I took the other. She seemed amiable enough, helping out with alacrity, but with that faint smile on her face that I find unsettling. Now she's relaxed, staring out the window, humming under her breath. I'm starting to wonder if I understand her at all. More worryingly, I'm wondering whether I can trust her. What do I know about her, besides that she's Darlene's daughter, and remembered me?

We encounter only one car on the way—an ancient Cadillac, with an elderly man at the wheel, his wife in the passenger seat beside him, driving slowly down the rutted road, both of them staring at us wide-eyed as we slip by them like salmon in a stream. Their mouths are open, like gaping holes, and their pale faces remind me of sad clowns, sliding silently past. The woman is wearing lipstick, a bright orange, and her hair is permed. I notice these details before they drive by, gone into the distance, who knows where.

We left Darlene at home, lying on the sofa, the fire built up. She drank a cup of coffee and ate some oatmeal, and all in all seemed in good spirits, although her skin still had a grayish cast and there was a sheen of sweat on her forehead. Still, she smiled, grabbed my hand as I walked by with some firewood.

"You're a good girl," she said, squeezing my fingers, and I nearly dropped a log in her lap by accident. I smiled and slipped my hand from hers to steady the firewood in my arms. I could hear her wheeze as I went to the fireplace and dumped the logs in the wrought-iron rack my dad bought when I was in college. I remember him joking how he was gentrifying the place.

Before we left for Corville, I let the chickens out of the pump house, to their seeming relief; Kerry said they could peck around freely, as long as they were back inside by sunset, before the foxes or wolves or whatever else could get at them. Still, leaving both Darlene and the chickens, the cottage itself, is making me nervous. I want to get back, lock doors, and hunker down; and yet I'm desperate for news, for a sense of the world as it is now, even if it is just what I find in tiny, out-of-the-way Corville.

As we come to the junction at the edge of the town—a

lumber yard on one side and on the other an abandoned building that once housed the town's grocery store, until the big Foodland was built on the other side when I was a teenager—it looks just like it did when we were last here—how long ago now? Four days? *Only four days.*

"Nothing's changed," Mattie says eagerly, leaning forward, craning her neck. "Nothing!" She sounds exultant.

"Let's wait and see," I reply quietly, because what, after all, was meant to change with a lumber yard and a deserted building? I scan the empty road, feel the sense of stillness that's settled over it, and then I turn right toward the town. We drive in silence, and it feels as if we are all holding our breath, hoping, even as I know, I *know* we won't find Corville the way we did just four days ago.

After about a mile and a half, a straight shot and then curving down a hill, we get to the junction that leads into town —a gas station on the right, a big Catholic church and school across the street. The gas station is shuttered, a padlock on the door, along with a cardboard sign, handwritten in marker: NO GAS. NO FOOD.

I glance at Kerry, who shrugs as if I've asked a question. We drive on—down the hill, past the church, across the bridge. All the stores are shuttered, the parking lots empty. When we drive by the hipster coffee shop by the bridge, I see that the plate-glass window has been shattered. Inside, tables and stools are knocked over. A shudder goes through me. It's *real*. Whatever we thought had happened, hoped hadn't, has. That much I know, absolutely, just from what I've seen so far, and it feels like grief.

I glance in the rear-view mirror; Mattie's arms are folded, her lower lip jutted out. I'd think she looked disappointed, but I know it's deeper than that. Here is proof that the world really has changed, despite her desperate hopes. Ruby, I see, is gazing down at her laced fingers in her lap, humming very softly under her breath, her own kind of coping mechanism. I turn to look at Kerry again, but she's staring out the window, that smile of hers gone; her eyes look bleak, the lines from her nose to her mouth more deeply drawn, and I wonder what about this scene has made her drop her insouciant mask, if only for a moment.

"We should check out Foodland, anyway," she says tonelessly, still staring out the window, and I head over the bridge. At Foodland, we finally see people. They are milling around the parking lot, and someone with a megaphone is issuing instructions.

"Turn in," Kerry instructs, and I obey her without even thinking about it. A guy in a high-vis vest directs me to an area where a few trucks and vans are parked.

"What's going on?" Mattie asks, and I don't reply because I'm not sure. It looks like people are lining up at the front of the store; there's some kind of system going on, but I can't make out what it's for, or why.

"I'll go see," I tell them, and I get out of the car. It feels strange, to be among people again. There is a normality to it that feels odd. Off. No one is looking at me, or even at each other. Shoulders are hunched, faces averted. There's a feeling about the place like the aftermath of a tragedy, which I suppose is exactly what it is.

I walk toward the guy in the vest, the space between my shoulder blades prickling with awareness of feeling seen, even though I'm not sure I actually am. I manage a smile, although the guy doesn't look entirely friendly; he's a bit too officious for that, brandishing his megaphone like it gives him some kind of power.

"Hi there," I say. "What's going on?"

"We're distributing food," he replies curtly. "Get in line and you'll receive a box."

"Really?" I'm heartened by this; the world hasn't turned dog-eats-dog apocalyptic quite yet. Humanity has not descended to barbarity the way Daniel seemed to think it would. People are still trying to help each other.

"We figured it was better to give the food out fairly than have it looted," the man replies flatly. "That's happening everywhere as it is."

"Is it? Do you know anything?" I ask. "Do you have any news?"

The man shrugs again, more of a jerk of his shoulder. "Nobody really knows anything. The prime minister hasn't spoken or been seen. Some say Toronto and Vancouver were hit."

"Toronto?" That's only about two hundred and fifty miles away. A visceral shudder goes through me.

"That's what they're saying. There's no hydro, no water, no internet anywhere. And someone said the army at Petawawa has been mobilized."

"To do what?" How do you fight a nuclear bomb, except with another nuclear bomb?

"Who knows?" He jerks a thumb. "You should get in line if you want a box. It's not going to last forever."

"We heard the president of the US on the radio," I tell him, my tone insistent, a little bit whiny. "He said things would be up and running in a few days."

The man guffaws, and then spits on the ground, a bit too close to my boot. "I don't think so."

Which was exactly what Daniel said. *Daniel.* If he were here, he would take control of the situation; he would be the steadying presence I crave, now that it has been taken from me. Instead, *I* have to be it, and I feel myself failing at every turn. "Thank you," I tell the man, and he gives a brusque nod.

Back in the truck, I tell everyone what I've learned.

"We need to get some of the food," Kerry says immediately.

"We have a lot already—" I begin, only for her to give me a scornfully incredulous look.

"We could always use more."

Which is true, absolutely, and yet some deep-seated, half-forgotten altruistic notion, already from another age, compels me to persist, "But others need it more than we do—"

"Are you kidding me?" She leans forward, getting in my face. It takes effort not to jerk back. "We have five people to provide for, and most people here know how to hunt, fish, trap, all that. They'll be *fine*."

"Don't you know how to hunt?" I ask, and she snorts in derision, which I take for a no. I almost feel like laughing because why on earth did I ask this woman to live with me? I thought she—or really, her mother—could teach me something, but so far, the only lesson I've learned is to look out for yourself, and I think I knew that one already. But Kerry is right; if they're offering boxes of food, we ought to get one.

"All right," I tell everyone. "We'll line up for food."

Kerry is already shaking her head. "That line could take hours. There's got to be a hundred people in it. We don't have time."

"But you just said—" I begin in exasperation, only to have Kerry cut me off.

"We'll have to split up."

"*Split up...*" I speak incredulously because if Kerry thinks I'm letting her go off with my truck...

She nods. "I need someone to come with me, and then two people can stay here."

Kerry hasn't even told me where she's going, why she'll need a pair of bolt cutters. I hesitate and, in that second's uncertainty, Mattie speaks softly into the silence.

"I'll stay here and get the food," she says. "I can wait in the line."

"Not by yourself—" I retort. Absolutely not. Not in this Armageddon universe.

"Ruby can stay with me."

An even worse idea. Let both my children out of my sight? Never. Already I'm shaking my head.

Kerry snorts, and the sound puts me on even more of an edge. "Mattie's, what? Fourteen?" she asks, and her tone implies that I'm coddling my daughter, which, considering that we're in the middle of a nuclear holocaust, seems utterly absurd. "Besides, where we're going is right across the street," she continues. "It's like, two minutes away." She points, sticking her finger near my face to indicate past my shoulder. "That street of houses right over there. I can practically see the roof from here."

"It'll be fine, Mom," Mattie says. "There's lots of people around, and they look friendly." She nods toward the line, which does look like it's full of normal people, neighbors, some chatting quietly; there are children, even toddlers, holding their mothers' hands, a baby in a sling. "I want to do this."

"It's not safe—" I begin, only to have my daughter cut me off.

"It's *fine*. Besides, there are security guards and stuff."

If a guy in a high-vis vest counts as a security guard, I think, but I realize I'm considering the notion seriously. We need to get back to the cottage as soon as possible, and we can't all spend hours lining up for a single box of food. But to leave my daughters here alone... am I crazy—or just desperate?

I glance out of the car, at the neat line of people, some of them looking shell-shocked or resigned, but not feral. Not dangerous. The security guard is directing people, and it all seems orderly. Friendly, even, or almost. Safe. What exactly, I wonder, am I afraid of happening?

"Please, Mom," Mattie says softly. "I want to help."

I realize that, expediency aside, maybe I need to let Mattie do this for herself. Maybe, like me, she needs to *do* something because it helps her feel in control, even if we both know she's not. Nobody is.

"Okay," I say, and it feels like stepping into space,

freefalling. "Okay." My heart is starting to judder, my palms leaving damp marks on the steering wheel.

Mattie is already getting out of the truck, and a cry to stop her bottles in my throat and burns in my chest. "I'll text you if anything—" she begins, only to stop suddenly as she remembers that of course her phone doesn't work.

"I'm coming too," Ruby says suddenly, sliding out of the truck.

I throw out a hand. "Ruby, *no*—"

"It's better for them to be together," Kerry advises. "They'll be fine. And we'll be quick. Ten minutes, tops." She sounds so confident, so *insouciant*, and it makes me want to slap her. Why is this all such a *joke* to her? Doesn't she have anything—anyone —to lose?

"We'll be fine, Mom," Mattie promises, as if she can, and somehow, they are closing the door of the truck and heading off to join the end of the line, and I'm driving away, and all the while I don't quite know how it happened, how I let it happen.

"Turn here," Kerry says after just a few seconds, and I swing the truck down a street lined with ranch houses, just across from Foodland; I can see its roof from where we are, which comforts me a little. "Stop here," she says a few seconds later, and I park in front of a ranch house made of breeze blocks, with a garage attached.

"What now?" I ask her, and she brandishes the bolt cutters with a wolfish grin.

"Kerry, whose house is this?" I speak in a hushed whisper, glancing around to see if anyone notices us, but there is nobody around. The street is empty, and the curtains of every house are drawn tight. Kerry is already climbing out of the truck, and I do too, following her to the garage, which is padlocked.

"My aunt and uncle's," she replies, as she fits the bolt cutters to the lock. "They go to Florida every winter. They left a couple of weeks ago. They won't be back anytime soon." She wrestles with the bolt cutters for a few seconds, grunting a bit, and then, with a loud snap, she cuts the lock, holding it up in triumph before carelessly chucking it aside.

I wince as she pushes the garage's roller door up with a loud, protesting squeak, looking around to see if anyone is watching, but, as far as I can tell, no one is. Kerry steps inside the garage, which is neatly ordered—shelves, bins, plastic crates, a smell of gasoline and oil.

"What exactly are we here for?" I ask, as I follow her into the shadowy space.

She gestures to the shelves, the bins. "What do you think?"

"We're—taking it?"

She lets out a snort. "They don't need it. Obviously."

"But if they come back—"

"They're not coming back." Already she's peering at the neatly labelled shelves and bins, taking cans from the shelves and inspecting them—engine oil, lighter fluid, white spirit. "I guess we should take it all," she remarks. "Who knows what we'll need. After that we can check the house."

"The *house*." I'm still appalled, in a maiden aunt sort of way, that Kerry is actually looting her aunt and uncle's house.

She turns to me, impatient, a bit annoyed. "Yeah, the house. They're in Florida, if they're alive at all. Wasn't Miami hit?"

"I... think so."

She shrugs. "I think their condo is near there."

I can't believe how unemotional she seems. "So you think your aunt and uncle are dead?" I ask, and she shrugs again, her face closing up.

"Probably."

"Were you... close to them?"

"Not really. After my dad died, they pretty much cut us off." She purses her lips. "They weren't interested in helping my mom, that's for damned sure. They don't even help their own kid, and he lives right here in Corville."

"Your cousin? Do you want to try to find him?" I'm both appalled and curious as to how indifferent she seems to her own family... but then again, am I any better? I've barely let myself think about my brother, my sister, my mother, never mind find a way to help them.

"Nah," Kerry says, as she starts taking things off shelves and chucking them into a box. "He's a pain in the ass. Never held down a job, just sits around and plays Call of Duty all day. Get a box." She nods toward the truck. "Unless you want to be here all day?"

We work in time, in silence, shifting boxes of standard garage items—bungee cords, batteries, bicycle chains. Wrenches, pliers, hammers. Screws and nails. Spare tires. Folding chairs. We take it all, every last thing. I feel like the Grinch, stripping the Whos' houses of all their Christmas presents, right down to the last can of Who hash, which we find when Kerry busts the lock of the door into the house.

"The fridge will be empty," she says with regret as we walk through a neat laundry room. "Check those cabinets, though." She jerks a thumb back toward the washer and dryer.

I open the cabinets above the washing machine and find laundry detergent, dryer sheets. Numbly, I take them.

Kerry has already gone to the walk-in pantry, and her satisfied hoot both excites me and makes me tense. I follow her into a neat kitchen that smells only slightly stale.

"Look at this." She gestures to some shelves of canned soup, vegetables, meat, tuna. There are maybe fifty cans. She opens the garbage bag she brought and starts chucking them in.

"Check the other cabinets," she says, and I do, finding a couple packets of spaghetti, some jarred sauce. Under the sink there are cleaning products, sponges, J-cloths, dish soap. Everything goes.

"Ah, here's the real prize," she says, as she opens the cabinet above the oven. There is half a bottle of gin, another of whiskey. She cradles them like babies before depositing them in a box.

We take it all out to the truck, whose bed is now brimming. Kerry goes back in for another haul, and I follow her reluctantly because I'm starting to feel antsy. We have been gone for fifteen minutes, at least.

"I think we should go back," I tell her. She's in her uncle's bedroom, opening the drawers of his bureau.

"Check these out," she says, and tosses a couple of heavy knit sweaters toward me. Instinctively, I catch them.

"We don't need these—"

"Alex, stop living in your little dreamland," she tells me impatiently as she riffles through the next drawer. "We *need* this stuff. The world is never going back to the way it was." She doesn't sound all that bothered by the fact.

"Never? That's a bit extreme, don't you think?" I try for a laugh, but it comes out like a wheeze. "The world is still functioning, Kerry. In Tokyo, they're probably still going about their business—"

She gives me her standard well-duh look. "We're not in Tokyo."

"I know, but..." I'm clinging to the remnant of the reality I knew, the reality I *want*. "The president said—"

She huffs a hard laugh. "Whatever."

"At some point," I insist, needing to say it, to believe it, "we're going to get back to the way we were, or something like it. There are still so many people alive. Two-thirds of the US population, at least—" Or so I can guess. "Infrastructure will be repaired. Utilities will be restored. There are enough people around, enough infrastructure still left, armies and police and—"

"Yeah, two-thirds are alive for *now*," Kerry cuts me off, unimpressed. "But how many people do you think are going to die of air pollution? Contaminated water? Heart attack?

Disease? Untreated cancer?" She speaks without any emotion at all. "Didn't you ever watch *The Day After Tomorrow*? Or *I Am Legend*?" She shakes her head as if I'm too stupid to be borne, and I feel a flash of anger.

"Isn't *I Am Legend* about zombies?"

She shrugs, and I continue, my voice tight. "This isn't some dumb action movie, Kerry. This is real life. It's going to be different. It's going to be... realistic." Which is about the stupidest thing I've ever said, but I'm too angry—and too scared —to make sense. I don't want to live out some real-life version of one of those movies. "It's going to be different."

"Okay, sure, but meanwhile I'm taking these slippers." She holds up a pair of fuzzy slippers with a grin. "I've always wanted Uggs. They might be a little big, but..." She shrugs. "Have you checked the bathroom?"

"We need to go—"

"How much shampoo do you have back at your place?"

Four bottles, I recall from the inventory we did. I don't reply, but neither do I protest when she heads to the bathroom. I walk back outside to check on our stuff. The street is still empty, silent. The sky is still bright, and the air has that metallic edge that promises snow. I glance at the bed of the truck, filled with the bins and bags and crates of stuff I know we'll find useful. But if Kerry is right—if we're living in something out of a disaster movie—how long will any of our stuff last? A couple of months, maybe, if we eke it out?

And then what?

Kerry comes outside, holding another bag of stuff in one hand, the slippers in her other. "I didn't want them to get dirty," she says, tossing the bag in the back of the truck like some rene-gade Santa Claus. "There were *six* Costco-sized bottles of Head and Shoulders. I don't have dandruff, but I guess my uncle did. Beggars can't be choosers, eh?"

"It's almost like you're enjoying this," I tell her, and she shrugs.

"How would crying or wringing my hands help?"

"It wouldn't, but it would be... understandable."

"Yeah, well, I prefer to be practical." Her expression hardens. "Like you are, right? I mean, the only reason you asked my mom and me to live with you is because you wanted our stuff." She says it like a challenge, and I decide to be as blunt as she's being.

"For your stuff, and because I thought you and your mom actually knew something," I tell her. "Hunting, fishing, that kind of thing."

She lets out a huff of laughter. "Oh, so because we live out in the sticks, you think we should know how to skin a deer? Joke's on you then." She's smiling, but her eyes look flinty.

"Yes," I agree, as I climb into the truck. I feel too defeated to be angry, but I know I really dislike this woman. "Joke's on me."

Kerry strolls to the other side of the cab, her precious slippers in her hand. "It was nice of you," she says, somewhat grudgingly, as she slides into the truck, "to ask us. Even if you only did it for what you could get out of it. I don't think we would have survived, in my mum's house."

"What about your own place?" I ask, and she shakes her head.

"I don't have my own place." She pauses. "I used to live here in Corville, a couple of years ago. I worked in the hairdresser's, as a trainee." She stares out the window, and then gives herself a shake, like she's coming to. "Anyway," she says, a way to the end the conversation, and before I can think how to respond, a sudden crack splits the air, and then another. They're coming from over by the Foodland.

Gunshots.

TWELVE

DANIEL

December

He wakes to sunlight in his eyes, and he blinks slowly. He is staring at a ceiling, stained brown from nicotine, and the air is thick with the cloying smells of air freshener and stale cigarette smoke. He is lying in bed. His mind is a blank. He tries to move his limbs, and realizes, with a jolt of panic, that he is naked. His memories are fuzzy and unformed, shadows slipping away before he can grab onto them, turn them into recognizable shapes. *How did I get here?*

Then, in a sudden, sickening rush, it comes back to him, a flash of images, of memories. The nuclear strikes, Sam. The boat, the river, the push, the gunshots as he clambered to the other side. He ran through the night in soaking-wet clothes, stumbling, falling, and lurching up again, his lungs burning, bursting, the clothes freezing to his body, until he could run no more, having no idea if he was being chased, if he would be shot.

The last thing he remembers is falling hard to his knees in the dark and thinking, *Alex will never know how hard I tried.*

But if he's here, Daniel reasons, in a bed, then someone must have rescued him. Cared for him. And yet even as that thought heartens him, he realizes just how completely vulnerable he is, naked and weak and ill. Where are his clothes, his money, his *gun*? Presumably whoever found him took all his things. And they might not give them back.

He takes a deep breath that hurts his lungs and forces himself into a sitting position. The room spins and a clammy sweat breaks out across his skin. Still, he moves forward, staggering to his feet only to have the floor lurch beneath him, and he falls back to the bed with a grunt, defeated at the very first hurdle.

The door opens. A woman stands there, squat and short, her broad face completely expressionless. She is Native American, and dimly Daniel recalls that there is reserved land somewhere around here—except he doesn't know actually where *here* is.

"You're awake," she says unnecessarily. "Do you think you can eat?"

His head is still spinning, and his skin is damp and clammy. He feels weak, so weak. "I don't know," he replies honestly.

"Huh." She gives a nod. "I'll bring you some soup." And then she closes the door without waiting for a reply. Daniel sinks back onto the bed, his eyes closing. He falls asleep without realizing he is doing so.

When he wakes up, the woman is putting a bowl of Campbell's chicken noodle soup on the bedside table. He recognizes the smell from his childhood, days spent home sick from school—the tinny taste, rubbery chicken bobbing in broth, the way the noodles slid down his throat, loathsome and comforting at the same time.

"Thank you," he whispers. He realizes he's sprawled naked on top of the bedspread, and he tries to cover himself, fumbling for the covers. The woman lets out a huff of laughter and throws a blanket over him from the end of the bed.

"Don't worry, I've seen it all before," she tells him. "You've been here for a week."

He stares at her in blank horror. A *week*. A week away from Alex, from Ruby and Mattie, a week totally wasted, while the world burned. What will Sam be doing now? Where will he be —and how will he get there? He shakes his head uselessly.

"Eat," she advises. "You'll feel better."

And then she leaves him alone.

Somehow, he manages to ease up in the bed until his back is leaning against the wall, and slurp down the soup, even though it is lukewarm, greasy, making his stomach roil. He knows he needs to eat. He needs to get out of here. *A whole week.* He has to keep moving.

The woman returns, his clothes draped over one arm— khakis, shirt, his fleece vest, all washed and dried. But not his watch, he thinks, not his money, not his gun.

"Thank you," he says, as she puts the clothes on the bed.

"Are you strong enough to come out?" she asks, and he nods.

"Yes. Yes."

She leaves again.

He rises from the bed, his limbs rubbery and shaking. He can't believe how weak he feels, how utterly helpless. He's at the mercy of this woman, whoever she is. So far, she's been kind, but even so, he knows he can't trust her.

He pulls on his clothes, grateful not to be naked. Small mercies, he thinks, and almost smiles. Then he remembers Sam. Alex, Mattie, Ruby. Are they all right, back at Lost Lake? Will he ever see any of them again? He remembers how he held Alex, before he left, how it felt as if she wanted to burrow into him, and how he'd wanted her to. He'd wanted to say so much, to take back the last six months, to have been someone different, but at least he could be different now.

He opens the door and steps out into the hall. The walls are an off-white turned to an uneven brown, nicotine-stained like the ceiling, and the hall is covered in brown shag wall-to-wall carpet. He feels as if he has stepped into the 1970s. He follows the hall to the main room of the ranch house—there is an L-shaped sofa on one end, with a large TV, its flat screen black and silent, and a dining room table and chairs on the other. A man is sitting at the table, smoking. He has long gray hair tied back in a ponytail, and his face is utterly inscrutable. The woman comes in with cups of coffee and places them on the table before retreating to the doorway of the kitchen, where she stands with her hands on her hips.

"Thank you," Daniel says, knowing he sounds too formal, "for having me here." As if they asked him to stay.

The man blows out smoke and points to the chair opposite him. Daniel sits. The man takes one of the cups of coffee, and he realizes the other one is for him. He takes it with murmured thanks—it is instant, lukewarm, with no milk, undissolved granules floating in the murky liquid. It tastes bitter, but he's glad for it.

"Can you tell me what's been happening?" he asks after a moment when it seems as if no one is going to speak.

"We found you down by the point," the woman says, the words seeming to burst out of her. "You were half-dead from the cold, clothes frozen to your back." The man gives her a quelling look; he certainly seems more sparing with words than she is. Daniel takes another sip of coffee, doing his best not to wince at the acrid taste, the coffee granules catching on his tongue in bursts of bitterness.

"You got sick from being wet," the man states. His voice is low and gravelly. "Fever and all. You cross the river?"

"Yes." Daniel decides not to mention the border police, the gunshots. He thinks the man might know about them, anyway.

"Where are you going?"

"Clarkson, New York, near Syracuse. To get my son." His

voice throbs and he takes another sip from his coffee to hide his emotion, but his hands shake and he puts it down again. The man glances at his wife, whose lips are pursed. Daniel senses an unspoken conversation flowing around him like a river, currents pulling. Then the man sighs, shifts in his seat. He blows smoke to the ceiling, squinting up at the blue-tinged haze.

"Things have changed since you crossed," he states, and Daniel tenses.

"How have they changed?" he makes himself ask.

"People have been saying there have been more strikes."

"What?" He lurches forward in his seat as if he has been pushed from behind, his hands clenched and clasped between his knees. "*What?* How? Where?"

The man shrugs, still staring at the ceiling. "Some say Detroit. Buffalo."

"Omaha," the woman fills in. "I heard Omaha."

"Has there been any news? On the TV, the radio?" His questions come out in gasps; he had told Alex there might be more strikes, but he realizes in this moment that he hadn't really believed it. He had thought the worst had already happened because he'd so wanted it to be true. He'd *needed* it to be true.

"Sometimes on the radio," the man replies with a shrug. "But the power is out everywhere now. No electricity, no water, no internet, no nothing. No one hears or sees much of anything, these days. Don't even know where the nukes came from."

"It must be Russia," the woman said, sounding important.

The man shrugs. "Russia, China, who knows? Don't suppose it matters much, now."

"Is martial law still in effect?" Daniel asks, thinking it must be. The police will be out in force, the army too. There might be barricaded roads, helicopter surveillance, armed patrol... His mind is racing, picturing vague scenarios from disaster movies. It will be harder than ever to find a way to Clarkson.

The man glances at his wife again. She looks down at the

floor. "It's not how it was before," he says quietly. "When everyone was waiting for something to happen."

"What do you mean?" But already Daniel thinks he knows. The shocked lull after the first few strikes has come to an end, as he knew it would. What has replaced it?

"It's dangerous," the woman states flatly. "No one's in charge anymore, not the army, not the police. There's no law anywhere."

"And when the law does show up..." The man glances at his wife. She purses her lips. "Better if they don't," he finishes, and Daniel feels a chill of apprehension. How on earth is he going to get to Sam?

"Can I travel?" he asks. "Are the roads passable?"

"They're *passable*," the man says, and Daniel knows there's something he isn't saying.

"Please," he says, "just tell me. What's going on? What is it like out there?"

A silence falls, like a simmering. The man and woman look at each other again, and the woman gives a little shrug. Daniel realizes he's clenching his fists and he uncurls them, smooths them out on his lap like crumpled pieces of paper. Takes a slow, even breath because his heart is racing, and he's feeling dizzy.

"It's not safe," the man finally says. "Not anywhere, but especially any towns, cities. There are gangs. Violence. The police have as good as disappeared. The army..." He shook his head, his mouth twisting with disgust. "Sometimes, they come, in trucks, tanks even, they wave their guns around. Sometimes, they shoot them. They're as scared as the rest of us, and no one knows what's going on. The government—"

"There is no government," the woman bursts out, as if she could not stay silent a moment longer. "The president, pfft! He's disappeared, down into some bolt-hole. He doesn't care."

"What about other countries?" Daniel asks. "Have there been strikes in other countries?" Or is the rest of the world simply watching the United States get blown up? Enjoying it, even?

The man shrugs as he blows more smoke up at the ceiling. "Who knows."

"Has the US retaliated?" he asks, and he's met with more shrugs.

He needs to get out there and see for himself, Daniel realizes. Take his chances. He's crossed the border, he reminds himself. That was the hardest part. Hopefully. It's just a matter of miles between him and Sam, that's all.

"I need to go," he tells them. "My other things..." He trails off, tensing, because he doesn't know these people, isn't sure if they'll give him back his belongings. But they did take care of him, he reminds himself. They fed him, they kept him, and they didn't have to.

The woman seems to read his expression, his uncertainty, because she stiffens, drawing herself up with dignity, wide shoulders thrown back, managing to look down her nose at him even though she's a foot shorter than he is. "I will get your things," she states with dignity, and Daniel feels ashamed.

She leaves the room, returning a minute later with his backpack, his rifle, his watch, everything. The money he'd put into different pockets has all been taken out, paperclipped together in a wad of crinkly bills.

"They had to dry," she explains stiffly. "It's all there. Count it, if you want."

"Thank you." He takes the money without counting it, even though part of him still wants to.

"The rifle dried out," the man adds. "But I don't know about your ammo. If it got too wet, it might not work. You'll have to see."

"Thank you," Daniel says again. He is, quite suddenly, overcome by their kindness. They could have left him to freeze to death. Why didn't they?

"You should stay the night," the man advises. "It's nearly dark, and you need the rest. Leave in the morning, early. Where did you say you were going?"

"Clarkson, between Utica and Syracuse."

"You'll have to avoid 81, any of the main roads, any towns." The man gestures to the woman, who goes to a drawer and takes out a map, the kind everyone used before phones, crinkly and creased, that were always impossible to refold.

The man unfolds it on the table, smooths out its deep creases before pointing with one gnarled, nicotine-stained finger to where they are—just outside Redwood, New York, Route 37, a few miles from the St Lawrence River. His finger traces various lines, avoiding all the highways. "Route 37 to 26 to 12, all the way to Utica," he muses, "but turn off before you get to the city itself, or even the outskirts. I heard some renegades had taken over the Home Depot just outside of Watertown, barricaded themselves in there... you just don't know." He hacks, spits into his empty coffee cup. Daniel realizes he has been chewing a wad of tobacco; his spittle is a deep, reddish brown. The man resumes tracing the route with his finger. "Then Route 46, maybe, to 31... there's Clarkson." He jabs at the map with his finger. "Don't go on 90. Keep to the back roads, skirt around any towns if you can, even small ones." He glances up, his expression somber, even sad. "It's got to be over a hundred miles."

A hundred if he'd been able to take the highway, but walking along all these meandering roads will add a lot of distance. A lot of time. Daniel swallows. How on earth is he going to do it?

The man refolds the map. "You won't be able to walk it," he tells him, a simple statement of fact.

Daniel looks down at his lap. He knows it is true. Even with all the other obstacles, he doesn't have enough food or enough stamina for that kind of journey, not now, when he's been in bed with a fever for a week.

"I have to," he says, also a statement of fact. He looks up to see the man nod slowly.

"We may have something," he says.

Daniel follows him out to the garage, blinking in the late-afternoon sunlight. The house is a ranch house off by itself, not another building in sight, facing the road, which stretches emptily through cornfields, now filled with brown, withered stalks.

The man opens the garage door, the screech loud in the stillness, making Daniel tense as he waits uncertainly, having no idea what he's going to be offered. Then the man emerges from the shadowy space, carrying a bicycle in one large hand. It is a child's bicycle, a girl's, with pink handlebars that have purple streamers attached, and a cushioned seat shaped like a banana, in pink and purple stripes. There is a purple, plastic basket hooked to the front, made to look like it has been woven, with a bright pink plastic flower attached to the front.

"I'll raise the seat," the man says, and Daniel has a sudden, wild urge to laugh. He's going to look like a clown on that bike, his knees practically up by his ears, and yet he's moved to a fierce tenderness for this stranger, for his inexplicable kindness.

A bicycle will, he knows, make a lot of difference. It might even make this journey possible.

"You don't need it?" he asks, and the man gives him a look.

"You think I'd fit on this thing?"

"Your daughter..." He's assuming they have a daughter, to have a bike like this, although he imagines she must be an adult now, judging by their age.

The man looks down at the bike, his face collapsing into sagging lines of sadness. "She lived in Chicago," he says quietly. "Moved there just a couple of months ago, for a job."

Chicago, hit in the first wave of strikes. The tenderness

Daniel feels is now touched with a deep, abiding pity. "I'm sorry."

The man shrugs. "We've all lost someone now. I hope your son is alive."

Daniel swallows. He has not let himself consider that Sam might not be. Clarkson wasn't near any strikes. As long as he had enough food, water... But of course there are so many dangers, not least other people. Sam might have left the college campus, gone... where?

No, he wouldn't, Daniel decides. He remembers a time when Sam was six, maybe seven. He'd taken him to the mall, was browsing in the men's section of Macy's when he turned around and Sam suddenly wasn't there. He hadn't panicked at first, had simply strolled through the racks of suits, looking for that familiar mop of dark hair, bright hazel eyes, but Sam was nowhere to be seen. Five minutes passed, nearing ten. A gentle exasperation had morphed into alarm, then panic, fear. He'd located a security guard; they'd agreed to use the sound system to ask if anyone had seen Sam. *If anyone has seen a dark-haired boy in a red T-shirt and jeans, could you please come forward...*

Then Sam, trotting toward him, looking perplexed. Daniel had taken him by the shoulders, his fear turned to fury for one blazing moment. "Where were you?" he'd demanded in a raw voice. "Where did you go?"

Sam had blinked up at him, looking both confused and a little bit annoyed. "I didn't go anywhere," he said. "I was right next to you. *You're* the one who moved."

Daniel had laughed and hugged his son to him. He holds that memory close now.

"Thank you for the bike," he says to the man, and he doesn't think he's ever meant anything more.

. . .

He rests for the remainder of the day, knowing he needs to keep up his strength. That evening he eats dinner with the man and woman—he hasn't asked their names, and they haven't offered them—a hash of dried meat and root vegetables cooked over a propane stove and tasting like mushy nothing.

While they eat, the man takes out the map again, tracing the suggested route with a red felt-tip marker. "Find shelter if you can, but be careful," he advises. "No one's friendly, these days. Not anymore."

You are, Daniel thinks, but he just nods, his gaze on the map, on the wavering, red line that will lead him to Sam.

The next morning, he washes in cold water drawn from a stream. He runs his hand over his face and the stubble that's grown there. He can't remember the last time he didn't shave for an entire week. He supposes he will grow a beard, something he's never done before. He dresses warmly and packs his backpack, straps his rifle over his shoulder. He no longer feels absurd, like he's play-acting at being a survivalist, a hero. He simply feels determined.

When he comes out into the living room, the woman silently hands him a bag. It is filled with food—granola bars, beef jerky, trail mix.

Daniel starts to hand it back. "You need this—"

The woman shakes her head, implacable. A lump forms in his throat and he swallows it down. "Thank you," he says simply.

They accompany him outside, stand by the front door as Daniel clambers onto the small bike, which is the right size for a ten-year-old girl. His knees are by his elbows, and it's going to be incredibly difficult to pedal. He doesn't care.

"Thank you," he says again, and then he starts pedaling, weaving down the driveway as he adjusts to the size of the bike; his thighs are already burning, and he raises himself off the seat, to give himself a bit more leverage. He feels the gaze of the man and woman tracking him as he bikes down their drive and then turns left onto the road, toward Watertown. There is not a car, not a person, in sight—just road and sky and husk-filled corn-fields, their dried stalks rustling and whispering in the frigid wind.

Improbably, as he starts down the road, his heart lifts.

THIRTEEN

"Put the butt high up on your chest, near your shoulder, and keep your elbows down. Put the stock against your cheek. Don't touch the trigger till you're ready to shoot. Eyes on the prize."

I speak as if I'm an expert because I have to. Mattie takes in all my instructions, her body taut with concentration, her eyes narrowed against the white glare of the winter's sun, focused on the tin can fifty yards away.

"Ready?" I ask, and she nods before pulling the trigger. The crack of the gun splits the still air, and the recoil makes her take a startled step back. We both blink at the target, and then I let out a whoop. She's nicked the top of the can.

"Good job, Mattie!" My feet crunch through the dry, ice-encrusted leaves carpeting the ground as I jog over to right the can once more. "Very good job. Let's try again."

It's been three days since we went to Corville. Three days since I sprinted from Kerry's uncle's house to the parking lot of Foodland, my heart thundering in my chest as I fought down a feeling too elemental and consuming to simply be terror.

When I got to the parking lot, I slowed, then stopped, hovering on its edge, my gaze sweeping through the crowd for my daughters. An open-topped army jeep was on the side of the lot, a man in full body armor standing in the back of it, a machine gun aimed unwaveringly at the crowd. Everyone was frozen in a tableau of terror; this was the army, but it looked like the enemy.

"Put the food down," the man barked loudly. "Go back to your homes. Now."

"Why can't we take it?" one brave soul called out, lost in the crowd. "It will go to waste otherwise. This is fair."

"This is military property now," the soldier barked back. "You're not meant to be out of your homes."

"We need food," someone else called out, their tone more resentful than pleading. There was a sense among the crowd, I was realizing, of bitterness as much as fear.

"You'll get it," the solider snapped back. "It will be distributed by the army in due course. Now go!"

A few people began to drift away, while my gaze swung wildly through the crowd, looking for my children. Where were Ruby and Mattie?

Then, a gunshot, and the soldier's head whipped around, looking for the rebel. I recoiled instinctively, and before I could process where the shot had come from, I heard the rat-a-tat-tat of the soldier's machine gun spitting bullets. A gasp, a scream, and people began to scatter, running in every direction. The soldier kept his gun aimed at the crowd as they ran. Then, through the clearing crowd, I saw Mattie and Ruby huddled beneath an overturned shopping cart, hugging each other. I sprinted toward them, heedless of the soldier and his gun.

A sound escaped me, something between a sob and a gasp as I pulled them up and hugged them each, fiercely, in turn. "What happened?" I demanded. I glanced behind me; the jeep was parked in front of the supermarket, empty now, the soldiers having gone inside. A shudder went through me.

"The army showed up," Mattie whispered. "And they started shooting in the air."

"Look." This from Ruby, surprising us both. I turned to follow her pointed finger; there was a man sprawled in the parking lot, blood pumping out of his stomach. Everyone else had gone. Until that moment, I hadn't realized someone had actually been shot.

"Mom, can we do something?" Mattie whispered.

I shook my head, my gaze fixed on the dying man, a pool of dark red blood spreading around him. "I don't think so."

"*Please.*"

I glanced at the army jeep; I was terrified that one of us might be shot, but the soldiers were nowhere to be seen. Reluctantly, holding my daughters' hands, I walked toward the man. There was nothing we could do, I knew that already, but I was compelled to try, or at least show my daughters that I couldn't save him. I couldn't become the kind of person who walks away from a dying man. I couldn't let my daughters see that I had.

The man's eyes were open, his jaw clenched, one hand pressed to the bloody mess of his stomach. I couldn't look at it. His body convulsed.

"I'm sorry," I told him helplessly, touching his shoulder, offering him what paltry comfort I could because it was clear there was nothing else I could do.

"Damned army," he choked out. "Damned government." He convulsed again, thick, viscous blood leaking out between his fingers, making my stomach roil, and then his eyes closed. Ruby pressed her face into my shoulder. Mattie was rigid, staring at the man as if she wanted to imprint the memory of him on her mind, her soul. Had she ever seen a dead person before? The only person I'd ever seen die was my father—in a hospital bed, drifting off on a sea of morphine. This felt different, raw and wrong.

"Come on," I said quietly, glancing again at the door of the grocery store. "We need to go." I hugged them both again, tightly, in turn, as if I could impress the force of my feelings upon them, the depth of my regret. How could I have left them alone the way I had? And for what? A couple of cans of motor oil, some Kraft Macaroni and Cheese, and a bottle of gin?

"Where's Kerry?" Mattie asked.

A cold wave of realization washed over me because Kerry had stayed with the truck, and I suddenly realized how naive I had been. How utterly, utterly foolish. Kerry could have driven off and left us here, as easy as that. She could go hole up in our cottage, just her and Darlene, with all our food, our clothes, our *home*. She didn't need us, and I was pretty sure she knew it.

"She's across the street," I told Mattie, praying it was true. If she'd *left*... what would we do? It was twenty miles back to the cottage. "Come on," I said, grabbing both their hands. We had just started walking across to the road when Kerry swung into the parking lot, pulled right up in front of us, the driver's window rolled down, her elbow resting on the frame.

"Hop in," she said with a grin.

Kerry seemed unfazed when Mattie told her what had happened. "Typical, army coming in and bossing everyone around."

"They shot someone," Mattie whispered. "A gun went off, and they just started *shooting*."

"Well, you don't shoot your gun at the army," Kerry replied, her tone jarringly reasonable. "You don't even shoot your mouth off, especially when there's martial law in force." She shook her head.

"He *died*," Mattie said, her voice choking, and Kerry turned, her face briefly softening.

"I'm sorry you saw that," she said quietly, and it was the most empathetic, the most human, I'd ever seen her. "But at least we're all safe, and we can get back to the cottage now."

"What is all this stuff?" Mattie asked, as her gaze roved over the jumbled crates and bins we'd pillaged from Kerry's uncle's house, and I just shook my head. I couldn't explain to her that I'd put her life in danger for the sake of some *stuff*.

No one spoke on the drive back; Kerry seemed almost cheerful, humming under her breath, Ruby retreating into herself as she so often did, Mattie silent and thoughtful, her lips pursed as she stared out at the wintry landscape streaming by in a blur of brown.

For about ten miles, I let myself simply not think. I needed a respite from the fear, and in any case, I felt frozen inside, numb with both horror and shock; but as the miles passed in silence, not a car in sight, I started to thaw, to *think*.

As much as I kept trying to believe there was some kind of normal to get back to, after that encounter with the army, I was being forced to accept that there wasn't, that there might never be. We weren't going to be able to wait this out, and we couldn't subsist on whatever we could steal or forage or find. Not for long, anyway.

There had to be another solution. I thought of Daniel, back on that first day, sounding so reasonable and yet so ridiculous. *The cottage is actually the best place for us to be in this situation. We really can survive here, if we try.*

I'd mocked him, I remembered, because I hadn't wanted even to think about living that way.

But now I was coming to the conclusion that it was the only option, and it was one I wanted to make work, however I could. And so here I was, giving my daughter lessons in how to handle a gun when I could barely shoot myself.

Mattie turns to me, her dark hair flying out behind her in a ponytail, her expression fierce as she holds the rifle like she was born with it in her hand. "I don't want to waste the bullets."

Something has hardened in her too, these last three days. Gone is the girl raging about her phone, declaring she's bored. I'm proud of her, but I also ache with sadness. She shouldn't have to be this way. None of us should, and yet this is only the beginning.

"One more time," I tell her. "If you hit it again, we'll call it a day."

Mattie nods and positions the rifle against her shoulder. Her hair blows out behind her as she narrows her gaze, draws a breath, lets it out steady and slow. She takes aim, fires, and hits the can dead center. My heart explodes with something deeper than pride, fiercer than joy.

"That's my girl," I tell her. My wilderness girl.

The smile Mattie gives me is flinty, determined. She puts the safety catch on the rifle and props it against her shoulder. "What now?" she asks, like I have a plan.

I take a breath and let it filter slowly through me. I've been doing a lot of thinking these last three days, letting ideas form and coalesce. I've walked down the road as far as the gate, and hiked up through the woods, my boots crunching on the frozen ground, the forest stretching all around me in a grove of leafless trees, like stark and silent sentries. Our army. Our defense.

We can live here. We can make this work, just like Daniel said. We just have to figure out how.

"We need to do another inventory," I tell her, and Mattie nods, unsurprised, ready. "All the stuff Kerry brought, and that we got from Corville. I want to open the root cellar too. There might be stuff in there."

"Okay."

"And then we need to figure out a rationing system. How long all this stuff will actually last." I pause, and then continue with determination, "And then we need to figure out what we're going to do when it runs out."

Mattie stands with one hand on the butt of the rifle, one leg stuck out, her hair blowing in the wind. She looks like she belongs in some teen TV show. Kick-ass dystopian heroine, right here. It almost makes me smile.

"And what *are* we going to do when it runs out?" she asks, turning to me. The mirage of her fearlessness is revealed by the vulnerability I see in her eyes, despite the stubborn set of her chin. "What are we going to do for food?"

"I'm still figuring that out. We'll have to grow some—"

"In winter?" She scoffs, just as I once did.

"Maybe we can last till spring with what we have."

"And if we can't?"

"I don't know, Mats. I'm still thinking about it." I take another deep breath, let it out slowly. "Let's take it one step at a time, okay? Do the inventory, figure out a rationing schedule. Then we'll worry about what we'll do to make it till spring."

"Okay." Mattie nods. "Let's go."

I almost smile again at her determination, and we head back to the cottage. In the three days since we came back from Corville, not much has changed. Darlene is still mainly bedridden, although she perks up on occasion, and Kerry slopes around the house, taking everything in while doing nothing, and making me nervous. Part of me wonders if she's sizing everything up, or even if she'd kill us in our sleep. I don't believe that, not really, but worry gnaws at me because I still don't trust her, even if she came back with the truck.

Ruby has not spoken one word since we returned.

I've tried to get her to talk a couple of times, to no avail. The night we returned, I sat by her bed and stroked her hair until she fell asleep, murmuring assurances we both knew I couldn't really give, and yet I meant them. *It's going to be okay. I'll keep you safe. Daddy will be home soon.*

Ruby simply stared at me with her big, brown eyes, unblinking, utterly silent. After about half an hour, she turned her head away. It was another hour before she fell asleep.

The next day I tried again, as I made her breakfast oatmeal on the wood stove. "Would you like syrup on it, sweetie? Or brown sugar?" Not that we had much of either, but I wanted to give her a treat. I wanted her to *respond*.

She shook her head and took the bowl of oatmeal without anything on it, going to sit at the table, where she picked at it while Mattie fumed, struggling to hold on to her patience.

"Eat it, Ruby," she snapped. "Food is precious."

Her sister simply stared at her.

Now as we head back into the cottage, I tell myself I need to figure out other things too—like what to do about Kerry. Right now, she's a mouth to feed and not much else. I need to get her to engage, but it's hard when I'm more than a little bit scared of her.

"So, Kerry," I say, as I see her sprawled on the sofa in the living room. I sound like a gym teacher telling off the girls who try to hide in the locker room, claiming they're on their periods. "I thought we could take an inventory of everything, make a rationing schedule."

She gives me a guarded look. "Okay."

"I thought you could help."

She lets out a long sigh and then swings her legs off the sofa. "What do you want me to do?"

Her acquiescence throws me, and I scramble for a response, which I can tell she notices. "Um, you could write stuff down?"

"No."

To my shock, this refusal comes not from Kerry, but from Ruby. She was curled up in a chair in the corner of the room, reading as usual, but now she comes toward me, looking almost angry.

"No," she says again, louder this time. It's the first time she's spoken in three days. I stare at her in surprise.

"I think, Mom," Mattie says quietly from behind me, "Ruby wants to do the writing."

Of *course,* just as she did before.

"Guess I don't have a job then," Kerry says, with a smile for Ruby.

"You can still help," I reply quickly. "There will be lots to do, and you're—you're part of this, you know."

Kerry lifts her chin. "Am I?" she asks, a challenge, and I have no idea what to say. "Aren't you just waiting for an excuse to send me and my mom packing?" Kerry continues. "I know what you're thinking. Two more mouths to feed, and I don't even know how to hunt. We're both a waste of space as far as you're concerned." She speaks matter-of-factly, without bitterness but with utter certainty.

"That's not true." This from Mattie, sounding injured, certain. "We wouldn't do that. We want to help you."

Kerry merely lifts her eyebrows as she looks at me, daring me to contradict my daughter. To tell the truth.

"Mom." Mattie tugs on my sleeve, insistent. "Tell her. We wouldn't do that."

"We wouldn't," I say at last, with not nearly enough conviction. Kerry lets out a hard huff of laughter.

"*Mom.*" Mattie looks at me, her expression a mix of accusation and hurt. "What are you saying? Did you ask Darlene and Kerry here just for... for what they could give us?"

I feel myself flushing. I'm exposed, and I'm humiliated to realize how lowered I have become in my daughter's eyes.

"Hey, at least we brought the chickens," Kerry remarks. "Although, full disclosure, they stop laying in winter." Her chin lifts in challenge.

"That doesn't matter," I say stiffly, a beat too late. "I just want you to help out, like everyone else is doing."

Kerry throws an arm wide, her eyes glittering. "Lead the way."

. . .

For the next few hours, we work through all the stuff Kerry brought, as well as all the stuff we took from her uncle's house. We go through my dad's little tool room, with its clutter of odds and ends, and Ruby writes it all down, while Mattie collates the figures, seeming to enjoy the challenge, and Kerry helps me organize the supplies, her manner both calm and capable. Somehow, that tense little confrontation cleared the air, at least a little, and we work in surprising, brisk harmony.

"We have two bottles of white spirit from Grandad's room," Mattie says, "and four from the truck... what category does that go in?"

"Miscellaneous?" I suggest, and Kerry gives me a look.

"How about cleaning supplies?" she suggests, and I'm too embarrassed to admit I didn't know what white spirit is used for, but I think Kerry guessed that already.

"Good idea," I reply, and her look indeed assures me that she knew I didn't know, just as I suspect she knows I don't know a lot of things. But I'm learning.

We keep moving through the house, room by room, just as we did before, but this time with more purpose, more focus. Even Ruby is concentrating, her forehead puckered as she frowns down at her paper. *We need this*, I realize. We needed to have a plan, and now we do.

Occasionally, Kerry peels off to check on Darlene, who insists she's fine, but I'm not sure she is. Her breath is wheezy, and when she hefts herself from the sofa, it's with a groan, but at least she can move.

Outside we go through the pump house—two garden rakes, a hoe, a pitchfork, a pair of old oars, a canoe paddle, some life jackets that have been devastated by mice, bits of foam scattered all over the floor. We've moved the chickens from here to the screened-in gazebo, which has the hot tub, long since drained.

There's an actual chicken coop, a hundred years old but still standing, by the old barn down the road, but the gazebo is closer. It works for now; Kerry pinned up some tarps to cover the screens and give the hens some shelter. I guess she hasn't been just doing nothing, not exactly. She just doesn't make a big deal about it, which makes me feel guilty.

"What about in there?" she asks now, jerking her thumb toward the root cellar door. It was a big project when I was twelve or so, and my parents were still in their hardy-pioneer phase, but the truth is they never really used it except to put the trash in, in the summer, to keep it from stinking.

"I can't open the door," I tell her, and again she gives me one of those looks of hers, like I'm dumb as rocks but she's too polite to say.

"What have you tried?" she asks.

I shrug, which is my way of saying not much, because how do you open a door that's completely stuck? I can't look it up on WikiHow, watch a quick YouTube video, the way I normally would.

Kerry presses her lips together as she examines the door like an expert. "It's swollen shut," she announces, and my lips twitch. *No kidding.*

"There are ways to open it," she tells me, as stern as a schoolteacher, while Mattie, Ruby and I simply look on. "Let me get some sandpaper, for a start."

Sandpaper? I watch, bemused, as she goes to fetch some; thanks to our exhaustive inventory, she knows exactly where it is and how much we have. A minute or so later, Kerry returns, and runs the sandpaper all along the door's edges, the sides, underneath, and then stands on her tiptoes to reach the top. The rest of us just watch. She tosses the sandpaper aside and pulls at the door; to her credit, it shifts maybe a millimeter. Her breath comes out in a frustrated rush. I fold my arms. Ruby glances at me, and Mattie shrugs.

"What we need," Kerry announces, "is a source of heat. Do you have a hairdryer?"

"Yes, but no electricity," I remind her, and she rolls her eyes and points to the generator.

"I don't want to waste the propane."

"It's a *hairdryer*. For maybe five minutes. And then we'll open this door."

I'm not at all sure a hairdryer is going to open the door to the root cellar. I also don't think Kerry is really the expert that she's acting like right now, but I appreciate her desire and maybe even her need to feel useful. I'm also curious. I doubt there's anything in the root cellar, but it's worth a look, at least.

"All right," I relent.

A few minutes later, we've located a hairdryer and an extension cord—doing an inventory of the whole house has really helped with this sort of thing—and I've switched on the generator. The sound of it rumbling to life makes us all jump, even though I was expecting it. It feels, I think, like the sound of life.

Kerry turns on the hairdryer, which startles us again, simply by the normality of the sound. I picture Mattie in her old bathroom, lights all around the mirror, pouting at her reflection as she dries her hair.

Kerry starts drying the door around its edges, and I can't help but think she looks a bit ridiculous. Mattie must think so, too, because she gives me a small, secretive smile, and I find myself improbably suppressing a giggle. Ruby cocks her head, her expression quizzical. Kerry keeps on with the hairdryer, and after a few endless minutes—every second costing us precious propane—I open my mouth to tell her to stop, that this is a tremendous waste of time and energy.

Then she tries the door, and it budges a little, and she turns off the hairdryer.

"I need a crowbar," she says.

"I know where one is." Mattie runs to get a crowbar from the pump house while I watch, apprehensive, impressed.

"You'd better turn off the generator," Kerry tells me, and I hurry to do it, a little annoyed I hadn't thought of it first.

Mattie returns with a crowbar, and as we all hold our breath, Kerry fits it through the handle, and then, with immense effort, the tendons on her ropey arms standing out, her face screwed up in concentration, she pries open the door. It comes with a protesting creak and a gust of musty air, and she flings the crowbar aside, triumphant.

"Wow." Mattie sounds deeply impressed, like Kerry is her new idol.

"You're amazing, Kerry." I mean the sentiment, but for some reason my tone doesn't sound sincere. Kerry throws me a look and then makes an elaborate "after you" gesture. I walk into the root cellar, blinking in the dim light, making out the shapes of various barrels and boxes. There is more in here than I thought. A lot more.

Mattie and Ruby follow me, Kerry bringing up the rear.

"This looks promising," she remarks.

"I thought my parents just used this for holding trash and stuff."

"They used to keep some canned stuff in here," Kerry remarks. "I remember bringing it out with my mom."

Which reminds me, painfully, of how tied up she is with the cottage, almost as much as I am, albeit in a different way. It feels important to remember that.

"Yeah," she says, nudging a stack of boxes filled with Mason jars. "Look." I crouch down and see that it's about a dozen large jars of spaghetti sauce. Kerry reaches down and slides one jar out of its slot in the box. "A bumper crop of tomatoes that year, I seem to remember," she says, showing me the sticker on the front of the jar. In my mother's careful, block-like writing, it reads *Mom's Special Spaghetti Sauce 2001.*

"Ew," Mattie whispers. For some reason, we've all been

talking in hushed voices, as if we've entered a crypt. "That's over twenty years old. Can we still eat it?"

"I don't know." I glance at Kerry, and she shrugs.

"Why not?" She moves further into the root cellar. "What else is in here?"

We all start poking through the various barrels, buckets, and boxes; as I pry open the lid of an entire barrel of salt, I realize this stuff must be from the Y2K scare over twenty years ago, when my parents, in pioneer style, loaded up on all sorts of stuff in case the promised Armageddon arrived. Besides the salt, there are several lidded buckets of flour, another couple of sugar, and a box filled with about twenty packets of pasta.

"We've hit the jackpot," Kerry states with satisfaction. She holds up a packet of what I realize are seeds. "Your parents really were preparing for the end of the world. We've got tomato, green bean, onion, peas, corn, and even seed potatoes, although, I'll be honest with you, those are looking a little questionable." She makes a face as she closes up a bag of what look like desiccated potato seedlings.

I look around at it all, feeling both heartened and discouraged, or maybe just overwhelmed. "Surely after twenty years," I say slowly, "some of this stuff can't be any good. The flour..."

She opens one of the buckets of flour and brandishes a small packet. "Oxygen absorbers, keeps the flour fresh, along with the gasket lid. Your dad really knew his stuff."

I shake my head, reluctantly impressed. "How do you know about all this?"

"Are you kidding me? We were all preparing for Y2K up here. I think my mom was disappointed when nothing happened." She drops the packet back in the bucket of flour and then seals the lid. "We should try to open it as little as possible, to keep it fresh."

I put the lid back on the barrel of salt, and that's when I notice the handwriting on the label on top. It's my dad's writing, spidery yet neat, so familiar and yet also forgotten. *Salt, 20kgs.* I trace the writing with my fingertips; it's funny, how something so small can suddenly hit me straight in the heart, leave me breathless with missing him.

Kerry comes to stand beside me, glancing down at the barrel with its faded label. "He was one of the good ones," she says quietly, and it occurs to me that she must have memories of my dad, memories I don't have. I long to ask her about them, but I know now is not the time. The girls are here, and we need to work on our inventory. But along with that shaft of sorrow and grief, I feel something like solidarity. Kerry, of all people, understands a little of what I'm feeling.

I give her a fleeting smile, gesture to the girls, and step back out into the sunlight.

FOURTEEN

We have enough food, if we're very careful, for about four or five months. It's all there in front of me, in Ruby's laborious writing, painstakingly neat, a column of figures that in probably any other circumstances would be impressive. Certainly enough to withstand a blizzard, or even a siege. But when I broke it down, trying to think practically, it didn't actually end up feeling like very much. Worse, it didn't feel like enough.

Two packets of pasta, with two jars of sauce, will provide a week of dinners; we have enough of both for ten weeks. The flour, if it really is still usable, will make two loaves of bread a week for twelve weeks; we don't have any yeast but, according to Kerry, you can make it yourself, not that I know how. I'm not sure she does, either, but maybe we can figure it out. Together.

For breakfast, half a cup of oatmeal each, made with water, should last around the same amount of time. The turkey, if I eke it out, will last a couple of weeks, along with the eggs; all the fresh fruit and veg, along with the milk, will, of course, last only a week or two, if that, before it spoils. Juice, butter, and cheese, a bit longer. The frozen dinners and pizzas might add, at best, another couple of weeks to our total, as long as we don't have a thaw, but basically, best-case scenario, we're looking at running out of food in April or May, and that's not considering the vitamin and nutrient deficiencies we might be experiencing before then, without any fresh fruit or vegetables, meat or protein.

I asked Kerry when the chickens might start laying eggs again, and she said maybe in March, and that's only of course if they survive the winter.

"Regretting asking us here?" she asked sardonically, correctly reading the expression on my face, and I sighed.

"Look, I admit that I asked you here, at least in part, because of how you might be able to help. Wouldn't you have been the same?"

She was silent for a moment before she admitted slowly, "Yeah, I would have."

It felt like a truce, a ceasefire. That was the last time she made one of those remarks, gave me one of those knowing, smirking looks, which has been something of a relief.

Now I sit and stare out at the dark night as the fire burns low, and the cottage settles quietly all around me. It's eleven o'clock at night and everyone is in bed, hopefully asleep. I'm grateful for the moment's peace because while the future yawns emptily in front me, the days have felt distressingly full.

I glance down again at the list of food. *Enough till April.*

We can't start planting till May and, even then, whatever we plant, we wouldn't be able to start harvesting until July… and that's assuming we can actually live off what we plant, which I'm not at all sure about. I have never actually gardened before, besides planting some begonias in pots, although I watched my mom when I was little. She was always happy in the garden, knees right down in the soil, hands covered in earth.

I reach for my wine glass and take a sip; Daniel and I bought a case of wine at the LCBO in Kingston on the way up, and while I know it's precious, I felt like I needed a drink tonight. I need the edges of everything to soften, just a little, for just a little while. I also need to think.

For once, despite the wine, my mind feels clear. I'm not numb, I'm not panicked, I'm not cringing inwardly and cowering with fear. Of course, if I let myself think about any of it too much—the army in Corville, the fact that Daniel has been gone for an entire week, the state of the entire *world*—I'll go into a tailspin of terror.

But right now, I have a very clear, basic problem, and I'm determined to solve it. We need food. Better yet, we need a *source* of food. And I'm going to find it. It feels like one of the word problems Mattie had in seventh grade—*there are five people and each one eats two pounds of food a day...* How much more do we need?

Not just a month's worth, or even two months' worth. Kerry, I suspect, would suggest another raid on someone's house, maybe a supermarket or some warehouse the rest of the world miraculously hasn't thought of. But we can't keep doing that, even if it is a tempting short-term solution. We need to figure out a way to make our own food. To be completely self-sufficient, the way Daniel envisioned.

How?

My gaze moves around the darkened living room, the light from the fire casting long, dancing shadows across the floor and furniture. We need to hunt, I decide, no matter what I sneered to Daniel about how we couldn't skin a deer. We'll have to figure it out. And what about vegetables? The obvious solution is to somehow build a greenhouse. Will fruit and veg even grow in a greenhouse in December in Canada? Maybe not tomatoes or melons, but what about potatoes? Carrots? If we're going to do that, we need to have started yesterday.

I take a steadying breath and then another sip of my wine. There's no point being defeatist. We'll start tomorrow.

It feels good to be proactive, to be problem-solving instead of mired down in the worry and the grief. At dinnertime, as I made turkey meatballs over the wood stove—made more of breadcrumbs than shredded turkey—Ruby came to stand by my side, pressing in as she stared down at the meatballs frying in as little oil as I could possibly spare.

"Bricco," she said softly, and for a second, I was too startled to hear her speak to answer, and even after that, I was confused.

"Bricco? You mean Restaurant Bricco, back in West Hartford?"

She nodded, looking solemn. The penny finally dropped, with a soft, sorrowful patter of understanding. "You always ordered the meatballs." She nodded again, and I put my arm around her, drawing her even closer. "You miss those meatballs." In reply, she pressed her face into my shoulder.

"I miss Barb's pizza," Mattie said. She was standing in the doorway of the kitchen, one shoulder propped against the wall. "With Italian sausage and hot peppers, extra cheese."

"I miss the *dulce de leche* pastries from Abby's Bakery," I said, deciding to enter into the game rather than redirect them, which had been my instinct. Caramel icing on a soft butter cookie—eye-wateringly sweet and wonderfully delicious. "And Dunkin' Donuts coffee," I added. "A large latte, extra sugar."

"Dunkin' Donuts strawberry lemonade," Mattie fired back immediately, and then it really was a game, and we began naming foods and restaurants that we missed—Girl Scout cookies, microwave popcorn, Pop-Tarts, chocolate milk, Hershey's Kisses. We smiled in memory, trying not to think about never having any of them ever again—but of course the knowledge was there, like a weight pressing down on us. None of us could get out from under it.

But that's not how I want to be now, looking back. I want—I need—to look forward. To find solutions.

A movement from the corner of the room has me stiffening, and I lean forward, peering into the darkness. "Kerry?"

"No," the voice wheezes back. "Darlene."

She comes closer, into the light, shuffling slowly, clutching one of my mom's crocheted afghans that she's thrown over her shoulders. She eases herself into the wicker chair by the fire with a groan of satisfaction. "I couldn't sleep."

"I couldn't, either." I haven't talked much to Darlene since she arrived, over a week ago now; she's been sleeping or resting, and I've felt too busy, too frantic, to sit down with her and have a chat. But there's nothing to keep us from having a conversation now; I think about why I invited Darlene and Kerry to come live here in the first place, and I wonder if *can you show me how to hunt* is too random or demanding a question. Kerry might not know how to hunt, but I'm pretty sure Darlene does.

In any case, Darlene speaks first. "I've been thinking about your mum and dad," she says, and I let out a muffled whimper because it's not what I expected and after seeing my dad's handwriting on that barrel in the root cellar—such a tiny thing—I'm feeling raw, when it comes to my parents. To the grief and loss I feel for them both, here, the place they loved most, where their absence is like an emptiness inside me, one I carry around like a weight.

"What..." I have to stop, swallow, start again. "What have you been thinking about, with them?"

Darlene lets out a gusty sigh as she gazes into the fire, drawing my mother's afghan more closely around her shoulders. "Just how much they loved it here. It was part of them, you know? Right down in their very bones."

"Yes." I nod, my gaze on the fire. "I know."

"I remember," Darlene says slowly, "when your dad first got sick. He didn't want to leave even though he had symptoms because he was afraid that he would never be able to come back. I think he knew it, really, and he still held on."

"Yes." My throat grows tight, and I have to swallow to ease it. Every time a doctor came into my dad's hospital room when he was first diagnosed with cancer, he'd ask, a bit desperately, "When can I get back to the cottage?"

He did go back, that summer, for two poignant months. Then in October he got sick again, and by Christmas we were planning his funeral.

"He's still here," Darlene says softly, and I tense because I don't think I can handle a he's-an-angel-watching-over-me speech right now. I know Darlene has been going to the little country church down the road for her whole life, and my parents did too while they were up here.

"He's not, though," I say quietly. Gently, because I don't want to hurt her feelings... but he's really not.

"I don't mean that he's really here," Darlene says, and my relief is tinged with a stupid little flash of disappointment. Did I think she was going to give me a little divine inspiration? "But you can feel him, can't you? And your mum. All around you." She nods to the chair next to her. "So many times your mum sat there, and I sat here with a cup of coffee... I remember after your dad died, she'd shake her head and tell me, 'I still don't know what to do without him.'" Her eyes turn glassy, and she brushes at a tear. "I didn't know what to tell her. It's not easy." Darlene's husband, I recall, died about fifteen years ago, a sudden heart attack. Kerry's dad, I realize, and for some reason, this feels like a new thought, even though I recall she'd already mentioned him herself. "You've just got to have faith," Darlene finishes, a pronouncement, and I let out a hollow laugh.

"Really, Darlene?" I ask, as nicely as I can. "I mean, I get it, and that's a nice sentiment, but how can you have faith now, when the entire world has been destroyed? What is there left to have faith *in*?"

She gives me a smile that is tender with sympathy. "Sweetheart, *that's* when you've got to have faith most of all. It's not much of a faith, is it, if life's going fine and dandy?"

I realize she has a point. I stare into the fire, the glowing embers shifting and already starting to die out, their edges whitening into ash. "We don't have enough food to last until spring," I tell her quietly. "It's hard to have faith when I'm facing that. I don't want to watch my children starve." Darlene is silent, and I turn to look at her. "What do you think I should do?" I ask bleakly.

She's silent for a long moment. "You don't have to starve," she says at last. "God knows. I grew up in these woods, and our cupboards were much barer than yours are, honey. We didn't starve."

"But you could go to the grocery store and buy something," I feel I have to point out.

She gives me a quiet, knowing look. "Not always," she says, and I feel ashamed. I knew Darlene grew up poor; everyone around here grew up poor. But I didn't really think about it much more than that.

"So, what should I do?" I ask again. "I could learn to hunt, maybe." I speak dubiously because I have only nicked that damned tin can once. Mattie is a better shot than I am. Maybe she can hunt, if Darlene can teach us, which, considering the state of her health, she probably can't.

"You could," Darlene agrees, sounding as dubious as I did, "but fishing and trapping are better options. Kerry should have taken some traps from my place. I had some, anyway."

"I don't know to trap."

"There's not much to it." She shrugs, smiling; there is the faintest trace of gentle derision in her eyes, at how obviously feeble I'm being. "You set the trap, and you put it out somewhere in the woods. Then you go back to check it out, hopefully before something else does."

She makes it sound so simple, but I don't think it can be. "Okay..." I say after a moment.

"And you don't mind too much, about eating rabbit or

squirrel or beaver," she adds, a definite note of amusement in her voice, and I swallow hard.

Beaver? "I don't mind," I say.

Darlene lurches forward, alarming me with the sudden movement, but then she simply takes my hand in her soft, plump one. "Your dad would be proud of you, Alex," she says quietly.

Again, I have to swallow. Try to speak, even though it's hard. "I don't know that he would, Darlene," I manage. "I don't know how to do any of this. I don't really want to learn." At least, I don't want to have to learn. I don't want this to be my life, my children's lives. What future is there for any of us?

"And your dad would say it's not about knowing something, but admitting what you don't know and being willing to learn it," Darlene replied steadily. "It's not about succeeding, but being willing to try, fail, and then try again."

She sounds so much like my dad, it's as if I can hear his voice. He is in the room with us, right now; if I turn, I'll see him in the recliner in the corner, his gaze cast to the ceiling as he makes such a pronouncement, his tone kindly and reflective, a small whimsical smile curving his mouth.

I try to thank her, but I can barely speak, and Darlene seems to understand. She squeezes my hand and then she lets go, leaning back into her chair with a groan.

The next morning, I'm ready to work. To try. I make oatmeal—half a cup each, with water, which feels like nothing—and I smile at Mattie and Ruby as I give them their breakfast. To their credit, they don't turn their noses up at the watery gruel, sprinkled with a scant quarter-teaspoon of brown sugar. They simply reach for their bowls and start eating.

"We're going to do stuff today," I tell them, and Mattie looks instantly alert, Ruby wary. "We need to figure out a way to find more food," I continue. "Darlene is going to show us how to set traps."

"Traps," Mattie repeats thoughtfully, and Ruby's eyes widen.

"Trap animals?" she asks in a horrified whisper, and belatedly I realize that my animal-loving eleven-year-old—last year for her birthday she asked for a donation to be made to the Worldwide Fund for Nature—might not take kindly to the idea of trapping animals and then eating them.

"We have to, Rubes," Mattie says before I can think how to reply. "Because we need to eat. It's quick and painless, I promise." I'm not sure it actually is, but I certainly don't say that. Mattie gives Ruby a reassuring smile, but my youngest child doesn't look convinced. She eats the rest of her pathetic breakfast in silence.

"Does Darlene have, like, actual traps?" Mattie asks curiously once we've washed and dried the dishes. Neither Kerry nor Darlene have made an appearance yet this morning, but it's not yet eight o'clock. For some reason, we've all become early risers. I was up at six, hauling water from the lake; the ice is thick enough now that I need an axe to hack through it, and there are several inches of snow, dusting the trees, softening the stark and leafless branches, the hard, frozen ground.

"Yes, I think so. She said she had some back at her place, and we brought pretty much everything she owned from there."

"And she knows how to set a trap?"

"I hope so," I reply with a smile, "because I certainly don't." Along with a lot of other things. "I don't know how to skin a deer or weave a basket or can fruit," I tell Mattie wryly. "Or..." I try to think of some other skill that belongs in *Little House on the Prairie*. "I don't even know what I don't know," I finish on a sigh. "But if I did, I'd try to learn it."

Mattie smiles back at me, and I'm heartened, but then Ruby

makes a sound like a small animal—something between a gasp and a squeak—and runs out of the kitchen.

I sigh, trying to curb my worry. Mattie glances at me, a frown settling between her brows, a question in her eyes. *What now?* In response I give a little shrug. *I don't know.*

Then Ruby returns, holding an ancient-looking book, its cover and its pages tattered, almost falling out. It's a paperback, the size of a textbook, and as she comes closer, I realize I recognize it—it's been on the bottom shelf of one of the bookcases built around the fireplace, made from the weathered wood of the old barn; my parents must have bought the book when they first built this place, back in the seventies. Ruby is holding it like an offering, like it's the Holy Grail.

"Rubes?" I ask uncertainly, and she holds the book out to me. I take it and read the title out loud. "*The Complete Book of Self-Sufficiency* by John Seymour." I open and read some of the table of contents with a growing sense of wonder—"The way to self-sufficiency. The one-acre holding. The food-producing garden." There's absolutely everything in here. It's like having the internet at my fingertips, but maybe even better. "*Ruby.* How did you find this book?" I know it's been on the same shelf for about forty years, but why did she even take a look at it? We didn't inventory the books; I didn't see the point, which I realize now might have been a huge oversight.

She shrugs, and I think of how for the last week she has always been reading, losing herself in the world of books as she so often does. I thought she was skimming *Archie* comics; it turns out she might have been doing something far more useful.

"This is amazing, Rubes," I tell her, putting down the book to give her a hug; she clings to me, arms wrapped tightly around my waist. "You're amazing for finding it."

Mattie has picked up the book and is leafing carefully through it, making sure the pages don't fall out. "So, is there a page about setting traps?" she asks, ever practical.

. . .

We spend the rest of the morning, with Darlene's help, learning how to set a snare for a rabbit. It's not a trap so much as some wire, tied in a loop with a slipknot. Simple enough that even Ruby can do it, and she does, silently, her forehead furrowed with concentration. Figuring out how to trap a rabbit—and then how to skin it and eat it—is, I fear, going to be much more challenging. But it's a start, and I'm trying, and that knowledge strengthens me.

The beaver trap Darlene brought from her house is another matter entirely—a bulky thing made of iron, with a square frame, a strong spring, and a chain that reminds me of a manacle. It looks like something that belongs in the Yukon, or maybe a dungeon's torture chamber.

"My dad used these," Darlene tells us. Since she's started to teach us some skills, she's become more animated and energetic, although she still wheezes as she talks. "Remember, Kerry?" she asks her daughter, who nods. Kerry hasn't said much since we started; she seems unusually pensive. She didn't know how to set a snare either, but she learned pretty quickly, her lean fingers flying as she made the knot. "I've never used 'em myself," Darlene continues. "I always liked beavers. Cute little critters." At this remark, I glance at Ruby in apprehension, but she's completely focused on the trap in Darlene's hands. "Beaver meat is actually pretty darn tasty," Darlene continues, as she picks up one of the clanking traps. "Red and rich and delicious —my father used to call it poor man's beef."

"Where do we set the beaver traps?" I ask Darlene, and she gives a knowing nod.

"That's the tricky part. Easy enough to make a trap, harder to catch something in it!" She lets out a wheezy laugh. "Usually along the shoreline. What would you say, Ker?" She turns to her daughter, who frowns in thought. I wonder what experience she has of such things, and acknowledge that, whatever it is, it is more than mine. My dad never trapped a beaver on this lake; he liked to see them cutting placidly through the water. Plus, they kept the water level high. But things have changed now. Obviously.

"It has to be in the beaver's travel path or dam crossover," Kerry says, and now she really does sound like an expert. Darlene nods in agreement. "There's a dam on the far side of the lake," Kerry continues. "In that little inlet in the southeast corner. Maybe there."

Mattie and I glance at each other, surprised by her air of knowledgeability. Kerry looks at me. "We'll have to walk around. The ice isn't thick enough to step on yet. Although you might want to work through all your turkey first before you try to trap a beaver."

"Well, we can keep it outside to freeze," I reply. "Or we have enough salt to preserve it." Not that I even know how to preserve meat, but it's in Ruby's book.

I see a flicker of something almost like respect in Kerry's eyes, and she nods. I feel a surge of triumph; I haven't done much yet, hardly anything at all, and yet I've started. *I can do this*, I think. We can do this together. We already are.

FIFTEEN

We set seven rabbit snares and three beaver traps that afternoon; Kerry and I walked around the lake and then hunted in the reeds by the shoreline, looking for evidence of a beaver's travel path.

"Do you even know what you're looking for?" I ask dubiously, because until today Kerry hadn't seemed as much of a backwoods woman as I'd thought she was.

"Yeah, because I've watched *Lady and the Tramp*." I stare at her blankly, and she lets out a laugh. "Don't you remember, the beaver who gnaws off Lady's muzzle?"

"Oh..." I dimly recall that scene in the movie; I haven't watched it with the girls in years. "Yeah."

She shakes her head, still laughing. "Forget it. We're looking for beaver tracks—webbed back feet and front feet like little handprints. Plus, sometimes, you'll get the imprint of a tail in the mud. Other signs to look for are gnawed branches or felled trees. Kinda obvious, the last one."

"Okay."

"And I know all this," Kerry continues, even though I haven't asked the question, "because I used to date a guy who trapped. Kevin." She bends down to inspect a branch. "He was into all this stuff."

"You did?" I realize just how little I know about her life.

"Yeah, for a couple of years." She sounds indifferent about it, but I wonder if that hides a deeper emotion.

"What happened?" I ask, and she sighs.

"Well, it didn't work out. Obviously." She clearly doesn't want to tell me anything more.

"How old are you?" I ask, because I realize I don't know.

She gives me another one of her humorous, but slightly sneering looks. "Thirty-six. Ten years younger than you."

How does she know how old I am? Kerry answers as if I've spoken aloud. "You babysat me when you were sixteen and I was six. You'd just gotten your driver's license, and you were pestering your dad, asking to borrow the truck."

"Oh…" Vaguely, I remember driving my dad's truck into Corville for poutine. It seems like not one but several lifetimes ago now. "Was I annoying?" I ask suddenly, and she lets out a little laugh.

"Not as much as I was."

"I don't really remember," I tell her, like an apology.

She waves a hand in easy dismissal. "If I'd been sixteen, I wouldn't have either. Okay, here we go." She nods toward some tiny tracks frozen in the mud by the lake's shoreline. "I don't know how old these are, since the ground's been frozen, but we might as well try."

A sudden, terrible thought occurs to me. "Do beavers hibernate?"

She laughs. "I hope not." I can't tell if she's joking or not, and she must see my apprehension because she laughs again, not unkindly. "Relax, I'm pretty sure they don't. They swim under the ice." She starts setting the trap, her movements brisk and efficient, while I watch.

"Did you ever see your boyfriend butcher a beaver?" I ask, and she looks up.

"No, that stuff grosses me out. You're on your own there. Sorry."

"Fair enough." I take a breath. "I want to build a green-house," I tell her. "We'll need fresh vegetables."

Kerry straightens, dusting her mud-speckled hands on her jeans. "A greenhouse in Ontario in winter?" She sounds more curious than incredulous, and that heartens me.

"Why shouldn't it be possible?" In Ruby's book, there was a two-page spread on greenhouses, and the author wrote about using them year-round. "If there's a heat source, it can work," I add, and Kerry raises her eyebrows.

"What heat source is strong enough in below-zero temperatures?"

"Well... we have the chiminea out on the deck," I say, wincing a little at how lame it sounds. "If we built a greenhouse against the cottage with the chiminea inside... the deck is south-facing and gets a lot of sun. Maybe..."

Kerry nods slowly. "So, how do we build a greenhouse?"

"Your mom had one in her yard. I thought maybe we could... shift it somehow."

She raises her eyebrows. "Shift it?"

"Yeah, take it apart in pieces? Panes, I guess?" I wish I could search how to on the internet; Ruby's book did not include advice on how to move a greenhouse, just what to put in one.

"It's possible," Kerry allows after a moment's thought. "Maybe. We could maybe keep it in big sections, rather than take it apart completely."

I'm grateful she hasn't completely shot down my idea; it sounded ludicrous to me. "Okay. Let's do that."

She sighs, shaking her head, but with a small smile twitching at her lips. "You know I used to want to get *out* of the woods? I was going to move to Renfrew." She speaks of it as if it is a big city, rather than a town an hour away with a population of about eight thousand. Still, I certainly understand about broken dreams.

"What happened?" I ask.

"My dad died, and my mom's health wasn't so great." She shrugs. "It didn't feel like the right time to go, and then somehow it never was. I worked in Corville until my mom needed more care, and then I moved out to be with her." She sighs again, the sound one of both sorrow and acceptance. "That's life, I guess."

Fifteen years ago—Kerry would have been about eighteen, on the cusp of everything, or at least Renfrew, which probably felt like a lot. I feel sad for her, although that old heartache is nothing compared to what we're facing now.

"Anyway." Kerry turns back toward the cottage. "We should head over to my mom's place before it gets dark if we want to get that greenhouse."

Twenty minutes later, we are in the truck bumping down the dirt road. I feel apprehensive at leaving the cottage again, even though we're only going four miles away. Mattie insisted on coming, saying we'd need the help, and Ruby stayed back with Darlene.

"I'll look out for my sweetheart," Darlene said, putting an arm around my daughter. "She's great company. Will you read to me, darlin'?"

Ruby nodded, and I tried to hide my surprise. *Read to Darlene?* The way Darlene spoke, it sounded like something Ruby had done before. How much had I missed, worrying about everything, bustling around, making lists and plans? And yet I was glad; if Darlene could be an honorary grandma to my daughters, all the better.

We drive in silence to Darlene's place, but when I turn in the little dirt drive, I inhale sharply, and Kerry lets out a groan.

"What's happened?" Mattie clambers forward, craning her neck over the seats.

"Someone's taken a baseball bat to my mom's house," Kerry replies flatly, shaking her head. She gets out of the truck slowly while I hesitate, alert to dangers. "No one's here," she calls back, her tone weary now, and then she steps over a jumble of broken glass, inside the house. After another second's pause, Mattie and I follow.

Inside, the house has been comprehensively and pointlessly trashed. The windows are all knocked out, the TV that we left smashed to pieces. Everything that could be wrecked—and there wasn't that much left—was. The mattresses have been shredded with a knife; even the bathroom mirror is shattered. Glass crunches under our boots as we go through the house—all four rooms of it—in silent dismay.

"What a waste." Kerry stands in the kitchen, her gaze distant as she looks around at the mess. "I don't think they even took anything, just trashed it all. Probably some nutjob out of his mind on fenty."

"Look." Mattie points to the window, and Kerry and I both turn to look out at Darlene's once neat yard; the chicken coop has been kicked down, and the greenhouse is nothing but a frame with shattered shards of glass clinging to it.

Kerry sighs again. "Well, so much for that."

The buoyant optimism I was feeling earlier drains away, leaving me cold and so very tired. "What do we do now?" I wonder aloud.

"There are some old windows in the barn," Mattie ventures. "Aren't there? Could we use those?"

Build a greenhouse ourselves from some old windows? I have no idea how even to begin that project. "I suppose we could try," I say, but I'm not feeling optimistic. Just this one small project overwhelms me—what about all the rest?

Kerry presses her lips together. "We need to go back to Corville."

"What?" I stare at her in surprise, and no small amount of dismay. "Last time we were there, my daughters were shot at. We are not going back."

"If we want to build a greenhouse, we need some more tools," Kerry replies evenly. "Wall studs, bigger screws, lumber. We can't do it otherwise." She stares at me levelly, a cool challenge in her eyes, as well as a flicker of sympathy. "The army will be long gone. They were never going to stick around. They've probably gone to some other town, to take the food and tell us how they're going to redistribute it."

She speaks so sardonically that I'm compelled to ask, "You don't think they did?"

"Who knows? But they were sure willing to shoot at the people they're meant to protect. Anyway, they won't be there, and we might be able to find some stuff somewhere."

"You think the Country Depot won't be stripped like Foodland was going to be?"

"Other places. Churches, the school, maybe. Places people won't think of, that will have supplies."

"The school," Mattie repeats in excitement. "They'll have a kitchen too. They might have tons of food."

I stare at them both, a sense of futility swamping me, because already I sense that they are both right. We need more supplies—tools, lumber, food. Still, I don't want to go back to Corville. Everything in me resists it.

"My dad has a circular saw," I say, a bit feebly. "And we've got plenty of wood. We can cut down a tree, for heaven's sake..."

"And wall studs?" Kerry asks. I barely know what those are.

"I think we should, Mom," Mattie says quietly. "There might be all sorts of stuff we need."

I'm being swayed, but I don't want to be. It will be danger-ous. I know it will be. I feel it in my bones, in my gut.

"The army will be gone, like Kerry said," Mattie says, her tone strangely gentle. "And everyone else there was nice, help-ful. I don't think it will be dangerous."

I can't believe how much my daughter has grown up in the space of a few short weeks. A couple of weeks ago, she was screeching about the lack of Wi-Fi.

"Okay," I say at last. "Fine. We'll go, early tomorrow, when it will hopefully be quiet. And we won't stay long."

Kerry and Mattie share a complicit, triumphant look; another relationship has been growing there, and I'm not sure how I feel about it.

We leave the next morning, just after dawn. Ruby stays back with Darlene, and while I once again resist leaving them alone, leaving the cottage at *all*, I feel I have no choice. As we drive down the road, shrouded in dawn mist, I can't decide if I'm doing something risky but smart, or just dangerously stupid. What would Daniel do in this situation?

I know immediately; he would go to Corville by himself, and make sure we stayed safe at home. Why didn't I appreciate his selflessness more, I wonder, even as I acknowledge it's the kind of thing you only appreciate when a person is gone. Even with our financial troubles, I know Daniel was trying to think about the family. I was so angry that he hid it from me, but he did it to keep us from being worried. I wish I'd been willing to understand that before he left. I hope I have a chance to tell him if—when—he returns. There are a lot of things I want to say to him, things I need him to know.

The roads are empty, at least, but as we drive onward, I know I have no idea what we'll find in Corville. If Darlene's place, out in the middle of nowhere, could be trashed, what about the homes and businesses of a once-thriving town? I'm trying to prepare myself for devastation, but I know it will still be a shock to come face to face with it.

When we get to the first crossroads, with the lumber yard on one side and the empty grocery store on the other, we already see signs of havoc having been wrought. The stacked lumber is gone, and the windows of the store are all broken, even though there couldn't have been anything inside. *Why,* I wonder, and then I ask aloud, "Why is this happening?" Both Kerry and Mattie look at me like I'm stupid. "I mean, why in rural Ontario?" I continue. "Canada wasn't hit, was it? There shouldn't be the same kind of chaos as in the US, right?"

Kerry shrugs. "Maybe it was hit. I mean, if the army is going around trying to boss people around, something must have happened. Or maybe it's just the US, but everyone's scared we'll be next. Who knows?"

The thought that Canada might have been targeted too chills me. I had, without even realizing it, believed that all the attacks had already happened, that they were over. I thought I knew the extent of the damage, at least in terms of localities, but of course I don't know anything. No one does, which is why the windows of an empty supermarket have been broken.

I take a deep breath and let it out, and then I start to turn toward the town.

"Hold it!" Kerry barks, and I jam on the brakes, my heart starting to race.

"What—"

"Someone's left a couple of two-by-fours in the lumber yard. We could use those. Pull in."

I do as she says, and I wait in the truck in case we need a quick getaway while she and Mattie dump half a dozen two-by-fours in the back.

"Good haul," Kerry says with satisfaction as she climbs back in the truck. She glances at Mattie, who smiles back and agrees, "Yeah, good haul."

I pull out of the parking lot and head toward town. We made a wish list of what we hoped to find in Corville today—everything we could possibly think of that we might need, and even stuff I'm pretty sure we won't. Lumber, a nail gun, sheets of plexiglas—all of it could be found at Country Depot if it hasn't been looted, but I'm pretty positive that it has. And then other, more wistful things—papers, pens, books, boots that fit Mattie and Ruby, hand lotion, chocolate.

"Even looters leave stuff," Kerry said when I, in typical pessimistic fashion, pointed out once again that we probably wouldn't find anything. "They won't take everything. It's just a lot of grab-and-go."

"Even up here, where people can find a use for anything?" I countered.

Kerry gave me a wry smile. "Fair point."

Now, as we come into town, it is clear things have changed —a lot—since we were last here, when, at least in the parking lot of Foodland, I felt a sense of goodwill from the people waiting in line. Now there are broken windows, both in houses and in stores, and the very air feels bristling and dangerous. I see a man on a street corner, a rifle strapped to his chest; a woman pushing a shopping cart full of what looks like looters' leftovers down the street, two small children following behind her, one of them kicking a deflated soccer ball. As we drive past, all four people look at me silently, eyes wide and empty. It's only been a week, and yet it feels like an age. Back when we went to Foodland, it all felt new, strange; now this has become the reality.

There are signs around too, I can see, written in Sharpie on cardboard or on scraps of wood, posted or nailed to storefronts, doors of houses, even to telephone poles. WE HAVE NO FOOD. WE ARE ARMED AND WE WILL SHOOT. JESUS LOVES YOU.

"Corville's never looked so good, huh?" Kerry says, and Mattie lets out a gurgle of laughter. When I look in the rearview mirror, though, I see her face is pale and shocked.

"Stop here," Kerry instructs, and goes so far as to put one hand on the steering wheel to direct me to the pharmacy on the right-hand side of the road.

I pull up onto the curb with a screech of tires, swearing under my breath. "You could have caused an accident," I accuse, and she rolls her eyes.

"Yeah right. Do you see another car on the road? Let's see what's left in the pharmacy." She starts climbing out of the car, and Mattie scrambles to follow her.

"Wait," I say. "Let's just... wait. Mattie, maybe you should stay with me."

Mattie looks as obdurate as she did when we were wrestling about her phone. "I want to see what's in the store."

"There won't be anything in the store."

"There might be, Mom. Come on."

I shake my head. "I'll stay with the truck." If we lose the truck, we are in seriously bad shape. I give Kerry as commanding and forbidding a look as I can. "Be careful. And watch out for Mattie."

"I'm not a baby, Mom, I can take care of—"

"We're in a *nuclear holocaust*, Mattie," I bark at her, "and I'm not taking chances!" I can't believe we're having this conversation, that we're *arguing* about it. It almost makes me laugh, except it really, really doesn't.

"Of course, I'll take care of her," Kerry says, almost sounding offended. She glances at Mattie, who smiles back at her. I watch as they step through the broken plate-glass window and into the pharmacy, whose shelves I can see from here are depressingly empty.

As Kerry and my daughter disappear further into the store, I let out a shaky breath and lean my head back against the seat. I don't think I've ever felt so tense, so *scared*. My breathing is shallow, and every second feels endless as I wait for them to return. I scan the street, but I don't see anyone; the hardware across the road looks as looted as the pharmacy. We're never going to find plexiglas, I think, or a nail gun. We are not going to be able to build a greenhouse. Why on earth did we come here? Why did I let myself be persuaded?

For a moment, I let my mind drift beyond that immediate and necessary horizon. Problem-solving about a greenhouse is comforting, familiar, even safe. A difficult problem, but one with a potential solution. But what about after? What about the rest of our lives? What on earth can my future—Mattie and Ruby and Sam's future—even look like? And then I let myself think about things that were once tedious nuisances, like getting our teeth cleaned. Having my moles checked by a dermatologist. Ruby getting braces. Or little luxuries, seeming so utterly frivolous now—a back massage. A haircut. A manicure.

Never again?

Kerry and Mattie emerge from the store, their arms full of stuff, their expressions triumphant. I'm too nervous even to be curious about what they found. "Get *in*," I bark, as Kerry opens the door of the truck.

"Relax, Alex." As ever, Kerry looks amused. "This isn't World War Three, you know. Not quite."

"Actually, it is," I snap, and she just laughs.

"Mom, look what we got." Mattie is bubbling with excitement as she brandishes her new treasures—a bottle of nail polish, a box of Band-Aids, a jar of gummy vitamins. She looks thrilled.

"Wow," I manage weakly. "Good job, sweetheart." I glance at Kerry. "What did you get?"

"Most everything was gone. All the prescription stuff. Pfft. Not a chance."

"I told you—"

"Still, I found some good stuff." She gives me a canary-eating grin as she shows me her loot—a bottle of over-the-counter sleeping pills, a six-pack of soap, a box of condoms, and a tube of ointment for vaginal thrush.

"Seriously?" I ask, and she shrugs, still grinning.

"You never know," she tells me. "Either way."

I let out a reluctant laugh as I shake my head and start the truck.

I reverse out of the parking lot as Kerry says, "Let's try the school, down by the church."

"Has everywhere been looted?" Mattie asks. "What about the hospitals? What about the cancer patients?" For the first time in a long while, she sounds troubled, frightened. "What's happened to them?"

"Nothing good," Kerry returns flatly. "I mean, anyone on life support has already bitten the dust, for sure. It was probably a mercy."

"*Kerry*," I admonish, and she gives me one of her looks.

"What? You think a fourteen-year-old should be shielded from that kind of common sense? The world as we know it is over, Alex." For the first time, she sounds angry about that fact; her insouciance really is a cover. "I think Mattie gets that more than you do."

"Maybe it is better to go quickly," Mattie says quietly. What a sentiment for a fourteen-year-old to have, and yet I think I agree with her.

We drive to the parochial school attached to the big Catholic church, which looks empty, its windows still intact. My hearts lifts in hope, just a little.

"It looks like it hasn't been touched," Mattie says excitedly. "And they'll have so much stuff. Books, papers, art stuff... you could homeschool us! Or at least Ruby," she amends quickly. "I don't need to be homeschooled."

Of course not. "We'll see," I reply, still apprehensive. I just want to get back to the safety of the cottage. We shouldn't have come out at all.

We park behind the school, facing the woods and the river, where no one can see us. As far as I can tell, the school still looks secure.

"How do we get in?" Mattie asks. Her cheeks are flushed, and she's springing up onto her toes, clearly excited by the prospect of finding out what's inside.

"Break a window," Kerry says decisively. "Quietly."

How do you break a window quietly? I find out when Kerry shrugs off her coat, wraps her hand in it, and then, in one swift, certain movement, punches through a classroom window by the back door.

"Ouch," she says ruefully as she massages her fist. "That hurt a *lot* more than I thought it would. I saw it in a movie, and it looked way easier."

Mattie is already clearing the rest of the broken glass away with a stick she found somewhere. I'm watching, struggling to keep up with their cool-headed sense of authority and purpose.

Just a few minutes later, we are in the school. It is eerily quiet, the air both frigid and stale. Our shoes squeak on the floor. I pause by a notice for an audition for a play, two weeks ago. *Please prepare a monologue, no more than two minutes long.* I trace my fingers over the words; a world forever gone.

"Mom." Mattie has stridden ahead of me, toward the class-rooms. "Come *on.*"

Within a few minutes, it's clear we have, in some senses, hit the jackpot here. There are textbooks, pens, papers, paints, craft supplies. Mattie is stacking it all by the door while Kerry ventures farther into the school, no doubt looking for the kitchen.

I follow her, casting my eye at the empty classrooms; there is something ghostly about it all. "What about a nail gun?" I ask.

"Do you think there might be one, in a janitor's closet somewhere? Or if the school has a carpentry shop?"

"I don't know." Her tone is diffident, distracted; she's found the kitchen, and she strides forward, past long, industrial counters made of metal, to a walk-in pantry in the back. As she opens the door, she whistles softly. I stand behind her, peering over her shoulder.

There is a lot of food in there—gallon vats of tomato sauce, cans and cans of vegetables, sacks of flour, five-kilogram packets of pasta and rice. For a second, I can only stare; then my heart fills, swells. There is enough food here to last well into summer, I'm sure of it.

"This is awesome," Kerry breathes. "We've got to move quickly, though, in case someone sees us. Do you think there's a dolly somewhere, or something?"

"I can look." I turn, intent on finding a janitor's closet. There must be one around here somewhere. I start opening doors, peering into cupboards, focused on securing all this wonderful food, when the silence of the empty school is pierced by a terrible, jagged sound.

My daughter's scream.

SIXTEEN

DANIEL

It took Daniel four days to bike from Watertown to Utica, a distance of some seventy miles on Route 12, although it was farther on the back roads he sometimes took to avoid the few towns peppered along the route—Copenhagen, Lowville, Boonville, Port Leyden. He rode at night, to avoid detection, and slept during the day wherever he could hide—deep in a cornfield, in an abandoned barn, behind a billboard—huddling in his sleeping bag as the days grew colder, the nights colder still.

He allowed himself only two pieces of beef jerky and a handful of Ritz crackers or a granola bar every day, and supplemented with whatever he found along the way. The second day, he ate some old apples rotting on the ground of an abandoned orchard; he lost half a day of travel to stomach cramps and diarrhea as a result. After that he stuck to dried goods—in a looted Texaco on the outskirts of Lowville he found a bag of Fritos and, to his amazement, a Milky Way bar, the only things left in the whole minimart. As hungry as he was—and he was starving—he slipped the chocolate into his rucksack. It was Ruby's favorite candy bar.

He washed and brushed his teeth in the gas station bathroom, and, when he glanced at his reflection, he was jolted to realize he didn't actually recognize his own face. Several weeks' growth of patchy gray beard, hollowed-out cheeks, a stringy gauntness to his neck; but most alarming of all was the look in his eyes—a kind of dazed weariness. He looked like he wouldn't be surprised, or even care, if someone shot him, and he supposed in some ways that was how he felt.

He wanted to get to Sam; he *needed* to get to Sam... but he was more than half convinced that he'd die trying, and, even more worryingly, he was somewhat okay with that.

Mostly the route was quiet, but not always. On the Walmart on the outskirts of Boonville, a homegrown militia had formed. Men with bushy beards dressed in combat fatigues, armed to the teeth with knives and pistols and semi-automatic rifles, the kind that would absolutely obliterate a deer, patrolled the sweeping drive up to the Walmart, which they seemed to have made their headquarters. They looked like they would shoot at anything, and gladly.

Daniel, hiding behind a road sign down the road, quietly biked back the way he had come, and took a long, meandering country lane around the whole town, even though he'd been hoping to find some food somewhere among its stores and houses.

Somewhere between Lowville and Boonville, a dozen or so fighter jets raced across the night sky, in perfect formation. Daniel was heartened at this sign of military organization, of some sign there was still a government, an attempt, at least, at law and order, or maybe just restoring it. But he had no idea where they were going, and his lonely journey along the empty road continued on.

One particularly cold day, when snow dusted the ground, he crept into a barn on the outskirts of a farm and curled up in a corner, planning to sleep for just an hour or two, hoping he wouldn't be discovered. He woke when a wild-eyed farmer prodded him hard with his shotgun, aiming it right between his eyes as Daniel blinked away sleep.

"Get the hell out of here," the man said in a low, gravelly voice. "Now."

Daniel stared at the man, saw a coldness in his eyes that suggested he would pull the trigger as easily as one of those jacked-up guys outside the Walmart would. What, Daniel wondered, had happened to people?

He scrambled up slowly from the haystack, arms flung up in the air. "I'm going," he said, his voice a rasp. "Don't shoot."

The farmer's rifle didn't move a millimeter. His heart beating with slow, heavy thuds, Daniel wondered if the man would shoot him just for the hell of it. He walked backward out of the barn, his hands still held up, his panicked gaze never leaving the farmer's face. When he got to the door, he started to run. He felt the space between his shoulder blades prickling as he pelted down the road, toward his bike, which he'd hidden in a field, along with his backpack.

When he finally got to Utica, he slowed down, did his best to stay hidden. It was clear something was going on here; there were barricades, police cars, army trucks, a sense of a menacing presence. He thought of what the couple back in Watertown had said, about how it was better if the police or army didn't show up.

He had to get through Utica somehow; he kept to the outskirts of the town, skirting it along Route 169, which headed southwest toward Albany, and toward Clarkson just another twenty or thirty miles west.

One night, as darkness fell and he started to bike, he heard the staccato sound of gunshots—not just from one gun, but several, many. It sounded like warfare, and he wondered if that was what was happening. What, he'd wondered many times as he'd biked from Watertown to Utica, was happening in the world? Just how bad was it all? The glimpses he saw—the men bristling with guns and ammunition outside the Walmart, the looted stores, the farmer who had pointed his rifle in his face— suggested that it was very bad indeed, and yet he found he still couldn't grasp the how and why of it. Why wasn't the army imposing order? Why weren't things getting back to normal at least a little, in places that couldn't be too badly affected—like Utica, over two hundred miles from any of the blast sites? Unless, of course, other cities had been hit—like Omaha, as the woman had said back in Watertown. Where else? He was troubled not just by what he saw, but what it had to mean.

When he was biking, he tended to let his mind empty out, focusing on the burn in his legs and the open road before him and nothing else. But when he rested or slept, the thoughts came, along with the deep and terrible fears. What if he couldn't get to Sam? What if he made it to Clarkson, but couldn't find him? It had already been over two weeks since the first blasts, after all. Would Sam really have stayed in his dorm, or even in Clarkson at all, for that length of time? And if he'd left, where would he have gone? The thought of reaching his destination and yet not finding his son was too dispiriting, and so Daniel tried not to dwell on it. He tried to believe in some providential force of nature or deity that meant he had to find Sam, simply because he'd come this far. It couldn't be all for nothing.

At other times, he let himself think about Alex and Mattie and Ruby. He told himself that they had to be safe since they were at the cottage; there was enough food to last a month or two at the very least, so if they just stayed put, hunkered down until he came home…

And yet he knew that was not in his wife's nature. Moreover, he feared how others in the area knew about the cottage, its resources, its acreage, its private lake… They'd known for years, for decades, ever since Alex's parents had rocked up to this remote corner of Canada, two well-to-do Americans, and built their own cabin, and gamely played at homesteading, while everybody local had looked on, more than a little skeptical.

When Daniel couldn't bear to think about his family anymore, he thought about the world. He considered the places he would never see again, that the children of the future would only know from photographs—the Statue of Liberty, the Metropolitan Museum of Art, the White House, the Lincoln Memorial, the Hollywood sign, the Golden Gate Bridge... all gone. It was inconceivable, *still*. Sometimes, he played number games in his head, with time—three months ago he was living in Westport, worried about money and finding a job. Six months ago, he was starting his new job, full of hope, looking toward summer. A year ago, he hadn't been fired even for the first time, never mind the second; his biggest worry had been what college Sam might get into, keeping Mattie on track, helping Ruby with her social challenges.

Those worries felt so absurd now, and yet so precious. He thought he'd give just about anything to have the luxury of being worried about such small things again. The luxury of being *annoyed* by something—a delayed train, an overflowing trash can, a hangnail.

Thinking about Alex was hardest of all. He thought of their last night together, the way he'd held her in his arms, and she'd let him. The way she'd felt, tucked into him, their legs twined, her head on his shoulder... he ached to feel that again. To believe it would happen.

On the eastern side of Utica, as night draws in and the wind turns bitter, he pauses outside a farmhouse—made of white clapboard, with a wide front porch, everything neatly tended, an American flag waving from one of the porch's posts. Surprisingly, the curtains haven't been drawn and he can see into their front room—two children curled up on a sofa, reading a book by the light of an oil lamp. It is so cozy, so lovely, so deeply, painfully *familiar*, that he feels a lump rising in his throat, an ache in his chest, and for a second, he's afraid he might weep. It could have been Mattie and Ruby on that sofa, legs tangled together, a book in front of them, Mattie pointing out the pictures, Alex watching on from the kitchen as she bustled about, making dinner, humming under her breath...

Then the front door opens, and a man steps out on the porch, his tread heavy in his boots. He's holding a rifle clasped against his chest.

"You out there," he calls. "You gonna move on?"

Daniel starts; for a second, it felt almost as if he were dreaming. "Sorry," he calls, his hands tightening on the handlebars of his bike. "Sorry. Yes. I'm moving on."

The man squints as he watches him wheel the bike around, but as Daniel prepares to cycle away, his voice calling from the porch stops him. "Wait."

Daniel tenses, knowing he can't outrun a gun, praying this isn't the end of everything.

"When's the last time you've eaten?" the man asks.

The question is so unexpected that it takes him a few seconds to respond. "I've had some beef jerky a few hours ago," he finally says.

"I mean," the man replies gruffly, "a square meal."

Daniel turns around slowly, his hands resting on the handlebars of the bike. "Five days ago."

The man stares at him for a long moment and then he jerks a thumb toward the house. "You can share our supper, if you want."

Daniel hesitates, ashamed to realize he's worried this might be a trick. Can he not accept simple hospitality? Is it worth the risk?

"We don't bite," the man says, a trace of humor in his voice. "Not even Rocky, our German Shepherd."

Daniel manages a hoarse sound that was meant to be a laugh. This is the first human interaction he's had since the couple who rescued him from the river, and he realizes he craves it. He needs to feel normal again, if only for a few moments. "All right," he replies. "Thank you."

As he wheels the bike toward the house, the man nods to it. "Best bring that inside."

"All right," Daniel says again.

"I'm Tom," the man tells him as he comes onto the porch, bumping the bike up the steps.

"Daniel."

Inside the children have scrambled off the sofa and are standing in the doorway of the living room, wide-eyed and silent. The youngest, maybe four or five years old, sucks his thumb, clutching a grubby square of blue blanket, one corner a little rabbit's head with silky ears.

"That's Noah," the man says. "And this here's Hannah." He nods toward the girl, who looks about eight or so. "My wife Abby is in the kitchen with the baby."

"Nice to meet you all," Daniel murmurs. It feels completely surreal, to walk into a family home full of warmth and light, and make introductions like he's at a party. The normality of it feels both beautiful and miraculous. He takes off his rucksack, props it against the wall, feeling a bit bereft without his things, his rifle. Then he follows Tom back to the kitchen, where his wife Abby is standing at a wood stove, stirring a pot. A baby in a highchair is banging a spoon on his tray, and Rocky, the German Shepherd, is sprawled under the table; his head lifts as Daniel comes into the room. Abby's eyes widen as she catches sight of him, and he realizes he must look a sight—wild-eyed, unshaven, dirty. He probably smells.

"Sorry," he blurts. "I've been on the road for the last week."

"This here's Daniel," Tom tells his wife. "I said we'd share our supper."

Abby, seeming unsurprised by this statement, gives one brief nod of acceptance. "All right then," she says. She glances at Daniel. "You'd best sit down and make yourself comfortable."

"Thank you," Daniel murmurs, too overwhelmed by these people's simple and easy generosity to say more. He sits down at the table, next to the baby, who stares at him with avid openness before letting out a sudden, ear-splitting shriek.

Abby smiles and gives a self-conscious laugh. "Sorry, he always does that. He figured out he could make that noise a couple of days ago and he hasn't stopped."

"Isaac's got a good set of lungs on him," Tom agrees comfortably. "Can I get you something to drink? We don't drink alcohol." He says it without apology, simply a statement, and Daniel smiles.

"A glass of water would be wonderful."

He watches as Tom dips a pitcher into a barrel of water in the corner of the room, so similar to the barrel back at the cottage that he feels a pang of longing assail him; it would have sent him to his knees if he hadn't already been sitting. He wants to be home. He wants to be home with his family around him like Tom is.

"So, Daniel," Tom asks, as he hands him a glass of water, "where you headed?"

"Clarkson, out toward Syracuse. My son is at college there, and I want to bring him home."

Tom nods slowly. "Must be about thirty miles between here and there."

"Yes." He's come so much farther, though, he reminds himself. He's come over two hundred miles already.

"You come all that way on that little girl's bike?" Tom continues, his eyebrows raised. "I don't think it's big enough even for our Hannah."

"Only the last seventy," Daniel replies. "I had a car before then."

Tom nods again and sits at the table opposite him; Noah scrambles into his lap and he puts his arm around the boy, drawing him close in a way that's unthinking and easy, and makes Daniel ache to put his arms around his own children. His own wife. "I'll check the tires before you go on," Tom tells him. "The front one looked a little low."

Startled, Daniel can only gulp and nod. "Thank you," he manages after a moment. "You're very kind."

"It's our Christian duty," Tom says simply, in a way that suggests there is no more to say than that. He gives Abby a significant glance, and she purses her lips and nods. Daniel isn't sure what communication has taken place, only that one has.

"We eat plain food," Tom continues, as Abby starts dishing out what looks like a stew of potatoes and a bit of stringy beef, swimming in thin gravy. "Got to be careful, these days, but we're blessed in that we have a farm, our own land and source of water."

"This looks delicious." Daniel's mouth is already watering; in that moment he realizes just how empty his belly truly is.

"Hannah, Noah, wash your hands," Tom instructs, and the children do so in silent obedience, before sliding into their seats at the table, Noah still clutching his little rabbit blanket. Abby sits next to the baby and puts a few bits of food on his tray, which he immediately picks up in one chubby fist and then smears onto his face. Daniel has already picked up his fork when Tom begins to intone grace, and he stills immediately, bowing his head.

"Dear Lord, thank you for this food you have so graciously given us. Thank you that you always provide everything we need. And thank you for Daniel, that he found our house tonight, and we pray for his safe journey to his son, who may, in your goodwill, be found safely and in good time. Amen."

"Amen," everyone murmurs, and for a second, Daniel can't lift his head; when he does, he has to wipe his eyes.

"Thank you," he whispers. Tom nods his reply and starts eating with the methodical gusto of a man who has worked up an appetite.

"Can you tell me what's been going on?" Daniel ventures after they've been eating for a few minutes; the taste of hot food, potatoes and beef, is so good it is making his head swim. "I haven't had any news for nearly a week, and even then not much."

"We don't know much ourselves," Tom replies. "I guess you know about the first blasts, about two and a half weeks ago now?"

"Seventeen days," Abby states quietly, her head bowed over her food.

"Yes, I know about those." Seventeen days, and yet an absolute age, an *eon*. "And then there were others, I'd heard?"

Tom nods. "About a week ago now, I'd say. Kansas City, Columbus, Denver. It's rumored that some cities in Europe were hit too, though I don't know if that's true..." He glances at Abby. "Where else, that you heard?"

"Toronto," Abby says softly, and Tom's expression turns regretful as he briefly puts his hand over his wife's.

"And Toronto," he agrees quietly. "Abby's brother lives there," he explains to Daniel. "With his wife and three girls." He's silent for a moment, and Daniel swallows a piece of potato, wondering whether to offer condolences. The cottage is four hours from Toronto. Far, but not that far. Closer than he'd ever wish.

Tom resumes, "Vancouver, too, I recall, and Regina... some other places. We heard on the radio, but there haven't been any broadcasts for a while now. Still, I try, of an evening. I've got my own ham radio, so I can pick up all kinds of stuff, from all over the world."

"Daddy heard someone in Tokyo," Hannah pipes up, and then falls abruptly silent.

Tom smiles at her. "That I did. Couldn't make out a word of it, of course, but the guy sounded pretty upset." He lapses into silence, looking sad himself, and Daniel doesn't know what to say.

"What have you heard more locally?" he finally asks, wanting to know more, even as he dreads hearing it, fearing even worse news.

"Usually, it's just another ham like me, looking for news. We share what we know, but it isn't much." He gives a little sigh as he forks a potato. "It isn't much at all."

They all lapse into silence once more; Hannah and Noah have finished everything on their plates, every last drop of gravy, and Daniel feels a shaft of guilt. Did they get less because of him? Abby cleared the whole pot when she served everyone; there will be no seconds.

These children have it better than many, but will they slowly starve to death, he wonders. *Will his?*

"Why?" The word bursts out of him suddenly, making the baby screech again. Abby shushes him, feeding him a spoonful of mashed potato, which he eats with smacking lips, some of it dribbling from the corners of his mouth as he grins at Daniel. He takes a steadying breath and resumes in a quieter voice, "Why has it happened like this? Why are they bombing cities, and not the nuclear missile sites? Why so suddenly, with no warning?"

Tom shrugs, shoveling in the last of his meal. "Maybe they want to cause the most damage, without actually blowing up the whole world."

"Except it seems that's what they're doing," Daniel replies bitterly, shaking his head. "Has it stopped, do you think? The bombing?"

"I reckon so. Haven't seen the sky turn red like that for six days now." He glances again at his wife. "It was Rochester, you reckoned, wasn't it?" She nods.

Rochester, Daniel thinks, appalled. A no-name city in the middle of New York's Rust Belt, with a population of maybe two hundred thousand? And *it* was nuked? It makes no sense, and yet, he supposes, in a terrible way it does. Maximum damage, maximum fear, with targets spaced throughout the country so everywhere is affected, nowhere untouched, no one knowing what innocuous place will be next. He takes another bite of his supper and then struggles to swallow it. What if Syracuse has been bombed, as well? It is a similar size to Rochester, and it's only twenty miles from Clarkson.

"What is the government doing?" he asks Tom. "The police?"

"Not much, not anymore." Tom shakes his head. "Our neighbor was in the reserves, he was called up when it first happened, went to report to duty at Griffiss Air Force Base, about fifteen miles from here. But half the reserves called up didn't show, and the other half didn't want to do as they were told. It was dangerous, I guess, what with the blast zones and the fallout and whatnot, and when the second round of missiles came, everybody just ran. They disbanded a couple of days ago. Same with the police."

Daniel stares at him for a moment, absorbing the meaning of his words. "So there's no law and order at all?" he asks.

Tom shrugs. "Not much, as far as I can see. The regular army might be still doing something. I've seen some fighter jets and such. But down here on the ground? Seems like it's every man for himself now."

"Some people have formed militias," Abby puts in quietly. "And others have formed gangs, although I don't know that there's much difference between the two. One of them has taken up in the high school in town, won't let anybody in or out."

Tom nods his agreement. "Something of a fortress, that, with these big stone walls all around. They raided the Costco, brought it all in with them. Same thing happened with the hospital."

"Took everything from Price Chopper *and* Hannaford," Abby adds.

"Everybody's scared about food," Tom says. "Understandable."

"But... but..." Daniel is spluttering, still unable to get his head around it all. "How could they have refused to help, the reserves?" He thinks of the patriotic army posters from his childhood, the sense of pride in duty and sacrifice. *Uncle Sam Needs You.* The feeling has waned in recent years, with the shift in culture, he knows that, but... "Wasn't anything —enforced?"

"I reckon the higher-ups didn't do much about it," Tom replies. "It was all pretty dangerous, obviously, and well—futile, I guess. I mean, when a place is flattened, on fire... well, nobody wants to die of radiation poisoning or what have you. And they don't want to leave their own families behind." He shakes his head regretfully. "That's not the way the world works anymore, is it? Sacrificing yourself for another, for a higher cause?"

And yet here these people were, feeding him, a stranger, with food they could scarcely afford to share. "I heard the president say things would be restored in a couple of weeks," Daniel says. He thinks of the man's reedy voice, proclaiming peace from a bunker. He hadn't believed him, at least he *thought* he hadn't, and he'd told Alex as much, but right now, he realized he had, at least a little bit. He'd wanted to, so much.

"We heard that too," Tom answers, "but that was before the second set of blasts. And the looting and the gangs... all of it. I don't see how order is going to be restored, not for a long time, anyway. We do our best to live as we're called to live, with honor and respect and charity. But it's going to get tougher for everyone." He glances at Hannah and Noah, who are sitting silently, their heads bowed over their empty plates, and for a second, his face is suffused with sadness. "Those up there in the high school are going to run out of food one day. Costco isn't that big."

And then would those gangs and militia come for good, honest people like these? Daniel isn't about to say as much in front of the children, but he sees the resigned truth of it in Tom's face, and his heart aches for the man, for his family.

"I should go," he says, as he rises from the table and takes his plate to the sink. "You've been very kind and generous." He realizes he's unconsciously mimicking Tom's slow, country drawl. "Thank you."

"I'll fix that tire for you." Tom rises from his seat. "And if you want to spend the night, sleep in a bed, you're welcome. You can leave in the morning, at first light, get a good day's travel in."

Daniel hesitates. The thought of a pillow, a mattress, clean sheets, is so very tempting. Maybe even a wash and a shave. "I usually travel by night," he tells Tom, his voice filled with regret at what he's passing up—but he knows he needs to get to Sam as soon as he can. Every day that passes is a danger. "But thank you."

Tom nods, accepting; he's not going to argue the point. As Tom leaves the warmth of the kitchen, Daniel glances back longingly—Hannah and Noah are crouching on the floor, playing with the dog, and Abby is wiping baby Isaac's face. The look on her face is calm but also resigned, the same as her husband's. Stoic, even as she turns to speak gently to one of the children. Daniel has a strong and powerful urge to stay in that comfortable room, enjoy its warmth, these people's kindness, but he can't. He knows he can't.

Outside by the barn, Tom pumps up both his tires, tests them with his thumb. "Seems okay," he remarks. "I hope they last you."

"Thank you—"

"Here." Daniel turns to see Abby coming down the steps, toward the barn. She's carrying a bag, which she thrusts at him. "Some food to keep you going. God bless you. I pray you find your son." She blinks rapidly, and he thinks of the people she has lost—her brother, his wife, their three girls. Who else?

"Thank you," he says again. He doubts he will ever see these people again, and yet he feels a rush of affection for them, deep and true. "I don't know how to thank you—" he confesses helplessly, and he hears the throb of emotion in his voice, the threat of tears.

"Find your son and get yourself back home," Tom says gruffly. "That's plenty thanks enough." He puts his arm around Abby. "We'd best get inside. Not always safe out here now. You take care."

Daniel nods, and then as Tom and his wife turn away, he gets back on his bike.

SEVENTEEN

I am running out of the kitchen, my heart in my throat, when Kerry grabs me by the arm, wrenches me around so hard it feels as if she's pulled my shoulder out of its socket. "Don't," she hisses, and I stare at her wildly.

"*Mattie*—"

"There's someone else here, and you'll just walk right into them." She pushes me back into the kitchen, and I want to kick and claw at her, howl my outrage. I *need* to go to my daughter. "I'm serious, Alex," she whispers. "You won't help Mattie by running out there like that." She nods toward the gun I have strapped to my chest, more of an afterthought than anything else. "Do you even know how to shoot that thing?"

"I will if I have to." My voice trembles, and I unstrap the gun with shaking hands. The school has gone completely silent, which terrifies me. *What's happened to Mattie?* "How do you know someone else is here?" I whisper to Kerry.

"I heard them, right before Mattie screamed."

Everything in me goes icy and empty. I tighten my grip on the gun. "What did you hear?" I whisper.

"A guy, maybe two. They were muttering something."

"Why didn't you say—"

"It happened too fast."

I nod my acceptance, take a breath, and then glance toward the hallway that leads back to the classrooms, shadowy and empty. Before I can even take a single step down it, a man emerges from one of the classrooms. He's fiftyish, with a patchy gray beard, wild hair under a baseball cap, a paunch under his plaid shirt. He's got a gun, and I'm pretty sure he knows how to use it a lot better than I do.

"You can just put that gun down right now, missy," he says, aiming his right at me. "*Right* now."

If I put the gun down, we might as well all be dead. "Where's my daughter?" I demand, and I'm heartened that my voice comes out strong.

"Mom..." Mattie's voice wavers as a second man emerges, as scruffy and weather-beaten as the first. His arm is hooked around my daughter's neck, so she's forced to stumble in front of him, a human shield.

"Now this here is a very pretty girl," the man says, and he slowly, lasciviously, runs his free hand down my daughter's body, over her small breasts, her flat belly, and then cups it between her legs. "*Very* pretty."

Mattie lets out a whimper, trapped against him, unable to move. Rage burns in my veins, boils up from my gut. I want to kill these men. I want to shoot them in their kneecaps, their groins; I want to watch them bleed out. The depth of my rage, the *viciousness* of it, shocks me, but it also gives me strength. I will shoot this gun if I need to. I will kill these bastards, and gladly.

"Let her go," I state coldly.

The man chuckles, a rasping sound. "Why should I?" His hand travels back up her body, squeezes her breast, hard enough to make her wince. "I think I'm enjoying myself too much."

"And I like the look of the skinny one," the other man says, swinging his rifle toward Kerry. "She looks like a fighter." Kerry makes some small sound of protest as he chuckles, and my stomach heaves, then hollows out. The reality of our situation slams into me. These men could rape and kill us; in fact, it's *probable* they will, or at least try. They're both armed, and I'm a bad shot. I can't risk shooting the man who has Mattie, and the other man looks like he knows his way around his gun. I have no idea what to do.

I glance at Kerry, half hoping she's got some solution up her sleeve, but she doesn't even look at me. She's staring hard at the man with the gun, her eyes narrowed in a glare, her arms folded across her body.

"Look," I say, trying to sound strong. "You don't want to try anything. Because if you do, at least one of you is going to go down. We're all fighters, and you're going to get hurt."

The man holding Mattie chuckles and spits tobacco juice onto the floor. "You think so, missy? Because I reckon we could take you. Pretty damned easily, in fact."

"Why?" There is a desperate edge to my voice now; am I really going to appeal to these men's better nature? I gaze at the man holding Mattie; his face is deeply seamed with wrinkles, and there are broken veins across his nose, grey whiskery stubble on his chin and cheeks. His eyes are small and dark and pitiless. The other man is still pointing his rifle at me, his expression almost indifferent. I'm nothing to him, I realize, nothing, and yet something to be taken, had. Still, foolishly, I persevere. "We're just trying to survive, the same as you are."

"Well," he replies, his hand moving back down Mattie's body, "there's survival, and then there's *survival*." Once again, he goes for her crotch, and my vision blurs with rage. I have to do something. Now.

The man takes a step toward me. The man with the rifle glances at his partner, distracted for a single second, and I take the only chance I'll probably get.

"*Duck*," I scream at Mattie, and then I pull the trigger. The sound in the enclosed place is far louder than I expected, hurting my eardrums, bouncing off the walls, and I jump, nearly dropping the gun. By the time I blink the world back into focus, Mattie has wrenched herself out of the man's grasp and she and Kerry are huddled by the door. The man with the rifle has it pointed at me.

"You *bitch*," he states coldly. "You're going to pay for that. Slowly."

"You will too, if you think you can shoot me without getting shot yourself." My voice is trembling, but my hands are not. I aim the gun right back at him but then I glance at the other man; his shoulder is bloody, and he's doubled over, gasping in pain. I actually hit him. I can't believe it. And that's my mistake, that single glance, because while I'm distracted, the man shoots.

The sound of the gunshot explodes through the room, and I feel the blaze through my shoulder, more heat than pain, at least at first.

"That was because I don't want to kill you," the man says, as he stalks toward me while I reel, trying to hold on to the gun even though one of my arms now feels useless. "Yet." He grabs my hair, yanking my head back so hard I yelp. Then he's throwing me to the ground, and my head slams into the concrete, so for a second, I see stars. The gun falls from my hands, clattering on the floor as I try to twist away from the man, who is now straddling my body, his eyes narrowed, his lips flecked with spittle as he wraps his dirt-stained fingers around my throat, the other hand holding his rifle, aimed at my head.

"Run," I gasp out to Kerry and Mattie, my voice choking because he's squeezing that hard. I'm going to die like this, I realize numbly, but first I'll be raped. But not my daughter. *Please, not my daughter.*

The man lessens the pressure on my throat, so I'm able to take a single, gasping breath before he leans into me, his eyes boring into mine. "I'm going to enjoy this," he tells me as he grinds against me. I feel too numb to be afraid; my shoulder is now blazing with pain, and his hand is still around my throat, so I can barely breathe. The world is darkening at the edges, and it almost feels like a relief.

He reaches down to yank at my jeans, his hands fumbling with the zip, his fingers brushing my bare navel while I do my best to buck against him, my legs scrabbling on the floor, my head swimming. With my jeans halfway down my hips, he pats my pocket. "Well, looky here," he says, and withdraws the keys to the truck. "Isn't this nice. You ladies have yourself a vehicle."

"Take it," I choke out. "Take it, and let us go."

"I don't think this is an either/or situation," he replies with a rasping chuckle, and then he pulls my jeans down to my knees before he reaches for the fly of his own pants.

"*Mom*," Mattie whimpers.

"Damn it, Keith," the other man wheezes from behind him, still stooped, blood trickling out from between his fingers. "Let's just go. I'm bleeding out here."

"You got hit in the shoulder," the man scoffs. "Relax." He slides his hand in my jeans; the feel of his fingers makes me rear up before he pushes me down again.

"Get off her, you filthy bastard." Kerry's voice is low and deadly. She's holding my rifle; she must have crept up and got it while the man was busy with me. "Get off her, or I *will* shoot."

"Oh, yeah?" The man twists around, a sneer on his face; he's not afraid of us, even with a rifle pointed at his face. "You really think so, honey?" he jeers, and, without a qualm, he reaches out to wrap his hand around the butt of the rifle, wrenching it out of Kerry's grasp with a single twist of his wrist. She wasn't expecting such a bold, swift move, and, after a brief tug-of-war, the gun clatters to the ground. She lunges for it, and he laughs, punching her on the side of her head so she falls in a heap, dazed.

It's enough, at least, for me to scramble away from him; I try to yank my jeans up as I look wildly around for Mattie, but she's nowhere to be seen. I hope she's run, far and fast. Saved herself.

Meanwhile, I realize, the man now has our rifle and the keys to the truck. Even if we get out of here alive, we're screwed.

Kerry manages to get up on her hands and knees. Her face is pale, her eyes glittering with fury, her breath coming in gasps. The man is holding a gun in each hand, lounging back a little, clearly enjoying the moment.

"Keith," the other man says from behind him, still dripping blood. "Let's *go.*"

"I told you to relax." Keith sounds annoyed now. As he glances back at his partner, Mattie suddenly catapults out of the kitchen, a gallon can of chopped tomatoes held aloft between her hands. With a scream, she hurls it at the man; it hits him in the side of the head, and he staggers back, the guns swinging wildly.

"*Run,*" I shout, and we all hurtle toward the kitchen. I hear the men swearing behind us, and Kerry slams the door shut as the sound of a gun goes off. They will kill us, I think numbly, if they can.

"There's a door on the other end," Kerry chokes out, and I stagger down the length of the kitchen, my shoulder blazing with pain, as Kerry kicks open the fire door. She and Mattie burst out into the back parking lot of the school, and I follow behind, stumbling, my head swimming; I've lost more blood than I realized.

"Down to the river," Kerry gasps, and then we are sprinting and staggering down a steep hillside, half running, half falling, bare branches tearing at my hair, my face. Guttural sounds are coming out of my mouth, and I don't know whether I'm weeping or screaming or praying, as Kerry leads the way, Mattie behind her. Another gunshot; Mattie staggers.

"Mattie!" I scream, but she keeps going, until we reach the

bottom of the hill, where the river rushes by, chunks of ice bobbing in its freezing water. Kerry pulls us along, grabbing my hand then Mattie's, all of us stumbling along the bank, for another few minutes until I finally fall to my knees, unable to go any farther.

"I can't," I gasp out, and then my vision blurs, and I feel myself crumple as the world goes black.

EIGHTEEN

When I come to, I'm lying stretched out on the cold ground, Kerry's coat over me. I'm shivering, the frozen ground seeping into me, my shoulder throbbing with pain. My vision is blurry even after I blink, and I feel incredibly tired, my head thick, my body leaden.

"You're awake," Kerry states, her expression grim as she looms over me. "Good."

"How... long was I... out?" The words come slowly, like I have to fish them out of the murk. Everything aches.

"An hour, maybe? We bandaged your shoulder. It didn't break a bone, as far as I can tell, but you did lose a lot of blood."

"Mattie...?"

"I'm here." She kneels next to me, taking my cold hand between hers. Her eyes blaze determination. "I'm okay, Mom. I'm fine."

I press her hand to my cheek, grateful simply to see her face. "I thought you got shot."

"He nicked me." She sounds almost proud as she sweeps her hair out of the way to show where a bit of her ear has been bloodied, a chunk now missing.

Another few inches and she would have been killed. I close my eyes against the thought, and tears seep out, trickle coldly down my cheeks. We came so close to dying, and we've lost everything. The truck. The gun. The stuff in the school that could have seen us through winter...

"It's okay, Mom," Mattie says gently. "We're okay."

"We're not." I force my eyes open. "How are we going to get back to the cottage? And the gun..." We no longer have a gun. How can we defend ourselves? How are we going to survive? And worst of all, beneath that question is a far more hopeless one—*why should we even want to?* I don't like this world. I don't want this life.

"Well, truth be told," Kerry says with a smile, "you couldn't shoot that thing, anyway." Her tone is wryly upbeat, but her eyes are soft with sympathy. "I'm not sure how much use it was, Alex."

I can't match her mood; right now, I feel overcome with hopelessness, with despair. "And the truck," I say. My dad's truck. For a second, I'm hit with a wave of the most inconvenient grief. I miss my dad's *truck*, of all things. Seven years on it no longer had the smell of him, but I can still remember it—cigarettes, his old-fashioned aftershave, leather and soil. My *dad*. I close my eyes again, wanting to block out the whole world.

His old baseball cap was kept in the side pocket of the truck, and he had a Bible verse he'd handwritten tucked into the sun visor. *The strength of the hills is his also.* Psalm 95. My dad said he thought of it every time he looked out at the hill rising above the cottage, thick with pine.

I wish I'd taken that little slip of paper out of the truck, kept it with me. I wish I had it to remember him by. But what does that even matter when we might not survive today? And what about Ruby, back at the cottage with Darlene, waiting for us? A choked sound escapes me. I can see no way through this. No way out.

"Mom." Mattie pats my good shoulder, like a parent comforting a small child. "Mom, it's going to be okay."

I lift my head and blink her and Kerry into focus, standing above me. "How are we going to get back? It's twenty miles, at least."

"We can walk twenty miles," Mattie says staunchly, and I don't bother to reply because I don't think my daughter has walked five miles in her life, never mind twenty. This is the girl who had a dozen different excuses for missing gym class. I appreciate she's become tougher, stronger, and I'm *glad*, but twenty miles is twenty miles, and I'm not sure *I* could walk it, especially in winter, while recovering from a gunshot wound.

"We need a car," Kerry states, like it's obvious, which I suppose it is. But she makes it sound like it's simple.

"Well, yeah." I manage a laugh-like sound, hollow and utterly humorless. "Let's head over to the car lot and pick one out, shall we? A nice big SUV? With heated seats and built-in Wi-Fi, perhaps?"

"Well, the Wi-Fi wouldn't help us much now," Kerry points out. She purses her lips, unfazed. "It's too bad there isn't a car lot in Corville, though. You have to go to Pembroke to buy a car." I just shake my head. "As it happens," she continues, "I know someone in Corville who has a car, so we'll have to make do with that."

This is news to me. "Who?" I ask.

"My cousin Kyle." She rolls her eyes. "The gamer? Also a pothead, but whatever. He has a car. At least, he did."

"And you think he'll just give you his car?" I ask, sounding far wearier than hopeful. "He might not even be in Corville. He might not even be *alive*."

"Do you have a better idea?" Kerry asks, and of course I don't. I turn my face away, and she kneels by my side, her expression turning almost gentle. "It's not over yet, Alex," she says quietly. Her gaze moves over my body. "Are you okay?" she

213

asks in an even lower voice, and I know she doesn't mean my shoulder.

I think of that man's hand on my body, his hips pushing against mine, and I manage to nod.

"Okay, then," she says, her tone bracing yet still gentle. "This is our best chance. We've got to take it." Reluctantly, I turn to look at her, and her gaze bores into mine. "What other choice do we have? Do *you* have?" she says quietly, more of a statement than a question, and we both know the answer. I might feel ready right now to give up for my own sake, but I can't for Mattie's. For Ruby's.

And yet...

"I just don't know," I whisper, closing my eyes. "My shoulder..."

"I know you're hurting." Kerry's voice is soft. "We'll help you."

"Mom." Mattie's voice is as gentle as Kerry's. "You can do it. I know you can."

I'm not sure I can, but I know I have to try. "Okay," I say slowly, and then with a groan I attempt to struggle to a seated position; my shoulder rages with pain, and I feel like passing out and throwing up at the same. I take a breath, swallow it down, and heave again as Mattie and Kerry each take an elbow to help me up. Somehow, I manage to stand, putting far too much weight on both of their helping hands. "How far is it?"

"Not too far," Kerry assures me. "Just across the river."

Across the river *is* far, but I don't bother pointing that out. I just start to trudge forward, one weary foot in front of the other as Kerry and Mattie carefully back away, letting me try to make it on my own. I manage to do it, slowly, achingly, but still.

"I think it's best if we follow the river into town," Kerry suggests, "away from any buildings or people, just in case."

"What about crossing it?" Mattie asks.

"We might be able to get across under the bridge," Kerry

says. "There are some flat stones that go almost all the way across, I think."

I recall just weeks ago, when Mattie, Ruby, and I jumped across those flat stones. How I told them my mom and I used to pretend to be pioneers. I felt burdened at the time, I remember; now the ability to worry, to care about such things feels like a decadent luxury. Mattie must be remembering as I am because she gives me a small, sad smile, and then, stiffening her shoulders, she starts walking.

We walk along the riverbank, all three of us silent and wary, our narrowed gazes scanning the stark treeline, the few buildings above us that we can see from down here. Corville is an old mill town, built above the river, on either side of its steep banks, with the one bridge spanning its width in the center of town, and we are walking toward that bridge.

My shoulder hurts so much, and I feel so tired and dizzy that I can barely take anything in—a muted landscape of gray and brown, the town in the distance. It's all I can do simply to put one foot in front of the other. Mattie and Kerry are more alert, every single noise, no matter how small, making them either still or jump. Where did those backwoods bastards go, with my dad's truck? Are they waiting for us somewhere, angry and bent on vengeance? The thought would make me shudder if I weren't so weary. We're more vulnerable now than we've ever been before; we've got *nothing*. Absolutely nothing. But I can't let myself think that way, or I won't be able to go on.

None of us speaks as we pick our way along the riverbank, trying to keep to the few trees, and I feel too muzzy-headed to try to think practically, plan next steps, after this unbearable setback. I don't even want to, which feels worse; I want someone else to pick up the slack, to care for me, because I'm not sure I do anymore. Not after today.

When we reach the bridge, we discover the river is rushing far too fast to cross on the stones, the way Mattie, Ruby and I pretended to, just a few weeks ago. One of them is completely submerged by rushing water now; chunks of ice bob in the torrent.

Kerry surveys the rushing, icy river, her hands on her hips. "Well, *that* sucks," she states matter-of-factly. "We'll have to cross over the bridge." She makes it sound like no more than a minor inconvenience, but when she cautiously scrambles halfway up the bank to get a view of the bridge, keeping low and out of sight simply by instinct, she shakes her head at us as she slides back down the bank.

"More crazies up there," she tells us in a low voice. "It's been barricaded off with a whole heap of junk and guarded by guys in full camo." Her voice is full of derision.

"The number of guys who have been *hoping* for this," she says in disgust, shaking her head. "They actually *want* World War Three, you know? They're wetting themselves over it."

"What are we going to do?" Mattie whispers. For the first time since she was grabbed by that animal with the rifle, she sounds scared, her hands lost in the sleeves of her coat, her shoulders hunched. We are huddled right beneath the bridge, less than a hundred feet from a homegrown, hostile militia. I press my hand to my shoulder, which Kerry bandaged with part of her shirt, swaying slightly where I stand. I can't manage to put two thoughts together.

Kerry is silent, thinking, and I realize how much I've come to depend on her for a practical solution, but she doesn't seem to have one now. And then a memory slips through my mind like a ripple in water.

"We can cross further down," I tell them. I recall a sepia-tinted fragment of memory of a long-ago picnic with my parents and siblings, by the caves near here, along the banks of the river. I must have been seven or eight; I swam in the river with my sister, where it was still. My feet touched the rocky bottom. "Isn't there a little waterfall along here, Kerry?" I ask. "And then the water empties into a pool, and becomes pretty calm?" I'm picturing myself paddling in that little pool while my parents watched on and my brother skimmed stones.

"I don't know," she replies, shrugging. "I didn't hang out down here, you know?"

"There are some flat stones there, I think," I say. I picture my skinny, seven-year-old self, lying spread-eagled on one of the sun-warmed stones, eyes closed, face tilted up to the light.

"I'm pretty sure there is," I go on, with far more firmness than I feel. "We can cross there."

Silently, we walk along the riverbank, away from the town. There are no trees, just rocky ground and brown, winter-dead grass dusted with snow, and once again it takes all my strength, all my concentration, simply to keep going. For about two hundred feet, we're pretty much completely exposed to the guys on the bridge, as well as anyone else who might be watching. I have no idea if they'd care about a group of women walking along the river, or if they're the sort of people who use innocent strangers for target practice. Considering the men we've met so far, I'm not holding out much hope. In this brave, new world, I don't know anything anymore, only that I can no longer trust in basic human decency.

"They're not looking," Kerry mutters. "They're focused on the road. Idiots."

Walking ahead of me, Mattie gives a jerky nod of understanding, her eyes on the ground, her slender body practically vibrating with tension. My poor daughter. How much has she already endured? And yet there is likely more to come.

When we finally reach the cover of the trees again, we all breathe shaky sighs of relief, giving each other oddly shame-faced looks, as if fear is something we shouldn't feel, when right now it's *all* we feel.

Another couple hundred feet and we find it—a short spill of frothing water, and then a small, still pool with several flat stones stretching across, almost to the other shore, but not quite. In fact, I realize with a weary, sinking sensation in my gut because nothing, it seems, can ever be even close to easy, very much not quite. There's a good ten feet between the last stone and the opposite shore—too far to jump, if I even had the strength to jump, which I'm not sure I do.

"I think this is the best we're going to get," Kerry states matter-of-factly, and I have the jolting feeling that I spoke aloud, even though I know I didn't.

"How are we going to get across?" Mattie asks.

Kerry's expression firms. "We'll have to wade the last few feet. It's not that deep."

"But it's freezing—" I protest feebly.

"We don't have a choice, Alex." She speaks plainly, but also with sympathy. "Will you do it?"

I force a nod.

The water is cold, barely above freezing, with chunks of ice floating in it. If it were just a little colder, it would have frozen over, which would have been a lot simpler. I press one hand to my shoulder, fling the other one out to keep my balance as we start across the stones—Kerry first, then Mattie in the middle, me last. When I step into the river, off the last stone, the water comes rushing well past my kneecaps and I almost fall over.

I put my other foot in the water, and both my legs are instantly, entirely numb. I have a sudden urge to let the icy water sweep me away; how long would it be before I lost consciousness? A matter of moments, and then, sweet oblivion. It's frighteningly tempting.

"You can do it, Mom," Mattie calls softly, and so I grit my teeth and keep walking; ten feet isn't any distance at all, or so I tell myself, but right now, it feels endless. I glance ahead at Mattie, her arms flung out for balance. The water goes up even higher on her, all the way to her thighs, rushing around us fast enough, I think, to knock her off her feet. I may have been tempted to let myself fall, but I don't want Mattie to.

Step by faltering step, the rocky riverbed shifting under our feet, we finally make it to the far side. When I clamber out, hauling myself onto the bank, my legs feel as if they are on fire, and my shoulder throbs worse than ever.

We stand on the opposite shore, all of us shivering uncontrollably, our jeans already starting to freeze right onto our skin.

"We'll need to get out of these clothes as soon as we get to Kyle's," Kerry says. Her teeth are chattering. "I don't think his place is too far from here."

The next fifteen minutes are a dazed blur; I'm so cold I feel as if my mind has slowed down, my thoughts trickling through me like molasses, or stalling completely, so I can't think at all. Even though I'm freezing, my shoulder still burns.

I follow Kerry through a maze of side streets and shabby buildings—I haven't been to this part of Corville, and I never realized the town was this big—with no idea where we're going, and I don't even care. The will to figure this out, to get past this and back to the sweet safety of the cottage, is slipping away from me once again. It all feels so hard, so *pointless*. I just want to lie down. *Lie down and close my eyes, drift away…*

"*Mom.*" Mattie slips her arm through mine, tugging me along none too gently. I realize, belatedly, that I have stopped walking and have been simply standing there, staring into space. "We've got to keep moving," she says, tugging on my arm again. "We're losing Kerry."

I blink and see that Kerry is striding ahead, into an alleyway between two dilapidated buildings, while we've fallen behind in a small, abandoned parking lot.

"Okay." I try to move faster, but it feels like I can't. I don't know how much longer I can keep trying, and for what. It all feels so *futile*. We get the car, we get back home, and *then* what?

"Mom," Mattie says again, and I focus on my daughter's face. She's shivering like I am, her eyes dark and her skin pale and clammy, but she's still so young and vibrant and beautiful, her whole life ahead of her, even if I have no idea what it might look like, what world she'll live in. Yet for her sake, and Ruby's, and Sam's as well, I know I have to keep going.

"I'm okay," I tell her, and I squeeze her hand. "I'm okay."

Five minutes later, we are in an apartment building, a squat two-story building of fake brick, the kind that's papered on over concrete blocks, with a roof of peeling tiles. The front door is hanging off its hinges, and the whole place has a deserted, dese-crated air. People have either left or are hiding.

Kerry heads up the narrow staircase in the middle of the building, to the apartment at the end. There is trash in the hall-way, old pizza boxes and junk mail, a broken stroller and even a single, dirty sneaker. In the air is a stomach-roiling smell of sewage, trash, and rotting food—at least I hope it is food that's rotting, and not something worse. I breathe through my mouth, but I'm not sure that's any better. The air feels thick, like I can taste it on my tongue.

"Man, this place was always a dump," Kerry mutters, "but this is something else." She taps, quietly but firmly, on the flimsy front door of Kyle's apartment, paint peeling off plywood, while Mattie and I wait behind, shivering, gazes darting nervously around. I feel watched, even though there's no one else here, and the whole complex has an air of abandonment to it.

"Kyle," Kerry calls, softly at first, and then more loudly, enough that Mattie and I jump a little. "*Kyle!* It's your cousin, Kerry. Open up. I can help you."

She can help *him*? I glance at Mattie, who shrugs back. Kerry swears under her breath and then, taking a step back, she kicks the door down. It doesn't take much; the thing comes off its hinges like it was made of cardboard.

She steps into the hallway, and we follow; the smell in here is worse than outside. I glance at the open doorway across from us and nearly gag; it's a bathroom, and the toilet is overflowing with excrement. Mattie covers her mouth and nose with her sweater, her eyes wide and dark above her hand.

"Kyle," Kerry calls, her sweatshirt up above her face. "God help me, Kyle, this place is a *pit*."

A man—a boy, really, only a little older than Sam—stumbles out of the living room. He's greasy-haired, pimply-faced, slight and sour-smelling. I take an instinctive step back as his odor wafts toward me.

"Aw, man, Kerry," he says, his voice a nasal whine with a strong Ontario accent, "why did you have to go and break down my door?"

"You weren't answering."

"I was *coming*." He hunches his shoulders, sinking his hands into the front pockets of his very dirty hoodie. "What are you doing here, anyway?"

Kerry gives him a no-nonsense look, her sweatshirt still up over her face. "Do you still have your car?"

He shrugs, indifferent, miserable. "Yeah, I guess, if it's in the lot. I don't know."

"I need it."

"What? Why—"

"Someone stole our truck." She shakes her head slowly. "What have you been doing, Kyle, since this all happened? And why the hell are you crapping in your own toilet, when you must know it can't flush without water?"

He hunches his shoulders even further, looking truly miserable as well as pathetic. "Where else am I supposed to go?"

"Oh, I don't know, outside maybe?" She shakes her head again. "I always knew you weren't the sharpest tool in the shed, but come on." She holds out her hand. "Where are your keys?"

He stares at her, looking more hurt than angry, and very young. "What, you're just going to take my car?"

"You can come with us if you want and drive it back."

"You can't get over the bridge. It's guarded."

Kerry blows out a breath. "What about at Douglas?" Kyle shrugs. "What do these crazies even want?" she demands, for which of course none of us has an answer. "What are they guarding the bridge for?"

"I don't know, they're holed up in the Bank of Montreal, I think," Kyle replies. "Have been for a few weeks. Most people have left. I think I'm the last one in the building."

"Where did they all go?" Mattie asks, and he glances at her without interest.

"Somewhere else."

"Why didn't you leave?" Kerry asks, and Kyle gives her a look that's bleak in its honesty.

"Where would I go?"

She sighs, shaking her head. "Okay, well, we'll have to try to get across."

Having fallen into something of a stupor, my shoulder throbbing, my legs aching, I become more alert at that. "Try crossing the bridge?" I repeat. "Kerry, those men are *armed—*"

"And we're in a car." She shrugs, raising her eyebrows. "You got any better ideas?"

Mutely I shake my head.

"First, though, we've got to change." She turns to Kyle. "You got any clean clothes you haven't crapped in?"

He shrugs. Kerry shakes her head. "Come on, Kyle, man up, okay? You're better than this. At least, my mom always told me you were, even if your own parents didn't believe it."

He sniffs, running a dirty hand under his nose. "You think my parents are dead?" he asks, a wobble in his voice, his gaze lowered to the floor.

Her expression softens, just for a mere millisecond. "Yeah, I think they probably are," she tells him briskly. "Now, come on, let's get going."

Kyle nods slowly, accepting, defeated, and Kerry goes into his bedroom and starts riffling through his drawer. "So? What have you been doing since it all happened?" she asks him as he stands in the doorway, watching her.

He shrugs, hands in the pockets of his baggy sweatpants. "I don't know. Just sitting around. Waiting."

"What about food? And water?" she asks.

He shrugs again. "I had some, and I got some from the Foodland when they were handing it out. And my neighbor shared some stuff. I don't know. I'm hungry."

"All right, these don't seem too dirty." She throws a pair of sweatpants at me, and another pair at Mattie. "Do you need help?" she asks, and I nod and shrug at the same time because I'm not sure.

Kyle clocks my wounded shoulder for the first time. "What happened to you?"

"She got shot," Kerry replies. "Two rednecks broke into the school where we were trying to get some stuff."

"There's been a couple of gangs around," Kyle says with a sniff. "That's why I've been staying inside. Why so many people have left." He sounds so pitiful, so young and so alone, that I feel a flicker of sympathy for him, even in his disgusting, disheveled state.

Kerry, however, is all practicality. "Have you even changed your clothes in three weeks, Kyle?" she asks, and he shrugs again, looking lost. "Well, put something clean on now," she orders, and throws him a T-shirt from his drawer.

We all change as quickly as we can; I manage to peel the frozen jeans from my reddened skin and put on a pair of only somewhat clean sweatpants that hang about my hips. I've lost weight in the last few weeks, I realize, probably a fair few pounds. *The Armageddon diet works wonders.* I leave my shirt on, even though it's damp, because I'm not brave enough to try to pull it over my shoulder.

Kerry bundles our wet jeans into a plastic shopping bag she finds in the kitchen. Then she glances around the apartment, which is a disgusting mess, looking as if she's assessing whether there's anything worth taking, and then deciding that there isn't. "Okay," she says. "Let's go."

"How are we getting across the river?" Mattie asks.

"By car," Kerry says, which is no answer at all.

We head outside to a day that's both dusky and freezing; the sky is already darkening, the metallic tang of snow in the air. Kyle's crummy little rust bucket of a Toyota is one of the only vehicles left in the weedy little lot behind the building. Mattie and I sit in the back, Kerry driving, and Kyle in the passenger seat. He turns to me.

"Who are you?" he asks.

I open my mouth to reply and find I don't have the energy to explain. After a second's silence, Kerry answers for me.

"She's a Benson," she tells Kyle.

A Benson. My parents were Bensons; at one point up here the name meant something, caused eyes to widen, heads to nod. *The Americans*, people might say. *The ones who actually stayed.* Kyle, however, just looks blank.

"Benson, Kyle!" Kerry exclaims impatiently. "You know, the American family with the cottage that my mom looked after?"

"Um, yeah, I guess," he mumbles, and she blows out an exasperated breath. It's then that I realize what she's doing. She's heading straight across the bridge, toward the three guys bristling with weapons, standing in the center of the road, in front of a clumsy, jumbled blockade of chairs, sofas, wooden pallets, even a stroller.

"Kerry," I exclaim in a yelp of fear. "What—"

"I'm so *sick* of this," she exclaims, and she presses the gas until she's halfway across the bridge, heading straight toward the barricade. A camo-man with various knives strapped to his body points a semi-automatic rifle at the driver's window. Kerry rolls it down, unfazed.

"What do you think you're—" he begins, only to have her push the gun away from her face as if she's swatting a fly.

"I'm crossing this bridge, is what I'm doing," she snaps. "And you or one of your thugs can shoot me, but what's the point? You guys keep playing king of the Bonnechere River, and we'll be on our way."

"Where are you going?" the man blusters. He clearly hasn't prepared for pushback.

"Home. I've picked up my cousin, and I'm heading out of this shithole. So just let me pass, unless you really want to die for absolutely nothing? Because I'll happily run you over, just saying." She stares him down, unblinking, while everyone else in the car remains completely still, holding our breaths, not daring to move an inch. A millimeter.

"Fine, whatever," the man grumbles, and he steps aside. There is a space between an old sofa, its springs coming through the cushions, and a couple of oilcans. Kerry floors the car, so it practically jumps across the road, crashing through the barrier, and a shriek escapes Mattie—or maybe me—as debris flies, both side mirrors come off the car, and then Kerry starts weaving all over the road.

"Kerry, what—" I exclaim, grabbing onto the door handle as Mattie and I slide across the seat.

"Just in case they were thinking about shooting out my tires," Kerry replies. She slows down, staying on her side of the road, as she comes around the bend. The car is looking a lot worse for wear, but at least it's still drivable. For now.

"Kerry," Kyle breathes, his expression alight with awe, "that was *seriously* badass."

She grins at him. "Yeah, well, take notes," she tells him, and drives on.

I exhale quietly, relief making me sag in my seat. *We've made it*, I think, even though I know we haven't, not really. Not yet. Not for twenty more miles, and even then...

Then Kerry swings sharply left, and I blink the school into focus.

"*What...*"

"You didn't think we were leaving without getting something, did you?" Kerry says, twisting back to give me a mocking grin, although her eyes look hard. "After everything we've been through?"

"Kerry," I begin, shaking my head, filled with more fear than fury, "the last time we were here—"

"You'll stay in the car."

"This is way too dangerous—"

"I'm going too," Mattie says.

I turn to her, one hand flung out. "Mattie, no, you are absolutely not—"

"Mom." She gives me a look, the kind of look I normally give her—commanding, reproving, in control. "I want to go."

I don't think I can bear to let her go another time, but I also know I don't have the strength to make her stay. I lean my head back against the seat and close my eyes as my arm throbs.

I hear Kerry and Kyle climb out of the car, and then, to my surprise, I feel Mattie's hand on my shoulder. I open my eyes.

"I'll stay," she says quietly, and she slides into the driver's seat. "You can't drive with that arm."

"If you see anyone," Kerry instructs her, "honk the horn and then get the hell out of here. We'll meet you outside of town, by the lumber yard."

Mattie has never driven before, but I'm not about to argue that point now. "Okay," I croak, and she nods.

"Those guys are long gone, Alex," Kerry tells me. "We'll be fine."

I lock the doors and lean back against the seat, as Mattie

rests her hands on the steering wheel. "Do you know how to drive this thing?" I ask, with a hint of a smile.

Her hands tighten on the wheel. "I can figure it out."

"I know you can." I reach over with my good arm to touch her shoulder. "Are you okay?" I ask quietly.

She glances at me, her expression dark and uncertain, and in her eyes, I see the child she still is, even if she is determined to act as if she isn't. "Yeah," she says, looking away. "I'm okay."

Everything is quiet, the parking lot completely empty. The men who were here before, who stole my dad's truck, are long gone, just as Kerry said.

I breathe in and out. Think of Ruby and Darlene, back at the cottage. Daniel, somewhere between here and Clarkson. *Sam...*

I just want my family back.

I hear a noise like laughter, high and wild, and I jerk around in the seat. Kerry is running, Kyle behind her, both their arms full. At first, I think they are running from something, someone, but as I scramble to unlock the car doors, I realize they are running just because, a liberation.

"Let's go," Kerry says, as she dumps a bunch of cans in the footwell of the passenger seat. Kyle gets in the back while Mattie scrambles from the driver's side.

"What did you get?" she asks eagerly.

Kerry glances at me. "Are you okay?"

I nod. "I think so."

"We'll have a good look at your shoulder when we get home," she tells me. "Put a few stitches in if we need to."

I don't want to think about having stitches put in without any anesthetic, or Kerry being the one to put them in, when I doubt she can sew. "So, what did you get?" I ask, and I realize I am almost as curious as Mattie. Mattie leans forward from the back.

"All kinds of stuff," Kerry replies. "A bunch of cans from the kitchen, and Kyle got some stuff from the chemistry lab—"

Oh great, I think, *is he going to try to make meth in my kitchen?* Just what I need—an amateur episode of *Breaking Bad*, Armageddon-style.

"What did you want from the chemistry lab?" I ask him, and he shrugs, seeming abashed.

"I got a microscope and a fire extinguisher," he says proudly, holding them up. "I don't know, I thought they might be useful."

Kerry shakes her head. "Never the sharpest tool in the shed, were you, Kyle?" she says again—something of a family joke, I gather—but she's smiling, and he smiles back. As for what we'll do with a microscope or a fire extinguisher... well, I guess they can't go amiss.

"Anything else?" Mattie asks, and Kerry shoots her a grin.

"Did you think I forgot about you? We got some books. Textbooks, seventh-grade stuff. For Ruby."

"Oh, great," Mattie exclaims, sounding genuinely pleased, and this little exchange is enough to make my throat tighten.

We don't talk on the way back to the cottage; after the exuberance of getting the stuff from the school, everyone has turned solemn. Maybe the events are catching up with us, or maybe it's the fact that, after living in that crap-filled apartment for three weeks, Kyle smells vile and no one wants to breathe it in. Kerry ends up opening the windows to get some fresh air, freezing as it is.

"Dude," Kerry says when we finally, thankfully turn onto the dirt road, not having seen a single car all the way from Corville, "you need a shower when you get back."

"There's no running water," Mattie reminds her in a muffled voice. She's brought her sweatshirt up to cover her mouth.

"Then I'll pour a bucket of water over his head," Kerry states flatly. "You smell, literally, like shit."

Mattie laughs at this, and I give Kerry a stupidly reproving look, which she shrugs off, obviously unrepentant.

As the cottage comes into view, I exhale quietly in relief. We're home. We're safe. Sort of. I have a wounded shoulder, and we have no truck and no gun, but we're back, and I'm very glad for it.

It's not until I walk inside and feel the silence like a tangible thing, a shroud hanging over us, that I sense something is wrong.

"Ruby?" I call, as I come into the living room, one hand pressed to my shoulder, which has started to bleed again. "Darlene?"

They are both there, Ruby sitting silently on the sofa in the twilit, shadow-filled room, Darlene stretched out next to her. Ruby is holding her hand, and Darlene is clearly dead.

NINETEEN

Outside, beyond the pump house, Kyle is digging a grave. The ground is frozen solid, iron-hard, and he's barely managed to dig a hole big enough to bury a hamster, never mind a well-proportioned woman like Darlene, but at least he's trying.

Kerry comes to stand next to me by the kitchen window, watching him silently. Last night, when we came home, she didn't even seem surprised that her mother was dead. For a long moment, she simply stared at her slack face, her skin already turning waxy and gray, before she said flatly, "I guess she had another heart attack, huh?"

I would have believed she didn't care at all except for the sheen of tears in her eyes, the tremble of her lips. She didn't speak about her mom again.

Kerry and Kyle carried Darlene out onto the porch, to keep her body cold until it could be buried; it reminded me of the only time I'd touched a dead person, when I kissed my father's forehead, right after he died. I remember how strange it felt, like kissing marble. You don't realize how alive someone feels until they're not. There's no breath, no warmth, no movement at all under the skin, just this absolute, utter stillness. It was unsettling, that kiss. I wished I hadn't done it. I wished I'd been like my mother, who hadn't wanted to stay in the hospital room for another five seconds after my dad died. She knew well enough he wasn't there anymore; I'd had to be convinced.

Well, Kerry clearly didn't need to be convinced as she hefted Darlene's body, with Kyle taking her feet. There's a reason they call it dead weight. As they positioned her as carefully and respectfully as they could by the woodpile, I saw Ruby standing in the doorway, watching.

She hadn't said a word since we'd come home an hour before; her expression hadn't even changed, her face as opaque as the surface of the lake on a gray day, revealing absolutely nothing. In some ways, she felt as unreachable as Darlene was, and that scared me.

"Rubes." I went to her and gave her a one-armed hug, but she didn't lean into me the way she normally would have, arms wrapped tight around my waist, head burrowed into my chest, which was probably a good thing, since it would have killed my shoulder, but I still craved a connection.

She simply stood there, completely still and straight, and waited until I released her. "It's going to be okay," I said, knowing what a banal platitude that was even as I said it, yet right then, I had no others. Ruby, of course, did not reply, her gaze moving from beyond me to where Darlene lay on the floor, next to the wood. Catching her gaze, Kyle covered his aunt with an old tarp that had been on top of the woodpile.

Now, a day later, Kerry stands silently next to me, both of us watching Kyle work.

"He's a good boy," she says finally, the words escaping on a sigh as she shakes her head. "Hopeless, though, in a lot of ways."

"His parents were the ones who went to Florida?"

"Yeah. They never really had time for him, to be honest. He

flunked out of school and never held down a job, except on the highway."

I know that around here the government offers people ten weeks or so a year working on the highway, in construction. Sometimes, like Kyle, it's the only job they have.

I watch him chip away at the hard earth, his shovel clanging against the dirt every time he tries to dig, and yet he continues, his expression set and grim. "Do you think he'll be able to dig a big enough hole?" I ask Kerry.

She blows out a breath. "Probably not, but who cares? We could chuck her in the woods, let the animals have at her. Why not? We're all going to end up that way, anyway, and, frankly, that's if we're lucky."

"Kerry!" I sound both stern and shocked, a bit disapproving, because I've never heard her talk like that. She's been irreverent, yes, but she's also been funny and, in her own way, hopeful. I've come to rely on that; I relied on it yesterday, when I felt so dispirited. A day later, with my shoulder bandaged—Kerry decided against stitches, after blanching when she saw the messy wound—and a slug of whiskey to numb the pain, I started to feel more myself. Not hopeful, not exactly, but more determined.

Kerry, however, looks almost lifeless, her expression slack as she watches Kyle dig her mother's grave.

"I need a cigarette," she says abruptly. "I'm all out. Have you got one?"

I think of my parents' crumpled pack from years ago and nod. Silently, I turn from the window and root around for the cigarettes in a drawer. Kerry takes them from me without a word and heads out front, to the deck. After a second's pause, I follow her, past Mattie and Ruby, who are curled up on the sofa by the fire; Mattie is reading to Ruby from one of my childhood books she found up in the loft, an old Enid Blyton. It's a touching sight, one I would have given my right arm for just a few months ago, when I couldn't pry Mattie off her phone or make her interested in her sister, but now, for some reason, something about them curled up together like that makes me sad.

I close the door quietly behind me as I step out onto the deck. Kerry has already lit up, and she inhales deeply, blowing smoke toward the blue sky as she gazes out at the lake. It's frozen now, only just, a sheet of rippling glass, lightly dusted with snow. It's not thick enough to walk on yet, but it took Kerry ten minutes to chop through it this morning to fetch our water.

"I'm sorry about your mom," I tell her. "She was a good woman."

Kerry twitches her shoulders in something like a shrug. "It's not that."

"What is it then?"

"Everything else." She keeps staring at the frozen lake, her back to me, as she smokes the cigarette with a sort of fervent, desperate determination. The air is still and cold, starting to penetrate through my thick fleece and jeans, and making my shoulder ache. I try not to shiver. "I mean, what are we doing here, Alex?" Kerry asks after a moment. She tosses the cigarette into the snow before turning around to face me. "Really? What are we hoping to achieve?"

"Achieve?" I stare at her, registering the weariness in her face, the indifference, the hopelessness I see even more clearly now. "I don't know that I would use that word, exactly. We're trying to survive."

"But what for?"

I can tell this isn't a throwaway question; she genuinely wants an answer, and the truth is, I struggle to give her one. "What's the alternative?" I ask instead, my tone veering between seriousness and levity. "Suicide?"

She eyes me levelly, unfazed. "That might be preferable to getting raped and killed by some backwoods extras from *Deliverance*."

"That was yesterday," I say, deadpan, and Kerry lets out a huff of admiring laughter before stating flatly,

"And could be tomorrow."

I feel compelled to admit something that's been nagging at me since we lost the truck; I haven't wanted to think about it, but I know I have to. "The truck," I tell her, and Kerry nods, already understanding.

"There might have been something in it with the cottage's address. I thought about that."

"Maybe not?" I offer, not even half-hearted.

She gives another humorless huff of laughter. "Really? Not an old envelope, some junk mail under the seat, anything? What about the truck's registration, in the glove compartment?"

"I don't know," I admit.

"If they find it..." She presses her lips together. "We can take down the road sign."

"Camouflage the lane a bit more," I add. "Remove the gate."

"Yeah." She nods slowly. "That might help."

"It's not like they have a sat nav," I offer, and Kerry raises her eyebrows.

"They might have a map."

She glances back out over the frozen lake. "The thing is," she says slowly. "Those guys in the school, on the bridge? They're going to be all over the place. All over the world. And they'll find this place eventually, no matter how well we disguise it. They'll find us. And they'll take whatever they want, and we won't be able to stop them."

The image she paints in just a few flatly stated words is chilling. I can practically see those guys roaring up the dirt road in some monster truck, their raucous laughter echoing over the lake, the way they'd swarm the cottage, tipping over tables, grabbing my daughters—*no*. I can't let myself think like that. "Okay, then," I say after a moment, straightening, my shoulders thrown back as best as I can. "We'll have to prepare."

"How?" She raises her eyebrows. "We have one rifle left and a couple rounds of ammo. We're women and children and a useless teenager. How?" The cold challenge in her gaze chills me because it contains so much certainty. For Kerry, there is no *how*.

"Well, we look at our weaknesses and we address them," I say, which sounds like something off a corporate website. Ridiculous. Meaningless.

"Why, though?" Kerry presses, shaking her head. "I mean, why even try? What does the future hold, Alex, except more of the same? We carve out some pathetic pioneer life here, barely managing to survive, and for what? To just keep doing it until we die from cancer or pneumonia or who knows, a bug bite?"

"No one can know what the future holds—"

"Tell me about it." She reaches for another cigarette and lights it. "You know these are menthol, right? Disgusting."

"They were my parents'."

"So, they're about ten years old too? Well, better than nothing." She blows out a plume of smoke toward the sky. "I just don't see the point," she states wearily, "of anything."

"Things can change," I insist quietly. "It's only been a couple of weeks. There could be a future for us, Kerry, that's more than this place." I have to believe that, for my children's sake, if not my own.

She shrugs, as if it doesn't really matter either way, her gaze once more on the lake. "You know I was trying to get pregnant a few years ago?" she remarks after a few moments when the only sound has been the shifting of the ice, sudden cracking sounds like a gunshot as it expands and contracts. It startled me at first, those sudden booms, but then I remembered it from my childhood, how the lake is like a living thing, the ice too, moving and breathing.

"You were?" I ask.

"Yeah, with Kevin. The trapper. I don't think he was all that bothered either way, to be honest, but I really wanted a baby. It didn't happen, though. Obviously. Turned out I have ageing eggs, and there was a waiting list for the laser treatment to fix it —a couple of months, not too bad, but by that time Kevin wasn't around anymore." She lets out a weary sigh. "It's for the best now, I guess. But it's just one more thing I'll never do. Never have, not in this world."

"Kerry, you don't know that—"

"I kind of do." She turns to me, the ghost of one of her old smiles curving her mouth. "Come on, Alex. This is me you're talking to. Let's be real. Aren't you worried the same for Mattie? For Ruby? What kind of lives are they going to be able to have? They're so *young*. They've already been denied so much. What's their future going to look like?"

A visceral tremble goes through me, a shudder of fear, of grief, because that's something I have not let myself think about too much, if at all, and I won't let myself think about it now. "That's why we need to fight," I insist. "We need to prepare, for all eventualities. For them, for their future. And for yours."

"And what about yours?" She purses her lips thoughtfully. "Do you think Daniel is still alive?"

I jerk as if I've been electrocuted, or shot, *again*; she's really not pulling her punches today. "I don't know," I admit, the words drawn from me with painful honesty, deep reluctance. "I hope so."

"It's been three weeks."

"I know that." It's mid-December now, well below freezing every single day, and even colder at night. Is Daniel out there somewhere, a corpse in the snow? And what about Sam? Will I ever know?

"The likelihood," Kerry states matter-of-factly, but with a certain gentleness, "is that he's not coming back."

I press my lips together, hard enough to hurt, to keep from making the sound that threatens to escape me, small and wounded. "You can't know that for sure," I manage after a moment. "And right now, for the sake of my children, as well as my own, I'm choosing to hope that he is. That he *will*."

Kerry nods slowly, accepting if still clearly skeptical. I breathe out, forcing the images, the fears, from my mind. If I think too much about Daniel, about Sam, I will lose my focus, and I can't afford to do that now, or ever.

Kerry looks back out at the lake. "What about Kyle?" she asks after a moment.

I know what she means. "I think he should stay."

She turns back, one eyebrow arched. "Another mouth to feed?"

"A man around could be helpful. And where else is he going to go? Plus, we need the car." I've been surprised by my own sudden feelings of something approaching tenderness toward Kyle. Last night Kerry insisted he bathe before bed, and he undressed down to his boxers, shivering as he stood in the bathtub and Kerry dumped a bucket of not even tepid water over his head. Soaking wet he probably weighed less than I did; he was short and skinny, his ribs poking out, his shoulder blades like chicken wings.

And, oddly, because he was really nothing like him, he somehow reminded me of Mattie's boyfriend Drew. I'd been so harsh toward that boy, so dismissive and so scornful, certain he was bad news for my daughter, and maybe he *was*; but I never gave him a chance. I never even thought about giving him one. I'm not sure I can make myself regret that now, but it feels like I have a second chance, with Kyle. To be kinder, more accepting.

"Okay," Kerry says, accepting. "We keep Kyle."

"I think we need to call a meeting," I state, warming to the idea as I consider it. It feels proactive, purposeful. "Let everyone weigh in on how we can protect this place. How we can go forward in a way that works—for food, for protection, and even for fun. This doesn't just have to be about survival. We can make a life here. A real life." I've said as much before, but we keep getting derailed by events, by the outside. No more trips to Corville, I think. No more drawing attention to ourselves, and we can, maybe, make this work. At least, we can try.

"For *fun*?" Kerry shakes her head, but she's smiling, at least a little. "So, what are you thinking? An alarm system for the gate? We'll string tin cans along the road, so we know when someone's coming? A voluntary militia, out on patrol, with frying pans for shields, saucepans for helmets?" I know she's mocking me, but frankly it doesn't all sound like that bad an idea. "You sound like the Apple Dumpling Gang," she says with a short laugh. "Or maybe, I don't know, the Goonies."

I shrug, smiling back. "Whatever works." But I'm thinking about building a greenhouse, cutting more wood, trapping a beaver. Making maple syrup in March, planting the seeds my parents kept in the spring. Figuring out a way to live here long term, and worry about the marauders when they actually show up, if they ever do. Surely, we've got enough to be getting on with.

Kerry heaves a long-suffering sigh as she flicks her second cigarette into the snow, where it lands with a little hiss. "Okay, fine, we'll call this town meeting or whatever, but just remember, when we're being raped and killed by those rednecks, it was me who told you so."

"I'm sure that's exactly what I'll be thinking about at that particular moment," I reply, and Kerry laughs while, improbably, I feel myself grinning.

We're just about to head inside when Kyle appears at the door, looking as eager as a puppy—begging to be loved or even kicked. "I set a fire to thaw the ground so I can dig a big enough hole," he tells us. "Mattie's watching it, but I just wanted to check that was okay?"

Kerry's smile broadens as she ruffles his now-clean hair. "That's some good problem-solving skills right there, Kyle," she says, as she walks past him. "Good thing we're keeping you."

We bury Darlene that afternoon, under a sky white with snow that is yet to fall, in the hard, unforgiving earth. The fire Kyle set managed to thaw it enough to make a shallow grave; we wrapped her in the tarp and covered the mound with some brush. Kyle made a cross with two sticks, nailed together; she would have liked that, I know. She went to the little Baptist church on the road to Flintville every Sunday.

There are no hymns because we don't know any, and no one says any words because there doesn't seem to be any to say. We simply stand by the graveside, as silent as Ruby, as we each remember Darlene.

I think of her words to me, just a few weeks ago. *You are your father's daughter.* What would my dad have done in this situation? He would have looked out for everyone, I know that much, but I also know he would have been afraid. He was a man, not a superhero, but I know he always tried to do the right thing. He was generous, accepting, forgiving. Mostly, anyway, more than I've been. But he could also be irritable, short-tempered, moody. He wasn't perfect, but I loved him, and I'm thinking of him now, as we bury Darlene.

I think of my mother too. She was the counterfoil to my dad's bonhomie and dreaminess—utterly practical, sometimes ruthlessly so, thinking in terms of realities rather than wishes. Together, I think, they would have triumphed against this Armageddon disaster, the perfect team. They would have been excited by the challenges, I realize; in an entirely different way to those guys on the bridge, they'd been waiting for something like this, to put their homesteading to the test. Well, now it's our turn.

"Right," I say, as I turn away from Darlene's grave. "It's time to have a meeting."

TWENTY

DANIEL

A mere ten miles outside of Clarkson, he is attacked. Although *attacked* feels too violent a word; he's ambushed, waylaid even, by a couple of teenagers, barely more than kids, cruising around in a big black SUV, rap music blasting, almost like they would be before this all happened, except now they're just that much more reckless. There is a wildness in their eyes that Daniel recognizes in himself, a surge of something feral and uncontrolled he has so far kept at bay, all through his travels—through the farmer waving a gun in his face, and the camo-suited pretend soldiers parading in front of Walmart, the tanks he once saw heading down a country road, the fighter jets in the sky.

He kept himself hidden when he saw a bunch of drugged-up teenagers racing hospital stretchers down the street; he didn't think there were any patients on them, but he knew he couldn't truly be sure. He looked the other way when a gang robbed a mother and child of the pitiful amount of food they'd collected; the woman screamed and the child sobbed and Daniel stayed hidden.

While the world exploded around him, a frenzy of looting

and larceny, pillaging and marauding like something out of a medieval siege or a Mel Gibson movie, he'd stayed calm and controlled, guilt-ridden yet determined in his self-interest, but now he senses in himself the fraying of his tether, how soon it will snap. He's so close to Sam.

"Hey there, Grandpa," they call out, as they pull onto the side of the road with a spray of gravel. Some of it hits him in the cheek, stinging. He pauses, hands gripping the handlebars, his expression guarded, wary, alert.

One kid gets out of the passenger seat and sashays toward him, one hand resting on his belt buckle. He's Sam's age, if that; he still has pimples and he has a few hairs sprouting from his chin, not much more, but he's striding toward Daniel like he's Jesse James, or maybe just Clint Eastwood. *It's all games to these boys*, Daniel thinks. They're so terrified they can only play-act at life because none of them can bear for this to be real.

"What do you want?" he asks. His voice is a throaty rasp; he can't remember the last time he spoke out loud, and the sound of it surprises him. It has taken him two weeks to get from Utica to here, two weeks he does not wish to remember in any detail.

"What the hell are you doing on that little girl's bike?" the boy asks; it sounds like a genuine question, but his laugh ends in a sneer, and before Daniel can react, before he realizes what this *juvenile* is about to do, the kid wrenches the bike from under him, so he sprawls back onto the road, hitting his head hard enough to daze him.

By the time he blinks the world back into focus, the boy is raising the bike over his head and then, with a methodical and even bored indifference that makes Daniel all the more outraged, he smashes it onto the road. A tire pops and the frame becomes bent and twisted; it is ruined. *Ruined*, and for what? It didn't even look like this stupid teenager enjoyed his wanton act of destruction.

Daniel eases up onto his elbows as the boy smirks down at him. "What do you think of that, Grandpa?"

"What do I think of that?" Daniel asks, and something in his voice, the deadly matter-of-factness of it, or maybe the complete lack of fear, makes the boy's eyes widen just a little. The boys in the car who were watching, grinning, suddenly go still, their expressions turning wary. They are children, Daniel thinks, and yet they are his enemies.

Slowly, deliberately, he rises from the road. He dusts off his khakis while the boy waits, watching him uncertainly. And then, with an assuredness he feels right now in every atom of his body, he unstraps the rifle from his chest and points it unhesitatingly in the boy's face. "What I think," he states levelly, "is that you just made a big mistake."

The boy gulps. At a movement from the car, Daniel swings the rifle toward the driver's seat window, which is rolled down. "Everybody out of the car," he barks. "Slowly. No sudden movements. Trust me, I'm so trigger-happy right now, you don't even want to *think* about doing something stupid." He's never meant anything more; he knows part of him, a large part, would enjoy blasting the head off one of these stupid, stupid boys. Would positively *relish* it.

Slowly, looking scared and young, far too scared and young, the boys get out of the car. They're younger than Daniel thought, probably not even old enough to drive. Fourteen, maybe fifteen. Mattie's age. His rifle, trained on their uncertain forms, does not waver.

"Stand by the side of the road."

"Look, we didn't mean it. We were just joking—"

Joking, Daniel thinks, *joking in a nuclear fallout, this Armageddon dystopian nightmare?* There is no joking. "Move," he says. They shuffle to the side of the road. None of them have any weapons, not even a knife. How stupid are they, he wonders. What were they thinking, joyriding like this, with no weapons?

"Where are you from?" he asks them.

They look surprised by the question, a little wary, like he's going to trick them somehow. "Clarkson."

"Clarkson? At the college?" he demands sharply.

"No," one boy, the one who broke his bike, replies sulkily. "The town."

"What are you doing out here?" he demands.

A few of them shrug. "What else is there to do?" one says sullenly.

Daniel almost wants to laugh. They're *bored*, he realizes. Bored in a nuclear holocaust. "Aren't you worried about gangs?" he asks. "Violence?"

Another shrug. "There are Marines in the town," one boy says. "It's pretty safe."

Marines? He doesn't know if that's a good or bad thing; on the whole, he decides it is good. "Why are Marines in the town?"

"I dunno. They just are."

"What about your parents?" Silence. He waves the gun. "Well?"

"Mine are dead," one boy says. "They were in Boston for the day."

Daniel feels the very faintest flicker of pity, so easy to suppress. "And the rest of you?" he demands.

A few shrugs; some of the boys shift where they stand, stare at the ground. "Well?" Daniel roars, swinging the rifle between them.

One boy flings his hands up. "I don't know, man. Why do you care about our parents?"

Daniel suddenly finds himself laughing, a slow, rasping chuckle that turns loud and wild. The boys stare at him like he's crazy, and maybe he is, but he could be asking Sam's friends what they think they're doing out at this time of night, seeing them hang their heads or look rebellious. Nothing changes, he thinks, even when everything does.

"What happened to all the students at Clarkson?" he asks them, and again he's greeted with an uneasy silence. "Tell me!"

"I don't know, I think most of them left, went home to their parents and stuff," one boy says quickly. He sounds caught between annoyance and fear.

"Most?"

"Some stayed," another chimes in, his tone uneasy. "The international students did... although some of them went with friends. But some chose to stay because they thought it would be safer, with the Marines and all. They're guarding the campus."

"Do any of you know a boy," he demands, "a freshman, named Sam Elliot?"

They glance at each other again, and then shake their heads.

"Why did you leave Clarkson, if it's so safe?" he asks, and none of them answer. After everything he's seen, Daniel can't believe these teenagers are out *joyriding,* with no thought to the dangers. "Your parents," he asks, his voice shaking with disbelief, "the ones who are alive, they just let you wander around when the world is in this state? When there are men like me who could blow your heads off?"

"I doubt there are any bullets in that gun," one boy states suddenly. He starts striding toward him, a sneer twisting his face, one hand outstretched to take his gun, all cocksure arrogance.

Daniel doesn't think, just reacts. The sound of the gunshot echoes in the still air and the boy lets out a choked gasp as he clutches his chest.

"You... *shot* me," he says, his voice filled with incredulity, and Daniel gulps, his heart juddering. He thinks he might be sick. At least he didn't kill him, he thinks numbly as blood seeps from the boy's chest, too high up to hit any organ. The boy starts to cry, big, shuddering gulps, like a child. "I'm hurt," he exclaims, looking at his friends. "I'm *bleeding*." He sounds incredulous, but also scared. Slowly, he crumples to the ground, still clutching his chest. His face is gray, and his friends look terrified.

I shot a boy, Daniel thinks. *I shot a boy younger than Sam, and I didn't even have to.*

"I think you killed him, man," one boy says, his voice high-pitched and wavering. "I think you killed him!"

I didn't kill him, Daniel thinks. *I can't have killed him.* He stares down at the boy, feeling strangely dispassionate, almost indifferent. He turns back to the other boys, who are huddled together. "Are there any guard posts between here and the college?" he asks, and they stare at him dumbly, like they don't know what he's talking about. Has Clarkson been in its own little oasis, thanks to the Marines? Daniel shakes his head, impatient now. "Get to the side of the road," he tells them, and they all shuffle over, even the boy with the bullet wound whimpering softly, crawling on his hands and knees.

Daniel opens the driver's door of the SUV. One of the boys lets out a squawk of protest.

"That's my dad's car—"

"You shouldn't have wrecked my bike," he replies, and then he heaves himself in, slamming the door behind him. The cloud of dust as he pulls hard onto the road obscures the sight of the boys standing there, looking shocked and scared and so very young, the one he shot still huddled on the ground.

Daniel doesn't look back. He drives blindly for several minutes, the only sound the ragged gasps of his breathing, until he realizes he isn't just gasping, he's crying. Tears run down his dirty face, and he hits the steering wheel with the flat of his palm, as hard as he can, several times as a howl escapes him, and then another.

He can't believe he shot a man. A *boy*. And left him on the side of the road, with no way to get back home. It's four o'clock in the afternoon in the dead of winter and it's freezing. Will those boys die? He's become what he has despised, and even that is not what makes him sob in outrage and grief. It is that he doesn't even care.

Ten miles pass emptily, without a single car. Then he comes upon the town of Clarkson, which is like every other town he's seen, a mix of abandoned buildings and barricaded ones, home-made signs warning about private property, guard dogs, that trespassers will be shot. He sees a homegrown militia patrolling ahead and swings a hard right to avoid them. His breathing has evened out, and he wipes his face, composing himself. He's going to find Sam. In a few hours, maybe even a few minutes, he will see him.

At the gates of the college, he stops. There are half a dozen Marines, genuine military, barring the road. The college is on a hill, surrounded by a brick wall of middling height; no wonder it's being guarded. Just three months ago, he drove through those gates in his station wagon, Sam's stuff piled in the back, Sam practically bouncing in the backseat. They'd left Mattie and Ruby at home with family friends, so they could do this, the three of them—him, Alex, and Sam. He'd lost his job two months before, but they hadn't told Sam about it. He'd still been hiding the truth about the house. Really, that day was a mirage, a facade, but he remembered feeling happy.

Slowly, his hand shaking, his heart beating with slow, heavy thuds, Daniel rolls down the window. One of the Marines steps forward, eyes narrowed, his hand on the assault rifle strapped to his chest. Daniel knows he will use it in an instant, without a qualm, without a quaver.

"This is private property," he tells Daniel, his tone flatly forbidding. "You need to turn around right now." He doesn't say it like a threat, more a simple statement of fact; and yet Daniel feels his limbs go watery.

His hands tighten on the steering wheel as he takes a deep breath. "I'm looking," he says, his voice coming out strong, "for my son."

TWENTY-ONE

February, two months later

"I don't think I can do this."

"Well, I know *I* can't." Kerry's voice holds a hint of laughter as we stare down at the dead beaver lying on top of the picnic table. It was already enough of an effort simply to get it here from across the lake; fifty pounds of dead weight is no small thing, and the truth was I was doing my best not to touch it, at least not too much. The result being that Kerry and I heaved the thing onto a toboggan and sledged it across the frozen lake, trudging knee-deep in snow. Then we dragged it by its hind legs up to the cottage, probably not the best way to transport the animal. It was frozen solid, so we've had to wait to let it thaw out a bit before I get to do the dirty—skin and prepare it for its meat. Ruby's book on sustainable living doesn't cover wild animals, but there is a page on how to skin, joint, and disembowel a sheep, and I'm hoping that the process is at least somewhat similar. Not that I want to do any of it. Not remotely.

Still, this is what I signed up for, when I optimistically and officiously called our town meeting two months ago, and sold everyone on the idea of making life work here for all of us.

"Not just as a temporary measure," I explained, "but as a way to live. Because we don't know what the future holds, but we've got enough here to make a life for ourselves, if we want to. If we try."

"Thrive, not just survive," Mattie interjected, and I couldn't tell if she was being sarcastic or not.

"Well, yes," I agreed after a pause, although the idea of thriving in the middle of a nuclear holocaust seemed a little ridiculous even at the height of my optimism, but it was what Daniel had said we could do, and for his sake—and maybe his memory—I wanted to try.

And we *are* thriving, sort of, at least more than we were. Kyle and Mattie worked together to build a greenhouse, made out of the old windows and lumber from the barn and heated by the chiminea. Seeing my daughter confidently wielding a circular saw—we turned on the generator for that—made my heart swell with pride. It's not the strongest or most solid of structures, admittedly, but it catches the sunlight and keeps the heat in. Mostly.

Ruby planted the seed potatoes in the soil; we used the bags of old compost in the root cellar, mixed with vegetable and fruit peelings and cores, to give it more nutrients. It was Kerry who had suggested that; apparently, it was something her mother did. Darlene's wisdom lives on.

Three weeks ago, the first shoots sprouted through the soil, tender and green, the very definition, it felt like, of a miracle. Ruby hovers over them like a nursemaid, and we all work on a schedule to make sure to keep the chiminea well stocked and burning day and night. We had chosen to grow potatoes since they were hardy and, according to Ruby's book, which we now consult religiously, they preferred cooler soil.

We've had to cut more firewood, a never-ending need that's

left our hands blistered and our backs aching. Kyle and Kerry hauled deadwood from the other side of the lake, building a pile to dry out under a tarp, and Kyle went out to cut down as many of the smaller dead trees around the cottage as he could find. We all took turns, even Ruby, wielding the axe to split the trees into logs. Something that looks easy on *Lumberjacks: Extreme Competitive Loggersports*, which I'd watched a few minutes of, bemusedly, while flicking through TV channels, is, in reality, extremely difficult and exhausting work. But we did it, and now the basement and porch are both stacked high, and there is more outside—not enough, it's true, and it will always be a huge need. Heating the house and the greenhouse by wood alone means we burn through a *lot*.

We have fallen into a daily routine that seems to work for everyone, taking turns fetching water, making breakfast, building fires. Kyle, Kerry, and I each take turns on a patrol of the road, down to the end of the drive, going in pairs, simply to see if anyone has been about, but thankfully so far, we have been left entirely alone. The logs across the road, the removal of the gate and the road sign, are, I hope, enough to keep people away, even those crazed men from Corville.

Mattie wanted to take turns patrolling as well, but I refused. She helps Ruby with her schoolwork in the morning, and I have insisted that she at least do some of her own reading.

"I'm already getting an education, Mom," she told me with a theatrical eye-roll, gesturing to the cottage, the lake, the entirety of her existence.

"Yes," I agreed, "but you still need to read."

And so, she's working her way through my dad's library, an eclectic mix of classic novels, Isaac Asimov science fiction, and Louis L'Amour westerns. It's not the education I once wanted for her, but it is, in some ways, better than what she was getting.

We have had our moments of pleasure too—we dug out the ice skates and cleared a rectangular rink on the lake, once it had frozen solid, and both Mattie and Ruby learned to skate, Kyle slip-sliding in his sneakers, yelping with fear every time he nearly fell. We went sledding on the big hill behind the old barn, dragging out the old toboggan from my childhood, the same one that carried the dead beaver back home. We've had an epic tournament of Go Fish and Spit, with Mattie tabulating the rankings, and in the evenings, if we're not too exhausted—and often we are—we sit around the fire, listening to Kyle play my dad's old guitar. He can barely do more than pluck at a few chords, but it's enough for us. I'd missed music, I realized, along with so many other things. I used to miss the convenience of our old lives, but now I find I miss its beauty—music, art, a well-crafted film. Looking in the window of an art gallery and seeing a hand-thrown glass vase, colors glinting in the light. Reading an interesting opinion piece in the *New York Times*. I even miss the comforting hum of a coffeemaker, the whirr of a tumble dryer, sounds of security and safety, so unlike the quiet and stillness that permeates our lives now.

And yet there is beauty here, too, glorious beauty—in the untouched sweep of snow on the frozen lake, the sky a deep, frigid blue above. In the whisper of the wind through the trees, and the utter stillness after a snowstorm, when their boughs are heaped with snow, as softly mounded as icing. There is even beauty in the menacing—one morning I woke up early and, as the dawn mist was clearing the lake, I saw a lone wolf standing in the center of it, its head lifted to catch a scent, its eyes piercing and blue even all the way from where I stood by the window, cradling my cup of hot water, since we'd run out of coffee weeks ago.

The wolf stood there for a moment, its body perfectly still and taut, the moment feeling suspended in time, almost as if it could go on forever—and then it loped off, into the trees, leaving me alone, arrested by the stark, eerie beauty of the moment.

So, yes, we have created lives here, and, while I'm proud of all our achievements, there is still a ribbon of loss as well as fear running right through its center. This isn't the life I wanted for myself, or, more importantly, for my daughters. We're all making do, and trying to act like it's enough, when in the moments of silence, of sadness, when my arms are aching from chopping through the ice or hauling water, when the blisters burst on my hands and blood runs down to my wrist, when Ruby cries in her sleep and nothing I can do will comfort her, when I see Mattie staring off into the distance and I consider how lonely she must be, fighting despair at what her future holds, or, more importantly, *doesn't* hold, can never hold... the truth thuds through me that this will never be enough.

Worst of all is when I have let myself think about Daniel. It will be three months next week since he left us. I can't let myself believe he's actually gone, *dead*, even though the leaden certainty lining my stomach tells me he is. He must be. And so, most likely, must be Sam, as well as everyone else I can't bear to think about—my mother, my siblings. My friends. My children's friends. My neighbors. *Everyone*. And if they're not dead, then they're living lives like we are—a hand-to-mouth existence, teetering on the precipice of extinction. How long can it possibly last?

In a few weeks, we'll start tapping the trees to make maple syrup. I know it will make me think of Daniel, along with my parents, all the people I've lost who loved it here, even more than I ever did. Daniel belonged to the cottage just as much as I did, even if he came to it late.

Worse than the sense that this isn't enough is the fear that it will be taken away. We are only five people, four of them females, two of them children. We have just one rifle and a fairly paltry stash of ammunition. Besides that, we are living on the very brink of disaster—if someone gets hurt, or falls sick, or our measly potato crop fails... It would only take one of these to have our whole fragile existence rent completely apart.

I have been monitoring our food situation—the fresh fruit and veg are long gone, of course, as is the turkey, the frozen meat and meals, not to mention the treats we tried to ration—the bags of potato chips, the packets of cookies. Once, late at night, I discovered Kyle munching his way through our last roll of Oreos all by himself. I was on the verge of becoming incandescent with rage—about *Oreos*—when I remembered he had been hauling logs from across the lake for ten hours that day. Maybe he deserved a couple of Oreos, or even a round dozen.

Still, it's been hard, losing those little treats, that taste of what life used to be like, what we took for granted or even disdained. Now food is nothing but sustenance—a bowl of oatmeal for breakfast, along with an egg each, now that the chickens have started laying again. Lunch is a slice of bread—Ruby's book told us how to make yeast, with varying results and plenty of dense, flat loaves—spread with whatever we've decided to use that week: a precious tablespoon of peanut butter, or a sprinkling of tuna. We are slowly going through all our jars and cans of extras. For dinner, we unvaryingly have pasta with a few spoonfuls of my mother's vegetable-packed tomato sauce—some of it admittedly tastes a bit tired.

It's not really enough for any of us—we've all become thin and stringy, and when I looked in the mirror once—I don't very often—I saw I was scrawny and wizened, my hair turned gray, the skin around my face loose and wrinkled, old before my time.

Still, if we continue on this way, we can last for another two months, *maybe*, although after that it will become difficult—we will be out of oatmeal, pasta, and sauce, along with all the other accompaniments—peanut butter, honey, ketchup, tuna. But there is still flour for bread, and eggs from the chickens, and now there is a beaver, the first wild animal we've managed to trap. Maybe we can make it.

"So, how are you going to start?" Kerry asks, and I wonder, not for the first time, how I ended up with this job. Except, of course, I already know how; nobody else wanted it. I'd been hoping Kyle might have a hunter hiding inside him, but when we found the beaver in the trap a few days ago, he grimaced with distaste.

"No way, man. I used to eat stuff from the freezer, you know?"

Yes, I knew. Out of all of us, Kyle missed his junk food the most. I miss my coffee—in spring, I will try to make coffee from the ground and roasted roots of the wild chicory plant, if I can manage to find it. I know it won't be the same, but having run out of coffee over a month ago, I'm already looking forward to the attempt.

"I think I'm meant to cut it longwise through the belly," I say doubtfully. I'm holding a sharpened butcher's knife, but I'm not sure it's up to the job. I'm not sure *I'm* up to the job. I don't even like the sight of blood; Daniel had to deal with all the little first aid emergencies the kids had when they were little. A bloody nose or a chipped tooth were beyond me. And yet now I think I can slice open a beaver, and cut it up into steak-sized parcels we'll want to eat?

Yet I've done a lot of things I hadn't expected to. I've chopped wood and fired a gun and hauled water. I've faced down an attacker and missed my husband and buried my mother's friend.

I can do this.

"Start at the bottom," Kerry advises. She's standing well back, her arms folded, her gaze slightly averted from the beaver's carcass. My stomach is already roiling, and I haven't done anything yet.

"The bottom?"

"The base of the tail. Well, technically, the anus. Kevin told me that, I remember."

"Wow, that's some serious sweet talk," I reply, and she smiles faintly. I take a deep breath and start to cut. I don't put on nearly enough pressure because I'm nervous about cutting too deep and spilling out the beaver's guts, which apparently is another part of the process. I'm also squeamish, and I don't like the concept of putting a knife to flesh, never mind the actuality of it, pressing down, making an incision.

"Put some elbow grease into it, Alex," Kerry says, and I give her a not-so-mock glare.

"You're the expert, huh?"

"Kevin taught me a few tricks."

"Then why don't you do it?" I return, exasperated, and Kerry just smiles. I press harder, and the knife sinks through the animal's rough fur. I move it upward, my fingers clammy around the handle. It's not smooth, the way I'd hoped it would be, one seamless cut from bottom to top, like going through butter. Instead, maybe because the blade isn't sharp enough, or due to my own lack of confidence, it's a series of jagged jerks and pulls, the line along the beaver's belly looking more like a scar than a seam. I can *feel* that cut in a way that makes me suppress a shudder. But I do it, and after a few endless minutes, the animal is open. My mouth tastes metallic, and my stomach is definitely heaving. I haven't got to the hard part yet—cutting the pelt away from the beaver, and then opening it up to take out all the organs, before slicing up all the meat. I'm not sure I can.

"Are you sure Trapper Kevin can't do this?" I joke, and I'm surprised by Kerry's answering thoughtful silence.

"He could, for sure," she replies. "If we asked him."

I look up from the carcass, the bloody knife in my hand. "What? Are you serious?"

She shrugs. "If he's in his cabin, we could, I mean. *I* could. I guess."

I'm still staring at her because this is news. The way she talked about Kevin, I assumed he was long gone, far away, deep into the north woods, maybe. "Where does he live?"

"About four miles from here, through the woods, down one of the old logging roads." She nods toward the little wooden bridge that crosses the stream that feeds the lake, heading off into the woods. "That way."

I shake my head slowly. "Four *miles*? Why have you not told me this before?"

"Because I didn't think we were entertaining guests," she replies. "And, you know, I wasn't sure I wanted to see him. Or that he wanted to see me."

"But you think you might want to, now?" I'm still trying to process all this new information.

"Well..." Kerry smiles faintly. "We're all getting a bit stir crazy here, aren't we? Some new blood might be welcome." She waggles her eyebrows suggestively.

"*Kerry.*" I shake my head, as prudish as a nun, and she laughs.

"What? It's true. Although I don't even know if he'd be interested—in any of it. Kev always did like his own company." She sighs. "And he's probably got a pretty sweet set-up, you know?" She points to Ruby's book, on the bench next to me. "He could have written that thing."

"Then we definitely need him here," I say firmly. "I can't believe we haven't talked about this before." Kerry and I have talked about a lot of things over the last few months, and, while I feel closer to her than I ever have before, I'm still not at all sure I know or understand her. There's a remoteness at her center, maybe from her dad leaving, having to care for her mother. She keeps part of herself hidden away, although I suppose I do too. Maybe everyone does, to one degree or another, a kind of self-preservation. "Is there something about him I should know?" I ask. "Is he a secret serial killer?" It's not actually outside the realm of possibility. "Can you trust him?"

"I trust him not to kill us all in our beds," Kerry replies. "Or steal from us or anything stupid like that. But do I trust him not to just walk away when he feels like it?" There is a hurt, bitter edge to her voice that I don't think I have heard before. "No, I don't trust him not to do that."

"We can just ask him to help us with this, you know," I tell her quietly. "We don't have to invite him into our lives."

"I know." She recovers some of her old insouciance as she glances at me with a hard smile. "Don't worry about me, Alex. I'm not going to go soft."

Kerry heads over there that very afternoon, taking the rifle. I offered to go with her, but she said it was better if she went alone.

"Kevin doesn't like visitors," she explained, which made me wonder just what kind of mountain man we were inviting into our lives.

Mattie and Ruby are both intensely curious about the possibility of a visitor, the first new person we'll have seen since Kyle.

"He's Kerry ex-boyfriend?" Mattie exclaims, round-eyed; somehow, I'd managed to let that slip. "Seriously?"

"He's going to help us skin the beaver," I explain. "That's all, Mattie."

"Okay, sure." She laughs, and I shake my head.

I'm starting to feel uneasy about asking this stranger into our midst; all I know about him is what Kerry has told me, and she admitted she hasn't even seen him in several years. He might not be living in his cabin in the woods, or if he is, he might have gone off the deep end, cabin fever turning him into a conspiracy theorist or an axe-wielding serial killer, never mind what Kerry insisted about his character. I thought I'd learned my lesson—more than once—about being reckless, but maybe I haven't.

And really, I can skin the beaver myself, can't I? Even if it isn't done well, I'll learn and do the next one better. We don't *need* Trapper Kevin... except, considering the state of our food stores, maybe we do. Or, I wonder, maybe Kerry does. She certainly seemed willing to go in search of him.

I try to distract myself as we wait for Kerry to return with Kevin—or not. Ruby retreats into reading, and Mattie has gone ice skating; she's become more than proficient, practicing her figure eights all alone on the ice, a solitary figure swirling through the snow.

Kyle is flicking through the *Archie* comics in the loft, the same ones I read thirty years ago. I haven't been able to get him to read anything more challenging, not that I've tried too hard; he does enough without me nagging at him to improve his mind, much as it could probably use some improving.

I tidy up the kitchen and get started on supper, survey the food stores in the pantry that grow paltrier by the day and try not to worry. It's the middle of February, and we still have four or five months before we can hope to harvest anything much, although the potatoes should be ready soon. But even *then*... we've learned to go without so much already, we'll simply have to learn to go without even more.

I remind myself what it will be like here in summer—raspberries and blueberries bursting from bushes; apples and plums hanging low and sweet in the overgrown orchard by the old barn; wild rhubarb and sumac and chicory and who knows what else growing wild and rampant. I have been studying a book of wild herbs and plants, with beautiful watercolor drawings of each one, in the hopes that I will be able to identify these edibles and not poison everyone in the process.

If we can make it to summer, we can find a way. It's been my motto, my mantra, and I say it again now as the sky starts to whiten the way it does before twilight, and Mattie skates to the dock—repaired by Kyle and Kerry—to unlace her skates. In the loft Kyle sighs and tosses aside the *Archie* comics, and Ruby drifts up to me, a question in her eyes.

"I think they'll be here soon," I tell her, just as I hear the porch door open.

"Hello?" Kerry calls, and we all hurry to the kitchen, apprehensive, expectant.

Kerry is walking into the cottage with a man following silently behind her, and although I try not to show it, I'm taken aback by the sight of him. He's not at all what I expected—which was some sort of modern-day Jeremiah Johnson, complete with bushy beard and camo clothing. Trapper Kevin is dressed in a pair of jeans and a fisherman's knit sweater, hiking boots and a hunting vest bristling with knives, so yes, he's a *little* Jeremiah Johnson-like, but what surprises me about him is how quiet and sensitive he looks—a thin, fine-boned face, dark hair worn a little long. If you took away the hunting vest, I'd think he was a musician or an artist.

"Kevin," I say. "I'm Alex. Thank you so much for coming." Which makes it sound as if we're hosting a party, but he just nods without saying a word. "Can you help us with the beaver?" I ask, and he merely nods again. Kerry smiles at him, and there is a softening in her face that touches me. I don't think Kevin even notices.

He stays for a single night. He skins and guts the beaver, and slices the meat off so neatly and efficiently I feel like if I blinked, I'd miss it. Like a miracle we have stewing-sized chunks, steaks and roasts, all wrapped in wax paper and stored in the root cellar—around thirty pounds of meat, which is enough for quite a few meals.

"Does it taste like chicken?" I ask him, teasing, and he replies seriously, although with the faintest glint of humor in his eyes, "More like gamey beef." When he smiles, barely, I understand what Kerry must have seen in him. "Slow-cook it in broth," he adds, "or it will be as tough as an old boot."

That evening, he and Kerry sit outside on the deck in the frosty moonlight, while Kyle and Mattie play Go Fish and Ruby watches them. I watch Kerry and Kevin, pretending I'm not, but Mattie notices.

"Give them some privacy, Mom," she tells me after twenty minutes, when I've sat down, got up again, stoked the fire, sat down. "Jeez."

"If they want privacy, they could go just about anywhere else," I tell her, and she rolls her eyes.

When they come back in, an hour later, Kerry is pink-cheeked but quiet, and Kevin goes to bed, sharing Kyle's little box room, without a word. I tell the girls to get ready for bed, and when I try to catch Kerry's gaze, my eyebrows raised in query, she doesn't look at me.

That night I lie in my own bed, feeling the empty space next to me in a way I haven't let myself in a long time. I crave the warmth of Daniel's body, the sense of security I felt resting in his arms. I picture myself with my head against his chest, his slow and steady breathing as he drifted off to sleep. I want that so much it's like a physical ache inside me, relentless, pulsing.

The resentment I felt for his deception, the anger at how our life had been so disastrously dismantled—none of it matters now. It isn't even that life as it is now has put it into perspective, although of course it has. It's more that I've changed, that the things that once were important to me aren't anymore. All I want is my family back. Whatever life we can forge for ourselves, we'll do it together.

And yet... Daniel might be dead. It's a thought I try not to let myself think too often. It's been almost three months since he left. Three *months*. It seems an unbearable amount of time; when I think how new and raw everything was when he left, how we were all still reeling, having no idea what the world was like, it feels like an absolute eon. I've changed so much, and so have Mattie and Ruby. Has Daniel? Has Sam?

Sam. If Daniel is dead, is Sam? Did he even manage to find him? The thought that I will most likely never know tears at me, and alone in my bed, in a spill of silvery moonlight, I give way to my grief—silently, my face pressed into the pillow, my body shaking with sobs, the emptiness stretching all around me. I don't feel any better for it; in fact, I realize, I feel worse. It was better when I repressed all the fear and sadness, and soldiered on. Now that I've opened that Pandora's box of emotion, I have no idea if I'll be able to close it again.

The next morning, I wake early, gritty-eyed and freezing. The thermometer outside reads ten below zero, and it feels it, even with the triple layers I'm wearing; I can see my breath as I throw on another sweater. I stoke the fire and have just pulled on my coat and boots to head outside to fetch water when, to my surprise, I hear the creak of the deck steps and then the door, and Kevin is coming in with two brimming buckets.

"Th-thank you," I stammer in my surprise. He gives me one of his nods. "You didn't have to," I add, as he dumps the buckets into the barrel in the corner of the kitchen.

"I don't mind helping."

"You could stay," I blurt, because he's obviously so helpful, and we could use someone like him here. A lot.

He stills, saying nothing, and I feel like I've crossed a boundary, like I've suggested something rude. Then he takes the empty buckets and heads outside again, all without saying a word.

After breakfast, Kevin checks our rabbit snares, which have not caught a single rabbit, and shows us how we've been doing them wrong, tying a neater loop, setting them in better places. After that, he chops a hole in the ice in the middle of the lake—which is no mean feat, since it's over a foot thick—and explains, in his low, calm voice, using as few words as possible, how to fashion a tip-up ice trap with some wood and wire from my dad's cupboard, to catch trout.

"Use live bait and fish near the surface," he tells us. "Trout don't go too deep."

He even takes a look in our greenhouse, offers Ruby a few words of praise, telling her it looks like she has about sixty more days before the potatoes can be harvested. He also gives some advice to Mattie and Kyle about how to make it warmer—if we have any bubble wrap lying around, we can insulate the windows, and if we raise the beds a few inches off the ground they won't be subject to frost.

"Ventilation isn't a problem, at least," he says with one of his faint smiles; the greenhouse isn't well enough constructed.

All in all, Trapper Kevin feels like a gift from providence, a miracle heaven-sent and so desperately needed, teaching us so much in so little time. In his calm, quick actions, I see possibility; I see a future. If we fish, and trap, and plant in the spring, we can have enough food to survive. Just. Maybe.

And that's enough hope to keep me going, at least for now, despite the grief that still weighs me down like an anchor, steadying me and reminding me of who I am, yet still an unbearable weight.

Kevin leaves after lunch; I don't think he's said more than a hundred words the whole time he's been here, and yet I'm so thankful for what he has done. I considered asking him to stay again, but the absolute solitariness of him kept me from really even considering such a possibility.

And yet, as he leaves with a nod of farewell for Kerry and me—the girls are in the greenhouse and Kyle is inside—I see the look of naked grief pass across Kerry's face like a shadow, and I ache for her. She went to find Kevin as much for herself as for the beaver, if not more so; as he walks through the trees, I can see she's grieving not just the loss of the man himself, but the hope and possibility he presented—a partner, a family, a *life*, even in the midst of the hopeless scratching of our existence.

It's hard not to hope for more, even in the midst of so much difficulty; just as I hope Daniel and Sam will return, Kerry has hoped for this. And as Kevin disappears between the trees, back to his cabin, I see something harden in her face and I know that hope has died.

"Will he come back?" I ask quietly, and she shakes her head.

"No." She sounds so definitive, I wonder what they talked about last night, what promises he didn't make. I don't feel I can ask.

With a sigh, Kerry turns back to the cottage. "I knew he wouldn't," she says wearily. "So more fool me, eh?"

Did she ask him to? I wonder. Again, I don't press. "I'm sorry," I say instead, and she simply shakes her head.

As we head inside, a sudden, jagged cry splits the air and we both freeze.

"*What—*" The word comes out of me in a breath.

Then we hear Mattie's voice, high and panicked, caught between a screech and a sob. "*Mom!* Help me!"

TWENTY-TWO

The first thing I see is blood—so much blood, spurting up and dripping down, bright, bright red. Then I see the broken glass of the greenhouse, an entire pane nothing but jagged shards, and Ruby clutching her arm, her face pale, her body swaying. Before either Kerry or I have made it into the greenhouse, she crumples to the ground. Mattie's hands are pressed to her face as she looks down at her sister in a kind of dazed terror.

"What happened?" I demand. I kneel next to Ruby, turn her over and then blanch. There is a huge, jagged laceration on her arm. There is even more blood than I thought—it's soaking into the ground, into my jeans. My fingers are already smeared with it.

"She—she fell," Mattie whispers hoarsely. "Into the glass."

"We need to make a tourniquet." Kerry's voice is low and authoritative, urgent. "We need a scarf or something. Quick!"

"I'll get one," Mattie says, and starts sprinting away.

I cradle my daughter while blood continues to spurt out of her, feeling numb, sick, and utterly terrified. This is the kind of emergency I've been dreading, that I've been waiting for, knowing it could be the end of us. It could be the end of *Ruby*.

"What do we do?" I whisper to Kerry. I have no idea. I can't think; I can barely form sentences.

"I think she may have cut an artery." Kerry's voice is calm, but with a tremor in it. "We need to apply pressure, get the artery against the—the bone, I think, to help staunch the bleeding."

"Okay." I'm doing my best to stay calm, even though my brain is buzzing, and my tongue is thick in my mouth. I can't pass out now, I tell myself. Where is my maternal fortitude? Isn't it meant to kick in, in moments like these, a mother's instinct for survival, for her *child's* survival?

Mattie comes back with the scarf, an old woolen one that my mother made, in bright green cable knit.

Kerry takes it and makes the tourniquet on Ruby's upper arm, pulling it tightly and then bending her arm and bringing it close to her chest. Mattie has found an old sheet and is wrapping it around her arm to staunch the blood. I'm simply holding my daughter, willing her not to bleed out. We are all silent, unbearably tense, as the minutes tick by and Ruby bleeds bright red through the sheet.

"I think... I think it's slowing down," Mattie says in a low, trembling voice. Ruby lolls lifelessly, her face deathly pale, her eyes not even fluttering, but at least she's breathing. She's alive.

"Let's carry her inside," Kerry says. "Get her warmed up."

Gently, as if we are holding a priceless treasure—and we *are* —we carry her into the cottage and lay her on the sofa. Kyle comes in from his room, clearly oblivious, then does a double take when he sees Ruby lying there, so pale and still.

"What... what happened?" he asks, looking almost as if he might cry.

"She fell into the greenhouse window," I tell him. My lips feel numb, and my brain is still buzzing. The bleeding has slowed down, at least, but I have no idea what to do next, and there are no first aid books that I can find; this is where our sustainable living bible lets us down. It doesn't tell us what to do when things go so very wrong.

"She'll need to be stitched," Kerry states matter-of-factly. She looks at me as she says it.

"I..." If I couldn't cut up a beaver, I certainly can't stitch the gaping wound in my daughter's arm. And yet who else is going to do it? I can't let myself fail her. I won't.

"I'll help," Kerry tells me, a promise. Her voice is steady and strong. "We'll need needle and thread. We can sterilize the needle in white spirit, if we have any left."

I think of the bottle we took from Kerry's uncle's garage, what feels like a lifetime ago. I didn't know what it was used for. I could have never imagined this.

"I'll get it," Mattie says, and hurries off, while Kyle gazes down at Ruby, his face crumpled with worry.

"Is she going to be okay?"

"Yes, but we'll need some more bandages," Kerry tells him. "Can you cut a sheet into strips, Kyle?" He nods, and she turns back to me. "You can do this," she says quietly. "I know you can."

I nod mechanically. There's no Trapper Kevin for this. "Okay," I say. "Yes." I can do this. I have to do this. I *will* do it.

The next few minutes, or maybe even hours, pass in a dazed blur. Ruby stirs, moaning, and Kerry gives her a sip of brandy— also from her uncle's house—in the hopes it will calm her, but she sputters and chokes.

Kyle ends up having to hold her shoulders down to keep her still while she passes in and out of consciousness, and Mattie hands me the sterilized needle and thread. I take it with numb fingers; my whole body feels both wired and weird. There is a distinct possibility I might pass out or throw up or even both.

"You know how to sew, right?" Kerry asks, and a wobbly sound escapes me.

"Sort of." I've never been the craftiest of people; I think the last time I sewed a button was in seventh grade Home Ec.

Piercing my daughter's flesh with a needle, I discover, is far worse than cutting open a beaver with a knife. The sight of her jagged wound, the oozing blood, the striated layers of muscles that are visible, is so much worse than the beaver's body being cut into steak-sized pieces. I feel as if I'm hurting her, but even worse than that is the fear I won't be able to save her. What if she loses too much blood? There are no transfusions out here. No antibiotics, no IV drips, no X-rays or doctors to tell me what to do.

Yet somehow, I do it. I feel disembodied, as if I'm watching myself from afar. The first time the needle goes through, Ruby moans and starts to writhe, and I falter.

"Keep going," Kerry instructs me, holding my daughter's shoulders still.

"You can do it, Mom," Mattie whispers. Her face is almost as pale as Ruby's.

And so, somehow, I do. The stitches are lumpy and uneven, probably just about the worst patch-up job that's ever been done in the history of medicine, but they're close enough that the whole thing holds together, just. I tie it off with a shaky bow —thirty-two lumpen stitches—as my breath escapes me in a shaky rush. Kerry wraps Ruby's arm in the strips of sheet while I collapse back into a chair, my whole body shaking in the aftermath, fear coursing through me. Mattie gives me a quick, tight hug.

"Is she going to be okay?" she asks, her voice a desperate murmur against my shoulder.

"Yes, she's going to be fine," I tell my daughter. I know no such thing.

. . .

Kerry and I take turns staying up with Ruby all that night. Mostly she sleeps, and we've bandaged her arm in a makeshift sling to keep her from moving it too much and opening the wound.

Several hours before dawn, when the world is quiet and unrelentingly dark, the despair creeps in.

"I always knew something like this would happen," I tell Kerry in a low voice. Ruby is sleeping on the sofa, and I'm sitting on the other one, aching with tiredness yet utterly awake. "It just takes one thing, one little thing, to send us all plunging off the cliff."

"I know," Kerry replies simply, no prevarication, none of her usual wryly macabre humor, that hint of levity that I pretend to be appalled by but now realize I secretly need. "But it could have been worse."

"This time," I tell her, and she nods in agreement.

"Yes. This time."

We stare at each other, both of us weary and resigned, knowing there is nothing else to be said. Worse, there is nothing else to do, but keep on. And on. And on. Until what end? The determination I felt a few months ago, that in a little while—however long that turned out to be—the world would right itself, has seeped away in light of this fresh disaster. It is February, and, as far as I know, nothing has changed. If the government hasn't established order by now, will they ever? We haven't left the cottage to know if gangs are still roving about, barricading bridges and buildings, terrorizing women and children. I'm not about to try to find out.

Despite what Kerry has said, this time it *does* get worse. Two days after the accident, when it seems as if the wound is actually healing, the stitches holding together, Ruby develops a fever. I press my hand against her hot forehead and try not to worry. She stares up at me miserably, her gaze unfocused, before she drifts into a restless sleep.

When she wakes up again, she seems disorientated, flailing about before going absolutely still.

"Ruby..." I touch her shoulder, and she shrugs off my hands.

"Where's Daddy?"

"He's coming back, sweetheart, remember?" My voice trembles. "He went to get Sam."

"Do I have to go to school today?" she asks, and I stare at her, realizing she must be delirious. *It happens with fevers*, I tell myself. The fever will break, and she'll get better.

But what happens is her skin turns clammy and cold, tinged with gray, and beaded with sweat. The wound site turns an angry, inflamed red, worse than it was at the beginning. Then red streaks shoot across her skin like livid fireworks. I know what this is, and it terrifies me. Mattie hovers over her, her eyes wide and shocked.

"What's going on?" She almost sounds angry. "Why isn't she getting better?"

"I think..." I have to swallow hard. "I think her wound might have become septic."

"Septic?" Mattie swings around to glare at me, her expression one of accusation. "What does that mean?"

"It means her blood has become infected." Is it really such a surprise? We are so far from the sterile conditions of a hospital. "We need to give her antibiotics."

Mattie's lower lip trembles and she bites it hard. "But we don't have any."

"Then we'll have to get some," I reply, except I have no idea how.

Kerry and I huddle in the kitchen, while Mattie watches Ruby, to discuss our options. Outside it's already getting dark, colder than ever, with that metallic tinge to the air that promises yet more snow. I feel calm in a disconnected sort of way; my absolute and only focus is getting medicine for my daughter. Saving her life because I know that's what is at stake now. People with sepsis, left untreated, can die in hours. You read it in the news, you hear the tragic stories. *If only they'd caught it sooner…*

"The hospitals will have been cleared out of medicine, I'm sure of it," Kerry says, staring out at the dark night. "The pharmacies too."

"Where else then?" My mind is racing, but it has nowhere to go. I have no idea how to get antibiotics. "Do you know anyone who might have some? A nurse, a doctor—?" She doesn't reply and I grab her shoulder. "*Kerry*. Do you?"

"Alex, I'm *thinking*." She presses her hands to her cheeks, her eyes closed. "My mom had a home care nurse. Justine. She brought her her prescriptions, checked her out when she wasn't well enough to go out. She lives in Eagle Rapids. She might…" She sounds doubtful, but it's the only hope we have now.

"That's about five miles past Flintville, right?"

Kerry nods. "About that."

"Would she really have them?" I struggle between desperate hope and terrified doubt; we can't afford to go on a fool's errand, to make a single mistake. Time is not on our side. "If she's only a nurse? She couldn't prescribe anything, could she—"

"She delivered stuff, she had some access." Kerry drops her hand to look at me bleakly. "I can't think of anything else, Alex. I'm sorry."

I can't, either. I nod my acceptance. "You know where she lives?"

Kerry silently nods back.

We leave just ten minutes later, on the four-wheeler because the driveway hasn't been plowed—something we decided on to discourage any interlopers, back when we didn't want people finding us; we never thought about needing to get out. Mattie clings to me before we leave, uncharacteristically tearful.

"You'll get the antibiotics?"

"Yes," I tell her, my voice blazing certainty I don't feel.

She throws her arms around me, pressing into me. "It was my fault," she whispers, so only I can hear.

My arms close around her automatically, hold her close. "What...?"

"My fault. We were arguing. It was so *stupid*. She was saying the greenhouse was hers, and I said it belonged to both of us." She sniffs, the sound close to a sob. "I pushed her, and she fell through the glass. It's all my fault." As Mattie sobs into me, I pat her back, murmuring soothing words, my mind whirling. I don't have time to assuage her guilt; I need to get going.

"It's okay, Mattie," I tell her, giving her one last hug. "It's okay, I promise."

She steps back, sniffing. "Are you mad at me?"

"No, sweetheart. Of course not. It was an accident." Besides, I don't have it in me to think about anything other than getting Ruby what she needs. "I'm not mad, I promise. But we need to go."

A minute later, we are on the four-wheeler, plowing through the heavy, wet snow, Kerry clinging to my back. The wind is cutting, making my eyes water and my cheeks sting, even though I'm wearing a pair of old ski goggles and a woolen hat—another of my mother's knitted creations—pulled down as low as it can go. The temperature is hovering around ten degrees. It's about fifteen miles to Eagle Rapids, and the four-wheeler doesn't go much above thirty miles an hour, and that's in decent conditions—not on a cold, snowy night. That's a long time to be freezing more than half to death.

I don't want to die out here. Kerry doesn't either, based on the way she's burrowing into me.

"Damn, but it's cold," she says, her voice whipped away by the wind.

As I pull out onto the main road, my heart gives a little lurch. I haven't left the property since that terrible trip to Corville, over two months ago now. I have no idea what the world is like anymore; I don't *want* to know. And I don't really find out, as we head west, toward Flintville. The fields are covered in snow and the sky is stretched out above like an endless black canvas, glittering with the first few stars. The scattered farmhouses along the road between here and Flintville look dark, maybe even empty, an abandoned feel to just about everything. It could be any peaceful night in winter, except I'm driving a four-wheeler in the freezing dark, and my daughter might be dying.

We make it to Flintville without seeing a soul but, at its one intersection, a truck on monster wheels roars up to the shuttered gas station and Kerry leans over me to jerk the handlebars hard, so we run right into a ditch.

A startled groan escapes me as we plow straight into the snow, flipping the quad over and landing flat on our backs. I stare up at the sky, completely winded, as the four-wheeler's engine sputters and dies, plunging the world into sudden stillness.

"Don't move," Kerry whispers. "Don't say a word."

I'm still too winded to do either; it all happened so suddenly, I can't believe I haven't broken my neck. Kerry slithers on her stomach to the top of the ditch, peeking out over its edge. I manage to rise onto my elbows.

"What..." I whisper, barely a breath of sound.

"*Ssh.*" She turns to give me a fierce glare. I fall silent.

The night is perfectly still, with that eerie, wintry silence that only comes from a heavy blanket of snow, like the Earth itself is holding its breath. But it *isn't* silent, I realize; in the distance, I hear the crunch of boots on snow, low voices, a sudden, harsh-sounding laugh. My whole body tenses.

Our one rifle is strapped to my chest, and I've become a better shot over the last two months, but I know without even looking at them that I'm no match for those guys out there.

I peek over the top of the ditch to survey the scene and a startled gasp escapes me. Kerry presses hard on my shoulder, and I slither back down.

"The truck," I whisper. "It's my dad's."

She stares at me for a long, tense moment. "The same guys?" she whispers.

"I don't know. They've changed the wheels, but it's my dad's truck. I saw the bumper sticker on the back." *Honk if you love Jesus.* My stomach feels as if it is shriveling inside me, everything curling up in despair. How are we going to get past them? And why on earth are they out here?

What if they're already looking for us?

And yet we have to keep moving; we *have* to get to this nurse, if she's even where Kerry thinks she is. Maybe she's moved on; maybe she's dead. Maybe she's there, but she doesn't have any antibiotics. The sheer futility of everything swamps me, again, and I decide I'm not taking it lying down, which is what I'm literally doing.

"Let's go," I say, rising back up onto my elbows.

Kerry gives me an incredulous look. "Are you insane?"

"No, but my daughter is septic, and she will most likely die in a couple of hours. I don't *care* about these guys."

She shakes her head. "Alex, remember when I said about getting raped and killed by some backwoods guys?"

"Yeah," I hiss back, "extras from *Deliverance.* I remember."

She leans toward me. "That is *this* situation. Remember what almost happened in Corville? You go out on there on your four-wheeler, you might as well be riding a tricycle. They'll mow you down in *seconds*. And I hate to think what they'll do to you then."

"What if they stay there for hours?" I counter. "They might as well kill Ruby themselves."

"Then you have to think of Mattie," Kerry replies. "Getting killed yourself won't help her, you know. Ruby might be... past saving, but Mattie isn't." She stares at me steadily, and I have an urge to slap her face, to scream. I am *not* giving up on my daughter.

"I'm going," I state flatly, and I can tell Kerry doesn't believe me. "I mean it. I'll go cross country. They can't follow us through a field, right, even with those wheels?" I point to the farm fields stretching out on either side of the street. "That's the way to Eagle Rapids, isn't it?"

"Yes, but..." Kerry looks sympathetic but also reluctantly admiring of my reckless courage, or maybe my stupidity. "They'll just cut you off at the road, Alex. They'll wait till you come out by the bridge—"

The narrow, one-lane bridge spanning the Madawaska River. Eagle Rapids is maybe four miles past it. "Then I won't come out by the bridge."

"You'll have to."

"No," I tell her, "I won't. The river's frozen, isn't it? I'll just drive across."

Kerry's eyes widen; she hadn't considered this. "I don't know if it will be thick enough to hold a bike. Rivers don't freeze the way lakes do—"

"We'll find a place where it is."

"And then there's the bank. It's really steep—"

"I can make it down the bank. They can't, though." I sound far firmer than I feel, but I am that determined. "Kerry, my daughter is *dying*."

"Okay." She nods slowly, looking accepting, resigned. We

both know how unlikely it is that any of this will ever work. "Okay, let's do it."

As quietly as we can, we right the bike. We push it along the bottom of the ditch until we are behind the cover of some trees, and then together we heave it up the ditch's bank. We're a couple of hundred yards from the gas station, where the guys are still parked. They're strolling around like they own the place, and maybe they do. I can see their guns glinting in the moonlight from here; they've got several each, and knives, too, handles gleaming. I think I recognize one of the men—the crumpled red baseball cap, the plaid woolen jacket. He was the one who tried to rape me.

I glance at Kerry; her face is taut and pale, and she nods. I get on the bike, Kerry behind me. As soon as I start it up, I know, the guys will notice. They didn't hear us before because they were in the truck, but it's completely silent now; if one of us so much as coughed, they'd probably hear that too.

"Gun it straight across the road," Kerry whispers, so close to my ear that her lips brush my lobe. "And then through the field. Cut to the right as much as you can, to give us some distance. If you hit a fence, you'll have to drive alongside it until you come to a gate." She expels a shaky breath, right into my ear. "Honestly, Alex, I don't know if we're going to make it. If we don't..."

I can't think of what those men might do to us if they catch us. "If we don't, you can shoot me," I state without a single tremor in my voice. "And then shoot yourself... if you want to."

"Blowing my head off with a .22 rifle? Wow." She laughs softly, and improbably, I find myself smiling. "What a way to go. I'm not even sure it would kill me."

"Well, it would sting a bit," I reply, and she gives another soft laugh. I downshift into neutral, my thumb on the accelerator. My heart is thundering in my chest, and yet at the same time I feel weirdly, almost supernaturally calm. I take a deep breath and Kerry tightens her arms, wrapped around my waist.

Then I gun it.

The bike shoots out of the ditch, across the road, the world around us streaming by in a freezing blur. I think I hear shouts, but I'm not sure. I drive straight across, into the field; we hit a rock almost right away and nearly catapult off, but somehow, we manage to hold on and keep going. The engine whines in protest and I kick up a gear, snow flying up, stinging my face even though it's covered by the goggles and scarf.

The snow has a hardened crust, which, if we go fast enough, means we won't get stuck; but if the wheels sink too much, it will be slow going indeed. Kerry glances behind us and swears under her breath.

"They're in the truck, following us along the road."

I veer right, deeper into the field. The wheels are sinking, the engine groaning, but we're moving, at least. It's a clear view from us to the truck, and I can see their headlights in my peripheral vision, a menacing sweep of blazing white. I'm trying to focus on the field in front of me when a scream escapes Kerry as we hear the crack of a gunshot.

"They didn't hit me," Kerry shouts into my ear. "You?"

"No." At least I can't feel anything.

Another shot rings out. Kerry clings to my back. "Make for the trees, for the love of God, Alex!"

There is a fringe of pine trees separating the fields, and I drive toward it, while the guys in the truck shoot at us twice more. I don't know how close the bullets come, but there is a prickling in the center of my back; I'm bracing myself to be hit, to be killed. I don't know if I'm imagining their cackling laughter; I think I must be, from this distance, but I hear it echo in my ears all the same.

I drive along the fringe of trees until the next field; by this time, we are far away enough from the road that they can't get a clear shot. My breath is coming in ragged gasps, and so is Kerry's, and the quad bike sounds like it's gasping for air as well.

"I can't see them," Kerry says, as we clear the trees, and I cut the engine, just so I can take a breath. In the sudden stillness, we strain to hear the truck, and, after a few seconds, we do, a distant, menacing, gravelly purr.

"They're heading to the bridge," Kerry says dully. "I knew it."

"We'll go farther up then," I reply staunchly.

"They'll be listening for us—"

"This is our only chance, Kerry. We have to try to get across." I pause, knowing it's not fair to take her on this wild ride, a veritable suicide mission. "But if you want to get off here," I tell her, "walk back to the cottage, I'd understand." I twist around to face her. "I really would, absolutely. Just tell me how to find this nurse's house first."

Kerry stares at me for a second; in the darkness, I can't make out her expression. "After everything we've been through, Alex... all these months..." She pauses. "Do you really think I'd do that?" Her voice is caught between curiosity and hurt.

I'm touched, and I almost feel guilty for having asked the question at all. "Don't you think I have a duty to give you the choice?" I ask her.

She sighs and shakes her head, and in the glint of moonlight I see a small, sad smile quirk the corner of her mouth. "Start up the bike, Alex."

TWENTY-THREE

We drive for twenty minutes through the freezing dark, bumping through the snow, my fingers numb and aching in my gloves, curled around the handlebars. When we come out to the road, it's at least a quarter-mile past the bridge, and we'll have to double back to head to Eagle Rapids, which will add another twenty minutes, at least.

I cut the engine, and we stare at the darkened river in front of us, the road we need to travel down on the other side. The river is covered with snow; it *looks* frozen, but will it hold a four-wheeler? According to Kevin, the ice needs to be six inches thick for a person to walk on, seven or eight for a quad bike and a few inches more for a car. Is the ice that thick? It's nearly March; winter is on the wane. It's impossible to know if it will hold us.

And then, beyond the danger of the river, there's the bank on the other side; it's steep, practically a ninety-degree incline. If we manage to make it across, by the time we manage to get up it, *if* we get up it, the truck could be upon us.

"This is not looking good," Kerry says.

It's not feeling good either—there is nothing but one obstacle after another, with no relief, no respite, and we don't even know if we'll find this nurse or if she'll have antibiotics. I take a deep breath and press the gas.

We careen down the bank so fast I don't even have to touch the accelerator, and then we shoot across the river, so I don't think we'd have time for the ice to crack. In the distance I think I hear a shout, the sound of an engine starting up. Then it's up the bank, pushing as hard on the accelerator as I can, my thumb throbbing with the effort, everything straining, but, after just a few seconds, I can feel that we aren't going to make it. It's simply too steep. The engine hits a high-pitched whine, and we start sliding down, and Kerry and I both realize at the same time what is going to happen—the bike is going to flip over right on top of us. We simultaneously fling ourselves off, into the snow, and the quad rolls down the bank, handlebars over wheels, back to the river, where it sputters to a stop, lying on its side.

We're both breathing hard, bruised and shaken, and in the distance, we can hear the roar of the truck, coming for us.

"Leave the bike," Kerry whispers. "We'll have to go by foot. It's the only way."

So once again we'll be stranded. I know she's right, but I don't want to leave our only mode of transportation behind, *again*. I don't want to be so vulnerable, out here alone in the snow and the dark, with these evil predators searching for us. As quietly as I can, I crawl on my hands and knees to where the bike is resting, and then I reach over and take the key out of the ignition. I crawl back to Kerry, and we start to head along the river, back toward the bridge, pressing close to the bottom of the bank, while the truck roars above us and then slows, the engine idling right above our heads.

"Come on, now, little ladies," one of the guys calls, his voice sounding slurred. They're all probably drunk or drugged up or both. "We know you're down there. Don't be shy with us." Another one laughs, the ugly sound making the hairs on the nape of my neck prickle. We both know what these men are capable of.

I glance at Kerry, who makes a gagging face, and once again, utterly improbably, I almost laugh. I'm beyond terror now, I realize; I have the same disembodied sense I had when I was stitching up Ruby, only even more so. It's like I'm watching an action movie, and part of me is sitting on a sofa somewhere, wondering at what point I should go make the popcorn. Maybe that's the only way to get through this.

We continue to edge our way along the river, toward the bridge and Eagle Rapids, while the truck stays parked above. The men have climbed out of it; I can hear them walking around, their murmuring voices, the occasional hard laugh, but I don't know which direction they're heading. I don't think any of them wants to risk scrambling down the bank, but if they see us, they might take a shot, just because. We keep inching along, trying to be as quiet as possible.

"The ice is going to break up as we head toward the rapids," Kerry says in a low voice. "At some point we've got to get up the bank before we fall in."

"We'll do it when we're clear."

"And when will that be?" she asks dryly. "If ever?"

We haven't heard the guys for a few minutes; we might have left them behind. I can hope, anyway. "The truck hasn't moved," I tell Kerry, "and I don't think they can see us down here. They don't know which way we're going."

"They might come down and get the quad."

"They might."

We keep walking.

Another few minutes pass as we inch along and then, in the distance, we hear the truck start up. In the darkness, Kerry and I exchange a fathomless look and press up against the bank. The truck rumbles above our heads, and then drives on. I slowly let out the breath I hadn't realized I was holding. Are we safe, relatively speaking?

We remain still and tense for another minute, waiting for the sound of the truck to completely recede, and then I turn to Kerry.

"Let's go back and get the bike."

She shakes her head. "We won't be able to get it up the bank, Alex."

"We could try. We could pull it, maybe, or find a place where it's not so steep."

In reply, she simply glances up and down the river, where the bank is just as steep.

"Kerry, we're ten miles from the cottage. We don't even know if this Justine will be where you think she is. We don't have time to walk all this way. We need to try."

Kerry lets out a weary sigh. "I don't know why I let you convince me of these things," she says, shaking her head, as she heads back the way we came.

It takes fifteen minutes of trudging through the snow to get back to the bike. As Kerry goes forward to right it, a figure suddenly straightens from behind the quad. It's one of the guys from the truck—craggy-faced, squinty-eyed, holding a rifle, which he points right at Kerry. I don't recognize him, but I know what kind of man he is.

"Well, hello there, missy," he says. "We thought you might be back."

Kerry freezes; in the darkness, the guy hasn't seen me yet, standing about fifteen feet away. His rifle doesn't waver.

"Aren't you a pretty thing," he tells Kerry.

"In your dreams, Grandpa," she replies in a bored voice.

Fury flashes across his face. "You want to be nice to me," he warns her. "I'm the best of the bunch." And then he lets out a laugh that gives me the noise cover to unstrap the rifle from my chest. My fingers don't shake at all as I take aim. The man reaches for Kerry. I pull the trigger.

The crack sounds abnormally loud, echoing up and down the river, as the man freezes for a moment, looking stunned, and then falls backward, the rifle dropping from his hands.

Kerry spins toward me, looking about as stunned as he did. "I can't believe it," she says in an awed voice. "Alex, I think you killed him." I can't tell if she's horrified or impressed: maybe both.

I lower the rifle; my hands aren't shaking at all, and I feel strangely empty inside. I'm not sorry at all. "Get his gun," I tell Kerry. "And anything else he has."

Shaking her head slowly, she strips the guy of his weapons. It's very clear he's dead, and I try not to look at him. I still feel calm, but the shock and horror are there under the surface, the surging water under the black ice. I right the quad as Kerry slips on his coat, straps his gun across her chest.

"There's nothing else," she says, and in silence we get on the bike. I put the key in the ignition and then we are heading down the river, back toward the bridge.

It's clear after just a few minutes that we need to get off the river as soon as possible because the ice will start breaking up. The snow is soft in spots, and ahead are the rapids. I think of the churning water we saw in Corville just a few months ago, the chunks of ice bobbing in its frigid depths.

"Here," Kerry says, pointing to a place where the bank has a gentler incline, although it's still ridiculously steep. Silently, working in fluid synchronicity, we stand on either side of the quad and begin to push it up the bank. Our legs sink into the snow up to our knees as we heave and push, strain and pray, to absolutely no avail. Even with the two of us, we're not strong enough to do it.

Then Kerry loses her footing, and I can't hold the quad on my own. I fling myself out of the way as it rolls back toward the river, and we simply watch it go, too dispirited and exhausted to try to save it. A few seconds later, we hear a crack like a gunshot; we think it *is* a gunshot, and we both startle and jerk around, looking for our attacker. But our enemy now is the ice— the cracking sound was it breaking up, and we watch in silence as the ice begins to crack, and the bike begins to list. For a few seconds, it simply rests there, at a tilted angle like the *Titanic*, and then, slowly, it starts to sink. In about thirty seconds, it is gone.

"Well," Kerry says after a moment. "Good thing we weren't on it."

I find I can't reply. I'm numb and so very weary; there are too many things I can't think about, to process, to accept. My daughter, who might already be dead. The man I killed. The fact that our situation has never seemed more hopeless.

"Let's keep going," I say, and we scramble up the bank on our hands and knees.

The road is empty and silent, but we still keep to the trees as much as we can as we begin the four-mile walk toward Eagle Rapids. Above us the sky is scattered with stars and the night is still and clear; in another universe, in the life I used to take for granted, I would stand still for a moment and tilt my head toward the sky, breathe in the cold air and let my lungs and soul expand. The way I did the first night we arrived at the cottage, when I was so determined to believe we could have a fresh start, and yet already feeling so jaded.

Or at least I thought I was jaded. It was nothing to what I feel now, and yet in the midst of the cynicism and the weariness, there is a strength of conviction like a pillar of flame. I am *not* giving up. Not now, not ever.

We don't encounter anyone on that walk; we don't even hear the distant thrum of a motor, thankfully. We don't speak; we just trudge through the snow, putting one foot in front of the other.

By the time we reach Eagle Rapids, it is well after midnight and my feet and hands are numb. We look around the shuttered houses, half of them deserted; both the gas station and the tiny Food Mart are, of course, looted and empty.

"Do you know where Justine lives?" I ask Kerry.

She hesitates, peering around in the dark. "I picked up a prescription from her once... I think it was past the gas station, on the right."

She *thinks?* More and more I'm afraid this was a fool's errand, and the costliest one I could ever imagine. I don't say as much, though; I simply follow Kerry down the street, keeping to the shadows.

There are three shabby-looking ranch houses in a row, made of either clapboard or concrete, all of them looking dilapidated and forgotten and very unlived in. The hope I've been clinging to, as stubborn as a weed, wilts at its root. Surely, Justine can't still be here.

"The middle one, I think," Kerry says, sounding uncertain. The house is dark, the windows boarded up, but I don't suppose that actually means anything, these days.

"All right," I tell her, straightening and starting toward the door. "Let's do this."

No one answers my quiet knock, which I'd expect, and I can't peer in the windows, since they're boarded up from the inside. I don't want to draw attention to myself, but I need to be heard. I walk around the back, looking for signs of life, any evidence that someone still lives here. And then I find it, in the yard, under a tree. A snowman—crooked, lumpen, with twigs for arms and a stone for a nose, pebbles for a mouth and eyes, standing lopsided, protected by the spreading branches of an evergreen.

I stare at it for a moment, with its rictus smile and black, staring eyes, and it feels like both the saddest and most hopeful thing I've seen in a long time. I whirl toward the back door, and this time I hammer on it.

"Please. If you're in there, Justine, can you open the door? I'm a friend of Darlene Wasik's and my little girl needs antibiotics. She's got a wound that's gone septic—she'll die without them. *Please.* Darlene's daughter Kerry is here with me—she knows you. Please. Please." Eventually, I run out of words. No one stirs in the house. I think about breaking a window.

Then, amazingly, I see a face at the window—a woman has pushed aside one of the boards a few inches and she stands there, unsmiling. Her dark hair is pulled back in a braid, and she's staring at me with pitiless eyes. She's also holding a gun—not just an old .22 or .303 hunting rifle like I have, but a proper gun, something that shoots about a hundred rounds a minute. It looks like something a SWAT team would have, and I know by the grim set of her face that she means business.

"Please," I mouth, and wait.

She moves away from the window, and a few seconds later, she opens the door, that fearsome gun pointed right at me. Strangely, I don't feel any fear.

"You're not from around here," she says, and I shake my head.

"My parents had the cottage on Lost Lake."

She nods; she knows it. "You're holing up there?"

"Yes."

Another nod and then she gestures toward the door. "Get inside."

Kerry and I come in without a word.

I blink in the darkness; the place is tiny, and completely

dark with all the windows boarded. It's also set up like a battle-field—furniture tilted on its sides, for cover, I presume. I feel a shudder of apprehension, the first true emotion I've felt since I shot that man.

"Let's go down to the basement," the woman—I'm assuming she's Justine—says. She triple-locks the back door and then we head down to the cellar, which is a space of about twelve feet by twelve, and is clearly where she lives. There is a little girl of about three years old asleep on a nest of blankets in the corner. There is also an arsenal of weaponry stacked against one wall that rivals anything I've seen so far.

"My brother's," Justine explains briefly when she catches me staring. "He loved guns. Was waiting for a chance to use them. He killed himself the day after the first strikes."

I have no idea what to say to that. "Do you have antibi-otics?" I ask, and she stares at me levelly.

"Why should I give them to you?"

"Because my daughter will die without them." I mean to make it a statement, but it comes out like a question, a plea. In this new, cruel world we live in, why should this woman care about a stranger like me?

I glance at Kerry, who shrugs. There's not much we can do. Justine has the medicine—I think—and the weapons. We're at her mercy in more ways than one.

"I'll give them to you," Justine announces abruptly, "if you take me with you."

I stare at her, shocked. "You mean—"

"To Lost Lake. I've heard about that place. Darlene used to tell me about it. Private, its own lake, its own land. You could be safe there."

"What's it been like here?" Kerry asks quietly.

Justine gives her one skewering glance. "Bad. I don't know how much longer we can hold out. There's too many of them."

"The guys in the truck?" Kerry guesses, and Justine nods.

"They control the whole area. They've tried to break in four times. I've killed one of them, which makes them out for blood even more. The woman in the house across from me was raped and killed three days ago. She was sixty-five."

My stomach roils at that thought. I want to help Justine, just as I helped Kerry and Darlene and Kyle. I want to be that altruistic person, but we're on our very last food stores and we already have a lot of mouths to feed.

"How old is your little girl?" Kerry asks, and Justine softens.

"Phoebe. Four next month."

"Okay," I say, the word bursting out of me, because I know I have no choice and, in any case, I can't turn Justine away. How can I consign her child to this while asking her to help mine? "You can come. Both of you. Do you have a car?"

She nods. "A truck. I park it in the woods, about a quarter-mile from here."

Relief fills me, a cold, sweet rush that weakens my knees. We have a truck, we have guns, we have antibiotics.

As long as Ruby is still alive...

"Let's go," I tell her. "We've been away too long already."

It only takes a few minutes to mobilize; Justine gathers up her clothes and Kerry packs the guns and ammo in a duffle bag. There's not much food, just a couple of cans of beans and Chef Boyardee. As we wait by the foot of the stairs, Justine bends down and gently scoops up Phoebe into her arms; the little girl snuggles against her, and I feel an ache of longing like a physical pain for my own daughter.

Then we are slipping out into the night like shadows, like ghosts, and ten minutes later, we find her truck, deep in the woods, covered in brush and snow. We move silently, swiftly, dumping the stuff in the back and then climbing in the cab—a squeeze, with the three of us, Phoebe on Justine's lap. I'm driving, without any discussion about it; I'm not sure when it happened, but over the course of the night, I have become the person in charge. I tried to be it all along, heaven knows, throwing my weight around while leaning on Kerry all the while, but it is only tonight that I *feel* it.

I drive out of the woods and onto the road with steel in my heart.

TWENTY-FOUR

DANIEL

It is May, and the world is full of birdsong and beauty, when Daniel pulls onto the dirt road, the same road he turned into back in November, nearly six months ago, when he could feel the palpable tension between him and Alex in the car, and the thing he was most upset about was the loss of his self-respect.

It has been a long four and a half months since he found Sam. Four and a half months he longs to forget, yet remembers every time he closes his eyes. He's a different man than the one who left here in November, when he was both resolute and resigned, determined to do the right thing. He has seen too much even to know what the right thing is anymore.

He has done too much.

He and Sam are both silent as the wheels of the car—the fourth they've been in since Clarkson—crunch on the dirt road.

Everything is lush and green, the road overgrown with long grass in the middle and washed away by the snows at its edges, so it is a bumpy and uneven journey. It doesn't look as if anyone has been down this road in months, and he does not know whether that's a good or bad sign. He has no idea what—or who—he will find at the cottage. Six months has been a long time—not just for him and Sam, but for Alex. For Mattie and Ruby.

Are they even alive?

Daniel hasn't let himself consider the answer to that question.

The car bumps slowly down the road. Daniel breathes in and out evenly, but he feels as if he's holding his breath. Something in him is suspended—waiting, expectant, utterly apprehensive. He has imagined this moment, the glorious, joyous reunion, for so long that, now that he's on the cusp of it, he feels something close to terror.

They drive in silence.

When they reach the gate to the cottage's road, Daniel breathes in sharply. Sam looks at him in silent question. He doesn't remember the gate, of course. He can barely remember the cottage, beyond a few hazy memories.

But Daniel remembers. He remembers driving down the road, past the old wooden gate, its red paint peeling, just six months ago.

The gate is gone. The road is overgrown, far worse than the main road. The center verge is grassy, the stalks, waving gently in the spring breeze, at least two feet high. The trees and bushes have grown on either side, so the track is half-obscured, branches and leaves brushing the car as they drive up the lane.

Daniel is reminded of Prince Valiant, bravely cutting through the brambles to reach Sleeping Beauty's castle. But the sense of righteous adventure that fairytale prince must have felt is so far from what he feels now, his stomach hollowing out, tears already pricking his eyes. He tells himself that Alex would hardly have made a priority of maintaining the road, that he himself had cut down trees to disguise its use, and yet...

It feels like a harbinger of doom. Of death. Just as the last four months have been.

Next to him, Sam shifts in his seat and says nothing. Daniel glances at his son, the boyish curve of his jaw now hardened and lean. When he'd found him at Clarkson, Sam had been well fed and protected, in the little enclave surrounded by the Marines. If anything, boredom had been his biggest worry; he'd been given three careful meals a day, had been able to exercise on the quad, read books from the library. Order, in this one place at least, had been maintained.

But when the Marines had let his son go, when Daniel had clasped his arms around his form, tears pricking his eyes, unable to believe he'd actually made it... that was when everything had started to go wrong.

They'd made it only as far as Utica before they were stopped by one of the many militias springing up all over the country. Everything they'd had had been taken from them—his gun, his backpack, his money, even his car keys. They'd been left on the side of the road, next to naked, with nothing.

And that had only been the beginning.

Halfway up the road, as they reach the bottom of the hill before the old barn, they see a tree trunk lying across the road, resolutely immovable. It is not one that Daniel cut; Alex must have cut others. They won't be able to get across it. Daniel puts the car into park and slowly gets out; he moves like an old man now, every movement aching and deliberate. After a second, Sam climbs out too.

"Did it fall?" he wonders out loud.

Daniel walks slowly toward the stump on the side of the road. Although someone has done their best to cover it with branches and brush, the tree has been chopped down; the axe marks are fresh. When he touches the stump, his fingers come away with traces of sawdust. It was cut recently.

Silently, Sam walks over to join him. "What...?" he breathes, when he sees the hewn stump.

"It's a decoy," Daniel says quietly. "We cut a few trees before I left, to make outsiders think no one is here. Mom must have cut some more." At least he hopes that's the case. It must be why the gate is gone, the grass grown tall. *It must be.*

For the first time, he feels a wild, drunken lurch of hope.

"We can drive around it," he says, and Sam frowns.

"Can we?"

They do. It isn't easy, lurching through the long grass, half in a ditch, bumping and jostling, wheels spinning for a few seconds, but they do it. They crest the hill by the barn, Daniel swerving around the rock in the road, which is still there and somehow makes him feel almost happy. Some things haven't changed.

In fact, they haven't changed at all—he doesn't swerve far enough, and the rock of pink-flecked granite scrapes the bottom of the car. Sam winces. Daniel actually laughs, the first time in memory.

They keep driving—down the hill, around the bend, the cottage obscured by a stand of birch trees. In November, they'd been bare, but now they are leafy and green, and they hide the view of his home. Of his family.

Then, finally, the cottage comes into view. For a second, Daniel breathes easier. There are signs of life—the stretch of lawn that once served as a badminton court has been turned into a vegetable patch. On the driveway an old stump is being used as a chopping block for splitting wood; a well-worn axe that belonged to his father-in-law rests next to it. He pulls in front of the block, parks the car, and steps out, looking around in surprise and wonder.

He sees a greenhouse, made of what look like old windows, erected by the side of the house to catch the sun, and filled with burgeoning tomato plants; there is, amazingly, what looks like a deer hide pegged to a washing line, to dry. Signs of industry, of invention, are everywhere—another vegetable patch by the old gazebo, and a wooden locker by the porch that Daniel suspects is a *smokehouse*, of all things.

He's amazed, and unbelievably heartened—until a woman comes down the porch steps, holding what looks like a machine gun, aimed unwaveringly straight at his heart.

"Who the hell," she asks in a level voice, "are you?"

Daniel stares at this stranger with a gun as his stomach hollows out once more. "Who the hell are *you*?" he asks in just as level a tone.

"None of your damned business."

"Actually, it is, because this is my house." He stares her down, remarkably unfazed by the gun leveled at him. He's had a lot of guns aimed at him in the last few months. He's aimed a few of his own.

But he can't think about any of that. He won't.

"Where," he asks this woman, this invader, "is my wife?"

"*Daniel!*"

Alex's cry pierces him right through, and Daniel pivots to see her running from the front of the house, stumbling in her haste, her arms outstretched. She looks wonderfully the same and yet impossibly different—her hair is nearly completely gray, her body sinewy and strong, her skin weathered and tanned. She has aged, and yet she also looks younger. He can't make sense of the anomaly as she rushes into his arms, hugs the breath out of him.

"I thought you were dead," she whispers, her lips against his throat.

His arms close around her out of instinct, slowly drawing her to him; he's too dazed to act any faster than that.

"I know," he says quietly. Sometimes, he thought he was dead too. Sometimes, he wanted to be.

"Mom," Sam says softly, and Alex wrenches herself out of Daniel's arms to hurl herself at her son.

"Sam, *Sam*," she cries, weeping openly. Then Mattie and Ruby are running toward them—Ruby has grown three or four inches at least; she has that lovely, gawky coltishness of a young teenager. And Mattie, Daniel thinks in amazement, looks like a woman. There is a hardness in her face, a knowingness, that makes him both sad and thankful.

Then they are all hugging and crying, but after a few seconds, Mattie and Ruby step back, wiping their eyes, and the tears subside. They are all left staring at each other, shaking their heads, with far too many words to say and yet none that can fill the void stretching between them.

"How..." Alex begins, and then shakes her head firmly. She doesn't want to know. Daniel doesn't want to tell her.

"There's someone else here to see you," he says quietly, and then he goes to the back of the car and opens the door.

"Jenny," he says quietly to his mother-in-law, half dozing in the backseat, scrawny and small and almost entirely diminished. "You're home."

Alex lets out a stifled cry, her hands pressed to her cheeks, as she glimpses her mother in the back of the car, blinking dazedly up at her.

"Alex...?" she whispers, her voice little more than a croak, her gaze unfocused and confused.

After they'd been left by the side of the road, they'd found another car, looted an empty house. Daniel had become startlingly indifferent not just to the concept of stealing but the practicalities of it—the breaking of glass, the rifling of possessions. In one house they had broken into, an old woman, alone and unprotected, had cowered in an armchair, her arms flung over her face. Daniel had simply stepped over her to get to the kitchen and see what food she had for him to take.

When had he become that man? Had it been when he'd shot that boy? That had certainly been a turning point, but only one of many.

When they'd finally got to Jenny's nursing home, the place had been abandoned; they had walked through the entry hall, corpses in wheelchairs, the *smell*...

And yet Alex's mother had been alive. Just. She and another woman, Penelope, had been the only surviving residents of the memory care ward; the locked unit had probably been their salvation, hiding them behind high walls, safe from predators. Between them they'd had enough know-how—again, just—to provide for themselves, eking out an existence from what food remained in the nursing home kitchen. Fortunately, there had been enough bottled water for them to survive, although they'd been filthy and dehydrated. When Daniel had stood in front of his mother-in-law, swaying with exhaustion, overwhelmed with emotion and yet at the same time feeling utterly numb, she'd blinked up at him and then given him one of her knowing grins.

"Let me just get my things," she'd stated grandly, as if he were picking her up from a party. Maybe, in the confused corridors of her mind, he was.

He would have laughed if he could have summoned the energy, the emotion, but by then he'd felt as if he'd had nothing inside him, and yet in some ways that had just been the beginning.

They'd taken the other woman, Penelope, with them, as a moral duty, even though his moral standards by then had become questionable indeed. In any case, she'd died before they reached the state border.

But Daniel isn't going to tell Alex any of that now, as she takes her mother into her arms, presses a kiss to her wrinkled forehead.

"You're home, Mom," she whispers, kissing her again. "You're home, you're *home*."

An hour later, Jenny is settled in the guest bedroom, already asleep, and Mattie and Ruby are giving Sam a tour of the place, seeming self-important and excited, but also a little shy around their big brother. He and Alex are not the only ones, Daniel thinks, who will have to get to know each other all over again.

They have walked down to the dock, just the two of them, presumably to talk, although neither of them said as much. It is late afternoon, and the sun is gleaming on the water, burnishing its surface like a gold coin. Daniel has had introductions to the motley crew of residents, although he doesn't know how they came to be there, or why. They both have so much to say, to explain, and yet, in the silence of that mellow, golden afternoon, it seems as if neither of them wants to begin the reckoning.

They sit on the new boards of fresh pine, legs stretched out to the glinting lake. In the distance, a loon skims the water and then takes off, dark wings outstretched, into flight. The serene beauty of it all, after everything he has seen, feels like too heavy a weight to bear. He lets out a choked huff of sound, shaking his head. It is all he can manage.

"I know," Alex says quietly, and for a second, he wonders if she does. "I never expected you to find my mother," she continues after a moment, her tone reflective. "Never, not in a million years." He can't think how to respond. "I shouldn't have asked you to get Sam." Her voice is low, firm.

"I would have gone, anyway."

"Still."

He stares out over the water, squinting in his eyes in the sunlight. He thinks of the man he was, driving down that road, determined not to fail his wife again. That man seems like a naive stranger to him now—pompous in his certainty, in his willingness to sacrifice, without any idea of the true cost. That man had no idea. No idea at all that he would sell his soul, give it away willingly, in tattered pieces, simply to survive. That he would see things, say things, *do* things, he could never have imagined himself doing, over and over again. And that he wouldn't even care. Stealing food from those who needed it.

Ignoring others who begged for help. Killing in cold blood. All without pity, without guilt.

"It doesn't matter now," he says at last, and Alex nods.

"I know, but it still needed to be said."

He glances at her appraisingly; like him, she has changed, but in a different way. She seems settled, stronger, more accepting. There is a calmness at her center, while there is only an emptiness at his. He drove a thousand miles to get back home, and now he wonders if he will ever find his way back to his wife again. If it is even possible.

"You've done a lot here," he remarks, in the tone of someone commenting on a well watered yard. *Nice place you have here.*

"Not just me," Alex replies, but he can see she's bursting with pride. "Everyone has taken part. I couldn't have done this on my own, Daniel, not even a little bit." Her voice is heartfelt, sure. She has relationships with these people, he realizes. These strangers— Kerry, Kyle, the woman who leveled a gun at him and has a child. He can't remember her name. They are important to Alex in a way he can't begin to fathom, not after the last few months.

"How did they all come to be here?" he asks, although he's not sure he has the capacity to listen, to care.

Alex lets out a soft laugh. "It's a long story."

"Yes."

"It didn't happen all at once, but... everyone needed help. And everyone has had something to offer."

How sweet, Daniel thinks, with a sudden burst of savagery. How perfectly Hallmark. She's been taking in strays while he has willfully ignored anyone who might keep him from his purpose. Entirely unexpectedly, he's angry; he's absolutely filled with rage. Alex was playing at happy families while he and Sam were battling their way through hell. He does his best to swallow it down.

Alex reaches over and touches his hand. "I'm not saying it

was easy," she tells him gently, and he wonders how much of his thought process she understood.

"No," he agrees. The rage subsides as fast as it came, a wave receding, leaving him only achingly, unbearably tired. They are both silent, staring out at the water.

"When you're ready," Alex finally says, "can you tell me what it is like out there? If there is... any hope? With the government? Any sense of order?"

Daniel thinks of the man rotting in his wheelchair. The two-year-old standing in the middle of the highway, his dirty face streaked with tears, entirely alone, while Daniel drove by, looking the other way. The empty, abandoned farmhouse in Utica where he once felt at peace, the American flag on its porch post in tatters, a small square of grubby blue blanket, with its worn rabbit's head, the silky ears, lying on the floor, spattered with blood.

"I'll try," he tells Alex, but already he knows he won't. "You haven't had any... trouble?" he asks after a moment, his voice a parody of casual.

Alex is quiet for a moment. "Not recently," she says at last. "We haven't left the property in months. We've done our best to fly under the radar, to act invisible, but there have been dangers. Gangs." She pauses, swallows, and then falls silent, and he wonders what she's choosing not to tell him.

"I saw the tree."

She nods. "It's not much, but we hope it might discourage... people... from exploring. Like you said, hiding is a better strategy than building some big gates or something like that, which would make people wonder what we're trying to protect, and frankly we haven't got the manpower or the weaponry to handle some kind of mass attack."

She speaks so matter-of-factly that for the first time Daniel wonders what she's seen. How arrogant of him, he realizes, to think he has suffered more. And yet he can't shake the feeling that he has, that he *must* have.

She reaches over and touches his hand again. "It's okay now," she says softly, like she's comforting a child, or maybe taming a wild animal. "We're all together again. It's going to be okay."

Daniel stares out at the lake and does not respond.

TWENTY-FIVE

A week after Daniel and Sam have come home, I rise early, boiling water for my cup of morning coffee, enjoying the few moments of stillness. It was Justine who showed us that coffee—or really, a coffee-like drink—could be made from roasting the tiny seeds of sticky weed, known as cleavers; it takes hours to collect enough to roast for a single cup, but it is worth it. The nutty flavor is almost reminiscent of the taste of coffee, a ghostly echo of my Starbucks Americano.

I've enjoyed my quiet mornings, before everyone starts to stir and the day's round of chores begins. Our household has become so full, and our days so busy. With the arrival of Justine and Phoebe, the need to find ways to get more food became increasingly urgent, as our stores were dwindling at an even faster rate. Fortunately, we managed to trap several rabbits and another beaver, along with a passel of fish. Kevin was right; beaver does taste like gamey beef, and you do have to stew it for a long time. I skinned and cleaned it by myself, with determination if not quite precision.

In March, we made maple syrup, arms aching from tapping the trees with a hand drill, trudging through the snow, hanging buckets with hope. I recalled my parents, dogged with determination, doing the same thing when I was a child; I never really understood just how much grueling work it was until I was emptying pails and carrying buckets myself—forty gallons of sap for one measly gallon of syrup, but how we savored the sweetness.

It took us a few tries to get the hang of the thing; the first batch of syrup was appallingly bad—hours and hours of wasted work, tapping trees and boiling down the sap to a rich, amber liquid—but the second was passable, and everyone loved having it on their porridge, since the brown sugar had long ago run out. The morning after Daniel came back, I brought my mother a bowl of porridge with a golden dollop of syrup on top. It had been hard to discern her lucidity; at times she seemed confused but accepting, other times as sharp as a tack, and at yet other times completely out of it, asking where she was or, painfully, where my father was.

When she tasted the porridge with the syrup, though, her whole face brightened and she asked me with a sort of interested eagerness, "Did I make this?"

I took it as the highest compliment.

Having her here has been like a gift, a miracle, and one I never, ever expected to happen, for Daniel to make happen. I'm still amazed—and more than a little apprehensive—as to how he managed it, somehow getting all the way to Worcester from Clarkson... over a hundred miles, that much closer to the nuclear blasts. And yet I'm so grateful because my mother belongs here, more than I ever did. The cottage is part of the fabric of her soul; it's knit into her very being.

When the sun comes out and the deck is warm in the afternoons, I help her out there; we sit together and simply gaze at the lake. We don't speak much, but we don't need to. The memories are there, for the taking; we can simply sit and savor them, look at all the blueness and *be*, together, at last.

But this morning, as I stoke the fire in the wood stove to make my coffee, that sense of dreamy peace eludes me. Daniel has been home for a week, and he has barely spoken to me in all that time. He's barely spoken to anyone, and when he does speak, it's as if he has to find the words from a well deep inside him, draw them up slowly, then lay them down, each one a burden.

I was so excited to show him all our innovation and industry —the greenhouse that Ruby is the proud mistress of, the smokehouse that Justine and Kyle built, the bottles of maple syrup and the fields plowed for potatoes and oats, the first seedlings pushing up through the earth; the fish we've caught and smoked, the herbs we've collected and dried, the plans we have for preserving apples and raspberries and plums, and the more distant plans we're still dreaming of—solar panels, keeping bees, a rainwater harvesting and purification system. I've studied that book on self-sufficiency until I can practically recite every word. But Daniel hasn't seemed interested in any of it.

He's observed and he's helped—silently chopping and stacking wood with Kyle, checking the rabbit and beaver traps, weeding the fields, collecting water from the lake for the barrel in the kitchen. But it's without any enthusiasm or interest, without even a word, and when I think of how *he* was the one who first said we could make a life here, back when I scorned his idea of us pretending to be pioneers... well, the fact that we're doing it now and he doesn't seem to care makes me want to cry. Worse, it makes me afraid.

What happened to him out there? Do I even want to know?

"Up early again?"

I turn to see Kerry standing by the ladder to the loft; I didn't even hear her climb down. After Justine and Phoebe joined us, Kerry moved up to sleep with Mattie and Ruby and Justine took the guest bedroom; Kyle stayed in the box room, which he now shares with Sam, who sleeps on a mattress on the floor. It's crowded, and we can't really fit anyone else, but it's working so far.

"Yes, it's the best part of the day," I reply. I love watching the mist move over the lake, the sky lighten from indigo to pearly pink, before sunlight floods the windows, lights up the whole house.

Kerry walks into the kitchen, and I follow her, not wanting to wake anyone up with our conversation.

"I can't believe it, but this stuff is growing on me," she remarks, as she pours herself a cup of cleavers coffee. "Too bad it takes a zillion seeds to make a cup."

"Good, though, that sticky weed is everywhere around here."

"Always the optimist." She smiles at me, and I smile back; over the last few months our relationship has become a deep and abiding bond, forged in suffering and danger, honed by hard work and cooperation. I'm more grateful for her friendship than I ever could have imagined. She takes a sip of her coffee. "It will get better," she says quietly.

I don't pretend to misunderstand; we've come too far for that kind of useless prevarication. "I didn't even think about what it would be like," I reply, "when he came back, *if* he came back. I just wanted him home."

She nods and takes another sip. "I know."

"What do you think he saw out there?" I ask after a moment, a tremor in my voice because I don't really want to ask the question, never mind have it answered, and, in any case, I know Kerry can't really answer it.

She shrugs, giving a sigh. "Think about what we experienced in Corville, which is a tiny town on the edge of nowhere, and he must have had that, a thousand times worse or more. I can't even imagine it. I don't want to."

I swallow. "I don't, either." I've tried to put Corville behind me, as well as that night on the river; the fear that those men might find us has lessened, with time. They haven't come yet; why should they now, or ever?

"Then don't imagine it," Kerry says simply. "He might tell you one day, or maybe he won't. But we all need to move on from whatever happened before. We have a lot of work to do if we want to survive next winter, you know."

My stomach clenches at the thought. We're in the heyday of spring now, with everything burgeoning and blossoming with life, with possibility. The days are long and warm, the danger of frost is past, and the worst thing we've had to deal with are swarms of black flies. They rise in dark clouds over the dirt, and we've taken to fashioning elaborate headgear made of old mosquito netting, found in a cupboard, to keep the worst of them at bay.

But so much of life feels *possible* now, with the garden and the fields, the rabbits and fish and the berries that will burst onto the bushes in just a few weeks... and yet in just three months it will be turning cold again; there could be frost on the ground, maybe even snow, the growing season over, and we will have had to store enough food for an entire winter with ten people, and nothing in the pantry but what we put there ourselves. It's a terrifying prospect, and yet it also excites me because for the first time I feel we might actually be able to do it. Together.

But I want Daniel to be involved, interested, excited... like I am.

"Has he said anything good about out there?" Kerry asks. "Is anything getting better? It's been six months now since the blasts. It would be nice to think the government is starting to get its act together, that the world isn't you know, on *fire,* but who knows?"

I shake my head. "He hasn't said anything at all."

She nods slowly. "This might be the rest of our lives then." She sounds more philosophical about it than she has before, in part, I think, because of Trapper Kevin. He's come three more times in the last few months; he never stays for more than a day or two, helping and teaching us, and spending time with Kerry. When he disappears into the woods to head back to his cabin, she looks wistful but not as sad as she once might have.

But what about Mattie, Ruby? Sam? As pleased as I am about the fact that we actually are managing to survive out here, I don't really want this to be the rest of their lives, and so I hold on to hope that, if we can survive another winter, maybe, just maybe, things will improve. The world will right itself. How, I don't know. How we'd even find out, I haven't begun to think. I think of Mattie scornfully saying she's like Laura Ingalls Wilder on Mars and I realize she's not far off. We are completely cut off out here, and while that's been no bad thing, it means we wouldn't even know if life had got back to normal. Governments could be restarting, cities being rebuilt, and we'd have no idea. The other day, Ruby flicked the light switch up and down a few times "just to check". Nothing happened, of course, not yet.

And judging by my husband's attitude, the world is still a fierce and fearsome place.

"It's only been a week, remember," Kerry tells me, and I nod. I can wait. I have no choice, and these last few months have taught me to be patient. And in the meantime, there have been small joys; unlike his father, Sam has taken to our pioneering life with a seemingly unbridled enthusiasm. When we caught a rabbit in a snare, he was eager to try skinning it, claiming he had experience from a video game he played.

I'd started laughing when he admitted sheepishly that, in the game, you pressed a button on your controller and the animal was neatly skinned and packaged into meat, presto. It wasn't quite the same with an actual dead rabbit. But he did it, and he learned, and we had rabbit stew with wild roots for dinner. I wanted Daniel to be proud of him, but he barely seemed aware. It's as if he's become a zombie, the walking dead, with us in body but not in spirit. Where his spirit is, I shudder to think. It feels as if it has gone completely.

But maybe Kerry is right, and all he needs is time.

The sun has risen, and I can hear people stirring, the cottage coming to life. I need to make breakfast—we're on the last of our porridge oats—and weed the oat field, fetch water and stack wood and collect more cleaver seeds for coffee. Ruby and I were going to scout out apple and plum trees in the overgrown orchards by the old barn, and Mattie wanted to look for strawberries. She remembered how I'd told her how they grew here once, back when I was a girl. Maybe they still do.

There's a lot to accomplish. I don't have time to stand around and wish things could be different.

"Thanks," I tell her, and she smiles. Kerry has softened in the last few months, and in a way, I've hardened; the doubt that plagued me for so long has calcified into determination. And yet, as I put my coffee cup in the sink and head into the living room and the new day, a wave of doubt assails me. I've made a little kingdom here, one I'm deeply, fiercely proud of—and yet how long can it last?

We're better off than we used to be, and I want to believe we are safe, but I know we're still vulnerable. A few more guns, a couple more people, hasn't turned us into either a fortress or an army.

I pause in front of the picture window and stare out at the lake; the mist has melted away and everything dazzles, and for a second, the sunlight shimmering on the water feels like a mirage. For a second, I can imagine it disappearing, melting away just as the mist did, into the ether, into nothing.

An hour later, I have settled my mom on the sofa with a blanket over her knees and am helping her eat her bowl of watery porridge. She has aged so much since I last saw her, just over six months ago, before we came up to Canada. Her hands shake and her fingers have become curled and claw-like. Her back is humped, her shoulders rounded, her body so thin and frail, and yet when she looks at me, there's a gleam of understanding in her eyes, of knowledge. Whatever Alzheimer's has taken from her, it hasn't taken that spark of self, and for that I'm so grateful.

After I help my mom with breakfast, I head outside; Justine is already busy in the garden, Phoebe playing nearby. In the two months since Justine arrived here, she's maintained a somewhat wary distance with us all, although she certainly works hard, and her antibiotics saved my daughter's life. When we returned from Eagle Rapids, Ruby had fallen unconscious, her skin clammy with her raging fever. It was touch and go for two days before she finally responded to the medicine. Mattie had sobbed in my arms with relief; she'd been torturing herself with guilt the whole time for her part in their pointless argument.

Today Sam walks down the road with me to the oat field by the old barn; although the sun is warm, the breeze is chilly, but at least it keeps the worst of the black flies from us. We stroll along in easy companionship for a few minutes, and I revel in the simple fact that he's here. But as we crest the hill, keeping my voice casual, I ask the question that's been burning within me.

"How was the trip back here, Sam?"

My friendly tone doesn't reassure him; he turns tensely alert, giving me a guarded look. "What do you mean?"

"Well, how long did it take?" My tone is still friendly, like a teacher talking to a student she doesn't know. *Tell me something simple.*

He shrugs. "A little over four months? Dad came to Clarkson sometime in December."

"He did?" I'm jolted by that; I had assumed that whatever Daniel experienced, whatever he saw or did, happened before he got Sam. How else could Sam now seem so unscarred, so *insouciant*? And yet, maybe that's just an act because right now, my son doesn't seem either of those things.

"Yeah, around then. I don't remember, actually. We lost track of the days, you know?"

"Yes, I know." We had, as well; Christmas and New Year's had passed unnoticed, unmarked.

He shrugs. "Around then, anyway."

"But... why did it take so long to get back here?"

Now Sam looks distinctly uneasy. "Hasn't Dad told you about all that?"

About what? "Not really," I hedge.

Sam frowns. "It was hard... it took us maybe two or three weeks to get to Granny because there were blockades and gangs and stuff... we lost our stuff, and then we kept having to do detours. And we had to stop to find food sometimes... but Dad always found the food and had me wait with the car. It wasn't..." He blows out a breath. "Well, it could have been worse."

"And when you got to Granny?"

"Yeah, he didn't tell me about that. I mean, he went into the home by himself, and then he brought her to the car, where I was waiting... and he brought another old lady, too, from the home. They were the only two left, but she died a couple of days later."

"She did?" Why hasn't Daniel told me any of this? And yet did I really want to know?

"Yeah." Sam is quiet, his expression turning pensive, sorrowful. "Yeah. She was really weak. We... we could tell she wasn't going to make it."

I'm silent, absorbing just this, realizing how much more there is—this vast tundra of my ignorance, my husband and son's experience. "And then?" I finally ask.

Sam shrugs, his gaze sliding away. He looks like a little boy now, scared and defiant, not wanting to admit he broke my best lamp playing ball in the house.

"Sam?" I prompt gently.

"I don't know, Mom. It was all kind of a blur. Granny was really weak... we stayed in an empty house for a while, to help her recover, while Dad went out and got food."

"You did?"

"Yeah." He nods. "For a couple of weeks."

A couple of *weeks*? I'm trying to imagine my son and my mother stuck in some empty, dilapidated house—frightened, hungry, and alone. And then I ask the most mundane question —"What did you do all day?"

Sam is quiet for a moment. "There are worse things than boredom," he finally says, and I think of him at fifteen, complaining loudly and vociferously on vacations without a gaming console because there was nothing to do.

"How did Dad get food?"

Sam shakes his head. "He never told me, and I never asked. He said my job was to take care of Granny, and his job was to take care of me." He looks off into the distance, toward the lake, squinting his eyes in the glare of the sun. "To be honest, I didn't want to know."

"Did anything else happen?" I ask, and he turns to look at me with an expression of mingled disbelief and scorn.

"Lots of stuff happened, Mom. We got carjacked on 95— they threw us out of the car, took all our stuff, and drove off. We were lucky they didn't kill us. There was a time when we had to hide out from some gang—we spent nearly a month in a rat-infested apartment building outside Albany." He's silent for a moment. "Do you really want to hear about this?"

"No." I'm shaken, more than I expected to be. I knew something must have happened; as Kerry said, Daniel and Sam would have experienced far worse than we did, and what we experienced was bad enough. But my son, my firstborn, my *baby*... and my husband too. "I'm sorry, Sam," I say quietly, and he shrugs.

"I just want to move on. It's a lot better here."

We have come to the field of oats, the tender, new plants tiny green shoots in the soil, the lake glinting beyond. I take a deep breath of fresh air, let it fill my lungs. *Yes, let's move on,* I think. *Let's all move on.*

"Mom." Sam's voice is quiet, tense. I turn to him, only to see him nod at the long grass growing underneath a gnarled, old apple tree, on the edge of the field. "Where's that from?"

When I look down, it takes me a moment to see what he's nodding at—a crumpled can of Labatt Blue, a few cigarette butts scattered around, both clearly recent.

"Is that from someone here?" Sam asks in a low voice and, numbly, I shake my head. We don't have any beer. We ran out of my parents' old cigarettes months ago.

Someone else has been here.

TWENTY-SIX

A crumpled beer can catapults us into a state of emergency. Sam and I walk home quickly, half running, hearts beating hard, and then quietly tell both Kerry and Daniel what we saw. The three of us walk back to the field, the can. It's still there, looking just as innocuous and terrible.

"They smoked six cigarettes," Daniel remarks, counting the butts. His face is calm, expressionless, while I'm struggling to conceal my terror. "They must have been here for quite a while."

"Who still has any cigarettes?" Kerry demands, but her usual wry insouciance falls flat; she looks too scared. The old barn is only a quarter-mile from the cottage. They might as well have been in our living room.

"They were watching," Daniel states. "That's why they must have smoked so many. They stood here for half an hour at least and watched us." He glances up at the old apple tree, and nods slowly. "They must have been up there."

"What—" I want to sound scornful, but I don't.

Quickly, with an agility I didn't realize my husband possessed, he scrambles up in the tree. "You can see the cottage from here," he tells us. "And the deck, and the beach, and the dock. You can pretty much see everything." He speaks flatly, without any emotion, but Kerry and I stare at each other, completely chilled.

We've been discovered. I always feared this would happen, but I let myself be lulled into a sense of security, simply because I wanted it so much.

"Maybe it's just some rando," Kerry says, without any conviction. Neither Daniel nor I bother to reply.

He shimmies down the tree and brushes the dirt off his hands. "We'll have to take some precautions."

"What precautions?" I ask, torn between eagerness and despondency. I want there to be precautions to take, measures to put in place that will keep us safe, yet already I know, in my gut, in my bones, that there won't be. Not enough, anyway. Never enough.

Daniel rubs his chin in thought. "I'll have to think it through, but I should probably park the car somewhere hidden, where we can get to it if we need to. Pack it with provisions, just in case."

Kerry and I share uneasy glances. "You mean run away?" I finally ask, and Daniel gives me a level look.

"If it's necessary."

"What about defending this place?" I burst out, angry.

"How?" Daniel replies simply.

I spin away, my nails digging into my hands, tears of frustration rather than sorrow smarting my eyes. *This isn't fair*, I think, and I almost laugh at myself. What a pointless emotion, the foot-stomping cry of a child. Of course, this isn't fair. There has been nothing fair about what has happened for the last six months.

"I'm not saying we just give up, Alex," Daniel says quietly. "We can take other precautions too. But depending on how many there are..." He lets that idea fade away into silence.

"What other precautions?" I draw a shuddering breath; I'm determined to be pragmatic, but positive. We can do this. We can, at least, do something.

"We should have an armed guard." Daniel glances up at the loft of the old barn. "If the building is stable enough, someone could sit up there. You'd get a fairly decent view of the road."

"And if they saw someone?" Kerry asks. "How would they alert everyone back at the cottage?"

Daniel shrugs, and I find myself saying, "We have a pair of walkie-talkies back at the cottage. Kids' ones, but I think they would still work." Ruby found them in the loft in an old box of toys; I don't mention that they're pink Barbie ones.

Kerry gives me a dryly disbelieving look, and I remember her sardonic quip about stringing tin cans along the road, like something out of *The Goonies*. *Well*, I think, raising my chin a notch, *so be it*.

"I suppose that could work," Daniel replies slowly. "Do we have batteries?"

I think of the corroded batteries I threw out all those months ago, back when everything still felt theoretical. "We have some."

"All right. Then that's what we should do. And Mattie or Ruby shouldn't come down here, just to be safe. Or Phoebe."

"What about Sam?" I ask, and Daniel gives me a level look.

"Sam is an adult. He can make his own decisions."

I think of my eighteen-year-old son tripping merrily out to college, and I wonder just how much he has had to grow up since then.

We head back to the cottage in silence; by the time we get there, it's clear that everyone knows something is up. Kyle and Justine are standing by the back door, Phoebe perched on Justine's hip. Mattie and Ruby crowd behind them, looking anxious, and Sam is lurking behind the screen door, keeping an eye on my mother but clearly as concerned as everyone else.

"What's happened?" Justine asks quietly. Knowingly.

"Let's talk inside." Daniel speaks authoritatively; despite his seeming lack of interest in what we've been doing here, he has now become our leader, maybe because he knows what the outside world is like. He can guess what we might be facing more than we can... although when I think of the two men in Corville, the guys in the truck in Flintville, I'm afraid I *do* have a good idea, and I don't like it at all.

We all sit in the living room, sober and silent, as Daniel outlines what he thinks needs to happen. The two cars should be parked down the old logging road, filled with supplies and covered with brush. Someone in the old barn, on guard, at all times, even through the night. No one goes to the potato or oat field without an armed guard, and Ruby, Mattie, and Phoebe don't go at all. We cut a few more trees to block the road, not as a decoy, but a deterrent.

"And if they do come?" Justine asks quietly, clutching Phoebe to her. "What do we do then?"

"I guess it depends how many there are," Daniel replies.

"If it's those guys from Flintville, it'll be four or five," Justine tells him. "They've been terrorizing the whole area for months."

"We can take four or five guys," Sam states with authority; he sounds like he's talking about a shoot-out in a video game, some teenaged rumble.

"Maybe," Daniel replies. "Maybe not."

"So if it's looking bad, we just get in the cars and leave?" Kerry asks. She sounds matter-of-fact, without any of the outrage I showed earlier. "Leave everything we've worked here for?"

Daniel nods. "If we want to survive."

"How do we survive out there?" Justine demands. "Do you know what the world is like now?" She speaks scathingly, but Daniel doesn't rise to meet her fury.

"Yes," he answers quietly. "I know."

. . .

Later, when we are alone, getting ready for bed, we talk again. The whole day has felt subdued, as if we're already grieving. Mattie wanted to practice shooting; Ruby escaped into a book, barely saying a word. I fretted and paced and tried to figure out a plan—and came up with nothing. We are too vulnerable here, too defenseless against a mob. And a mob, I already know, is what it will be.

Now we are in our bedroom, the door closed, the lake outside the window gilded with moonlight, an illusion of serenity. In the distance, I hear the lonely, bittersweet sound of the whippoorwill, its mournful call tearing at me, reminding me of my childhood, of the sweetness of long-ago days.

"When we were traveling," Daniel says, as he slips on a T-shirt for bed, "we heard rumors about a community out near Buffalo."

I stare at him, nonplussed. "Buffalo?"

"It's on a Department of Defense military base. The military abandoned the base right after the second round of strikes, and some people took it over. Or so I heard. It might not be true, and even if it is, it might not still be there."

"Another homegrown militia?" I ask, scoffing.

"Maybe," he allows, "but one that isn't out for blood."

"You don't know that," I point out, and he nods.

"No, I don't. A few different people were talking about it, saying they're trying to make a community there, a protected place where people can be safe, but it was all whispers or rumors. More a hope than anything else, but still... it could give us a place to go, to aim for."

I'm silent, absorbing the idea, resisting it. I don't want to head for some unknown military base in Buffalo. I want to stay here, and harvest the potatoes, pick raspberries, *live*. Tears prick my eyes, and I swipe at them angrily. This is too deep for tears, too important for some childish emotional outburst.

"We were never going to be able to stay here forever, Alex," Daniel says gently.

Instinctively, like a child, I bristle. "You thought we could, back at the beginning. You said we could make a life here."

"I hoped, yes, but..." He lets out a long, low sigh. "What future is there for Mattie or Ruby, for Sam, in this place?" I've asked the question myself, but I haven't yet answered it. "We can't defend ourselves here," he continues. "The world is too wild. And yet... it's the *world*. This is bigger than survival, at least our survival. What about the survival of society, of civilization? I know those seem like ridiculous ideas right about now, but if we want our children to inherit a world that isn't eking out an existence entirely by ourselves, isolated and alone... then we have to go out there. Join with others, work together, if we can." He gives this little, inspiring speech in a voice that only sounds tired.

"Do you even think we could make it?" I ask abruptly. "Based on what you've seen? Sam told me a little bit about your journey here—"

Daniel shakes his head. "Sam only knows what he knows."

"What happened, Daniel?" My voice has turned soft, pleading. "What happened to you out there? Because I know something did."

He stares at me for a long moment, and I think—I am sure—that he's not going to answer. Then he says in a voice so low I strain to hear it, "If you knew, you wouldn't love me anymore."

I open my mouth, close it again. Something in me trembles; I can't speak. I have no idea what to say. To feel.

"I killed a man," I blurt. "Out near Eagle Rapids. Ruby had been injured, she was septic, and Kerry and I went to a nurse she knew of, for antibiotics—that was Justine. We went on the quad bike because the road wasn't plowed, so we couldn't take

Kyle's car. A bunch of guys in a truck chased us, they shot at us. And this guy was going to steal our bike, our only mode of transportation left. I couldn't let him do that. I wouldn't. And... and I didn't."

Daniel's shoulders slump, his face etched in lines of grief. He's reacting as if this is his failing, not mine, and I want—I *need*—to explain it to him. "I didn't feel anything when I shot him," I state matter-of-factly, my words coming in a rush. "Not sorrow, not guilt, not even relief. If anything, I felt... indifferent. He might as well have been a fly I swatted." I realize it's the first time I've said such a thing out loud. It's the first time I let myself think it. "Daniel, whatever... whatever happened, whatever you did, I'd understand. I know I would."

He shakes his head slowly, with utter certainty. "No," he says, and that seems to be the end of it.

The next few days creep by slowly; we tiptoe through them, trying to keep up with all our chores and activities, yet always looking over our shoulders, bracing for an assault, an ambush. Nothing happens. After three days, I start to breathe a bit easier. I can't live in a state of constant tension; no one can. You have to find hope; you have to nurture it. Thriving, not surviving, as Mattie said, I recall, and almost smile.

On a sunny day at the end of the month, Mattie and I go in search of strawberries. We take the old logging road that curves around the lake, now overgrown, barely visible through the bushes. Still I find it, tracing my steps, remembering the way, a heart memory born from instinct.

Daniel didn't want us to go, feared for our safety, but I have the .22 strapped across my chest and I can't live like I'm in prison. Not here, of all places. I'm even carrying the old glass of clear green plastic that I used as a child; I found it in the cupboard. I showed it to my mother, and she laughed and nodded; I think she actually remembered. I hope we find straw-berries today.

Mattie and I have agreed, without having to say anything, not to talk about the nebulous threats that can feel as if they surround us on every side. We simply want to enjoy the day—the sun pouring from the sky, the breeze whispering through the grass. The possibility of finding strawberries, out here, deep in the woods.

"Do you think we'll find any?" Mattie asks, her voice caught between skepticism and hope.

"I don't know. I haven't seen strawberries up here since I was younger than Ruby." But then, I'm not sure I ever really looked. Maybe the year or so after, with my mother, but not since then.

"Well, there's only one way to find out," Mattie says with determined optimism, a spring in her step, and I smile at her.

I almost don't recognize the little valley when we come upon it. The pine trees that were mere saplings in a wide field when I picked here with my mother now tower above us, blocking out the bright sun and making me feel like a child lost in a wood.

The only way to recognize the place is by the old farm gate, now just a rotting plank hanging from rusty hinges, the trees grown up around it, the remnants of the farmer's field, gone forever.

"Here?" Mattie asks dubiously, and I try to laugh, although I find I am suddenly close to tears. *So much has changed.* I knew that, of course I knew that; I've lived it every day, and yet I *feel* it now, right down to my marrow bones. The world is not what I once knew, what I still want it to be.

"Let's look, anyway," I tell my daughter, and I manage to keep the tremor from my voice. We look, hunting among the trees, even though I know in my heart we won't find them here in the shadows, where grass barely grows. They're gone;

they were gone a long time ago. I knew that, and yet I still feel grief.

"It's okay, Mom," Mattie says quietly, and I try to smile at her.

"I know it is." And it *is*, because, miraculously, my mother is back at the cottage, and we are all safe. For now.

"What about in the sunlight?" Mattie asks, wandering away from the gate and the trees, to a patch of grass that gets a little sun. I watch her kneeling in the grass, her dark hair falling in front of her face. She's nearly ten years older than I was when I picked with my mother, and yet right now she reminds me of me. I feel the passing of years like a physical thing, a turning inside me.

"*Mom!*" Mattie calls excitedly. "I think I've found one."

I come to look, not daring to believe, and I see my daughter with a tiny jewel-like strawberry nestled in the palm of her hand. I let out a cry of surprise, of hope, and then I kneel in the long grass with my daughter, and we hunt for strawberries.

We only find a few—a couple dozen at most, barely covering the bottom of my glass, and yet each one is like a precious pearl, a treasure.

"They still grow here," Mattie says eagerly. "We could find more."

"We could." I'm conscious we have been gone for more than an hour, and Daniel will be worried. "We should get back, though. We'll come again tomorrow and have a really good look."

We walk through the woods back to the logging road, the woods full of sound and light all around us, so different from when we came here in November and everything was barren and brown and eerily still. *It's been three days*, I think, nearly buoyant with hope. *Maybe they won't come. Maybe it wasn't anyone dangerous.*

As we walk along, Mattie turns to me with a serious look.

"You should give them to her. To Granny. Remind her of when you were little, and you guys played pioneers."

I'm touched that she remembers that story. "Well, we're not playing now, are we?" I tease gently, and she smiles.

Back at the cottage, I take my glass with its precious few strawberries, and I bring it to my mother. She's sitting on the deck, half dozing in the sunlight, looking diminished and fragile and yet still so very much herself.

"Mom." I speak gently, and she opens her eyes. For a moment, they cloud with confusion, and I hold my breath. She's never forgotten who I am before, but I know there has to be a first time. But then she smiles and stretches out one scrawny hand, and when she speaks, her voice is warm and rich with affection.

"Alex."

"Look." I kneel in front of her, and I press the glass into her hand. "Strawberries, wild ones. From the valley toward the other side of the lake. Do you remember?"

For a second, I think she doesn't, even though the older memories are the ones she still seems able to access the most. But then her face softens, and she looks down at the strawberries and then back up at me. "Pioneers," she says softly, and she presses her other hand, clawed and wrinkled, against my cheek. "My cottage girl."

Tears prick my eyes as I press my hand over hers and hold it against my cheek. My heart is overflowing—with love, with grief, the two so intertwined I can't tell one emotion from the other.

"You're a cottage girl too," I whisper. "The original, Mom."

She smiles and nods. "Always." Then she closes her eyes, and her hand falls away; she's already slipping into a doze. I let her go, rising from the deck as quietly as I can while my mother sleeps on.

. . .

She sleeps on that night, into death, as I think I knew she would, one day soon. She'd been fading since she came to the cottage, like a photograph losing its color, turning sepia in front of my eyes, corners curling up. When I go to bring her a bowl of oatmeal the next morning, I'm not surprised at all to see her lying there so still in her bed. There is no confusion, no uncertainty as to whether she's dead or not; like with my dad, I know it at once.

I take a deep breath, let it out, and simply stand there for a moment, acknowledging the moment, the surprising peace of it. As I'm turning from her room, I hear the crackle of the walkie-talkie from the kitchen; Kyle is on guard at the barn. He's used it before just to check in—and occasionally ask for snacks—so I'm not too worried.

But as I come into the kitchen, I hear his words clearly over the crackle, and everything in me goes icy and still.

"They're coming."

TWENTY-SEVEN

Kyle's voice is garbled, shrill with fear, but we get from him that there are three trucks, each one with a couple of men, minimum, all of them bristling with guns, and they are coming for the cottage.

"We can take them," Justine insists, her voice low and fierce, a rifle ready in her hands. "We have the stronger position, inside, up in the loft, at the windows. We can pick them off, one by one, as they come down the drive. *We can take them.*"

I so want to believe her. I *need* to believe her because what's the alternative? Surrendering the cottage and all we've worked for, to these renegades and rapists, these *destroyers,* without even a fight? I can't stand the thought.

"We could take a few," Daniel concedes, his voice steady. "But if there are ten, twelve men, all armed, with vehicles?" He shakes his head, a slow, firm back-and-forth. "No."

Justine lets out a huff of sound. "You're not even going to try?"

"If we try and fail, do you know what the price is?" Daniel returns evenly. "What these men will do to us? To you?"

Justine's face twists, her eyes flashing with both fury and despair. "Yes, I do. I've seen it myself."

Daniel doesn't reply; he just glances at Phoebe. Justine's face crumples and she hugs her daughter to her, closing her eyes. "Where else can we go?" she demands brokenly. "That's safe, that's even *possible*?"

"There's a military base near Buffalo," Daniel tells her, and he explains what he told me last night, about this mythical community that may or may not exist. And even if it exists, the people there may or may not let us in. And that's if we even get there in the first place. No one seems particularly enthused or impressed by the idea. How far away is that, anyway, I wonder? At least four hundred miles.

"Why haven't they come yet?" Mattie asks suddenly. "If Kyle saw them from the barn?" It's only been a minute, maybe two, since Kyle was shouting into the walkie-talkie, but she's right. Shouldn't they be roaring down the driveway now, whooping and hollering, firing their guns? There is only silence.

Daniel moves to the laundry room window, standing to the side, peering out cautiously. "Nothing," he says. "They must be planning an attack."

We are silent, absorbing this news. How will they attack us? When will it come? I look around the cottage living room—the blue wicker chair in the corner my dad always sat in, the clock on the mantle that's ticked the time for forty years, the bookcases filled with beloved old paperbacks, the wooden sign above the door to the deck that reads proudly, 'Lost Lake'. I imagine those men, those villains, in here, striding around, lolling on the sofa or breaking the pictures, and everything in me cries out *No*.

"We have to fight," I burst out. "We *have* to."

"There's more than one way to fight," Kerry says quietly. I look at her in confusion, but she just gives a little shake of her head. The rest of us remain immobile, undecided. Should we leave while we can, get away safely? It feels wrong somehow, as if we're giving the cottage away. We might as well leave a welcome note and a plate of cookies.

But if—*when*—they do attack, it will be far worse. Far more dangerous. I know what those men will do to us—to me, to Mattie and Ruby. I *know*. And, in reality, we might not get away at all.

Daniel glances out the window again, up toward the stand of pine trees on the hill; my dad planted them when they first bought this place, when I was just four years old. "I think I see them," he says quietly. "They're up in the trees."

Instinctively, I head toward the window to look, but he holds me back, hard, with one hand. "Don't," he says quietly. "They're getting into position. They'll shoot if they see any movement."

In an instant, the cottage feels like an empty stage we have all stepped onto, helpless and exposed under the glare of a spotlight. I look around at all the windows, imagine us being silently surrounded. My stomach drops, and my heart begins to thud, my head feeling fuzzy and light. I have to take several deep breaths just to stay upright. Next to me, Ruby begins to cry, the tears slipping silently down her cheeks. Mattie just looks furious, Sam sad.

"What about Kyle?" Kerry asks suddenly. "He's stuck back in the barn."

"We've said we'd meet at the car in case of trouble," Daniel reminds her. "If he slips out the back and stays down by the lake, he shouldn't be noticed."

"Yes, but..." Kerry frowns. I don't think any of us actually imagined this happening.

In the next second of silence, while we are all still absorbing the sudden sea change of our lives, it begins. I don't know what it is at first because I don't hear the gunshot. I simply see Justine clutch her chest, her eyes widening with surprise as she drops Phoebe and blood blooms between her fingers, spreads outward.

Daniel moves first, hitting the floor, pulling me with him. Everyone else follows while Phoebe begins to wail, and Daniel pulls her toward him.

Another bullet shatters the picture window into a million glittering fragments. We are all on our hands and knees, every single one of us completely terrified.

"How do we get out?" Sam gasps. "If we're already surrounded?"

"They won't be on the lake side." Kerry's voice is sure. "Not yet. We'll have to go out the front, right down to the lake."

"It's too exposed—" Justine protests in a gasp, her face pale with pain. I look at her chest, which is covered in blood. With a frisson of shocked wonder, I realize she's not going to make it.

She must see the truth of it in my face because she gives me a panicked, blazing look. "Phoebe—"

"Yes," I say quickly. "*Yes.*"

I glance at Kerry, who is looking at Justine, her face drawn in sadness. "Bastards," she whispers, and Justine's head falls back onto the floor with a thud. For a second, we are all silent; it's all the time we have for a memorial.

"Sam, you take Phoebe," Daniel instructs. "Ruby with me. Mattie, go with Mom." He turns to me in query. "Your mom—"

"She's dead." I can't believe I'd actually forgotten that fact for a few minutes. "In her sleep, last night. I went in this morning—" I stop because already something that happened ten minutes ago feels like a lifetime. It was, and it's irrelevant now.

Daniel nods, and I don't miss the relief that passes across his face. I realize I'm relieved too; I would never want my mother to see what is happening now, or to have to deal with her in this chaos.

"All right then," Daniel says. "We go out the door, down the steps, and straight into the brush by the lake. Stay as low as you can. Move quickly but quietly. I'll go last, to distract them."

"No," I say quickly. "You lead the way. I'll go last."

"Alex—"

"I mean it." I stare him down, and after a second, he nods.

Then, with his arm around Ruby, he starts crawling toward the door. Sam follows with Phoebe. Another bullet hits the far wall, embedding itself in it. I'm frozen with fear, but also with fury; I *still* don't want to leave. I can't give up this place I've worked so hard for, that's been so much a part of my life, to be used and destroyed by my enemies.

"Mom," Mattie whispers, pulling on my arm. "What are you going to do? How will you distract them?"

"I'll shoot." I crawl toward the window, rising onto my knees, my palms slick on my gun. I aim, knowing I won't hit anything; I can't even see out the window, but hopefully it will be enough to keep their focus. "Go, Mattie! *Go*." I shoot once, twice, and duck down when a volley of shots is the reply.

Mattie has crawled toward the door, but Kerry comes to kneel by my side. "We don't need to end it like this," she states quietly, and I turn to her.

"What do you mean?"

She nods toward the window, the hill. "Those guys. You know if they get the cottage, they'll turn it into some kind of citadel. They'll just become worse and worse, stronger and stronger. They'll hurt more people. We don't have to give it to them."

"How?"

She takes a handful of bullets from her pocket and holds them out. "You put a couple of these in the wood stove, and they'll have nothing left to fight for."

My heart leaps with something too raw to be hope, and yet that's what it feels like. This isn't the way I wanted it to end, but I'm already sure it is better than the alternative. "But will we have time to get out ourselves?" I ask.

"If you wrap them in a wet dishrag or something, we probably should, but it's still a risk." She pauses, her gaze level on me. "Are you willing to take it?"

I gaze back at her, crouched there on the floor, the rifle in my hand, and then I take the bullets from Kerry. They are solid, with copper casings, and as my fingers close around them, feeling their weight, something in me both stills and hardens.

"You go," I instruct Kerry. "I'll follow as soon as I can."

She nods and begins to crawl toward the door; Mattie is still on the threshold.

"Mattie, *go*," I hiss, and then I head for the kitchen, keeping low. I grab a dish towel from the counter, jerking in shock when a bullet whistles past me and lodges in the water barrel; a jet of water from the hole it has caused arcs out. I wet the rag in it and then wrap it around the bullets.

My heart is thundering now, and yet I feel calm. I know this is the right thing to do. For a second, no more, I let myself remember—curling up on my dad's lap by the fire; my mother finishing off the maple syrup on the stove. My brother and sister and me roasting marshmallows, playing cards, running down to the dock, our laughter floating away on the breeze, the sun setting over the lake, turning its surface pink and orange.

I clench my fingers around the bullets tucked inside the wet cloth, and then I open the door to the wood stove and hurl the bundle inside.

I don't have time to crawl carefully to the door, and so I stand up and sprint. I can hear the gunfire now; they must be closer. Something grazes my arm, but I don't feel the pain. I throw myself through the front door; Kerry and Mattie are halfway down the steps to the lake. Behind me I hear the explosion of the bullets in the stove, and, impossibly, I smile.

We are going to make it.

I hear the angry roar of one of our attackers as it echoes over the lake, close enough that I turn. A man is standing on the deck. They must have come closer than I'd realized. He has a bushy beard and wild eyes, and he could be anyone—the guys in Corville, or the ones who followed us on the truck to Eagle Rapids, or someone else entirely. He takes aim with his rifle, and Kerry looks back, a wild look of terror on her face as she suddenly hurls herself in front of Mattie.

The next moment feels like it happens in slow motion, and yet it's over in an instant. One second Kerry is there, her arms outstretched in front of Mattie, a look of fierce determination on her face, and the next she's crumpled on the ground, blood soaking her T-shirt.

"*Kerry!*" Mattie screams, and I lurch toward them, tripping on the steps, falling hard enough to knock the breath out of me. Gasping, I crawl toward Kerry.

"Get to the lake," I shout at Mattie. "*Go!*"

A sob escapes my daughter, but she obeys, her arms over her head, ducking low as she makes for the cover of the brush by the water. A volley of gunshot erupts from the deck, as she dives into the brush. I kneel in front of Kerry; she's still alive, but only just.

"What a way to go, huh?" she rasps, blood bubbling from her lips as she manages a smile. "Well, it could have been worse."

A broken laugh escapes me. "Kerry—"

"Get out of here, Alex," she insists with the last of her breath. "They can't do anything to me now. They won't take the cottage. *Go.*"

I know she's right, and yet I can't bear it. I hold her hands in mine and squeeze them once. "*Thank you*," I whisper, and she smiles faintly, the life spark already flickering out in her eyes.

The man on the deck takes aim as I crawl down the steps and then dodge and weave the gunfire across the beach before I throw myself into the brush, brambles tearing at my hands and face as I make my way down to the water. The staccato sound of gunfire echoes in my ears. Mattie is ahead of me, half crawling, half stumbling, toward the woods. I glance behind me once and see that the cottage has erupted into flames that lick orange into the sky. My mother's funeral pyre.

I keep going.

It's about a hundred feet to the edge of the brush, but it feels like forever, crawling on my hands and knees. Blood drips from my arm, and I know I've been shot, but only a flesh wound. Still, it hurts, more now that I've acknowledged it, and yet it's nothing compared to the grief I feel poised to crash over me, as soon as I let it. Kerry, *dead*... I know I can't think about that now. There will be time later. Too much time, perhaps.

As I get closer to the woods, I realize Daniel and Sam are shooting back, offering us covering fire, their faces fierce in focus, grim with determination. Kyle is there, too, I see with relief, shooting alongside them. When Mattie gets to the edge, Ruby, who has been holding Phoebe, pulls her across and they collapse on the ground, clutching each other, rocking back and forth. A few seconds later, I follow. Ruby takes my hand, and I pull her into my arms, pressing my face against her hair.

"Kerry?" Daniel asks, and, still holding Ruby, I shake my head.

"She saved my life," Mattie whispers, as Phoebe clambers into her arms. She holds the little girl tightly.

Daniel nods, grimly accepting, unsurprised. "Let's go," he says, and, with a few parting shots, he, Sam, and Kyle holster their rifles and we head through the woods, to the cars.

It's only a matter of seconds to sweep the brush from the car, clamber in. Daniel drives the SUV he arrived in, with Sam and Kyle. I take Justine's car, with Mattie, Ruby, and Phoebe, ignoring the pain firing up my arm. We bump over the old, overgrown road without any of us speaking, the only sound the ragged draw and tear of our breathing. We're half a mile, no more, from the cottage, and our only hope is that they don't realize we have a means of transportation—or that they don't care because they want what is left of the cottage and what we had built there.

As we reach the first curve, I twist around to see the horizon a livid orange from the fire, smoke billowing toward the sky. Then I turn back, step on the accelerator, and keep going. No one speaks as we drive along the abandoned road, branches and bushes swiping the windows, the dirt pitted with rocks and ruts that make us jolt and lurch every few seconds. Kerry had said the road came out somewhere near Foymount, around fifteen miles away.

After the first mile and then the next, we start to breathe easier. When we've driven for half an hour, deep into the woods, Daniel pulls over in front of me and I follow.

"Kyle needs his shoulder seen to," he explains. "He was shot, running across the beach. I think we're far enough away now to stop." He glances at me, noticing the dried blood up and down my arm for the first time.

"You're hurt—"

"It's nothing."

As Daniel tends to Kyle, I walk over to a mossy, fallen log and sit down. The woods are completely still, just like they were when we first came in November, but after a few seconds I start to hear other sounds—the chatter and chirp of birdsong, the hum and whine of insects and bees. The rustle of the wind in the grass and the trees.

Mattie comes to sit next to me, and Ruby trails along, holding Phoebe's hand. Phoebe's eyes are wide and watchful; does she know her mother is dead? She is my responsibility now, along with my own children. I can barely take it in, along with everything else.

We all sit in silence for a few minutes, the only sounds the ones of nature around us, the twitter and rustle and chirp, a peacefulness about the whole scene that feels utterly at odds with what I'm feeling.

"Kerry," Mattie finally whispers. It's all she can manage.

I put my good arm around her and draw her close. Already I miss Kerry with a fierce ache, like a missing limb, sawn off, hacked away. *She gave her life for my daughter.* I hope she knew how much I appreciated her. *Loved* her. I hope, because I never told her. Not in words, and now I never can.

With Kyle's arm bandaged, Daniel walks toward us, Sam behind.

"I don't think anyone is following us," he says. "I can't hear any engines." We all listen; it remains still. We're safe... for now.

But Justine, and *Kerry*...

I will always, always be grateful to her. I will always make sure my daughters remember her. And it's for her sake that I have to think of the future because she would have hated to die in vain.

"So, what now?" I ask, the words a challenge, and we all look around at each other, a silent question in our eyes, so much unknown in front of us.

"It's four hundred miles to Buffalo," Daniel states. "We have enough gas, and hopefully enough food. There's a good chance we'll be able to get there."

"And if we run into guys like those again?" Mattie asks, her tone suggesting it's only a matter of time.

Daniel straightens; his tone, when he speaks, is steely. "Then we fight because there's nothing left to lose."

A chill of fear steals through me, along with the burning fire of determination. I'm afraid, but I am brave. I stand up, drawing Mattie and Ruby up with me, my two wilderness girls. With my other hand, I reach over and take hold of Phoebe's.

"Then let's get going," I say firmly, and Daniel smiles faintly in response. Maybe one day he'll tell me what he did that now seems so unforgiveable; maybe one day we'll help to forge a new world from the ashes of this one. But first we have to begin—

here and now, starting down this wild, lonely road, not knowing where it goes.

As Mattie and Ruby get into the car, I turn back toward the cottage one final time, and I imagine I can see the last clouds of ash scudding across a pure blue sky.

Then I get in and start driving.

A LETTER FROM THE AUTHOR

Dear reader,

Huge thanks for reading *The Last Stars in the Sky*; I hope you were hooked on Alex and her family's journey. If you want to join other readers in hearing all about my new releases and bonus content, you can sign up here:

www.stormpublishing.co/kate-hewitt

If you enjoyed this book and could spare a few moments to leave a review that would be hugely appreciated. Even a short review can make all the difference in encouraging a reader to discover my books for the first time. Thank you so much!

I was inspired to write this book when I was visiting our family cottage in Canada that the cottage in *The Last Stars in the Sky* is based on, and reflected that, if some major world event happened, we wouldn't actually know about it! That led to a fascinating family discussion about all the what-ifs, and the genesis of this novel. Although this novel is clearly speculative, in some ways it is the closest to my own life because Alex's experiences with her family's cottage mirror my own. Like her, I was privileged to have the opportunity to be a "wilderness girl" growing up; many of her childhood memories are also my own. I hope you enjoyed this story of survival and togetherness, as I so enjoyed writing it.

Thanks again for being part of this amazing journey with me and I hope you'll stay in touch – I have so many more stories and ideas to entertain you with!

Kate

www.kate-hewitt.com

facebook.com/KateHewittAuthor

x.com/author_kate

instagram.com/katehewitt1

linkedin.com/in/kate-hewitt-38b445211a

ACKNOWLEDGMENTS

When I first came up with the idea for *The Last Stars in the Sky*, I wasn't sure I could write it, as it was so different than anything I'd written before. I'm very grateful first to Oliver Rhodes, who loved the idea when I pitched it to him, and to Kathryn Taussig, my editor, who so wonderfully helped me bring it to completion. Their confidence in my storytelling abilities, especially in this new genre, really helped me to keep going. Thank you also to my family, who have shared so many cottage memories with me. I have loved all the discussions we have had about how you would actually survive a nuclear holocaust at the cottage! Many of the details in this story are thanks to these conversations. I'd also like to thank my husband, Cliff, who was so supportive of me writing this story, and whose love of the cottage is as great as, if not greater than, my own. To my wilderness guy, I love you!

Printed in Great Britain
by Amazon

40842197R00192